VIRTUAL STRANGERS

Lynne Barrett-Lee

Published by Accent Press Ltd – 2008
ISBN 9781905170166
Copyright © Lynne Barrett-Lee 2008

The right of Lynne Barrett-Lee to be identified as the
author of this work has been asserted by her in
accordance with the Copyright, Designs and Patents Act 1988.

Printed and bound in the UK

Cover Design by Anna Torborg

The publisher acknowledges the financial support
of the Welsh Books Council

For Kim and Peter
Sometimes life does imitate art….

Night's candles are burnt out, and jocund day
Stands tiptoe on the misty mountain tops.

William Shakespeare, *Romeo and Juliet*

Chapter 1

MANY STORIES START WITH a trauma or crisis. My story starts with a modem.

Late September 2000. Thursday night. Eightish.

And quite a nice modem, if you happen to have an opinion about modem aesthetics. Dark grey, dinky lights, the usual plug-with-pretensions, and stuffed with such breathtaking technological wizardry that it could doubtless connect me to Alpha Centauri if I wanted, at the sparkling velocity of fifty-six K. I got it out of the plastic bag, out of the box, out of the polystyrene, out of another (more bijou) plastic bag and placed it on the desk by my elderly yucca.

'*Finally*,' muttered my son, Ben, eyeing the empty box with derision. He slipped the word in on a convenient out breath, in what I'd come to understand was the thirteen-year-old equivalent of 'Wey-hey! Whoopy-doo! I'm *so* excited!'

'Yes, *finally*,' I echoed, in similar vein.

Which wasn't hard, frankly. I'd been feeling pretty grey and grizzly all week, and spending one hundred and nineteen pounds on another lump of grey matter wasn't my idea of therapy. Therapy would have been the calf-length boots in Oasis. Serious therapy would have been two pairs of boots. But there is (or so I remember telling myself at the time) that other kind of therapy to consider. The therapy that involves making yourself feel better by doing something kind and unexpected for someone you love. So I walked past the footwear, and got Ben his modem.

He'd been on about getting tooled up on the internet front for the best part of a year; us being, apparently, the only family in the entire developed world who didn't have an internet connection. But then it wasn't him paying for it, was

1

it? Now his brother had left home, I felt Ben needed something more substantial than a hundred and fifty back copies of *GamesMaster* to replace him. Not in a yell, kick, punch, wind-up and generally torment kind of way, but something with which he could fill up the hours he and Dan would normally be filling with a selection of the above.

'Is it working?' he asked, shrugging his bag off and peering. He'd been out rugby training and smelt like compost. Which was better than chutney. At least better than that.

'Of course it's working,' I told him, feeling suddenly, reliably, and unsurprisingly, defensive. It went with the territory.

He looked suspicious. 'As in, it's up and running?'

I shook my head. 'As in, when I switched it on – like *so* – a selection of lights came on.'

He did a slow hand clap then perched on the edge of my chair. 'Excellent!' he said, changing deftly from unimpressed to patronising. '*And*?'

'And nothing. I've only just plugged the thing in.'

'Yeah, yeah,' he said, making it clear, with the sort of movement of the buttocks that only one's offspring could get away with, that it would be appropriate at this point for me to free up the swivel seat for him. 'Got here just in time then. Have you installed all the software? Done the filters?' He rummaged. 'Uh huh. This the box?'

'It's *here*.'

'Well, give it me then, Mum. Any tea made or anything?'

'No, there isn't. And Ben, I am really quite capable ...'

At which my son grinned. In his grinniest fashion.

'Yeah, right, Mum,' he chortled. 'Sure you can do it. But be quicker if *I* do it. Tea?'

Always a problem, of course. Torn as I was – and usually am – with the competing claims of maternal instinct (Goodness! What a very clever boy you are! How wondrous and ground-breaking your every thought turns out to be! Feel free to impress me with your enormous mental capacity, my child! etc.), and baser instinct (Look, you snivelling pubescent, who d'you think re-wired your bloody baby monitor when your father shorted it, eh? Eh?), the former, naturally, knocked the latter into touch. That's what we mums *do,* isn't it? We cultivate exactly the kind of toxic male arrogance that we abhor in men. Or is it just me?

Of *course* it would be quicker if Ben did it. Plus Ben would be able to be *proud* of the fact that it would be quicker because he was doing it. Plus Ben would *enjoy* doing it. Plus I would not.

Though certainly *could.* Which is the main point here.

Truth is, the tired cliché of thirty-something females' technophobia is exactly that. A tired cliché. A *moribund* cliché. In fact, not even a cliché, but a wicked falsehood. Women are not technophobic at all. (Witness washing-machine programmes.) Most women are not techno-obsessive, that's all. And quite right too. Yes, yes, yes, I know. There was the space programme and Teflon and so on. But has non-stick proved to be *the* development, cuisine-wise? Since Teflon have we not embraced Le Creuset instead? Since Teflon, have we not discovered balti and chips? Have Teflon, it seems, no particular big deal. Have Teflon, may well achieve pneumatic fried eggs, but will not achieve Masterchef any time soon.

Seems to me that anything that comes to you by way of copious advertising, and whining from juveniles, needs to be treated with a hefty dose of scepticism, life-enhancing-wise; i.e. expect much in the way of hype, technical blurb, financial shock horror, number of plug sockets required, etc. But expect little in the way of life enhancement. Rather, it occurs to me, like Channel Five.

Except I must admit that I *can* see an advantage in being online at home, offspring-wise. I can see that I, too, will be able to communicate with Daniel, and without the necessity for adopting a badgering / pleading tone and / or spurious excuses. Plus I will have a small but significant chance of my offspring responding. Also I could, if afflicted by boredom at weekends, cyber-shop for ab cradles, or whatever. If I like.

I won't like, I'm sure, but I'm happy enough.

Chapter 2

BECAUSE I DO HAVE a lot to be thankful for. I have my health, I still have one son at home to beetle around slavishly after, I have a respectable three-bed semi with very nice, very clean, very *desirable* new uPVC windows (my dad's contribution; he doesn't like draughts), I have a job which earns money (if not intellectual satisfaction), and now I have the whole World Wide Web at my feet.

I also have a communication from Daniel. Though not in response to the email I sent him, as it happens, but in the form of a postcard. Of Harrods' fish counter. Harrods? Fish counter? Dan?

Hi Mum.
Everything fine. Hope you're all OK. Bad hangover today, as we went to the freshers' ball last night. By the way, change of address. Best to email me on jnecrosis@ub.ac.uk. (which is different from the address I gave you before. This is Jack's. Less hassle.) Take care.
Dan.

I'm feeling tearful now, of course. And I'm concerned that feeling tearful will become my standard response to *any* communication from my firstborn (excluding requests for further money, which will trigger altogether different synapses). And who's Jack? And what ball? I wish I didn't have such in-depth first-hand knowledge of boat races, fizz buzz and vomiting down drains.

I have my own mega-hangover in place anyway. So I can't really send him a preachy cyber-missive, and must instead trust to the years of shaky but well-intentioned parenting that got him this far in the first place.

*   *   *

5

Despite Rose being the very best friend I have in the world, going to her and Matt's leaving party was the very last thing I felt like doing. It was bad enough my son going off, without losing the entire Griffith family as well. I would either be sober and morose, or drunk and maudlin – neither being particularly desirable attributes of the party-guest-about-town. I would have to be stern with myself, and then some.

I decided to set out on foot, telling myself I was walking because I needed to take myself in hand, exercise-wise. That I was carrying a litre of Rioja, a hundredweight of cutlery and a Victoria sponge in a biscuit tin (and could therefore manage nothing more strenuous than a vertically restrained gentle meander), was not sufficiently disabling for me to abandon my pretence of energetic fervour.

But I was walking because I intended to drink.

And I was drinking because I was taking my father.

Which sounded dreadful, but was entirely reasonable, I felt. My father had only been living with us for a month, but I was already having to learn coping strategies; given his long and illustrious history of embarrassing me, it made sense to forestall him by getting completely sloshed and embarrassing myself instead.

'What's this?' Rose asked, as he held out a tin to her. She was wearing her hair up, like a glossy black meringue, her glasses slung at her chest on a glittery chain. She scooped them up now and peered hopefully through them, squinting at the Tesco's Festive Selection triptych on the lid. When she'd asked for donations of puddings and drink, I wasn't sure this was quite what she had in mind.

'A Victoria sponge,' I said apologetically.

'With a stencilled dusting,' my father added proudly.

'Well, that's just lovely, Mr –'

'Tsk! Call me Leonard!' my father trumpeted. 'And filled with my prize-winning greengage and Tia Maria jam.'

Not an auspicious start.

While Rose bundled my father off to acquaint himself with

the facilities, I grabbed a drink and headed out into the garden, where a cheerful voice reached me almost instantly.

'On your own, then? No Phil?'

As was often the case, given the curious twilight world Great Western Trains rostering people seemed to inhabit, I didn't expect my boyfriend to arrive for a while. In the months that I'd been seeing him, we rarely arrived anywhere together; we generally turned up at most places in stages, like catalogue deliveries. I shook my head as Sheila Rawlins, Rose's next door neighbour, moved forward purposefully. I was invariably cornered by Sheila at parties, because, like me, she was divorced with two teenage children. And there our situational kinship ended. Nevertheless, Sheila's main role in my life seemed to be to do everything I did just a little bit earlier than me, mainly, it sometimes felt, so that she could ease my own passage with her wisdom and spirituality. She separated from her husband just before me, had a resident (incontinent) mother, and her eldest daughter went off to Cambridge last year. I suspected she would have words of encouragement and guidance to impart. And she did.

'Feeling a bit upsy-downsy right now, Charlie?'

Why fight it? She meant well. 'So-so,' I told her. 'More downsy, I guess.'

'Of *course* you are. Tearful? I wept buckets and buckets.'

I nodded. She smiled. We both sipped at our drinks. 'I'm OK. It's just bad timing, losing Rose and Matt at the same time as Dan. But I'll adjust.'

'You will, given time. And diversions, of course.'

'Which I have, now Dad's with us. Diversions aplenty.'

'Mmmm! Offspring out, elderly relative in. Modern life, eh? In good health?'

Dad's health was the least of my worries. Most were fixed on his culinary foibles. I could even now make out his form in the distance, unmistakably miming a full rolling boil.

'Excellent,' I said.

'But a strain on the family dynamic nevertheless. And a symbol, of course, of a new life-stage beckoning. And one for which most of us are *so* ill-prepared.' She shook her head slowly, then rolled her eyes. 'Tsh! Mid-life-crisis city, eh?'

I spotted Phil arriving, and waved a hand in greeting, but he'd already been scooped up by Matt for a drink. Why didn't Matt come and scoop me up too? Much as I liked Sheila, I really didn't want to talk about me any more. I finished my drink.

'Well,' I said, swilling my ice cube around a bit. 'Depends if I'm going to die at seventy-eight, I suppose. I hope not. How are *you*, anyway?'

Sheila, whose wide experience clearly failed to encompass understanding when someone wanted to change the conversational direction and tone, continued.

'Oh, middling. Over the worst now, of course. As *you* will be, before you can say Gordon Bennett. You do know that, don't you, Charlie?'

'Oh, of *course* I do, Sheila,' I enthused, changing tack. 'I know I'm just a product of my age, time and conditioning. I've just discovered that the whole justification for my existence is bound up in my role as mother, nurturer, Piagetian facilitator and so on, and that having been denied that role – well, fifty per cent of it, anyway – I am bound to be floundering in the morass of my latent insecurities, and will most probably be forced to sign on for a course in early Renaissance influences on the twentieth-century biscuit wrapper or something similarly diverting, in order to prove to myself that I still exist as a functioning human being. For the moment, at least. Do you know what I mean?'

Sheila blinked and then drained her own glass. Then, like a thwacked daddy longlegs, soldiered gamely on.

'Mmm-*mmm*,' she said, nodding. 'And you're right to be so positive. I find my floristry classes an enormous help. Plus, I can do something useful for the community. For the church, at any rate. They've been through a terrible time, what with the silk flowers and so on ...'

'Silk flowers?' I asked levelly. I really wanted to say, Sod the bloody silk flowers. I couldn't imagine a single anecdote about flowers (silk, plastic, organic or Venusian) that would be worth standing around holding an empty glass for, but then recognised in myself an unsettling new streak; I was, I realised, in danger of becoming a cynic. She forestalled me, in any case. With a whoop and a hand flap.

'Oh!' she cried. 'Enough! *Please* don't start me on them.'

None the wiser, I nodded a relieved farewell, as, duty done, she began making her excuses and heading off in pursuit of more sensible talk.

'Oh, Sheila!' I called. She turned.

'Something, Charlie?'

'Yes,' I said, suddenly dismayed at my crabbiness. 'Are you online round at your place? I thought I could give you my new email address.'

She stepped closer.

'*What* mail?'

'*E*mail. Computer?'

'Not me,' she said, shaking her head emphatically. 'No truck with that sort of jiggery whatname. But remember, if you want to telephone any time – *any* time, Charlie, you know where I am.'

Rose had hung night lights in jam jars from the trees and the bushes. Even Matt's runner-bean canes were bathed in pale light. It seemed impossible that after next week I would probably never set foot in this garden again. All those school holiday paddling-pool sessions with the children; all those wine-infused nights of debate on the lawn. I met Matt's Aunty Jenny at the edge of the patio.

'I can't believe they're going,' I said.

She gave my arm a reassuring squeeze and shook her thin neck. 'Me neither,' she agreed. 'But we can visit. Though what a dreadful, bone-rattling coach journey that'll be! I shall probably have to travel without my dentures. Ah,' she continued, 'and this must be Leonard. What a joy to be able to meet you at last.'

My father smiled engagingly. Feeling suddenly

sentimental, I told her he made the best jam in Britain.

'Ah!' she said. 'There's a sweeping assertion if ever I heard one! But if you're talking preserves, I've the very thing for you. *Jams, Jellies and Junkets* – just bought it. It's in its seventh edition, you know.' She gave him a wink. 'Rose has just finished with it. Like a borrow?' she asked.

'Rather!' said my dad, allowing himself to be swept back inside.

Rather? Rath-*er*? What was the plot here?

Alone again, I slopped a gloopy slug of punch (plus brown apple slices, miscellaneous citrus membranes, bits of twig etc.) into my glass and knocked it back, Cossack-style, through a colander fashioned from loosely gritted teeth. When I had finished choking on the twig (rosemary? rosebush?), I flipped my head back up to find Adam Jones beside me. Doctor bloody Adam bloody perfect bloody smoothie bloody Jones. A man so infuriatingly friendly and functional that there should have been a law against letting him out without a leash. A man also infuriatingly married to Davina Jones, my boss. So I had to be pleasant to him.

Not that you'd ever want to be less than pleasant to a guy so disarmingly good-looking, decent and thoughtful, even if he did exhibit a rather shaky taste in wives. Davina was good-looking too, certainly, and undeniably successful, but in her case, the words decent and thoughtful sprung rather less readily to mind. I had worked for her estate agency firm for several years now, and the only area so far where she'd gained my unqualified approval was in having had the good sense to marry such a man.

He looked down at me now with his brows slightly knitted.

'You OK?' he enquired. 'Want a back slap or something?'

''s all right,' I spluttered. 'It was only a stalk.'

'Hmm,' he said, raising one eyebrow and smiling. 'So. Daniel get off to Med school all right?'

Drat. The D word again. I waved an arm in an extravagant arc and to my astonishment, nearly overbalanced. Adam Jones put out a warm downy forearm to steady me.

'Gone,' I said. 'Flown the nest. Flown the coop. Flown the … um. Whatever. Anyway. Yes. Gone.' I peered distractedly into the sediment at the bottom of my glass.

'Uh huh. As they do,' he said encouragingly, patting me. ' He'll be fine.'

'I know.'

'Probably having a ball.'

'I know.'

'Best years of his life. Mine certainly were.'

'I know. So they say.'

'No, *really*.' He spread his arms to illustrate the point. 'One big round of parties and drinking and hah, hah … and, er … Are you all right?'

No no no no no no. I'm not. Oh God. Here we go again. What's happening to me? Why do I keep bursting into tears all the time?

'Fine, fine … erm. Just got to …. You know. Well.' And I plunged off through the French doors and into the house.

Where a posse made up of Rose, Aunty Jenny, Phil and my father were waiting in ambush in the kitchen to bar my way to the toilet and to Express Grave Concern.

'Ah! There you are! Oh! Charlotte! Are you all right?' Etc.

'Rath*er*, Dad!' I twerbled. 'Just a pip in my eye.'

'A pip?' Phil advanced on me. 'How did a pip get into your eye?'

I rubbed, but fruitlessly. Piplessly. Everyone's face (bar Phil's, of course; his had gathered itself into a grimace of concentration) was taking on that tell-tale expression. That one which says, 'We know you haven't *really* got anything in your eye and that you're actually crying, but we're far too polite to make reference to it and will simply await further cues.'

'A tomato pip,' I expanded, furiously. 'It must have been stuck on the back of my hand while I was trying to deal with the twig.' I slapped Phil's questing finger away. 'There's a lot of acid in tomatoes, you know.'

Silence fell around us like a batch of badly tossed drop

11

scones, onto which, thankfully, Rose soon stepped. 'They're those vine-ripened ones,' she said. 'Sharp as a lemon. Matt makes a big hoo-hah about their superior flavour, but he really only buys them because they have a stalk on and he thinks he can fool people into thinking they're his. Come on,' she pressed a warm hand into mine, 'let's hit the bathroom and salvage your make-up.'

As we left the kitchen I could pick out my father's voice. 'It's the change,' he expounded. 'Had the same with her mother. Thank goodness I'm around now to jolly her along.'

By midnight, the party had divided itself neatly into two. One half drinking coffee and being sensible in the house, and the other drinking everything else and being legless in the garden. Phil, typically, was doling out instant in the former while Rose and I, on the grass, were very much in the latter. Supine, in fact, on her picnic rug.

'Look at that arse,' she observed, sitting up.

I propped myself on my elbows and focused. It was the property of a young guy in combats. I considered. 'Nine point five. Whose is it?'

'Keiran's.'

'Who's Keiran?'

'Oh, you don't know him. New head of IT at school. Phew! How I shall miss that arse.'

'There'll be others, in Canterbury.'

She lay back on the blanket again and twiddled her glass stem.

'Don't get me wrong. This is a brilliant career move for Matt and everything, and I would hate to think he even had an inkling about the way I feel – he's *so* excited about it being so rural, and the size of the garden and growing bloody brassicas and potatoes and leeks ... Oh, and chickens! Did he run *that* one by you yet? The kids will love it, of course, but God, right now I really wish I wasn't going.'

Rose and Matt's two were both still in primary school. Rose was right, they would love it. 'You don't mean it ...'

'Oh, yes I do, Charlie girl. Nothing like having all your best friends in a glut to remind you just how much you'll miss them when you're gone.'

'It's not so far.'

'It is. It might as well have been Brussels.'

'I know. But we can visit, and …'

She sat up and gestured. 'Look at him, for instance.'

'Who? David Harris-Harper?' David Harris-Harper was new to the area, but had already established himself as Cefn Melin's resident hunky conveyancer. And was managing to exude androgens even through cords.

She nodded. 'How could there possibly be anyone in Canterbury as shaggable as that?'

'I'm sure there must be.'

'Yes, but *you* won't have seen them, will you?'

'So you'll have to describe them for me, won't you? We can exchange our shag lists via lurid letters – emails even, come to that. You could take furtive photographs and send them down the computer to me.'

The idea of the shag lists – our secret top ten of local blokedom – being committed to print and zapped along land-lines like an urgent DX bag, struck me as not only funny but strangely appealing. Rose laughed. 'Excellent idea! Which reminds me …'

She disappeared inside.

She was back moments later, swaying slightly, with a present.

'What's this for?'

'For you, silly.' She proffered the slim package. She'd wrapped it, very beautifully, as always, in tissue.

'Oh, you shouldn't have. What is it? Should I open it now?'

She nodded. 'If you like. You might want to change it. When I bought it, I thought it was a book about Everest, but when I got it home I realised it was actually about a peak in the Andes. And then I thought, well, no matter. It's still about mountains. I thought it might prove an inspiration while

13

you're planning your trip. But then I read it. Well, not read it, but read the captions with the photos. And read some of it, and then thought it wasn't really what I'd wanted. It looks a bit harrowing.'

It was called *Touching the Void*. 'So?' I shrugged. 'You know me.'

'Well, pratting about in Timberlands is one thing, and I know you love all this stuff, but I wondered if harrowing is what you really need right now. Do change it if you like –'

'Nonsense, Rose! I can be harrowed with the best of them!'

'Hmm,' she said. 'Don't be so sure of that, Charlie girl.'

We watched Phil approach, bearing mugs and two cushions. 'Damp grass,' he said.

'Therefore, damp arses,' Rose countered, dismissing the coffees.

We then laughed uproariously, clutching our tummies, despite us both knowing that, at least for the moment, life wasn't particularly uproarious at all.

Phil looked disdainful and re-proffered the mugs.

'We need *wine*, Phil!' Rose told him firmly.

Chapter 3

MONDAY. SIXISH. EXCEPTIONALLY STRESSED.

The unholy trinity of my current working life consists (in no particular hierarchy of tedium) of a) the property from hell, Cherry Ditchling, b) the delightful but mad pensioner, Minnie Drinkwater, and c) estate agency not being remotely connected with anything I ever really wanted to do.

Thus Mondays, particularly, throw most sharply into relief the huge gulf that exists between Charlie Simpson, intrepid sort of explorer-mountaineer / geology enthusiast / right-on anthropological and Everest expert etc., and Charlie Simpson, Willie Jones Jackson (Independent Estate Agents) negotiator.

Thus it is that my first utterance on returning from work is a heartfelt 'Sod that,' albeit under my breath.

Among my father's many and varied parts, lies an incongruous fondness for syrupy sentiment. Thus a side effect of his residence has been the arrival of a small clutch of little heart-warming books about the place, which he seems to consult on a regular basis, in an attempt, I presume, to lend thoughtful profundity to his daily routine. Opening the one on the hall table tonight at random, I was, I noted, instructed to be especially kind and courteous to older people. Hmmm. The word 'sod' seems understatement indeed.

Why, oh why, oh why did I do it? My brother, God bless him, has about eight million bedrooms. And a Jacuzzi bath. And a hectare. And a shed. And a Mediterranean style verandah-type thingy. And an antipodean address. And patience. So why? *Why?* Someone tell me, before I burst with the pressure of the terrible injustice I have done myself.

My home was once an unpretentious but cosy Georgian semi; not a palace, but certainly a comfortable refuge, a place

15

that was *me*, that I could *bring* people to. But no longer. Not now my father has filled it with strange and terrible smells. Today's is reminiscent of the bat cage at Bristol Zoo. And this is simply an overlay. Beneath it, the date-chutney poo smell still lingers, competing with the stale-vomit quince-relish stench. I live now, like that fictional nursery rhyme woman, in one enormous Branston pickle jar. Or is it vinegar bottle? Whatever. Every room seems to sag under a fog of malevolent molecules. Every piece of clothing is infused with noxious fumes. No wonder we need windows with one hundred per cent air containment integrity. Or people would talk, no question.

My father is driving me mad mad mad.

'You're driving me mad, Dad.'

There. I've said it. He smiles indulgently as I throw down my handbag and keys.

'Tsh! Good day, dear?'

Dreadful. Depressing. Unproductive. Sad.

'All right. I've had better. What are you making?'

He herds a heap of pips and slime a little further away down the worktop and returns to stirring the vat of bilge he has on the go.

'Jam,' he says, smiling happily, clinking sterilised coffee jars. 'It's my own adaptation. Windfall Surprise!'

Sounds gross.

'Sounds entertaining.' I say, scanning the debris for clues. 'This wasp an escapee?'

'Tsh! Don't be daft, dear.'

My kitchen has become a malodorous hobbit hole. 'I need a drink.'

'Tsh! Before dinner, Charlotte?'

Oh, *Christ.* 'Before dinner, *yes*. I generally do.'

I bang around stroppily, lobbing pots at the sink as I go. 'Like one?'

He shakes his head. 'Shepherd's pie's bubbling up nicely. There. Get yourself sorted. I plan to be straining at 7.05.'

16

I return to the hallway and kick off my shoes.

'By the way,' he calls out. 'Your friend Rosemary telephoned. Says they're in now, but in chaos, and she'll try to call later. I told her to make sure it's not after 8.30. There's a preserves programme – *Bottle it!* – on BBC2.'

I return to the kitchen and open the wine. Which is already three days into changing to vinegar, but my taste buds have now lost the power to tell.

So this is my lot for the foreseeable future. I am missing my son, I am missing my space, and my best friend is now two hundred miles away. In exchange for these losses, what compensations do I have? A father who inflames me, a man friend who doesn't, and (I checked at the cashpoint on the way home from work) a scant forty pounds for my Everest trip.

Chapter 4

I assume I am less stressed due to a blood supply re-route; I'm still digesting half a ton of massacred mince. I feel as if I now live in a parallel universe version of my previous home. I decide to hole up in the least smelly region with hardware and hummy noises and blinky lights and modem and a very large glass of restorative wine.

Two very large glasses of restorative wine later, I decide that I must make some serious lifestyle changes. I have simply *no one* to send an email to. I spend a few consoling minutes visiting various pages at the BBC, but soon realise that it's a strange sort of grown-up that pores over Blue Peter Summer Expedition reports. So I re-activate the search engine with buzz words: 'tectonic', 'mountain', 'Everest', and 'summit attempts'. But bring up, depressingly, George Mallory's body, plus an in-depth account of recent Himalayan deaths.

Frozen mountaineers are not greatly uplifting, so I make the search a touch more pedestrian instead. I end up (as one does) at the Sainsbury's website, which at least gives me the opportunity to send a terse little email regretting their removal of French Vanilla polish from stock. After which, well – what to do? Who to email? And then I remember. You silly cow, Simpson! Of *course* you can send email! You can send one to Rose!

griffith@cymserve.co.uk

Dear Rose,
Tra la! Tra la! Found your address, and here I am, at last. Many, many thanks for *Touching the Void*. I've read the whole thing, cover to cover, and feel one hundred per cent more

confident that if I come across a void of any sort (physiological or otherwise) on my trip, I'll know just how to deal with it. Though doubt whether I'll look as fetching in bobble hat. And hey! How about this! Simpson online finally! Impressed, or what? Doubtless you're knee-deep in packing cases and cleaning, but, as the principal leavee in your life, I have simply nothing to do but wail and weep and wonder what the hell I'm going to do without you. What *am* I going to do without you? In fact, I have an inkling I will be spending a lot of time in this study – which my father insists on calling the dining room, despite that fact that no one's dined in it in a decade, bar flies. I think it's a rearguard action towards reinstatement, actually. He doesn't approve of eating in the kitchen, which is rich considering he's the one causing the stink!!

Great party, by the way. I know I looked as if I'd rather be pulling hairs from my nipples most of the time, but I was in a real emotional nadir last week, having lost a big chunk of all the stuff I hold dear, and having, it seems, picked up an early Seventies daytime cookery programme for a lodger instead.

Bless him, but *God*, Dad is sending me nuts!

Email back soon.

Love Charliexx

I have not, as yet, any sense of the cyber-space-time-logging on and off again-continuum, but am still somewhat surprised that I have not received a response by the weekend. I imagined that 'happening' people dealt with cyber-mail daily. But apparently not. Or else mine got lost.

But I do remember that moving house is not only busy, but also the most stressful thing on the entire planet after shopping for trainers. Decide instead to phone again. I'm greeted, however, by a jocular ansafone message from Rose reinforcing that thought, *'Hey, we've just moved. Think we've got time to chat?'* followed by much family guffawing down the phone. Return to computer and send another email instead.

Dear Rose,
Guess you're pretty busy!
It's all happening this end. We <u>already</u> have our invite to

the Stableford firework night barbecue party. A record? That's we as in me, Phil, Ben *and* Dad. Though as Phil is on a Brontë Awareness (or whatever) coach trip that weekend, I will therefore have to trail around flanked by offspring and parent like a novelty wallflower, don't know if I'll bother to go. It'll only be the same old crowd, and much as I love Caroline, you know how I feel about what she puts on her skewers.

Still a bit fed up without Daniel / with Dad. Uncharacter-istically fed up, in fact. Can't remember feeling like this since Felix and I decided to file for divorce. Though I guess I do know where a lot of it stems from; not quite being able to quite believe that I am less than a year from my birthday and haven't even come close to fulfilling my one big ambition. Which is ridiculous – I could have started saving five years back! It's not as if I want to climb the wretched mountain even! Just stand at the bottom – how hard can that be? Ditto the new kitchen ambition, come to think of it. The one that I didn't inherit. The one that doesn't have cat-claw trails up the cupboard fronts and wodges of brown stuff in the cutlery drawer corners. The one that I went into a shop and *chose*. The mythical, mystical, X-Files, Star Trek Voyager kitchen of my dreams.

I must make a serious mental note to ask everybody I invite to my birthday party to bring me an MFI voucher (must check if exist!) or Nepalese currency, or high-energy biscuits and so on. Do you know what Phil said to me this morning? He said 'I thought it might be fun to go on one of those Murder Mystery weekends,' and all I could think was 'Weekend from hell'. We are so pathologically unsuited! And, nice as he is, he can be such a prat at times, don't you think? Have we a future, Rose? Seriously?

Still, on a lighter note, here, as promised, is my latest shag list;

New at 6: Hugh Chatsworth (who I'm afraid you'll just have to take my word for. He's the new boy at Willie JJ – Only 19! (Bless) Very short hair. Very long limbs. Bit nervous of me. Nervous of *me*! Lots of scope for a dom/sub scenario …)

5: Richard Potter (Who I spotted in town in his hard hat and boots last week. Yum yum. Would have climbed to number four if it hadn't been for …)

4: David Harris-Harper (WOW or what?)

3: Adam Jones (bedside manner on top form, as ever…)
2: Your Matt (except beard tendency a worry, I have to say.)
1: That new IT teacher at your party. Forgot his name/marital status. What *is* his name/marital status? *Must* know. Can't ask Ben for obvious reasons!!!

Email back soon,
Miss you.
Charliexx

PS Really sorry to dump all my moans on you. Humour me! I promise I will snap out of it soon.

Saturday lunchtime. A response at last! Though, has to be said, a disappointingly short one. Expect she is bogged down in dibbing or dobbing, or whatever it is that new post-downshifting ruralites do.

thesimpsons@cymserve.co.uk

Dear Charlie,
Sorry you're feeling morose. I expect you failed to establish either status because you had lost the power of decipherable speech before ten.
Why Adam Jones at number three?
Rose.

Teatime. Tried calling Rose for qualification of this worrisome and hitherto unremarked aspect of humiliation status, and possible further detail on the IT guy. New ansafone message (Matt, this time);
Hi Guys,

Matt and Rose are just too busy chilling. Hang up if you like or hold tight for the bleep. Leave a message by all means – then call again later. You know what we're like. Hah!

*Chilling? Hah? A s*eriously bizarre, yet somehow spookily inevitable development, Matt-wise. Didn't bother again, as I'm complete crap at talking to ansafones – saying 'Well!

21

there we are then! so! well! anyway! yes! anyway! so! well!
ho ho! yes! ooh! listen to me! anyway!' etc. etc. ad nauseam,
and sounding like an utter dingbat. Plus, ansafones are
seriously old-hat now anyway. Booted up (getting slick now)
and sent an email instead.

griffith@cymserve.co.uk

Dear Rose,
Didn't think much of your new ansafone message. Have you
gone all ironic on me? (*Please* say yes). Or is 'chilling' Kent-
speak for watching *Neighbours,* perhaps? Oh, and has Matt
started tilling the courgette bed yet? (only ask as I saw a
brilliant and stylish recipe for deep-fried courgette flowers on
celebrity *Ready Steady Cook* yesterday). As for the doc, I
dithered about putting David Harris-Harper at number three,
actually, as he's seriously shaggable and has a nose just like
Antonio Banderas. (His wife, apparently, is a very good friend
of Davina's, by the way. Hmm.) But I think AJ has the edge,
doesn't he? Even if (or because, perhaps!!) Davina is being
such a baggage right now. Have I told you about that? She is
permanently irritable about the impending image-
enhancement make-over Willie JJ are undergoing as a stand,
I presume, against Metro Homes swallowing them up. God,
it's *awful*. They've drafted in this woman (who looks like a
cross between Katharine Hepburn and Wilma Flintstone), who
is called Ianthe, of all things, and who will apparently wave her
sartorial and space-enhancement wand and bring Willie JJ
into the twenty-first century. I've never seen Davina so fired up
about fabrics. You know her – half a dozen Austin Reeds and
she's normally sorted, but just lately – well, suffice to say, it's
like working in a Moroccan bazaar. (Not that she'll have to
wear any of it anyway, so she can afford to be completely
cavalier about styling.)
    Wondered about continuing list-eligibility of Matt (ditto Phil).
As no longer available for groping, should I remove? Please
advise.
    More importantly, is IT guy really single/thirty-seven/not a
wuss (as Ben tells me)? Go on, torture me. I can take it!
    And exactly how ratted *was* I? Don't spare me. I need to

22

know.
Charliexx

In an attempt to dispel any lingering local rumours about Charlie Simpson, Soak Star, I do not, as previously planned, take Ben and Dad to the pub for tea, but instead stay in and allow latter to cook pork chops – I even consume a small quantity of his home-made Cheeky Chilli Chutney. I do note, however, that chutney is probably more detrimental to my gut lining than ten years hard wine-abuse could possibly be to my liver. Take a large jug of water to the study and log on.

thesimpsons@cymserve.co.uk

Dear Charlie,

Of course Matt should be dumped! He is probably on a new shag-list as I write. Move Adam Jones up to second position.

Rose.
PS You know exactly how ratted you were. And you *must* go to the Stablefords' party. If you shut yourself away you will become depressed and introspective. If you go late you won't have to eat anything.
PPS Just found out. Head of IT is gay.

Rats.
But I must accept the dreary reality that almost everybody within my preferred age, appearance, normality parameters, is either already married / co-habiting / coming to terms with the emotional trauma of a messy divorce / starring as comedy strand in a docusoap about singles' clubs / cruise ships or wildlife sanctuary rangers and are therefore best avoided etc. Or indeed, gay.
Plus I'm already going out with Phil, of course. Hmmm.

griffith@cymserve.co.uk

Dear Rose,

I'm *very* disappointed about the IT guy. But philosophical. Or should that be Phil-osophical? Have decided I must accept my disappointment as an indication of the fact that I shouldn't really be going out with Phil any more. Must make a decision and *very* soon. Certainly before any more brochures about heritage/activity/theme breaks land on the mat. (Am expecting Saga one any time now.)

And where is *your* latest shag list? Any worthy candidates in Canterbury yet? Have been considering cabinet re-shuffle since sad news about IT guy, and have decided must move scrumptious Harris-Harper into equal first position with delicious Doctor AJ. Have to report that Kim Harris-Harper turns out not to be as friendly a person as I originally thought. Saw her in the bank last week and she remarked a) that she didn't recognise me without the red flush, chortle, chortle, and b) that she would just *love* to be able to let her hair down like I did, but regrettably, as she was a professional woman, she always had to be nice to people in the morning. Yes, *really*. Like I just say, 'Wanna house, do you? Well tough! Fuck off!' Seems she is going to be right up there with Davina in the baggage department. Speaking of which, I have to report a distressing development at work. Walked into the staffroom yesterday and came upon Hugh Chatsworth (no. 6, remember?) in the middle of changing his shirt. (He has perspiration difficulties, apparently.) And guess what? He has nipple rings! Yes, *rings*. Times two. Which he holds in place under his shirt with two Mr Men plasters. (So as not to alarm elderly householders, presumably. Or would it be to do with electrical activity?) Anyway, so *he's* gay as well. Though of course he could just be one of those fetishist guys who go to clubs where they put each other on leads and wear spikes round their necks, etc. But, well, yuk.
Charliexx

PS Have to accept Stablefords' party invitation now anyway as Ben is suffering (sic) a major hormone eruption, and has confessed to a friendship (sic) with Francesca Stableford of a type which obviously does not include the swapping of Nintendo games or going into town and playing on the escalators/telephoning people called Smellie and saying poo. And does include a fair amount of being holed up in his room, and sitting in bed looking shifty. A Development, eh? In fact, *the* development. I'm so touched that he felt able to share all this with me (rather than looking furtive and saying 'Yeah, whatever' etc.) that I can hardly bring myself to change his sheets – because then he'll realise I might have seen something he'd find excruciatingly embarrassing to have to think about the fact of me seeing and so on, that I want to spare him the discomfort. Perhaps I'll just leave a clean sheet folded on the end of the bed from now on. Ha! You have all this to come!

PPS Talking of perspiration, I heard on the radio today that most roll-on antiperspirants leave a white residue that shows up under ultra-violet light and can be the cause of much embarrassment to young girls out clubbing. For some reason, I found that immensely funny. What a sad, strange little woman I am.

PPPS Oh, yes! and green! You would not *believe* the new Willie JJ makeover. We have had a visitation from the aptly named Ianthe (see below) who is clearly Cardiff's answer to Conran, and whose (obviously covert) brief it has been to makeover Willie JJ, not as a go-ahead service sector business, but in the style, it would appear, of amphibious life. (Ianthe was a Greek sea nymph – so it figures.) The uniform is so utterly grotesque I cannot even begin to describe it. I shall have to send you a photo. Suffice to say, it is green (think distemper, think stagnant pond) and to reflect (I quote) the essence of the main corporate tenets (which are independence, one-to-one service and commitment to the environment, apparently). It incorporates a cut-away half oak leaf motif on each lapel which, when the jacket is done up, form a sort of oakey montage. And it's all pulled together by a monster chartreuse-and-khaki bow. I don't know how much the whole package cost them but they've been had, big time, I can tell you. The woman must be coining it in.

Charliexx

Monday. AM.

A dreadful, dreadful start to the morning, as I had a major panic re possible untimely menopausal symptoms. Though they were largely allayed by the realisation that a) the colour of my face was a direct result of my proximity to the new Willie JJ attire and b) the thermostat had been interfered with by my father (bringing the whole house to the temperature of a robust Finnish sauna). Was plunged, nevertheless, into a minor depression, as I couldn't stop thinking that the whole sweaty, unpredictable yukkiness of it all, was, in reality, probably less than a decade away anyway. And I have not achieved one fifth of the plane fare to Nepal, or got so much as an MFI kitchen catalogue yet.

And it got worse. I took a pair of perfectly respectable fifty-somethings to view Cherry Ditchling and was just showing them the refurbished dressing room / en suite combo when the man threw up all over the place; hand-stitched Italian silk throw, carpet, chenille bath mat, arrangement of silk gerberas / curly willow etc. – the lot. He had apparently overindulged at a Masonic Lodge dinner and became nauseated at the smell of the (excessively oil-refreshed, admittedly) pot pourri. Hah! He should try living at *my* house. But I cannot *believe* some people. Nothing to clear up with, of course, because the Rutlands don't possess anything useful in the way of serious hardware. They have it bussed in three times a week by the Little Darlings Home Valet Squeaky Clean Co (or whatever). And all I had to hand was a pack of travel wipes. In the end I telephoned Little Darlings, who agreed to come out and scrub up for me, but only at a price.

Returned to the office to find a) that said couple had already called to say Cherry Ditchling was an overpriced heap and too close to the motorway anyway, and b) that there is absolutely nothing in the Willie Jones Jackson contract to cover vomit-related soiling accidents to clients' property whilst viewing.

Now nursing a headache and dehydration (thus the promise of a further headache later). I have nothing to look forward to for the foreseeable future except dithering over whether to tell Phil I don't want to see him any more, and, speaking of vomit, waiting for Dan to get in touch and tell me he is still alive / has

26

not succumbed to excesses of student life and is consequently lying face down in a similar pool. With Jack. Who no doubt is a bad influence all round. Oh, plus a no-frills dig-for-victory-style dinner at 18.46. Plus jam.

18.37. Bright moment in my day! Email from Rose.

thesimpsons@cymserve.co.uk

Dear Charlie,
They put masking tape over metals (earrings etc.) when people have operations in case they use diathermy (cauterising etc.). As nipple rings pierce the flesh, there is a danger of shorting, so you are on the right lines about the electrical aspect. Though, for day-to-day purposes, I suspect the plasters serve mainly to reduce chafing.

Intrigued about the armpit thing. It's these little windows of absurdity in the day that make life worth living, isn't it?

I'm going to have to press you on the Harris-Harper/Jones stalemate. Which one is number one? No ties allowed. For my part, I must say I'm relieved to be able to remove Phil from my list. Nice chap though he is, I was only being polite.
Rose.

Stalemate?

Griffith@cymserve.co.uk

Dear Rose,
You know perfectly well that there is really no contest. But are you terribly busy? How about hello, how are you, what have you been up to type stuff. Am beginning to think you can't be bothered any more. In which case, sulking. I expect seriously long email, and soon.
Charlie.

PS have to cut my own communication short as Ben is having a prophylactic asthma attack; prophylactic in that his grandfather asked him to accompany him after dinner to the village bulb sale, and in a financially-challenged moment he rashly agreed. Now, of course, he has love etc., and has no need of earthly pleasures such as CDs/the price of renting a video and so on.

18.49. And twenty-four bloody seconds.

'Oh for God's sake, Dad, I'm coming, OK?'

'Tsh! I don't know. You young things spend far too much time dashing about like headless chickens. Rush, rush, rush! Deadlines, deadlines, deadlines! And *now* look. The broccoli's had two minutes too long. Don't blame me if it's gone all flaccid.'

'Look, Dad, it's no big deal, OK?'

'Not to you, perhaps, but if a job's worth doing ... and where's that grandson of mine? Skulking? BEN! DINNER! ON THE DOUBLE! QUICK MARCH!'

I go to bed at half past eight in a foul mood. My life is totally devoid of passion / direction (except I *do* now have £73.00 in Everest / MFI fund). And I'm unloved by everyone except Dan (reciprocated tenfold, but absent), Dad (reciprocated, obviously, but guilt-inducing), Phil (not really reciprocated, and suffocating) and Ben (reciprocated tenfold again, but in any case suspect it is only provisional; dependent upon maternal decision re newly proposed weekend in London with Dan. But thirteen is very young to be exposed to underground system / real ale / ragga etc.)

Going to bed at half past eight is definitely not a good move, as I wake up at half past four. And fret almost hysterically about life / love / split ends / the fact that I am so sad that I have only two people to send emails to. Go to work and eat lunch at ten thirty-five. Exceedingly long afternoon.

thesimpsons@cymserve.co.uk

Dear Charlie,
Bandying words like prophylaxis around now, are we? You *must* be fed up. Big apologies for previous brevity. We have indeed been very busy. But not so busy that the idea of you

mooching around sulking and being obstreperous with your father isn't good enough reason to say 'Stuff the spring cabbage. I must email Charlie.'

Trouble is, there's busy and there's busy. And so little is happening here that I'm at a loss to know what to put. And just how much am I missing? Sound's like back there's where all the action is. And as you are clearly finding cyberspace such a rewarding and therapeutic outlet for your creative/emotional energies, please feel free to bang on at length about anything that takes your fancy (or mine, for that matter. Who's currently hip?)

Rose.

Rose's response, I note, when I discover this on Tuesday evening, came almost straight after my own was sent off. But when I telephone later, the ansafone answers. Matt again, this time, and at odds with the email;

Out on the tiles, I'm afraid! We're such slappers! And the babysitter's French and won't answer the phone. Leave a message, why don't you?

No thanks.

griffith@cymserve.co.uk

Dear Rose,

Action! I wish! And where the hell are you now?

The only action this week is yet another spate of high drama chez Willie JJ. Have decided that Hugh Chatsworth is not the man I thought he was (apart from possibly not being a man in the heterosexual sense, in any case, but that is neither here nor there.) He is such a low-life! Will tell you all about it when I get hold of you – IF!

Oh, and Ben had a *real* asthma attack yesterday (the boy who cried inhaler etc. etc.) and as a consequence failed to finish the school cross-country heats, which has put *him* in a seriously bad mood as well. There's so much sniping going on

around here that I feel like I'm occupying a trench at the Somme.
Charlie.

PS Scrub that bit about the Somme. That was in very poor taste and not worthy of me. Particularly as it's Poppy Week soon.

Speaking of which, pop! An immediate response! Wish I understood better how land-lines configured, as I cannot compute how Rose can send me an email while earlier evidence suggests she is out. But she has. If a short one.

thesimpsons@cymserve.co.uk

Dear Charlie,

I read in a book this week that the expression 'over the top' derives from the First World War. And it was actually used flippantly by civilians *during* the war, in fact, which must have irritated the soldiers somewhat. Why is Hugh Chatsworth a low-life?

Rose.

I have decided that Hugh Chatsworth is not merely a low-life, but a fat little soil-living tick. Had a gratifying end to the morning as I had received an offer from the Pringles (my clients) for 62 Bryn Coch (Hugh's clients' house). As Hugh was on viewings, I then telephoned Hugh's clients, who were happy to accept the offer my clients had made. Lovely, lovely. Indeed, especially lovely, as I had already sold my clients' house too.

Except not *that* lovely.

When I called back Mr Pringle to tell him, his secretary told me he would be out until two. At which time, she promised, he'd call me straight back. Though he couldn't, as I'd be on viewings by then.

No matter, I thought, when Hugh returned to the office.

30

When Mr Pringle called back, Hugh could tell him himself.

No matter! Huh! Charlie Simpleton, me!

'Yes, I know,' Hugh was saying to his telephone when I returned. He glanced up and grinned as I shrugged off my jacket and sat down.

'Yes, but you've got to appreciate my client's position,' he went on. '*His* client is holding *him* to the asking price. And budgets being budgets, they simply have no choice.'

He then said, 'Ah, but that was probably before *he'd* made *his* offer. And he's had to up it … I appreciate that … but we're only talking, what? Two and a half K here? I'm sure, if you want the house, you can stump up that much.'

I wasn't taking a whole lot of notice. But I'd just begun typing in 'pleasing water feature' when I heard him finish with, 'OK, Mr Pringle, I'll leave it with you.'

I stopped typing.

'Leave what with him?'

He smiled at me. 'Upping his offer.'

'What d'you mean? Upping his offer? They've already accepted it.' I pointed. 'It's there, on that scrap pad in front of you. Accepted this morning. No problem at all.'

At this point, Hugh clearly thought he was being deeply impressive, because he prefaced his coming outrage with a cheery 'Aha!'

'In theory, yes,' he conceded, warming to his task. 'But the Pringles didn't know that, did they? And you know and I know that they have a bit more than that to play with, don't they? They offered four grand more for that other house last month. Give it an hour and they'll be back with the asking price. You wait.' He sat back.

I held in my splutter.

'I won't wait,' I told him. I picked up my telephone. 'I shall call Mr Pringle and tell him the truth.'

The response was quite gratifying.

'What the *hell* are you on about?'

'The truth,' I said sniffily. 'That their offer's been accepted. I can't believe you'd even entertain doing anything

31

else.'

Hugh's eyes darted to the receiver and back. 'Don't be stupid,' he said. 'We're talking two and a half grand here.'

'Exactly. A big chunk of money.'

'Which they can afford.'

'But which they don't wish to pay. Not for *this* house.'

'It's worth it.'

'It might be. It's entirely subjective. And it's not the point anyway.'

'Of course it's the point. We have a duty to see we keep price levels sensible.'

'Oh, and 'sensible' means inflating them at every opportunity, does it?'

I began dialling Mr Pringle's office number. Hugh stood up. 'And what about the business? What about the difference in the *agency fee*?'

I came back in a flash, because I'd already computed it. 'In this case,' I said sweetly, 'a little over thirty-one pounds.'

My call was connected.

'It's not the point anyway. The point is –'

I stopped him. 'You, Hugh, can wheeler-deal all you want to. I'd like to do my job *without* telling lies. Ah, Mr Pringle. I have some excellent news for you …'

Never really expected to enjoy work a huge amount, but now I realise I won't really enjoy work at all.

Chapter 5

<u>Bizarre</u> event. Small cache of post (propped significantly – and portentously – by Dad, between mail-order shrub catalogue and *Britain: short breaks and tours with our heritage in mind*) includes a letter. Hand-written. In writing. From *Rose*.

Charlie, hi!

Sorry it's been such <u>aeons</u> since we connected. Can't <u>believe</u> where all the time has gone. Actually, I can. Matt's been zapping back and forth through Le Shuttle like a manic squid. We have more wine bottles than milk bottles!

Reserving judgement on the local primary. Though the kids seem to have settled in really well, there is a definite whiff of champagne socialism in the air. Joe has a new friend called Oberon (which says it all, does it not?), and Ellen has become almost pathologically attached to her teacher (thoroughbred home counties but aggressively <u>Ms</u>) who has a nose-ring and bunches and is a spit, apparently, of Angelica from RugRats.

But the comp, as you'd expect, looks reassuringly like a more dissolute place. Despite the location, there seems to be no shortage of surly and dysfunctional pubescents here, which, as you'd expect, makes me feel quite at home!

How are things with you? I hated leaving you at such a low ebb (hated leaving, period) – and what with all the chaos of your dad moving in and then Dan going off to Med School, you must be feeling quite strange and bereft. Again, apologies for being so wrapped up in things here that it's taken me this long to get in touch. At the moment I'm oscillating between knowing we've done the right thing (and being happy for Matt, of course; he's settled in well at work, and seems to be enjoying it) and an overwhelming sadness for everything we've left behind. I can't quite believe we'll find friends like those we've left. And you suddenly seem a long, long way away.

Anyway, finally re-connected to reality. After threats of sanctions on al fresco sex come the spring, Matt dragged himself inside and unpacked the computer last night – I swear he'd sleep outside if it weren't for the slugfest he's inspired with his hoeing. (So strange for a agrichemical whiz kid to be so enthusiastically organic, don't you think?) Send me your email address asap, so we can update the shag lists and share all the goss – your phone, I have to tell you, is always engaged. Does your dad have some sort of 0898 habit???!!!!

Miss you lots. Lots. Take care.
Rose. xxxxx

What? How? *Eh?*

Griffith@cymserve.co.uk

Dear Rose,
Very confused by your letter. It's great to hear you're all well etc. But what do you mean by 'it's been aeons since we connected'? It's been two days. And why don't you ever answer *your* phone? Please explain. Asap.
Charlie.
PS What's an 0898 habit?

7 p.m.

Telephone Rose. Matt says; *We're just too busy chilling* and so on. Leave a message. 'Rose, it's me. Where the bloody hell are you?'

Turf Ben off the computer.

7.30 p.m.

Telephone Rose. *We're just too busy chilling* etc. Leave another message (needs must). 'Me again. I guess you must be out. Sorry about the 'where the dot dot dot are you' bit earlier.

34

Hope you play this when you get home so you can wipe it before the children hear it. Sorry. Anyway. Call me soon as you can.

Turf Ben off the computer.

9 p.m.
Call Rose. *We're just too busy chilling etc.*
Turf Ben off the computer. Turf Dad out of the bath (through keyhole, obviously). Turf Ben into the bath. Turf hissing, smoking, stinking, spitting preserving pan with new black crackle-glaze interior out into the garden.

10 p.m.
Call Rose. *We're just too busy chilling* etc.
Put Ben in bed. Put Dad in place. But! Ah! Post! At last!

the simpsons@cymserve.co.uk

Dear Charlie,
Oops. Suspect I have been rumbled. I suppose it was only a matter of time. I apologise.
PS. 0898. If you don't know, I don't feel it's my place to enlighten you. Why d'you ask?

10.05 p.m.

griffith@cymserve.co.uk

Dear Rose,
What do you mean 'rumbled? What's been going on? Is that you, Matt? Is this some sort of joke?

10.10 p.m. Instant reply again. Spookily on-line.

thesimpsons@cymserve.co.uk

Dear Charlie,
Not exactly. But this isn't Rose. Or Matt. Sorry.

10.15 p.m. I'm beginning to feel as if I have stumbled across a left-over alien from the Outer Limits. Or a comedy extra from Star Wars. Whizz a terse reply back.

griffith@cymserve.co.uk

Dear whoever you are,
    Forgive me if I seem a little slow on the uptake, but are you telling me I've spent all this time sending emails to an absolute *stranger*? And what the hell are you playing at, replying? And just who are you anyway? Tell me *now*. And what *is* an 0898 habit?

10.45 p.m. Now suspiciously off-line.

griffith@cymserve.co.uk

Dear 'Rose'
I said *now*.

Ditto. Hmm.

3.48 a.m.
    I wake in a cold sweat as the contents of several weeks worth of mindless / pathetic / revelatory / bitchy etc. emails rain down like a shower of whitebait on my head. I could surely be sent to the colonies for less.

4.59 a.m.
    Oh, *God*! Harris-Harper! Dishy Jones! Richard Potter! Richard Potter *in boots!*

5.42 a.m.
    Who the hell is it? Who? Who? Who? That's it. I'm finished. I will never be able to show my face in Wales again. I will have to move to Canterbury and rent tent space among Matt's perpetual spinach. And grow a beard or something. Oh

oh oh.

6.31 a.m.

Christ! And I called Phil a prat!

6.32 a.m.

And Davina a baggage!

Friday. a.m.-ish.

Bad start to the day. Got ready for work harangued by the burgeoning horror that I have spent weeks communicating my personal romantic fantasies to a complete stranger via email. But who? *Who?* Population of Wales: three million. Population of south coast of Wales (Cymserve main area): two million. Population of south coast of Wales with computers ... er ... one and a half million? Pop. of south Wales with online capability ... er ... *can't* be more than one million, can it? Pop. of south coast of Wales actually *using* online capability (i.e. spending leisure time emailing, as opposed to watching rugby / watching documentaries about Welsh Assembly / sitting in pubs pretending to know all about the Welsh Assembly / in street answering questions from thrusting journalists about who, *exactly* local Euro MPs actually *are,* etc.) Half a million? *Half a million?* Only five hundred thousand. Could easily be someone *I actually know.*

And it got worse.

*If there's somewhere cool
in your neighbourhood
grab-yourself-a-pad
Call Metro!
Seen a hip townhouse
an' it looks real good
grab-yourself-a-pad
Call Metro!*

Yeuch.

No peace to be found. Couldn't even listen to the radio in the car as a diversion, for fear of further assault by the truly appalling din that is the new Metro Homes advertising campaign, which has suddenly burst into terrible life, with a vocally challenged rugby player as the all-wailing front man, pretending to be a Ghostbuster. I decided that I must alert the film company and advise them of this blatant pilfering, and thus wreak revenge on behalf of my ears.

Davina bursts into the office in her usual thrusting, in-your-face manner, causing almost total defoliation of our moribund weeping fig, and a swirling mound of leaf litter.

'Pah!' she says, glaring at me. Then (glaring again harder, or possibly narrowing her eyes to escape all the green), 'You know it's not my usual practice to gripe unnecessarily, Charlie, but do you really think looking like you've been through a rinse and spin cycle is in keeping with the new WJJ corporate image?'

Oh, sod off, Davina. 'I'm *really* sorry,' I say. 'I had a bit of a bad night. I hardly slept, and –'

She slides a jewel-coloured nail over a perfect arch of brow. 'Yes, yes, yes. We all have our problems. For goodness sake get yourself sorted, will you? Drag a comb through your hair. Plump your bow up a bit. I've got Austin Metro due here any minute and the window display is an utter shambles.'

Oh, Davina, Davina, *Davina*.

I don't know why I let Davina get to me so much. Actually, yes I do. And it's not that she's younger, richer, smarter (only sartorially), taller, leggier and, by some yardsticks, more successful than me. Bar the husband, the confidence and the flawless complexion, there's not a lot Davina has that I think I'd really want, but, somehow (daily – and I've worked here for years now) there is something in the way we interact with one another that makes *me* feel that *she* feels I wish that I did. Which is wholly preposterous and needles me greatly. Though why I needle her, I do not have a clue.

And why should *I* care if she wants to spend half her life sucking up to her ancient ex-boss? (Whose real name is, in fact, Austin Evans, as everyone well knows.) Nevertheless, the arrangement of my window is a thing very dear to me. 'I just did the window display!' I sniff.

'That's as may be, but as I came in I noticed a gap. Third panel. Bottom row. Second from the left.'

Ha! 'That's because I'm just adding the 'sold' sticker to it.' Ha ha ha. Yah boo sucks.

'Ah. 27 Peasdale?'

'Full asking price.' Ha!

Better. In anticipation of getting hold of a lovely lovely commission-enhanced salary cheque, I despatch an extra £300 to my MFI / Everest fund on my way home.

It is almost a whole week however, before I manage to get hold of Rose. She calls during the five-minute pre-straining run up, but sod the vegetables, I decide – this is important.

'Charlie! There you are! At last!'

'What do you mean, "at last"?'

'What I say! You're so hard to get hold of –'

'*I'm* so hard to get hold of –

'Your phone's always engaged, Charlie.'

'No it's not.'

'It sure is. It always is. I almost sent you a carrier pigeon today. I've been trying you non-stop since we got back from Majorca.'

'Majorca?'

'Half term. One of those last minute pot-luck breaks to Pollensa. Anyway, what's the panic? You filled up the tape.'

'Your letter.'

'What about it?'

'I'm addled about it.'

'Addled?'

'Seriously addled. About what's going on.'

'Oh? What *is* going on?'

'That's just it. I don't know. You know Dan kept on at me

about getting a modem and signing up with a server for the internet and so on, so I could email him?'

'Yes.'

'Well, I did all that, and ever since then that's just what I've been doing. Sending emails.'

'And?'

'Sending emails to *you*.'

'To me? *Have* you?'

'Absolutely. And you've been sending them back.'

'I certainly haven't. Our computer's been stuffed in a box.'

'Exactly!'

'Exactly?'

'*You* haven't been getting them. But they didn't come back. They got sent somewhere else.'

'Sent to where?'

'That's the problem. I haven't a clue! I only realised it wasn't you when I got your letter.'

'But that's ridiculous. What email address did you use?'

'Yours!'

'You can't have. You would have had them returned.'

'But I did! I checked. But could there be two?'

'I don't think that can happen. The system wouldn't allow it. Once an address has been registered, no one else can have it. Unless it's with a different server of course. Definitely Cymserve?'

'Definitely. Griffith-at-cymserve-dot-co-dot-uk. And there's worse. Obviously, whoever's been getting my emails has been getting everything you would. Mindless prattling, bitching, ranting, shag lists –'

'Hang on. *Hang* on, *griffith*@cymserve? That's not right. Our email address is m-n-r-griffith at cymserve.'

'MNR? *Is* it?'

'It is. For Matt 'n' Rose. Not what you put. You just typed *griffith*. Not the same address at all.'

'Cripes! No wonder! Then whose address *is* it?'

'Haven't a clue. And it's a very common name. There must be hundreds – even thousands – of Griffiths in Wales. But

40

someone who's been on the Net for some time. Plain Griffith would have been snapped up early on, is my bet.'

'Which tells me nothing. Other than that it's not Sheila Rawlins. Anyway, they said 'Sorry, you got me' or something like that, and I've not heard from them since.'

'So no harm done then, *really*.'

'But it could be anyone!'

'So ask them.'

'I did! They wouldn't tell me.'

' So don't worry. You don't know them, so what does it matter?'

'But I might. There's at least a one in five hundred thousand chance that I do.'

'How d'you work that out?'

'Statistically, *obviously*. Wales isn't *that* big. Though the odds are shorter now. How many actual Griffiths online in Wales, d'you think?'

'Who cares? So what? So what if some clam digger living in Tenby knows the top five shag icons in Cefn Melin? They don't know them either, do they? Forget it.'

'Do clam diggers generally email each other?'

'Tsh, Charlie! Get a grip. What does it matter, *really*? Besides, it all sounds as if it could be rather fun, if you ask me. Like a pen-friend, except without the dodgy syntax. Is it a man or a woman, do you think?'

'Haven't the foggiest. I thought it was you!'

'So why don't you email them back again and ask them? You did say your life lacked excitement just lately.'

'Hmm. By the way. What *is* an 0898 habit?'

'Charlie, my love? Stay as sweet as you are.'

Chapter 6

I've decided that Rose is absolutely right. That what I have is not a low-life but a potential new pen-friend. Feeling suddenly imbued with a delightful spirit of adventure. I feign a headache and so despatch Phil home early, then despatch a further email to my new mystery friend.

griffith@cymserve.co.uk

Hello stranger.
    My friend has suggested that you might be a clam digger from Tenby. Please advise.
Charlie.

Answer in ninety seconds! Mystery friend is obviously on the same virtual wavelength.

thesimpsons@cymserve.co.uk

Hello back!
    I wish. But I do not own a bucket. Not sure it would be a prudent career move in any case. When was the last time *you* ate a clam?
griffith.

Fun indeed! Collect pickled shallots and a wine glass from the kitchen.

'Charlotte?' my dad calls. 'Are you back in that dining room?'

He is concerned, I know, that I have not 'acclimatised' sufficiently (and that I will perhaps become etiolated if I stay here too long).

'I'm in the *study*,' I correct him. 'I'm, er … doing some research.'

griffith@cymserve.co.uk

Dear griffith,
I honestly cannot remember. Though, thinking about it, aren't clams what they use in spaghetti vongole? And don't they go around selling them from baskets, in pubs? Like cockles? And are you male or female, by the way? All this time, I've been working on the assumption that you are my friend (Rose, obviously) but now I realise I don't actually know the first thing about you, and I have this niggling anxiety that you are, in fact, a man. And that you've been getting off on imagining me imagining what I'd like to do to with the guys on my shag list, etc., and that … There I go! This is the trouble. I just do not know who <u>or what</u> I'm talking to. Which is unsettling. <u>Please</u> tell me you're a girl, or, if not, that you're not a stalker / deeply unattractive person with a penchant for slacks / gay. Actually, gay is fine.
Charlie
PS. You could use the shells to make novelty gift boxes. The trade's seasonal, obviously, but I've heard people are willing to pay as much as £1.50 for a trinket box these days.

thesimpsons@cymserve.co.uk

Dear Charlie
Definitely male (though not gay or a stalker). Which I know will make you wince, but there's not a great deal I can (or would want to) do about it, frankly. Does it matter so much? And why should my maleness cause you anxiety? Isn't the whole essence of this sort of thing that it is a meeting of minds unfettered by prejudice? Isn't the fact that it doesn't matter about gender or looks the reason it works?
griffith.
PS I'm not terribly artistic. Perhaps you could give me some pointers, trinket box-wise, so that I can assess my potential as a small-scale manufacturer.

Hmmm.

griffith@cymserve.co.uk

Dear griffith,
Suspected as much. Could detect a slight *frisson*. Though, having suspected, I am now a tad uncertain where to take this thing. I suppose the sensible decision would be to simply cease communicating with you – you are undoubtedly a bit of a rascal – but your (very erudite) comments concerning minds meeting and being unfettered and so on lead me to suppose that you'd rather like to press on. But is this a sex thing? How do I know that 'unfettered' isn't simply a euphemism for sex, for example? I wouldn't want to be the unwitting recipient of any improper suggestions. Besides, I have a face like a pizza, boils and a stoop.
  Plus, where do you stand on geology?

Charlie.

thesimpsons@cymserve.co.uk

Dear Charlie,
Is that a trick question? If so, I'm tempted to say that where I stand is a place rich in geologically fascinating features with mainly igneous sub-strata(though not seismically active these past millennia). Can you place it?
  Unfettered is not a euphemism for sex in any circles I inhabit, though I can't speak for Cardiff, obviously. However, I'm sure it has the capacity to double up euphemistically, should the occasion merit it. (As, of course, does 'double up'.)
  I'm very glad to have instigated a *frisson*. Would you *like* this to be a sex thing? We can exchange smutty web site addresses, if you like. And it's of absolutely no consequence which foodstuff your face resembles. Mine was once likened to a steak and mushroom cobbler.
  Where do <u>you</u> stand on Tchaikovsky?

griffith.

Rats. Computer anorak / classical music buff. Might have known.

griffith@cymserve.co.uk

Dear griffith,
Oh dear. You're not a dreary cultural whiz, are you? I was just about to suggest frantic cyber-sex in an unusual setting of your choosing, and then you spoilt it all by mentioning a C word. I now have a vision of you sitting in a tank top and cord trousers, thrumming energetically to some concerto or other.

I'm utterly hopeless with classical music. I buy compilations of bits they use in adverts. Sorry, bought. It's been a while. Though that's not to say I don't like any of it. *Pathetique* (No 6?) is a favourite of my father's and has, therefore, been subliminally grafted onto my brain. And I like Stravinsky's Rite of Spring, which I heard in *Fantasia* when I was little. You know the bit? With the evolution of earth/volcanoes/dinosaurs cartoon? It's the rocks again, I'm afraid.

Speaking of which, can't we get back to them?
Charlie.

thesimpsons@cymserve.co.uk

Dear Charlie,
I have to say rocks would not be my first choice for sex, cyber or otherwise, though I will confess to having wondered if the old earthquake simulator at the Natural History Museum might not be an attractive venue for a seismically enhanced event. It also has the benefit of rubber flooring, as I recall.

I have to go now as it is way past my bedtime. Lovely to talk to you. Can we do it some more?
griffithx

PS Stravinsky's a little unstructured for me. You liking it figures, somehow.

This is more like it. I find I am absurdly pleased to be considered unstructured. And take it as a cue to adopt an

45

unpredictable stance by not responding immediately. Also take as a definite affirmation that Simpson genes are infinitely better suited to the earnest exploration of geologically fascinating corners of the globe / aspects of ancient cultures etc., than to the buying and selling of suburban houses. Fancy too, that I would enjoy Tenby immensely – can picture myself clam digging while developing an ear for Tchaikovsky on my Walkman.

But into each cyber-life, a little reality must intrude. Thus, the following week;

griffith@cymserve.co.uk

Dear griffith,
Apologies for the lengthy delay in responding. Uuurgh! What a start to the week! I've had real hassles at work the last couple of days. I have a client called Minnie (did I tell you I worked for an estate agent? Just what *have* I told you, period?). Anyway, she's elderly and very confused and she's supposed to be exchanging contracts on her house in a couple of weeks. (She's moving into a home, but she's very agitated about it, and thinks the place is run by aliens.) Anyway, the survey was supposed to be done at the beginning of the week and she wouldn't let them in – thought they'd come to beam her away somewhere – and I couldn't get hold of her social worker, and the buyer's agents were going ballistic about it, and my boss (who is cranky at the best of times) is in permanent hyperventilation mode about it, and the trouble is they're all just making it worse. And of course when I finally persuaded Minnie to let me in yesterday, she hadn't let the cat out for three days – imagine!!! Anyway, it's all sorted now and the survey's been re-arranged for next week. I just have some decidedly rank washing with which to occupy whatever pockets of opportunity my frenetic social life will allow.

Charlie

PPS Sorry to rant. So pleased you think the word seismic is sexy. Did you actually say that? Or am I just talking nonsense? Please advise.

thesimpsons@cymserve.co.uk

Hi,
I don't remember actually typing it, but, yes, deeply sexy. Though geologists in general, less so. And vulcanologists are very often excessively hirsute, I've found. Mountaineers, on the other hand, though less academically switched on to tectonics and seismology, often display an engaging enthusiasm for geological features. I have a mountaineer friend who's climbed K2 and, I believe, Changtse. He knows his stuff. I should put you in touch.

Sorry to hear about your traumatic week. Is your boss giving you a really hard time? Your Minnie sounds rather an unfortunate lady. Does she have no family?

griffith.

Find 'deeply sexy' so deeply sexy that I spend Friday lunchtime in the bookshop, poring over large geological tomes and books about Andes / Himalayas. I also purchase a travel book for cool, unstructured people, called *Trekking in Nepal*. On first inspection, it promises to be a rich source of both geographical and anthropological facts with which to impress my new cyber-friend.

'What's this?' asks my father, pausing in his paring to inspect it when I get home from work.

'A guide for people going trekking in Nepal,' I reply, fully aware that the question is rhetorical.

He flips through the maps and black-and-white plates. 'Hmmm. Hippy book, then. Kale or broad beans?'

'Wheat grass, ideally.'

Head off into study.

griffith@cymserve.co.uk

Hello again!
Yes, yes, *yes* please! I have been in touch with every travel agent this side of Kathmandu (well, Swindon, at least) and am

encountering a worrisome lack of expertise in the logistics department. Most galling, yesterday, was holding on for about fifteen minutes for the 'trailbreaking' expert, only to have her ask me if Everest was in India or Japan!!!! I am considering writing to Chris Bonington for advice. What do you think?

Minnie continues to trouble me. No, she has no family to speak of. Her husband died about ten years back. There is a son called Edward, but he's in Australia or somewhere, and nobody seems to be able to find out anything about him. I've known her a couple of years now, and she certainly doesn't get letters or phone calls from him. The social worker thinks she lost a child very young, but they don't know any more than that. It's all very depressing. I took her one of my dad's Madeira cakes last week and she cried. I think she used to make them for her husband.

But listen to me! You don't want to hear me droning on about all the dreary bits of my life! Let's talk mountains – ever been up one? You sound quite knowledgeable.
Charliexx

thesimpsons@cymserve.co.uk

Dear Charlie,
More knowledgeable than some, far less so than others. I too have a lot of big dreary bits in my life, regrettably, so don't get to do half of the things I would like to. On which note, I spotted the two kisses. This is new, isn't it? Does it signify a subtle development in our relationship? I wonder what the conventions of this sort of thing are.
griffithxxx

griffith@cymserve.co.uk

Dear griffith,
Three kisses – you raver, you! Actually, I could do with a little more passion in my life; I am concerned that my virtual relationship is looking like becoming more exciting than my actual one (with Phil, to whom you've already been (virtually) introduced, and who – bless him – has had a rather bad press). He's a good, kind, sweet man, but I don't think he's the man for me. Come to think of it, if you have to point out that

someone is good, kind and sweet then you're on a hiding to nothing, are you not? Trouble is, I can't seem to find the right moment to finish it, you know? Which is all a bit pathetic for a woman of my age.

Listen to me! What has my age got to do with anything? This isn't the real world, so I can be what I like! There's a thought. Perhaps I should develop an alter-cyber-ego. Call myself something like Gentian Foxglove, and regale you with lurid suggestions for sex games and so on (there must be a copy of Razzle or Rustler or Hustler or whatever around the house somewhere; there've been times when I couldn't change a bed-sheet without finding myself face to face with a crotch).
Charliexxx

'Gentian Foxglove! You sad person, you! Though I have to say, it does rather suit you. You've always had a Kate Bush-ish flower fairy kind of look. Mind you, I've heard a lot about this sort of thing. There's a maths teacher at school who has been having cyber-sex with a professor from Baltimore for two years now, apparently.'

Rose, who has spent much of the intervening week failing to get hold of me by telephone, wants to know just what it is that is so compelling about my clam digger.

'Oh, there's none of that,' I tell her. 'He's just really nice, that's all.'

Which is a lie. There's plenty of 'that'. In my head at least. I hear her tut.

'Must be. You're spending a heck of a lot of time emailing him. Is this a twice-a-week obsession or are you getting a fix daily.'

'It's getting that way. God, Rose, am I that sad?'

'Hmm. Depends on what your intentions are, I guess. Should I mention the P word?'

For a second, I think she's referring to the phone bill. Which says it all, really, as she actually means Phil.

'Fair comment. OK. And yes. I guess you should. And yes, you are right. I should do something about things. And yes, you're right again. I should do it forthwith.'

She sighs. 'But Charlie, are you – you know, with this email stuff – barking up a dead horse here?'

'And you Head of English! Yeah, right again. OK, I probably am. *Definitely* am. But I haven't any other livestock on the go right now, have I? It's just a bit of fun, Rose. A bit of zing in my life.'

And speaking of zing – good grief! Almost November already. 11.57 p.m.

griffith@cymserve.co.uk

Dear griffith,
Oh dear. I'm pathetic and then some. Had absolutely decided to – what's the word here – chuck? Give the elbow to? Dump? Whatever. *End* it with Phil yesterday. But failed miserably. Status all very much quo still. Well, what was I to do? I didn't ask to go to the cinema, did I? And yes, I know I could have said, no, I don't want to go and see a film, couldn't I? But *how* could I? He was so keen to see it. Plus he'd already got tickets over the phone, which made it worse. As it would, wouldn't it? And how can you compete with surround sound? And then, of course, the film was the *only* thing he wanted to talk about, and, God, I've already invited him over for Sunday lunch! And I feel so guilty about it all – what with you and everything, and – Oh, listen to me! Sorry. <u>Sorry</u>. The deal is that we don't talk about this stuff, isn't it? You never talk about this stuff. Ever. I know nothing about you. If we were having an *actual* relationship it would be a bit one-sided, wouldn't it? In fact, pretend I didn't send this. Though I will anyway, *obviously*.
Charliexxx

12.32. Twelve thirty-two in the morning!

thesimpsons@cymserve.co.uk

Dear Charlie,

I don't remember making any deals of that nature. And wouldn't dream of doing so. What did you mean 'what with you and everything'? I'm online right now, by the way.

Love griffithxxx

Oh!

griffith@cymserve.co.uk

Dear griffith,

I'm not sure what I meant. What do *you* think?
Charliexxx

thesimpsons@cymserve.co.uk

Dear Charlie,
I don't know. It's not my situation, is it? But if your relationship with Phil is not giving you anything you need, then he's probably not getting much out of it either. So you should end it, shouldn't you? For both your sakes. Move on and all that stuff.
griffithxxxx

Ah, but move on to what?

griffith@cymserve.co.uk
Dear griffith,
Move on as in staying in a lot, you mean?

thesimpsons@cymserve.co.uk

I doubt that. I'm sure you get plenty of male attention.

griffith@cymserve.co.uk

Dear griffith,
How would *you* know? Anyway, I was thinking more along the lines of reflection and yoga. And I meant staying in as in sitting at the computer emailing you, by the way. Which is male

attention of a sort, isn't it?

thesimpsons@cymserve.com

Which would certainly be good from this end. As Gentian Foxglove? She's grown on me.

griffith@cymserve.co.uk

No. As me. Such a shame you're only ephemeral.

thesimpsons@cymserve.co.uk

I'm just as real as you are, Charlie. Though virtual, certainly. But why ephemeral? I'm not going anywhere, am I?

griffith@cymserve.co.uk

Ephemeral precisely *because* you are virtual, griffith. Does the phrase 'get a life' strike a chord? Anyway, stop playing with words. The fact is you *could* have a face like a pudding, couldn't you? In which case I think you should email a picture of your horrific self *now* to give me some incentive to get out more.

thesimpsons@cymserve.co.uk

I'm sure you get out plenty. Just with the wrong guy.

griffith@cymserve.co.uk

I know, I know, I know. Plus, you must think I'm completely pathetic. Do you?

thesimpsons@cymserve.co.uk

Charlie, is what *I* think a factor here?

Yes, it is, griffith.
    Yes-very-much-so, come to think of it. God, Simpson. *Sad.* I have to pause to collect the fizzy sensations that are

52

presumably trying to pass for my thoughts at the moment. I pause some more. What is it with this guy? What is it *about* this guy?

griffith@cymserve.co.uk

What exactly do you get out of all this, griffith? I mean, it's all a bit of a novelty for me, of course. Plus, it's great to have this complete stranger dispensing wisdom on my shambolic love life and so on. But what are *you* in it for? Is your life crap too? no, scrub that. My life's not crap, just a bit lacking in whatever it is that means most normal happy people don't spend their evenings staring at screens. Plus I'm a bit nonplussed by life right now. Plus *you* seem to ... Plus I can't help but think ... God! Listen to me!

thesimpsons@cymserve.co.uk

I *like* listening to you. I like that you enjoy *being* listened to. Anyway, I could listen for Wales. It's what I do best (cursor based or otherwise).

griffith@cymserve.com

OK. Listen to this, then. I had this dream. And, in it, I lost your email address. I mean *really* lost it. I ran through my whole hard disk and it had gone. Completely. And I couldn't seem to remember what it was. I was trying, oh, I don't know – every surname in the phone book – sending emails in this mad frenzy. And no one responded. Every one came back. Then I woke up – as one does – and I thought 'this is crazy!'. This is just some guy I swap emails with. Probably with a face like ... no, scrub that. We've done that bit, haven't we! Anyhow, the point is that if I'm having ridiculous dreams about guys who don't even really exist (bodily speaking), then I really should pluck up the courage and call it a day with Phil, right?

thesimpsons@cymserve.co.uk

Dear Charlie,
You said it. But, for God's sake, get on with it, will you? Life is far too short to waste your time on anything that doesn't make you happy. Oh, and how about this – I read it just this morning, and I thought of you (it's a quote by Colleen McCulloch): 'the lovely thing about being forty is that you can appreciate 25 year old men more'. So it makes sense, doesn't it? Do it. Do it now. Then you'll still have plenty of time to appreciate a twenty-five year old man or two.
griffithxxxx
Or three. Though perhaps one will be enough.

griffith@cymserve.co.uk

Dear griffith,
Wow! You're surely not twenty-five, are you? It never occurred to me! What a wonderful, uplifting thought! Actually, it all makes sense. What with Bill Gates and silicon valley and so on. (Though he *is* forty-odd by now, isn't he?) But, hey! What a lovely surprise; a toy-cyber-boy! How <u>exactly</u> would you like to be appreciated? Tell me now.
      Yours, in feverish anticipation,
Charliexxxx and X

I have to wait twenty-four hours for a response, but as I'm still sailing blissfully on a high fluffy cloud of silliness, anything-being-possible and ridiculous speculation, I care little. I care not a jot.

thesimpsons@cymserve.co.uk

Dear Charlie,
Oh dear. Sorry, but I'm going to have to disappoint you. Not *quite* twenty-five, I'm afraid. But feel free to pretend, if it makes you feel better. And what I lack in muscle tone I can certainly make up for in imagination. And in a dim light – no – forget that. When you reach a certain age you're not so demanding about that sort of thing anyway. I'm certainly not. Give me enthusiasm and a big bed and, well … Did I say 'disappoint'?
griffith.XXXXX

griffith@cymserve.co.uk

Dear griffith,
Much relieved. There's nothing so daunting as the sight of young flesh rippling with great expectations. Because while I've no doubt I could give it a run for its money, I'm less certain the concept would hang together so well, once the flesh in question clapped eyes on my almost-forty-year-old packaging...

I pause to grope for an appropriate adjectival grouping and find myself suddenly transfixed. Hang on a minute. Hang *on* a minute. I bring up the last few emails and re-read them more carefully (at least, with less childish emphasis on the bits *between* the type). Aha. Hang. On. A. Minute. Delete email, and send instead;

Hang on a minute. How did you know I'm going to be forty?

Await answer. Make tea. Await answer. Drink tea. Await answer. Take mug back to kitchen and wash up. Await answer. I have been here before. *Do not get answer*. I type;

Come on. I'm waiting. And this silence feels guilty.

And unexpectedly scary. I send the email and wait some more. Then go to bed.
  Well, what else is there *to* do? I come down obscenely early in the morning but there's *still* no post. I spend some minutes groaning and pulling on my fringe. Spend a further few thinking, then groan a bit more. Type;

griffith@cymserve.co.uk

Oh, God. So it *is* true, isn't it? All this time and you've done it to me again! I can't believe it! I can't believe *me*. You *do* know me, don't you? You know exactly who I am. Oh my God. You bastard. Grrrrrr. I am <u>so</u> cross with you. I can see I'm just

55

going to have to move to Canterbury. God, I hate you. I'm
going back to bed.

I click hard on the mouse and send the email in high dudgeon.
I recall also what griffith said about action. I'll give him
action. But who him? *Who* him?

I have ample opportunity to consider his identity, as I do
not receive a response until late Saturday night.

thesimpsons@cymserve.co.uk

Look Charlie,
I'm sorry. I'm sorry. I'm sorry. And you don't hate me. Really. I
can see you might be a little riled, but it has been a laugh,
hasn't it? And, believe me, I wouldn't dream of telling anyone
anything you told me. I'm not that kind of guy. Look, can't we
just forget all about this?
griffith.

Sunday. Late a.m.

Stomping irresolute and irritable around the house while
the implications of my admission of my (albeit wistful rather
than actionable) sexual inclinations flood nerve-janglingly into
the quagmire of my consciousness. I telephone Rose to run
this depressing development by her.

'How d'you know?'

'Rose, believe me. I just *know*.'

'How? Give me evidence. Oh. In fact, no. Hold on. I have
to turn my parsnips. Hold on … There. Sorted. So. How do
you know?'

'Because he knew I was going to be forty next birthday.'

'But you could have told him that, surely. It's a big thing in
your life.'

'Oh, don't *you* start. And I didn't, for definite. I went
through my old emails; every single one. The nearest I got was
the fact that I mentioned it was going to be my birthday and
that I hadn't been to Nepal yet and so on.'

'So he could have guessed forty then, couldn't he? It's *the*

56

big birthday, after all.'

'Ah, but I know he didn't. When I challenged him he didn't email me back for hours and hours. And then when I emailed him again and ranted at him and told him I hated him, he emailed back and said, "You don't hate me, really." As if making a point, you know?'

'Hmm, I suppose. But not necessarily.'

'And now I've gone through the old emails again, little things strike me. Like him mentioning Cardiff. I never told him where I lived, ever.'

'Hmm. Fairly conclusive then.'

'Completely conclusive. He knows who I am. He knows all about me. And yet I don't have the first clue who he is. God, this is awful! Awful! Perhaps it's better if I don't know. I'll never be able to look anyone in the eye, ever again.'

Sunday. Still p.m. Drag, drag, drag.

Phil arrived, on schedule, for lunch, clutching a bottle of red and a pot of chrysanthemums for me.

'You always get your money's worth with a pot mum,' declared my father happily. 'Cut that back, Charlotte, and it'll flower again for you. You can even take cuttings and grow new ones with those.'

Oh, God. Oh, *God.* If you were a flower, I thought miserably, then what would you be? A lily? A briar rose? An orchid, perhaps? Charlie Simpson, of course, would be a small pot chrysanthemum; cheerful, no-nonsense, with big bile-coloured blooms. Long-lived, dependable, bright, undemanding; a flower so completely without pretension or attitude that only the most evil and foul-tempered person could consider it anything but, well, *jolly* nice.

Phil, who had doubtless simply scooped up what was to hand in the Spar, and who, anyway, had probably not the remotest idea why a gift of a potted chrysanthemum would cause me anything but grateful delight (and why should he?), nodded cheerfully as he took off his raincoat.

'Something smells good!' he chirruped. I made off with the

wine.

The trouble with Phil – the trouble with *us* – was that we had never reached a degree of closeness that would be sufficient for me to be able to say 'I'm sorry, but I actually can't *stand* chrysanthemums' and so on, and now, six months on, it was too late to start. Which is why, I suddenly realised, with breathtaking conviction, one should never contemplate adult (sex-inclusive) relationships with people for whom we feel less than compulsive desire. It wasn't that I didn't fancy Phil. Indeed, the first couple of times we disrobed and got down to it, I recall it as being immensely enjoyable. But then I recall that for some weeks, eight years back, I felt like that about playing Sonic The Hedgehog as well.

While Phil laid the table and Dad beat up a horseradish, I just sat and drank wine and felt stroppy and guilty and glared at the pot bloody yellow bloody mum.

But, then again, *had* they been lilies, just how would I have felt?

'So,' Phil announced, while my father doled out roast potatoes. 'My trip's all fixed up. I'm off Friday teatime. You going to go the Stablefords' then?'

He addressed this to me, but it was my father who answered.

'Looking forward to it, Phillip. It'll be nice to get to know the locals, so to speak. And can't have Charlie turning up on her own, now, can we? A girl needs an escort.'

Phil looked at me carefully, presumably to ascertain whether my father was making some sort of point here (which he was), and whether I was in agreement with it (which I wasn't). I had never indicated the least irritation about him trolling off up the dales without me, principally because he had asked me if I'd wanted to come when he'd booked it, and I had said no. So the fact of my father intimating that some archaic rule had been broken, coupled with Phil looking / feeling / acting even remotely guilty about it, coupled with the fact that I had all these ridiculous but unsettling stirrings about a man I was swapping emails with, made me even more irritable than I already was. I didn't need escorting anywhere, thank you. I rolled my eyes to emphasise the fact, and, quite without consciously realising I was doing it, reached out and plucked a bud – *pop!* – from the chrysanthemum. My father took the roasting tin back to the kitchen.

'Do you have a problem, Charlie?' Phil enquired quietly.

My scarlet face clashed with the forlorn yellow petals.

'I'm sorry. I don't know why I did that,' I said.

Grrr. I wish I was in Canterbury. Wish I was eating parsnips from Rose's Raeburn, instead of disgusting grey roast beef and rag-rug cabbage, plus jam roly-poly, with Ben and Phil and Dad. Wish I had gone with subversive plan B and snuck off with Ben to the Sports Café and eaten nachos and chilli dogs while playing slam-dunk or playing on the complimentary Playstation console. *Anything*. Wish I hadn't invited Phil over *at all*. Wish I could pluck up enough resolve to tell Phil that I'm very much *not* an English Heritage type person. Wish I could pluck up enough courage to tell Phil I'm actually very much not a *Phil* type person. Wish I could take Ben and Dan up a very large mountain and explain cols / moraines / screes, etc., while marvelling at the inspirational new perspective on life afforded by the breathtaking high altitude aspect. Wish I could get a new perspective, period. Wish mainly that I could persuade myself that mystery griffith was really of not the slightest importance at all.

'*Is* there something up?' This was Phil, while we were loading the dishwasher. 'You've not seemed yourself over the last few weeks.'

Crash, clatter, fumble, bang.

'Look,' I said. 'I'm sorry about the chrysanthemum, OK? And, no. No, there isn't. Phil – *up*side down. The cutlery has to go in *up*side down or it doesn't get clean. See? And if you put all the knives in together like that, the blades stick to each other and you end up having to wash them all again. There. No. No, I'm fine.'

'No you're not.' He rattled the cutlery basket. 'Feeling a bit low? Hormones?'

Hormones? Why do men say that? Do they *really* think it will cast them in a saintly, so-switched-on-to-women's-issues type light?

'Yes. I have the usual complement, thank you.'

'What?'

'Of hormones.' I slapped down the meat tin and a big glob of fat hit his trouserleg. 'As do you. But if *you're* in a strop, I don't ask after the state of your adrenals, do I?'

'I only asked. It's not like you to be testy and irritable. Is it Rose going? Is it me?'

'Of course not,' I said, in my instinctive, not facing up to the issue at large, usual ineffectual Simpson manner. 'It's just that I really can't *be* with someone who insists on slapdash dishwasher procedures.'

Phil flapped his tea towel and said, rather sneerily, 'A touch anal for someone who prides herself on being a bit of a 'wild child', isn't it?' *And* put finger quote marks around the wild child bit. Pah!

'Pshaw! When did I ever say I was *that*?'

'You didn't need to,' he sniffed, launching a spoon at the cutlery basket. 'It's a bit of a *persona* thing with you. You know – the free spirit bit. Don't pretend you don't ham it up.'

What?

'Ham it up? Persona bit? What are you on about? Just because I don't want to spend every waking moment footling around appreciating architraves and first editions of worthy biographies, and going to the bloody opera, doesn't make me a 'wild child' you know.' (Even though I *was* rather pleased with the label, which sat rather well with my 'unstructured' flower fairy tag.) 'And,' I finished, ' I'm *certainly* not anal.'

He laughed (Cheek!) as he reached for the dishwasher powder. 'You bloody are.'

'Don't swear,' I snapped back, quick as you like. 'Ben might be around.'

'Oh, and of course he wouldn't know any *swear* words, would he? And I must say I take offence at 'footling'. I don't footle.'

'If I do a 'persona bit' then you bloody footle. And that teaspoon's gone through the mesh. Get it out, please, before you switch it on, or the spinner won't work.'

Sunday evening.

Nothing sorted. No progress. Have failed to finish with Phil. Have failed to communicate with Phil in *any* sense. In fact, I've been having conversations with Phil which are so banal that I am almost convinced that I've been married to him for twenty years and have simply neglected to remember. And I am considered anal. I am most definitely not anal. Phil is the anal one, as he is so concerned about food debris soiling skin / hair / clothes, etc., that he cannot bring himself to execute the risky manoeuvre involved in loading cutlery in the drainer basket tines / blades up. Hah. Anal in the *extreme*. Whereas my own stance is based purely on the practical consideration of the inefficiency and irritation involved in retrieving still-dirty cutlery. I'm concerned however re the 'wild child' tag. Though uplifting on the face of it, the 'persona' angle is rather disquieting. Do not wish to be considered a poser among my friends. Will henceforth have to keep quiet about my Everest ambition, or I will appear pretentious.

It's clearer still that I am definitely stringing out the Phil / ending it debacle through a subconscious terror of total existential aloneness. Plus (if I'm honest) practical aloneness in social function situations. I cannot take a virtual stranger to the Dog and Trouserleg. But now I do have Dad to take out with me. So I *must* end it. (But must pay for the dry cleaning of Phil's trousers first.)

4 a.m.

Wake suddenly and re-run old emails in brain. *God*. Who the hell *is* griffith? I just don't know *anyone* by that name. Except … except … think, Simpson. Think!

4.22 a.m.

Ratted! That's it! Yes! *Ratted!*

Monday. Decisive. Before work (*after* strenuous attention to hair / bow alignment, as extent of carpet / upholstery cleaning at Cherry Ditchling is sure to become known any day. Do not wish to antagonise Davina further.)

griffith@cymserve.co.uk

Right, griffith. Moment of truth time, or else. I now realise that you were at Rose and Matt's leaving party, and do not intend to rest until I have deduced your identity. Am going to phone cymserve as soon as I log off. If I tell them you're stalking my modem with improper suggestions, I'm sure they'll supply the information I need.
Charlotte Simpson.
cc. cymserve.co.uk

Hah! cc. a nice touch. That should do the trick!

Dinner time. Stressed.
　　Turfed Ben off computer at 7 p.m. sharp with the promise of a quality-time, activity-based weekend next week. (But still held out over decision regarding his desired encroachment into low-life activities with his brother in London.)
　　Bing! went computer. You have post! Imagining myself as a cute yet feisty Meg Ryan character (except hair too curly, too long, too split-endy, plus not mega-buck movie star, plus doesn't *everyone* like to think they're bloody Meg Ryan?, plus oops! must anyway refrain from adopting personas), I cyber-walked to my post room and retrieved the latest email.

thesimpsons@cymserve.co.uk

Dear Charlotte Simpson (if we must),
Though the idea of stalking your modem with improper suggestions has definite appeal (despite boils/stoop/pizza caveat), I am beginning to feel rather embarrassed about this whole business. Please believe me when I say that all your

secrets are safe with me, and that I think it really would be best if we left it at that. Hope you make Everest. And get your kitchen. Though personally, I'd put my cash into the trip and make it a great one. A new kitchen is fine, but it won't make you happy. Being (almost) on top of the world certainly will.
Griffithxx

Thought; Oh! Griffith! With a capital G! Ah! Griffith with a capital G, who is male, who knows me, who knows I was ratted at Rose and Matt's party, who thinks it would *really* be best if we left it at that. Oh, *really*. I'll *bet*. But not a chance, buster. Not an earthly chance. Will work on a process of elimination from Rose and Matt's party guest list just as soon as Rose digs it up and emails it to me. Oh, *yes*. And if the list fails to establish mystery-griffith identity, I will simply trap all passing men-friends and engage them in fact-finding disingenuous light conversation at every social engagement until the matter is resolved. (Plus Everest thing very – very *something*. Very what?) So send;

griffith@cymserve.co.uk

Dear Griffith,
Sweet-talk all you like, it's still not good enough. But, OK, let's do a deal. We will take this no further. But to that end we must work on the need-to-know principle. If you want this to end, you'll appreciate that I need to know who you are. And if you don't want me to spend any more time trying to find out (and I will – I have a guest list, and it's a simple case of elimination), then *you* need to tell me who you are. End of cyber-dialogue.
Charlotte Simpson.

PS But before I go – what about that guy you know who can give me the advice about my trip? You never told me who he was, and I think you at least owe me that.

'Mum, what are you doing? It's quarter to six in the morning!'
    'Er, nothing, Ben. Just popping a plant stick in my yucca.'
    'At this time? So why's the computer on then?'

'Erm … silly me. Must have left it on overnight.'

'No you didn't. I used it last, remember. Unless you've been – Mum, you do know you're on-line, don't you?'

'Erm … ooops! Er … that's because … in fact … LOOK! What *is* this? Twenty questions? If you're up, make yourself useful and put the kettle on or something! Don't come in here quizzing me about … well, about anything, quite frankly. Go on then! Don't just stand there!'

'OK, OK, OK! Moo-*dy* or what?'

And all that for a deeply uninformative;

thesimpsons@cymserve.co.uk

Dear Charlotte Simpson,
I know I owe you that, but if I tell you who he is then you'll find out who I am, won't you? So, regrettably, I can't. I'm sorry I said I would put you in touch – I wasn't thinking. I will find out anything I can, however, and get it to you, promise.
Griffith.

Pah! On the way to work I compile a mental list of the male contingent of Rose and Matt's party and come to the depressing realisation that, to the best of my belief, all men-friends of my acquaintance at said party are either married / have partners or are somebody's grandad. Or are gauche teenage sons of more mature friends. So Griffith is either a rogue pensioner, an unusually eloquent juvenile, or a furtive, unavailable, *out of bounds* man.

Hmmm. Cyber-flirtatiousness is *not* a good idea.

Chapter 7

DEFINITELY NOT GOOD IDEA. Stableford Saturday. Late p.m. Tense.

What a funny thing. Having started the week in a mood of strident indignation and full of zeal about exposing my phantom email stalker etc., I find that I have ended the week in an unexpected romantically charged flap. I waved Phil off on Thursday with a peculiar surge of end-of-term excitement, imagining myself and griffith engaged in a frantic clinch at the much talked about Stableford Bonfire Night barbecue – which I am certain beyond question griffith will attend.

I'm now oscillating between cogitating anxiously about what to wear and being very angry about having developed the worrying (nay, *pathetic*) perception that what I look like merits any anxiety in the first place. I look like I look, and will look so whatever, i.e. unremarkable, pretty-ish, reasonable bustline, topped off with reliably unruly hair.

Having considered the miserable possibility of griffith being gorgeous stroke married stroke (arrrgh!) one of shaggable top six etc., I have instead decided he is allowed to be none of above. I have decided, rather, that griffith is / was an elusive, enigmatic, box of Black Magic chocolates type character, who has hovered mysteriously on the fringes of the Cefn Melin social scene keeping a profile too low even for eagle-eyed Simpson consideration. Indeed, I have expanded griffith into a figure of almost legendary and iconic proportions and imagined a whole saga-type international airport novel around him.

Except set in Tenby, of course.

11 p.m.

But perhaps I shouldn't have gone after all.

Well there wasn't any point in *not* going, was there? Not

going would have involved spending Saturday evening watching *Family Fortunes* or *Casualty* or some ropey film effort, while absorbing a relentless whining commentary from Dad about how he'd gone to a lot of trouble making a Sussex Pond Pudding (True. But why?) and how he'd told all sorts of people he'd be going to the party and that they'd be very disappointed if he didn't show (false, *surely?*). Plus, I knew Ben would never forgive me as his hormone surge is threatening to take him over entirely, with spot clusters rampant and claiming ever more territory, in the manner of bacteria on nutrient agar jelly. Plus, and mainly, as there had been not a single communication from mystery griffith all week, I was, I realised, practically hyperventilating with frustration about his steadfast refusal to spill the beans re his ID.

So we went.

Early reconnaissance revealed any number of prospective griffiths. Stableford parties always include a large male corporate contingent (from Bill Stableford's cutting edge of technology type firm in Cardiff Bay), some of which could have been at Rose and Matt's do also, given the complex dynamics of pairings and blood ties and, quite possibly, phases of the moon. And with Cardiff being Cardiff, you could sign up for a course in small mammal husbandry in the Amazon Basin and still expect to find someone you knew in the queue.

But conscious that I was in danger of looking like an old mad crone with mystical vision who could see people's spectral auras and so on, I decided being pro-active in griffith detection was a bit of a non-starter. I'd just have to bide my time, keep my wits about me, and hope.

I joined in, therefore, with all the usual firework barbecue party type activities, draping myself alluringly over the Stablefords' swing-seat, and making appropriate weee! wow! noises as rockets expired in their milk bottles and Catherine wheels whizzed enthusiastically shedwards – I even took charge of an ironic sparkler contingent (the average child age being fourteen or so). None of which proved to be productive romantically, so eventually, spying a lone adult male, I went and holed up under the jaunty green barbecue awning instead.

And found myself with a like-minded soul at last. Richard Potter, whose general air of skittishness might have led one less astute than myself to jump to erroneous cyber-conclusions, was never a contender for covert emailing stunts. Despite his glorious, dancing, come-to-bed eyebrows, over which he seemed to have little control, Richard sent out only signals of terror – terror lest anyone female and his side of eighty might leap up and shove their tits in his face. (This being due to a recent extra-marital-shenanigans crisis, and his subsequent – if now reversed – harrowing relocation by wife Julia to a lino-infested flat in Cathays.)

I came upon him lurking by the condiments trestle, where, whilst ripping the skin from his chicken, crocodile fashion, he'd launched a volley of translucent pink blobs at his shirt.

'Death by defrosted drumstick!' I quipped.

Blank look. Engineer. No food hygiene awareness. 'Really?' he said, eyeing the stump with alarm.

'Only joking,' I chortled. 'I'm sure it tastes lovely. Ha ha. Here, let me help you. Have a dab with my tissue.'

'Thanks. Here on your own?'

'I guess so. In spirit. Dad and Ben are here somewhere, but Phil's at some sort of Brontë weekend. How's Julia?'

'Oh, fine,' he said, instantly (and endearingly) blushing. We moved on to a hard landscaping and quarrying imbroglio till Caroline Stableford bore down upon us with yet another assortment of speared flesh, nestling invitingly in a bath of leached bodily fluids.

'Try a brochette,' she urged. 'They're surf and – don't laugh – hen coop. Ha, ha. The green bits (the black bits) are deep-fried radish leaves.'

'I'm allergic,' I improvised. 'Prawns make my face go all blotchy.'

'These won't. They're fresh ones.'

And still trying to breast-stroke through the chicken plasma, by the look of them. I shook my head. 'No, really. I simply can't risk it.'

'Hmm,' she said. Adding by way of her eyebrows that going all blotchy was my natural party look anyway, and more a mulled wine than shellfish-based facial response.

'Richard, then. Tempt you?'

His left eyebrow tangoed. Then lowered with relief as she gave up and left.

But one could never be far from a Stableford in Cefn Melin.

'No Phil, then?' Bill asked, moments later. He was doing the rounds with a Vin de Pays winebox. I was sucking a Twiglet, and thus unable to answer. I shook my head.

'Weekend in Yorkshire,' explained Richard. 'A coach trip.'

'Oh? He never mentioned,' said Bill.

'Never mentioned what?'

'Last night. About a coach trip. When I saw him in the Flag. Office do, was it? Or just a Friday night piss-up?'

Piss-up? What piss-up? *Phil* at a piss-up?

'This was last night?' I asked, feeling suddenly stupid.

'No Phil, then?' echoed Adam Jones, who'd just wandered across.

'No sirree,' Bill confirmed with a headshake, as Caroline returned, forcing Adam to deflect the brochette-laden tray.

'Just been saying,' Bill added, before I could. 'He's away on a coach trip. Yorkshire, you say, Charlie? Don't envy him two-fifty miles on a coach!'

I irritably scooped up a handful of peanuts.

'But they were setting off at tea-time. He was leaving work early.'

'Well he must have done that – amount he had on board.'

Phil *drunk*?

'Perhaps the coach was delayed.' This was Adam Jones again – interjecting in typical spit-spot Mary Poppins crisis management style. 'I expect they stopped off for a drink.'

Of course, I thought. And I'm Judith Chalmers.

'No Phil, then?' Davina, now. 'Pass the mayo, Adam.'

'Just saying,' said Bill. 'He's off bussing round Yorkshire.

With er ...'

'With Charlotte Brontë, apparently!' chortled Caroline, skewering Bill with a covert, but still perfectly obvious, look.

Which everyone saw. And then pretended to not see. Mouthfuls were taken. Throats were cleared. I picked up my drink.

'Well,' I said. 'No doubt I'll soon hear all about it. Ah! There's my father. And it's almost eleven. Better liberate Francesca before Ben does. Um. Yes.'

Back in the bloody toilet, and crying! What *was* it with me lately?

Caroline Stableford's downstairs loo had a cream stencilled muslin bag thing on a small coat hanger hanging from the radiator. Which cheered me up no end. Principally because it had *eleven* toilet rolls in it. Which led me to conjecture that there must be precious few crises one could find oneself in where a ten-toilet-roll complement would find itself lacking. Having run out of Handy Andies, I used an extravagant dozen or so sheets to mop up the trails of mascara. And then wondered what perverse personality facet would lead to Caroline's toilet arrangements making me feel better. But, nevertheless, it did.

Far less cheering, however, was emerging from the cloakroom to find both Adam and Davina Jones hovering by the door.

Davina thrust a finger into the airspace between us. 'Ah, Charlie!' she said. 'The Drinkwater survey. Is it booked, or has Minnie been stalling again?'

I cleared my throat. Smiled at her. 'Monday. 10.30. I'll be there. Don't worry.'

'Uh-huh. I hope so. Well, I'm off. See you next. Adam, keys.' She flattened her palm to receive them, then pecked his cheek lightly and tripped off down the hall.

'Right-ho,' I said to her back. Then, slightly embarrassed to find myself once again in a snivelling situation with the good doctor (who surely, by now, considered me a complete flake),

'Did you, er … want to use …'

'Yes, I did,' he confirmed, nodding and stepping back slightly so I could move around him. 'But d'you want this? You've a bit of something …'

He gestured to my (puff-o-puffy) eye, then smiled and plucked something from a pocket. He dangled it in front of me. It was a hankie. Unused, ironed, and depressingly snowy.

I took it and sighed.

'Why it is some people *always* have a clean hankie?' I burbled. 'I try telling myself it's not a particularly life-enhancing virtue, but, deep down, it makes me feel really inadequate.'

As did any overt display of effective household linen management. Dan's pitiful pants supply leapt to mind.

Adam Jones looked at me with the sort of facial arrangement that probably swelled the gynaecological surgery queue tenfold, then batted the air in a deprecatory arc.

'Sheer fortuitousness,' he said. 'Cleaning lady came today, that's all.'

'Oh, don't mind me,' I said, glad Davina hadn't actually ironed it herself. 'Stupid, stupid, stupid!'

He hovered, smiling benignly, while I began dabbing hopefully with the hankie. 'Look,' he said. 'Do you want to go back in and use the mirror first?'

'No, no. You go right on in,' I assured him.

'No, really … please. Go ahead,' he urged.

For God's sake! 'For goodness sake! Really, I'm *fine!*'

His forehead creased and he looked at me quizzically. 'You don't look it.'

This was getting ridiculous. He'd be offering to take my pulse next. '*Really,*' I insisted. 'Can't a girl have a small eyelash / cornea fusion crisis without everybody –'

He laughed. A sort of trrrhgh! Then shook his head. His hair, I noticed, didn't shake with it. Very short, very wavy, very thick, very dense.

'You have *such* a wacky turn of phrase,' he said. To which there was really no answer. Other than 'Bugger off, will you?'

which, under the circumstances, didn't seem like a terribly good idea. Which made me crosser. I was beginning to feel like I was getting the measles. Breaking out in offbeat descriptive quips all over the place.

'That's me!' I sang. 'A ditty, a smile, a merry quip and so on. Excuse me, won't you? My face,' I explained, 'is collapsing again.'

Eleven.

No Phil then, indeed. I'll give them no bloody Phil then. I'll give *Phil* no bloody Phil then.

I'm in the doghouse, of course, with Father. He has discovered a new friend, in the shape of Hester, Stableford granny (Don't know which side. Don't much care) and fellow preserves enthusiast, and wishes to be left to wow her with his extensive repertoire of facts about pectin. In the doghouse also with Ben. *He* has discovered new Facets Of Francesca and wishes to be left to wow her with his (albeit, I hope, less extensive) repertoire of ways to get inside her bra.

We march home in a terse and uncommunicative crocodile, punctuated by dissident mutterings and belches from behind, and, in my case, a feeling that life is happening somewhere else altogether (in mystery-griffith style pine-clad shag-piled sixties penthouse, in Cadbury-mauve lounge suit and fur mules etc.)

Midnight. *No Phil, then*. What's the matter with them all? Like, 'Yes! here he is! I keep him in a special pouch in my knickers, you ninnies!'

There will, of course, be an innocent explanation. Like; Phil was just on his way to the coach stop when he bumped into an old school friend and, seeing that he had an hour to kill (being an ulcer-containment hour early for everything), he decided to go for a drink with him to talk about old times, and one thing led to another and …

No. The only one thing that leads to another with Phil is it being seven o'clock and then it being eight o'clock and so on.

OK. Phil missed the coach.

No. Never.

OK. Phil got on the coach, realised he'd left his wallet or something …

No. Never.

OK. Phil got on the coach and the coach set off, but it broke down en route, and they all got off and went to the pub while it was fixed (or whatever) and by the time the coach was ready to go they were all a bit worse for wear, and he wasn't able to call me because Ben was surfing the net all evening and our phone was constantly engaged (*must* get extra line), and he couldn't call me today because he was indeed on the coach all day with a hangover, and probably fully intends to call me tomorrow. And may even have tried to call me this evening, of course. Yes.

No. the Flag and Fulcrum is in the middle of Queen Street, which is nowhere near the coach station, but *is* very close to Phil's office.

OK. Phil lied.

No. *Surely* not.

OK. Phil … um …Phil … Yes. Yes! Phil … No. Never.

OK. Phil lied.

Trouble is, I really can't believe that he did. Phil simply isn't that kind of a guy. He's straight, uncomplicated; a man with integrity. A man with – oh, hell. How would I know, *really*? All I really know about Phil is that he *appears* uncomplicated. But how can a forty-year-old divorcee *ever* be that uncomplicated? He has a whole chunk of past that does not include me. And as he steadfastly refuses to talk about any of it, I haven't a real handle on what makes him tick. Perhaps that's it. Perhaps that's why we don't work. Because we're starting from scratch, without reference to anything. Always skimming the surface – not plumbing the depths. But still …Phil lie? To what end? For what purpose? But just as the idea of Phil lying seems crazy, I have simply no reason to know that he won't.

One a.m.

I'm beginning to feel that a small hours cyber-meander could be a possible route to inner calm and stress reduction. Strange odours are always marginally less intense in the study (or nasal sensitivity is possibly cyclical, like sleep), plus the surfaces are not clogged with cooling preserves. Also I can surf the Net for pictures of obscure geological features and perhaps find details of a previously unadvertised June trek to the Himalayas, without the need for jostling with son two re Net time. Or perhaps I can find a friend with which to share love of plate tectonics. With GSOH, FSH etc. Or even stray griffith, perhaps? In any event I can send a cheap rate email to Dan about pant preferences, in preparation for providing a well-stocked clothing holdall next term. Make tea. Boot computer. Switch blow heater on. Pour tea. Sit down. Look up to find new unread email to view.

thesimpsons@cymserve.co.uk

Hello stranger.
Just wanted to check if you were all right.
Griffith.

Yes! No! Tsk! I'll give him bloody *G*riffith. And then, hmmm. Curious. I check the time it was sent. Well, well, well. Only fifteen minutes ago. Curiouser. Maybe … Consider pausing to reflect. Consider not answering his email until I've had a chance to order my thought processes and sharpen my investigative powers. Consider saving till morning for a very small percentage of a second, then, as minimum billing time with cymserve is one minute anyway, type;

griffith@cymserve.co.uk

Dear G̲riffith,
What makes you think I'm not?
C.

thesimpsons@cymserve.co.uk

Dear Charlie,
Look, I was just concerned. That was all.
Griffith.

griffith@cymserve.co.uk.

Dear Griffith,
What's with the capital G? And what do you mean
"concerned"? How concerned? And *why* concerned? And
what do you mean by typing 'Look' in that aggressive tone?
And why aren't you in bed? And why aren't *I* in bed, for that
matter? It's one in the morning, and my house smells of
hobgoblins, and my boyfriend (laughable; ho, ho, ho etc.) has
been sighted, inebriated, in a sleaze-bag pub in town when he
should have been hot-footing it up to Castle Howard or
wherever it was the Brontës hung out, and admiring the view
from the dormer, and so on – and all for reasons best known
to himself, and certainly not to me. And everyone else –
Caroline Stableford, particularly – seems to know all about it
and- and, well, like I said. *Why* concerned? You were *there*,
weren't you? Tell me your name.
C.
Now.

thesimpsons@cymserve.co.uk

Dear Charlie,
But you didn't really want to see him any more, anyway, did
you? To be fair. So you can hardly feel aggrieved about it.
Surely it's a blessing?
Griffith.

Tsk!

griffith@cymserve.co.uk

Dear, *dear* Griffith,
That's not the point. Anyway, I'm beginning to have a very

74

ambivalent feeling about this conversation. And you haven't answered my question.

C.

PS And scrub that bit about Castle Howard. That was Brideshead Revisited. It was Haworth I meant. I wouldn't want you to think I was stupid or anything. I've read that as well, actually.

And I must have read *something* by Emily Brontë. *Must* have. Was she *Northanger Abbey*? And what about Ann? (Anne?) And what the hell did Bram (Bramwell? Brom? Bromwich?) write? Very irritated by the fact that Phil, undoubtedly, has all the answers. Slurp tea and await bing. Bing!

thesimpsons@cymserve.co.uk

Dear Charlie,

I didn't think so for an instant. And I haven't. Jane Eyre was torture. And Brideshead was considered passé at college. We all thought it was Poncey.

Why ambivalent?

Griffith

College! Aha!

griffith@cymserve.co.uk

Dear Griffith,

Ambivalent because much as I want to find out who you are, there is a part of me that's apprehensive about it – supposing you have got a face like a scone-topping, or worse – supposing you're drop-dead gorgeous? Actually, I'm not sure which is worse. Yes I am – absolute worst will be if you're someone I know and really don't like, which is what always happens, isn't it?

I beg to differ about Brideshead (though Jeremy Irons *has* become a bit of an over-earnest thespian since then). And who's 'we'? And you still haven't answered my question. And most importantly, which college? And which course? A Clamtec diploma?

C.

thesimpsons@cymserve.co.uk

But, Charlie, it's not going to be a problem, is it? Because you're <u>not</u> going to find out who I am. Then we can carry on our chats without worrying. Anyway, which question was it you wanted answered? G.

griffith@cymserve.co.uk

Dear Griffith,
Stop pratting about. I've started so I'll finish.
   1. The question about how you knew there was anything to be concerned about.
   2. The question about who 'we' were.
   3. The question about who *you* are.
   4. The question about what the hell I'm doing sending emails to a qualified clam digger from Tenby.
   5. The question about *whether you were there*.
C.

PS – the underlining is a new departure. Is it significant?

thesimpsons@cymserve.co.uk

Significant only in that my typing has improved no end these last few weeks. I even do *italics* now. *And* **bold**. Impressed?
   Answers;
   1. You already told me about the Phil situation (it was an all purpose 'are you all right').
   2. My fellow clam diggers. We preferred Amis. (Martin.)
   3. Pass.
   4. Enjoying it.
   5. Pass.
G.

griffith@cymserve.co.uk

Griffith, you're a rat. So how come you emailed me at one in the morning?

thesimpsons@cymserve.co.uk

Fortuitousness.
   Oh, and the boxing being on.

Boxing? Huh? But I am just about to type 'what *about* the
boxing?' when a strange and hair-prickling sensation comes
over me; a sensation I am beginning to recognise as one that
should be attended to at all costs. Scan brain. Slurp tea. Scan
brain some more. Say 'fortuitousness' in soft tones to myself,
then 'look', then 'GOOD GOD' then 'fortuitousness' again.
Go into kitchen and retrieve the hankie from my jacket, ball
into my fist, then walk back into the study. Sit down, open fist,
spread out hankie on desktop, peer in light from computer at
monogrammed corner.
   Read; A G J.
   A *G* J. A **G** J. Blink. Sit back. Read again. Say out loud.
Lean forward. Type;

griffith@cymserve.co.uk

I have your handkerchief. Don't email me again.

Then I switch off the computer and go straight to bed.

Chapter 8

And carefully noted, as a *totally* pyroclastic moment in my life. Pyroclastic in that free flowing sensations of utter consternation / churning stomach / disbelief etc. are now tumbling in an almost seismic wave over the landscape of my psyche, while boulders of angst rise and bob on the surface: married-boulder, Davina-boulder, pillar of community-boulder, boss-boulder, blanket horror-boulder etc. If I was given to hand-wringing I would most certainly wring my hands.

The future is a strange and scary landscape; all at once full of excitement and promise, and at the same time, the risk of eternal damnation. Or some such waffle. It's corny, I know, and overstating the obvious, but such was the enormity of the truth I'd uncovered, that only the wildest and most clichéd of sentiments seemed to do justice to the situation I now found myself in.

Which was some situation. Here was a guy who was married to my boss and who, at the same time, and *with full knowledge of what he was doing*, was carrying on an email correspondence with *me*. And it wasn't just anyone. It was Adam Jones. Adam Jones the GP. Adam Jones the *utterly gorgeous* GP. A guy that, well – a guy that I really, really, *really* liked. A guy whom I not only liked but admired. A guy that I knew *everyone* liked and admired – and why wouldn't they? He was a kind, caring man. Whose wife was Davina. Oh God. *Davina*. How – how on *earth* – would I deal with Davina? How would I face her, knowing what I knew now?

And then there was sex. There was a sex thing at work here. Oh, *Lord*, I couldn't even begin to think about that.

So this is what I did. About fifteen seconds after I went to bed,

78

I got up again, went back downstairs, re-booted the computer and signed on to Cymserve. But there was nothing. Zippo. So I went back to bed.

About fifteen seconds after that, I went down and did it all again. But there was (infuriatingly now) *still* nothing. So, feeling stupid, I stomped back to bed once again.

And stared at the ceiling until it finally, amazingly, inexplicably hit me (possibly by means of the very mystical vision I have always been so sneery about) how the whole excruciating business might just have happened. In any event, a Willie JJ compliment slip became suddenly, horribly, mind-numbingly clear. So I went back downstairs and dug out my diary – an eighties style sliced-loaf sized mock leather organiser, within whose stout poppered cover resided some fifteen years' worth of administrative data (plus a perspex ruler and London underground map. There also used to be a page detailing important international feast days, but as it faced Z in the address book section, the text had been totally obliterated by rabid doodles and tear stains – my divorce solicitor being one Clemenzia Zoot).

The diary sprung open – a decade and a half's scraps are surprisingly springy – and I was soon ferreting feverishly among the snippets in 'G'. And at last, there they were, in my own spiky writing: the fateful words 'griffith@cymserve.co.uk'.

It was seven forty-two, but I called Rose regardless. I knew she'd be whisking the pigswill or something.

'So that's how,' I told her, having dropped my new bombshell. 'I wrote this down for *Davina*. Must have been, oh … a good eighteen months back, if not longer. There was some sort of contract she needed to look at and she wanted the guy to email her at home. Austin Metro I think it was. Funny thing is, I can even remember thinking it was a strange address at the time. But you know how it is – she rattled on so much about how important it was that the guy got the right address when he phoned, that I never got around to it. It was one of those things you just do and forget. You know?'

'Slow *down*,' she advised. Then, 'Hmm. *What* a business! But how come you thought it was ours?'

'God, that's just it! It was me! You know what I'm like with admin – six months in the handbag, three in the desk tidy and so on – when it surfaced in my handbag again, I simply copied it into the address book itself under G.'

'And ours?'

'Under R, of course. For Rose. I'm looking at it right now. It's a system of sorts.'

'Not when you then look us up under G for Griffith. Mind you, when was the last time you'd have looked us up anyway?'

'Exactly! Must have been ten years ago.'

'And your methods with most things are generally arbitrary. You must have had a filing-by-Christian-name moment.' She whistled. 'And Adam Jones ended up with *my* email. This is going to take some time to sink in! But – God! – just think – Davina could have seen some –'

'The first thing I thought of!' (Not strictly. The first thing, as I said, was more along the lines of Oh God Adam Jones Wow Christ Not Not Fair Oh Wow). 'But then I would have known about it like a shot, wouldn't I? And *then* I remembered that Davina has her own PC at home now. I remember her getting it. It's like Computers 'R Us at their place. They've got a study each, too.'

'No kids yet.'

I could hardly bear discuss this. 'Exactly.'

'And they're both workaholics. Though it tickles me to think of Adam Jones holed up in his study, furtively sending you emails.'

I wasn't sure *I* felt tickled. 'There was never anything furtive about it,' I reminded her.

Rose laughed. A dark chocolate laugh, swirled with nuggets of emphasis. 'Not for you, maybe, but certainly for him,' she purred. 'Don't forget, *he* knew who he was sending them to.'

*   *   *

My father tootled in half an hour or so later, bearing tea and the pained look he's recently developed, and could possibly patent.

'What on *earth* is that smell?' he whinnied, casting around.

Distracted and impatient, I shrugged irritably at him. 'What smell?' I barked.

'*What* smell?' he countered. 'Goodness me, Charlotte, has your nose gone on holiday?'

Regrettably, no. I exhaled then inhaled. Still breathing at least. Still functioning. Just. 'But *what* smell? What sort of sme—'

'Ah! Here's the culprits! Charlotte, what on earth have you been doing? Look at these!'

He bent down and picked up the blow-heater. Plus my flip flops. Which were spot-welded to the top.

Note; must make an ENT appointment sooner rather than later as I suspect I have suffered necrosis of the nasal mucus membrane, by spice.

Midday.

Am tempted to attach my hand to the kitchen door handle in order to stop a new and disconcerting involuntary log-on spasm, which is threatening to take over my entire day. Fortunately, I have a diversion in place, as my father is making a big splash at the Cefn Melin Xmas Food and Craft Extravaganza this afternoon with entries in several categories of the preserves section.

Also I am belatedly (oh, be still my beating heart!) re-aware that the Phil situation is still unresolved. Am tempted to surf the Net for obscure Brontëan factual trivia (as a lie-detector) but am deflected by the realisation that it is simply a symptom of the same involuntary log-on spasm. I'm anticipating a call from Phil with a mixed bag of irritable / nonchalant mind-sets (though my mind is almost fully occupied with the Adam Jones Development) and am actually, I realise now, dreading a bona fide explanation for his movements.

Am also tempted to email Daniel to glean pointers to his Possible Christmas Movements. But I know without doubt that any enquiry about Possible Christmas Movements will elicit a cavalcade of diatribes about personal space and its importance in parent / child duty-related negotiations (followed by a long period of non-contact as penance). Therefore I must accept that this is simply yet another symptom of my involuntary log-on spasm also, as I'm generally very mindful of filial sensitivities.

Early evening – bleak and cheerless time of early winter afternoon, during which all hope seems lost; all optimism pointless. Must beware of getting SAD – should I book a low-season week in Benalmadena, perhaps?

Dad won in both the chutney and the jam categories, and his lemon cheese came a respectable fourth in Miscellaneous Preserves (respectable because this, he told me, was only his second venture into the world of curds). We celebrated by sitting in the warm, dusky kitchen and eating an entire whisked sponge.

'The secret,' he told me, 'where lemons are concerned, is to look out for the ones with the really thin skins and to keep a tight rein on the temperature.'

All of which looked like becoming uncomfortably pertinent when Phil's car pulled up outside some moments later.

He hadn't called. And it had already struck me that whatever he'd been up to on Friday night, it wasn't simply a case of him drinking. Phil drank, but only in the most social of settings, and even then, only in small, straight-sided glasses. Him being drunk then, was not actually about drinking, but more likely about wanting to be drunk. For which he must have had a reason. And if it was a reason he felt disinclined to share with me, then it must have been *about* me. Or, more precisely, about someone else. Though we'd only been seeing each other for a while, I'd known Phil, in a chit chat at parties

82

kind of way, for ages. And as far as I knew (God, how little I *did* know), he really only drank when he was unhappy. As the security light illuminated his slim form on the driveway, I had the uncomfortable sensation that whatever manoeuvres I'd had in mind about ending things, I was about to be beaten to it.

'How Haworth?' I sang as I answered the door. (Bizarrely, some part of my brain seemed to think that a jocular tone was required.)

'Oh,' he said, wrong-footed, as he wiped his feet rhythmically. 'Oh, er. Small, dark, atmospheric. Um.'

He hovered in the hall while I entirely neglected to usher him anywhere – busy as I was with the diversionary tactic of straightening the ruck in the doormat. Phil had never really become *truly* comfortable in our house; never taken his shoes off or made himself tea, for instance. I'd taken this to be more about having two proprietorial young males (and latterly, an aged one too) prowling around, than about not actually *feeling* comfortable – Phil was always sensitive to proprieties – but seeing him now, I decided it wasn't about that at all. There were, it suddenly seemed, other forces at work. His eyes were the colour of sticky toffee pudding; dark lashed and intense, and quite his best feature. Looking back, I could now see it was the eyes that had swung it. The carpet, tonight though, was the chief beneficiary.

'And so *on*,' I repeated, for no good reason. 'Kitchen? Cake?' I started moving down the hall, but was immediately aware that he wasn't following. I turned around.

'Charlie, I need to talk to you,' he said quietly.

I said 'Ah!' (Why, exactly?) then, 'It's OK. Dad's watching *Your Favourite Hymns*.' I beckoned to the kitchen. 'And Ben's at Francesca's.'

Seemingly satisfied that we wouldn't be interrupted by requests for cheese strings or cups of tea or throat lozenges, he followed me in and perched himself up on the stool by the fridge. Where he sat and said nothing for a good fifteen seconds, having decided, I presumed, that my 'ah!' was indicative of the fact that I already knew what he was going to say and that I'd therefore take the conversational lead. Which I decided I'd better, or we'd be here all night. I said 'Ah,' again, but this time without the exclamatory nuance. Then 'Well? So?', which seemed to gee him up a bit.

'You know my weekend?' he began. I folded my arms and nodded. He slapped his hands down on his knees, as if starting a symphony. 'Well, I didn't actually go on it.'

He paused to let this sink in. As I'd already suspected as much, I nodded again, fairly immediately. 'I know.'

He looked startled. 'You do?'

'You were spotted in the Flag and Fulcrum. Late Friday night. And you didn't phone at all, so I was pretty sure. Why didn't you go?'

He jerked his head up and looked as shocked as if I'd just suggested energetic sex on the vinyl. Which, in other circumstances, would have been faintly amusing. What did he expect me to ask?

'Because Karen's been in touch. She's back. And we ...and she –' He stopped here and peeled my flexible *You Fat Cow* fridge magnet off the fridge. Then stuck it back on higher up. Karen, then. *Karen.* As in the ex-wife. As in the- no-go-discursive-region. As in – well, anyway. I had to find out about her sometime. It may as well be now.

'Well, anyway,' he said. 'She's back –'

'Back?'

'Back. In Cardiff. She – we – well, since the divorce she's been living in Bristol. But she's got a new job – the hospital. She's a nurse. She –' I nodded. This much I recalled. 'Anyway,' he went on awkwardly. 'She wanted to talk, so I met up with her on Friday evening and, well, I've been giving things a great deal of thought and I don't think you'd disagree that things haven't been all they could be between us lately, and I, well, I –'

'Think we should stop seeing one another.' I took a breath. 'So do I.'

'You do?'

'You seem surprised.'

'No, I … Well, yes. I suppose I am. This is all a bit sudden, isn't it? I mean, I only really began to think in those terms on Friday. You know, with Karen and everything. I suppose it hadn't occurred to me that –'

I unfolded my arms. I needed to move. 'Sure you wouldn't like tea?' I asked. Somehow, conversations of this nature were more palatable with a side dish of routine domestic pottering. I pulled my sleeves up. 'I'm having one.'

'I don't think so,' he said, while I slopped out the teapot. 'I have to be getting back. I have a … well, it's of no consequence really, is it? Charlie, look. Did you really mean what you said? Were you already thinking we should, you know, call it a day? Because I feel pretty bad about … well, we're neither of us getting any younger. It's not as if we … well, I just hope you don't feel I've … well. The thing with Karen and me, well, it's never really gone away, has it? I mean, I know we're divorced now but, well … Well, it's never really been sorted out, has it?'

How would I know? It had never even been *alluded* to, as far as I could recall. What a very dark horse. I shrugged. He sighed. 'And I feel bad about that,' he went on. 'I would hate to feel you're just putting a brave face on things.'

He paused (for breath, presumably) and then slid from the stool. I took a mug from the dishwasher and wondered how best to deal with this slight. It was one thing to have your control of the situation usurped by a pre-emptive strike; quite another to be assumed not to have had any in the first place. But to say 'Yeah, well, I'd gone off you anyway' seemed, though compelling, rather needlessly juvenile. So I settled for,

'Not at all. It's the right thing for both of us. I think we both knew it wasn't really going anywhere, didn't we?'

I'd stressed the 'both' – and the 'didn't', and he nodded gravely. Then tipped his head to one side.

'I suppose we're all looking for that elusive *something*, aren't we? Doesn't matter how old, how wise, how pragmatic we get, we still want perfection in our relationships. And why shouldn't we? But the problem is, have we a right to expect it?'

Which strange and unsettling piece of wisdom was not only the most profound exchange of thought we had ever shared as a couple, but also seemed to signal the end of our brief entanglement, as he then re-sited the fridge magnet again (why? With what significance?) and made all the movements that herald a parting; saying 'anyway', 'right-ho', and patting his keys. I followed him back through the hall, still digesting his words.

'I think we have every right,' I said. 'But whether we find it or not is quite another matter. I hope you do, Phil. I hope things work out with Karen this time.'

Her name felt unfamiliar on my tongue, and I half wished it didn't. Why had we never talked about this?

'Hmm,' he said. 'We'll see.'

I opened the front door and watched him stride down the path. In retreat mode he seemed somehow more elusive and desirable, but even as I stood and absorbed the loss of a man I never really had in the first place, I knew the feeling to be treacherous; as borne out by the memory of countless failed re-kindlings of teenage affairs. I brought to mind our brief history of sexual encounters. His flat. My house. His flat. My house again. Two beds. Two bodies. Two very separate people. No rush of desire, no wild passion, no great *need*. I'd never really desired Phil as wholeheartedly as I ought to have done. Just convinced myself I had, in the way that you do when you face the stark possibility that fluttering hearts are the exclusive domain of the young.

We did all the waving and earnest cheerio-ing that the situation called for, then I shut the front door on the dour winter night.

Back in the kitchen, two things occurred to me. One was my magnet – now positioned top left – and the peculiar part it had played as we talked. The other, and altogether more … more … well, *something*, was the feeling that skirted the edge of my stomach when the words 'Adam Jones' floated back into my mind. Not a fluttering exactly, but a definite stirring.

Affirmation, at any rate, of a functioning heart.

My father slopped in. (Oh dear. Men in mules. Yeuch.)

'Look at that,' I said, pointing. 'Take a set square to that magnet, you'd be hard pushed to better it. Perfectly perpendicular with the top of the fridge.'

'Do what, my love?'

'Right angles, Dad. Their importance in the scheme of things. Or lack of. Just thinking about the big picture. You know?'

Anal. Just like I'd said all along.

Midnight.

A half dozen hours down the line, and I look into my heart and do not like what I see. I suppose I expected to feel something a little more meaningful than just plain old nonplussed about Phil, but why? Why should I? I was nonplussed with him; now I'm nonplussed without him. No big difference there. The real trouble is the something else that's whizzed in where the feelings of loss and aloneness should be. Hmm.

In short, I have taken to bed an emotion that I don't quite know what to do with, plus cocoa in a stupid, difficult to drink out of, lump-of-chocolate shaped promotional mug. Plus, I've also taken to bed a print-out of email from Dan to Ben (Hi Short! How you doing? Twisted Mum's arm yet? etc. etc.) and (ohmyGod) another email from griffith. Or Griffith? Or Clam Digger From Tenby, perhaps? Every incarnation is markedly less stressful-to-deal-with than 'Adam Jones; friend, shag listee, general practitioner, *boss's husband'* etc. Whatever.

The email reads; *Charlie, don't quite know what to say, except how sorry I am. And that it seems such a shame we have to stop all this now. It's been fun, hasn't it? Thank you. Adam.*

I experience a smidgen of irritation at that specific underlining. Thank you for what? A good laugh at my expense?

I creep mournfully under a blanket depression at the futility of hearts stirring / fluttering (indeed doing anything other than that which is strictly necessary for pumping blood about) *per se*. And Benalmadena is clearly impossible due to big lack in Everest / MFI fund. No. Everest fund, period. I am an unstructured free spirit and have no need of round-nosed granite-effect worktops or Shaker-style pale mustard cupboard fronts. Rose? Canterbury? Ben/Dan reunion? I think yes.

Chapter 9

Why would anyone want to be an estate agent? Bad press, bad stress, and now a really bad uniform, to boot. So bad that I'm worrying about being seen in public and considered part of some obscure religious sect. Together, hip young Metro Homes staff must be laughing their socks off. And I cannot believe some people. Actually, I can, if I'm honest, as the person in question is Minnie Drinkwater, who though very much my most favourite local octogenarian and friend, is also completely barking. I arrived on schedule to facilitate the continued forward motion of her house sale, and spent an unproductive – though utterly predictable – ten minutes trying to persuade her to allow the surveyor to complete the full, structural, costly, etc. survey that the situation demanded. Failed even to negotiate access to the property, as Minnie was determined upon her immovable non-sale intentions – again.

I've known Minnie a couple of years now (because we've already visited this whole debacle once), and as much as I have grown to love her – and I'm still bemused that there's (literally) no one else, to my knowledge, who does – I couldn't help but want to throttle her.

'The thing is,' I explained carefully, 'that you've told the Applebys that you'll sell them the house. You've accepted their offer and you are about to exchange contracts with them. And they've spent lots of money on legal fees already, and they've got someone to buy their house. If you change your mind now it will make things very difficult for everyone and may cost you a great deal of money. And besides, you've got your place at The Maltings all sorted. You're due to be moving in next month. What's the matter, Minnie? What's brought all this on?'

'Changed my mind,' she said. 'My hellebores are just

sprouting. And who said anything about The Maltings? Dreadful place. They have radioactive carrots.'

'But …'

'Send that man away. He's throwing a shadow on the doorstep. I'll not have moss in my flagstones, thank you very much.'

Drat. Sometimes I wonder why I bother. Computed that today made the eighth offer accepted and then rejected, though (uurgh) the first this close to contract exchange. Do I need all this right now? Do I? Doesn't matter how much I care about Minnie Drinkwater. I do not need this. Do not know the next best move. Back in the office, cowering under a Davina-generated dust-storm, I was struck once again by the apposite 'baggage' tag. Very uncomfortable at the thought of a heap of incriminating / embarrassing material on the hard disk of a computer in my scary boss's very own house, plus extremely nervous about making eye contact with her on the first day post-my realisation of the griffith identity – indeed, decided that I would perhaps have to develop a mirror sunglasses habit.

And / or a new job habit.

This was all I needed.

Took the stroppy phone call from Austin Metro himself.

'What the hell are you people playing at?' he barked. 'I've got the Applebys absolutely apoplectic here. What the hell's going on?'

'I'm really sorry,' I told him. 'Minnie's an elderly lady, and she gets a little confused at times. I'm absolutely sure we'll be able to sort things out. When I've got some cover in the office, I'm going to go back and see her. My colleague should be back in an hour or so. He's …'

'Bah! This is ridiculous! Why can't you people ever do a job properly? Jesus Christ – you are so inefficient! Just get Davina to call me. OK?'

'Not inefficient,' I told him, as politely as the bellyful of abuse he was heaping upon an elderly confused lady with hardly a friend in the world would allow. 'As I said, she's rather old, and she gets very muddled, but I'm sure it's absolutely nothing to worry about. I will go round there as soon as my colleague gets back from his viewings. And I'm going to speak to her social worker, and between us we'll get it sorted out. I'll ring you as –'

There was an exhalation large enough to propel spit fifty yards. 'Sorted out? SORTED OUT! I'll give you bloody social workers. I'm trying to run a business here, in case you haven't noticed, and I don't give a stuff about mad old biddies. D'you hear? Not a stuff!'

What a scumbag.

I said, 'You've made that much clear. But ranting at me isn't going to help any, is it?'

He snorted. 'Helps me, darling. And that's why I'm here and you're there.'

By which I presume he meant as in sitting behind a mock-Georgian shopfront in town, while I languished in a mock-stagnant swamp in the sticks. But still ... 'I know where I'd rather be, thank you. Bullying senior citizens isn't part of my brief.'

'Oh, it will be, love. It will be.' He snorted again. 'But then again your brief might be shorter than you think, love. Just get the boss for me. And soon. OK?'

'Very happy not to have to talk to you any more. Byeee.'

Oh dear. Oh dear. Davina-wrath imminent. Still, sod her. Sod him. Sod the whole bloody lot of them. How dare they treat Minnie with such disrespect! Still, I was happy to note that I had suddenly discovered a whole uncharted area of abandon and pleasing *que sera sera* sanguinity. Sod the old buzzard and his grab-a-pad jingles. Whichever way you looked at it, Austin Metro was a very silly name.

I went back to Minnie's at tea-time and took a packet of jam tarts, plus cat food supplies.

She was really such a very sweet lady. A proper gran, deprived of her duty as such. She was ripping the '2nd pre-paid' corner from an envelope, to put in her little pot of stamps for the blind. 'Hmm,' she said, grimacing. 'Bad goings on at The Maltings. D'you know what I heard on the radio earlier?'

She moved back to the elderly wing chair she habitually sat in. It had, I suspected, been with her for decades. 'Not as yet,' I said, taking the stool. 'But I'm prepared for the worst.'

'And it is,' she said, pulling a tart out and sniffing it. 'Three people dead in an ambush, apparently. A bad business.'

'I think that was actually in Africa somewhere.'

'They say that. Of course they do. That's how they do it. These from Tesco? They've got a most peculiar flavour.'

'It's only apricot. Shall I feed Kipling for you?'

'Blinking foreign jams.' She waggled her finger. ' That's what you get for accepting that funny fifty pence piece they minted. You see? I've always said, if everyone had just said no at the time, then none of this would have happened. You all right dear? You look drawn.'

'I've come to see what we're going to do about selling your house, Minnie. You have to move. You know you do.'

She flexed her index finger. 'I know diddly-squat about that, young lady.'

I nodded. 'You know you do, Minnie. You can't manage here. Have you heard anything from Edward?'

She shook her head and stroked the cat. 'And never you mind about that. So. Tell me all your news. I don't see a living soul from one week to the next. How are those babies of yours?'

'Daniel's left home now, Minnie.'

'That was careless of you.'

'To go to medical school. And Ben's thirteen now –'

'And no better than he should be, I'm sure. And what will you do now? Have some more?' She took another jam tart out of the packet.

'Heavens, no!' I said. 'I'm going to climb Everest, aren't I?' Even with Minnie, such lofty ambitions sounded silly and pointless and trumped up, somehow. I recanted. 'Well, not really climb it exactly. But visit it. Trek there. To Nepal. It's always been an ambition of mine.'

'It was just outside Delhi I lost Iris, you know. A cobra.' Her gaze shifted, then returned to the packet. 'Will you have a tart? I just had them delivered this morning.'

I shook my head. Iris. The name of her daughter?

'A cobra?'

'Oh, yes, dear. Straight into the pram. The heat, you see. Shade. Tart or not? Eh?'

I took this to mean that the subject was now closed. 'Jam and I have fallen out big time,' I told her. 'Now. Moving. We've got to get that surveyor back round as soon as possible.'

She shifted in her armchair and pouted at me. 'Must we?'

'We'll both be in big trouble otherwise.'

'Oh, well. He can take what he likes. I've no strength left to argue. And I wouldn't want you having to go to prison on my account.'

'I won't have to go to prison, Minnie. And he's not coming to take anything. He just needs to look at the house itself to make sure ...' I stopped. 'What are you doing?'

Minnie had got up and was wrestling with the loose cover on her armchair. She gave it a sharp tug and it finally sloughed off.

'Ah!' She said, feeling beneath the seat. 'Still here. You never know, do you?'

I shook my head. 'Never know what?'

'Who's around. What might happen. You'd do well to get away, my lovely. There. Well, go on, then. Take it.' She pressed a coin into my hand.

'What's this?'

'Twenty pence, silly. Towards your fare to Nepal.'

On my way home, I looked in on Mr Williams at number seventeen. Minnie wasn't allowed to take Kipling to The Maltings, so Mr Williams was supposed to be having him for her. He had a cat of his own, an arthritic old tabby, which I suspected Kipling would comprehensively terrorise.

''Ow do,' he said. 'How's the old boiler today?'

'Boiling,' I said. 'And particularly truculent. But I think we're winning.'

He sucked on his dentures. 'Then you're as batty as she is.'

But perhaps not quite as astute.

Midnight.

Everest fund now seven hundred and forty-two pounds and twenty pence. Very, very touched.

But I've been thinking about the 'baggage' tag some more. Being a baggage is generally a symptom of hormone imbalance (in which case, cyclical), pathological persuasion (in which case, terminal), stress at work (in which case, actionable) or unhappiness generally. In which case ... in which case, is it a symptom of marital dysfunction? In which case is it a symptom of infidelity? Childlessness? Disharmony? Boredom? Ideological Drift? In which case is griffith in the grip of a relationship crisis? Is griffith, in short, unhappy too?

Dangerous, stormy seas; speculative avenue.

Click icon; re-read email you've already read.

Email reads; Charlie, don't quite know what to say, except how sorry I am. And that it seems such a shame we have to stop all this now. It's been fun, hasn't it? Thank you. Adam.

Hmmm.

OK. Bottom line. End of cyber-friendship.

Very, with a very capital V, fed up.

Tuesday.

And then some. Am in receipt of the largest domestic phone bill on the entire planet. Must compute the exact distance between North Cardiff / Everest, as it looks like I will have to walk the entire way.

But have, at least, enough petrol for London.

'Right,' said Daniel, once it had been established that though it was completely illegal to have Ben sleep on the floor of his hall of residence room, it would, in fact, be absolutely OK, because the warden of the hall of residence was, in fact,

Dan's mate, Simon, who was doing the job part-time for the year as he was seriously strapped for cash, and had, in fact, said he wouldn't tell anyone, and if anyone was suspicious he'd say Ben had been taken ill at the station or something and that it would, in fact, have been irresponsible to let him travel home alone. (Which patent fiction I went happily along with. Being, as I seemed to be, such a sub-standard parent.) 'This is the plan. You drive here with Ben after work on the Friday, have the curry, dump him, head off to Rose's, then pick him up when you drive back on Sunday night. Sound cool?'

I resisted the urge to enquire about pants. But would definitely pack some anyway.

Wednesday. Sad or what.

'It's ridiculous, Rose! I can't stop thinking about him. And how embarrassing this all is. And how I'm going to get into such a state next time I see him somewhere. Can you imagine? I shall be scarlet! And what do I do? Do I pretend nothing happened? Do I wink at him or something? And what about Davina? It's hard enough as it is, having to face her at work!'

'Just play it by ear. If he winks, wink back. If he doesn't, don't. If he acts as if he doesn't know you fancy the pants off him, then carry on as if he doesn't. It's no big deal, Charlie. It was just a bit of fun.'

Which is exactly what it wasn't. Didn't feel like now, at any rate. I said so.

'But you have just finished with Phil, after all. It's probably a knock-on effect. Cumulative, you know? Give it a few weeks and everything will be back to normal. After all, people have fancied each other since the dawn of time. It doesn't matter that he knows you fancy him. It's not going to change anything. Besides, he knows you fancy half a dozen other guys as well. Knows I do as well, come to that.'

'Yes, but I put him in joint first place with David Harris-Harper and when he emailed back and said I couldn't have stalemates, I told him he knew perfectly well that there was no contest really.'

'Wasn't there?'

'No.'

'But you always used to fancy Richard Potter the most, didn't you?'

'Not after him being unfaithful to Julia, I didn't. It didn't seem appropriate, somehow. Left a bit of a taste in my mouth.'

'Mine too. In fact, now I come to think of it, didn't you tell me all this at my leaving party?'

'God knows! I was ratted, wasn't I? God, yes! He said so! He said I'd lost the power of decipherable speech before ten! Oh, this is awful.'

'Ha ha! But also irrelevant. A woman's shag list is nobody's affair but her own.'

'Exactly! Which is why it's all so awful that he's seen it! I'll never be able to have a proper, intelligent conversation with him ever again.'

'Don't be daft, Charlie. Don't think for a minute that the guys don't sit around discussing the women. Our shag lists probably read like Janet and John compared to an average night's banter in the Dog and Trouserleg. Personally, I reckon there's scope for some very enjoyable *im*proper conversations with him.'

'God, don't even think such a thing.'

'No. I guess I can safely leave that to you. Anyway, Friday week. Can't wait. Bring your wellies.'

Leave that to me? What exactly did she mean by that?

Truth is, there's no getting away from the unconscious invention of sexual / romantic fantasies. It is normal adult behaviour. It is as nature intended. But it is also, at times, a pain.

Chapter 10

FRIDAY. GRIM.

'A shambles! I agree! That's exactly what it is! An utter shambles!'

Davina hooked her ankle round a chair and yanked it towards her. I pushed my nose deeper between the pages of *HomeScene*.

'Bah!' she said next, transferring the phone to her other ear. 'What's the point? Charlie!' I looked up. 'This social worker of yours. What's her name?'

I told her. She told Austin Metro. 'And you're sure she said Monday?'

I nodded. 'At ten.'

'At ten,' said Davina to the phone. Then, 'Oh, Austin, don't bother! These people simply will not respond to your pathetic faux-gangland bully-boy tactics. You forget, they spend most of their time dealing with the sort of people who'd ram a traffic cone up your backside for the price of ten cigarettes. A softie like you isn't going to cut any ice.'

Then she laughed.

'Yes, you are! Always were, always will be.'

Then again.

'Whoah! You're outrageous! Now look. Got to go. See you next – What was that?'

She rose from the chair then laughed again, loudly. Then glanced at me. 'I'll remind you that you said that,' she purred down the receiver, then plopped it back down on its rest on my desk.

'Right,' she said. 'Third and last time for Mrs Drinkwater. Or that's it. She'll just have to stay there and rot.'

It occurred to me that it would be so much better if Minnie *did* leave the house before we tried to sell it, but without selling she simply couldn't afford The Maltings's fees. She could, of course, go to the council home first, but it was pretty grim there, and miles away too; the few friends she had wouldn't be able to visit – I certainly wouldn't have much opportunity. And once there, she'd stay there, house sale or no house sale. The trauma of just moving once would be bad enough. I didn't think she'd cope well with moving again.

'Things will be fine,' I said. Just like everyone knows that an iced bun is ten calories.

'Things will be fine,' Ben assured me as we hurtled into the maelstrom under the Hammersmith flyover that evening. 'I'm not a *child*, Mum. I do know how to look after myself.'

None of which reassured me in the least. My misgivings, already robust and fast-growing, had been busy self-seeding baby misgivings all week. Which were amply manured by the dark London streets, which were inhabited, it seemed, by every species of low-life. Even the men selling papers on corners looked like drug barons, rapists or yardie gang heads.

The west end itself though, was more reassuring. The familiar throng of tourists filled every inch of festive pavement, and the traffic nosed along like a lava flow with motivational difficulties. Because there seemed to be nowhere on the street I could leave the car for the evening, we buried it instead in an underground car park just off Regent Street, the fee for which would have bought a perfectly adequate tent. Then we set off on foot to Euston Square station; the place where we'd agreed to meet Dan and Jack.

Which we did, soon after. And were introduced by Dan to Jack, only to find that Jack was not the beefy, hairy, real-ale swilling blokey young buck I had envisaged, but female. In fact, the same dour-looking, pop-eyed female in a cardigan who had been loitering on the corner with us for the last five minutes, while we waited for Dan. And also strenuously ignoring us. Moments of embarrassed (slightly hysterical) laughter (on my own part in relation to the sex mistake, on her part, presumably, in relation to the fact that woman plus pre-pubescent boy plus backpack plus Nicholson Streetfinder obviously meant *nothing*) were finally put to an end when Jack remarked that she didn't expect me to be quite as young as I was in a manner that made it seem as if I was five and she was ninety-two. Not impressed at all.

We then dumped Ben's stuff in Dan's room at the hall of residence and headed off by tube for our curry.

Which I was sorely tempted to shovel down her front.

Warning bells rang as soon as we entered. For though we were in approximately the right postal area, this was no curry house. Not in the sense that it existed as a place to eat basic Indian food for not much money and with lashings of beer. Instead we were treated to lavish flock wallpaper, amber paraffin lamps, bronze-effect plastic tableaus of elephants and multi-limbed women in saris, a fishtank (three fish, one neon fairytale castle, much algae), corner bar (red PVC quilted frontage), and a matched pair of Cona coffee filter machines. This was, in short, not your bona fide turn of the century curry house, but rather, I suspected, a chic retro version; a rather cynical early seventies theming of one. For which, I realised sadly, there was no small demand; it was filled not with students, but with what looked suspiciously more like clutches of post-modern thirty-something male novelists (who may, I supposed, account for much of the student population anyway), all no doubt making mental notes on the stream-of-consciousness-drunken-curry-experience that seemed obligatory in much contemporary writing these days, and about which, no doubt, they were soon going to write.

To my mind such prose had long outlived its charm. There's only so many times you can read about throwing up in your korma without actually wanting to do so yourself.

'Vinod! Hi! Lovely to see you!' Jack chanted, her strings of runes clicking together like the feet of so many scuttling cockroaches. 'Our table OK?' And she headed off down the aisle towards an ornamental fountain. With an expression that could have been read as respect or embarrassment (the latter, I judged), Dan hurried after her, leaving Ben and I to troll along in their wake, like Sherpas.

'Been coming here for oh, *ever*, haven't I, Vinod? Daddy used to bring me for the lunch buffet, didn't he? When he was on biz here. It's the absolute best.'

'Is this Brick Lane then, Dan?' asked Ben.

'Harharhar! No! Goodness me! That's so nineties!' twittered Jack. 'Now, Mrs Simpson, shall I explain the menu to you? I'm thinking nothing too spicy, right? Lamb Pasanda's quite nice. And if I were you, I'd go for the Kabli kebab as a starter. It's fabulous; not too hot, not too bland – plenty of depth of flavour without the burn. You know?'

'I don't care what I have,' Ben said, 'as long as no one expects me to give them any of my naan. OK? OK, Mum? I always end up having to share it with someone. And I get sick and tired –'

'Yes, yes, that's fine, Ben,' I snarled. 'Now, let me see ...'

'Or a korma? Wouldn't a korma be safest? Or actually – *act*ually, I think your mother would *prob*ably be OK with a bhoona, don't you, Dan? – that's a dryish dish, Mrs Simpson, with fried onions and peppers –'

'And I want a *whole* rice, Mum,' said Ben. 'I'm not sharing your one.'

'– or ... yes! There's a thought! Chicken Moglai!' She leaned across, hugging the PVC menu. 'Yes. Have that. I think you'll be pleasantly surprised.'

The choking fit was nothing to do with my Vindaloo, of course. It was simply that I had inhaled a cardamom pod.

Ben passed me his napkin, and I dabbed some of the sweat from my brow.

'She's always doing this sort of thing,' he told Jack happily. 'Last Christmas when she was carving the turkey, she sliced off the whole top of one of her knuckles. There was blood, like, *every*where – all over the meat, and –'

'Speaking of Christmas,' Dan started, fork waggling as diversion. 'I've er ... been invited to spend it at Jack's place this year.' He plunged his fork into a large chunk of chicken and studied the gummy green stains on the flock.

'Jack's place?' I spluttered.

Jack nodded enthusiastically, and made a little um-hum noise through her spinach. 'Yes,' she confirmed. 'Firmed up with Daddy just on Thursday. Dan's very welcome to join us for Crimble. Be nice for him to meet my people, won't it, Dan? If that's all right with you, of course, Mrs Simpson. More Keema Naan?'

10 pm. Grimmer.

Am pathetic beyond belief. Am lacking backbone, self-control and also a packet of antacids. I cannot believe I am driving down the M25 in tears simply because my adult son has made arrangements to spend Christmas day with a goggle-eyed witch called Jack and-her-people. Like death and taxes, children growing up / leaving home / deciding to spend Christmas elsewhere is a perfectly normal, expected phenomenon and should not give rise to feelings of hopelessness, despair, and abandonment, but, rather, to feelings of elation / liberation / pride in a job well done / solvency etc. (Solvency does lift spirits marginally as Everest fund in extremis at present and fare is in region of £1200 even allowing for eight billion Air Miles so far amassed.)

But no Dan! The stark realisation bobs like a rabbit in my headlamps, accompanied by a picture of a pathetic Bob Cratchit-sized turkey and a leftover cracker in the box come New Year.

I stop at Clacket Lane services to refuel / find a box of chocolates that look as if it's actually bought from a stylish shop, and am faced with a veritable sea of magazines urging Christmas Craft Frenzy; free stencils, free cookie cutters, free gold icing pens, free pom-pom frame even, and am faced with another stark reality; that I have spent many, many previous Christmasses not getting around to doing anything creative with free stencils, free cookie cutters, free gold icing pens, etc. (though did use a free snowflake stamper as a fancy dress party face paint for Daniel once, though indelible so a bad move). And that *it is now almost too late*. I eventually plump for a magazine promising Small Budget Big Style! Xmas repast plus free tasteful partridge-in-a-pear-tree stencil. I could possibly help Ben design / construct tasteful and individual personalised wrapping paper / gift box selection for Francesca. Could possibly even invite Francesca to Xmas lunch. Could possibly invite entire Stableford contingent to Christmas lunch in wild-child break with tradition innovation.

I am obviously in an emotional crevasse right now.

'Hello! Hello! Hello!' says Rose, as she clutches me to her bosom. Though it has only been three months since I last saw her, I fall upon her lovely flowers mixed with school-hall polish scent as if I haven't seen her in years.

'Well!' I say. 'Here at last! I can almost smell the parsnips!'

Rose reins me in then pushes me away to arms length and says 'Are you all right?' in her teacherly way, and I have to take a firm grip on myself before I dissolve again.

'Parsnips,' I clarify. 'I remember you talking to me about parsnips recently and I remember thinking how idyllic all this (I fan an arm around to take in the entire hall / idyll conglomeration) sounded. I can't really smell parsnips, of course. It was just a little picture I had in my head. Of you, at your Raeburn, basting a tray of parsnips that Matt had grown himself – something to look forward to, and –'

'Shit! Pellets!' says Matt enigmatically, rolling his eyes and walking away.

'I could do you some parsnips, if you like,' Rose offers. 'Matt's just pulled a few. Only I thought you said you were having a curry with Dan. Come along. Come through. Let me give you the tour.'

We make it as far as the guest bedroom-cum-study where she flops onto the duvet and then bursts into tears.

Which throws me completely. 'What on earth is it?' I begin, but she jiggles her head wildly, then gesticulates that I should close the door. I do so, then go back and sit down on the end of the bed beside her. She sniffs and snorts a bit, then turns to face me. By the look of her now, she has been crying a lot.

'Rose, what *is* it?'

'God!' she says, finally. 'Get a grip, Griffith!' Then turns to me. 'Charlie, I've had a bitch of a month here. I've got some sort of growth, and the pit's-end of symptoms. And – well, I won't bore you with the gruesome details, but I've got to have a hysterectomy. They're not sure, exactly. Fibroids, most likely, but they're concerned that – well, shit. Cancer, basically. *Cancer*. Can you credit it? *Cancer!* Perhaps. They say they don't think so, but, well, I've had some dodgy cells so they seem to think it's best to whip it all out. Whatever. I'm trying not to get hysterical about it. The chances are it's all perfectly benign and nothing to worry about, but, well, there you go. What a bitch, eh? Anyway. There it is.' She wipes her cheeks with the back of her hand. 'So. What have you done? Have you emailed him back about his mountaineer friend, then? I think you should. You should.' She grabs my wrist. 'Don't put it off,' she says. 'Don't back-seat your dreams.'

Her eyes swim again and I pull her against me. 'Rose, I don't care about that! What about *you*? Oh, God. This is dreadful news. How long has this all been going on?'

She pulls away, stands up then sits straight down again. 'Few weeks, that's all,' she says, visibly regaining composure. 'I saw the GP and then – well, whoosh, basically. Consultant, biopsy, Consultant again. It's all been so quick. Which is why it's so scary. They keep telling me not to worry, and that they don't think it *is* cancer, but how can I not? Anyway, I'm waiting to hear when I'm going to go in. After Christmas, at least.'

'Not before?'

She shakes her head.

'Well that's encouraging, isn't it?'

'Not necessarily.' She looks suddenly sheepish. 'I turned down a slot in two weeks. School Nativity.'

'Oh, Rose, *why*? Surely this is a priority? And couldn't you go private? Have it done now? Is it horrendously expensive?

You know, I do have a bit saved up. If you want some, you only have to –'

'Oh, Charlie, that's so sweet, but really, we're fine. It's only a few weeks away after all. And I'd rather get Christmas over with first anyway. If I'm going to be laid up like a stuffed duck for a month, it may as well be when there's not much doing anyway.'

'I guess so. But you know you only have to ask, don't you?'

She nods, then stands up again.

'Come on,' she says. 'Subject closed for the weekend. Lets get some bloody wine open and get ourselves drunk.'

Sunday night.

True to her words, Rose refused to allow further discussion of her medical problems for the remainder of the weekend, and not for the first time, I marvelled at her strength and composure, in the face of such potentially cataclysmic news. Her only concession was to promise to take me up on my offer to help if I could.

So, when I met up with Dan and Ben again, it was with a profound sense of gratitude for all the years I had spent with my children thus far.

Though less so about last forty minutes of driving, which have featured music so vile and vibrato and peculiar that I fear for the integrity of not just my fillings but my teeth. But I'm anxious to keep up with my son's post-Oasis musical preferences, even if I'm rendered permanently disfigured as result.

I feel shell-shocked. Yet streaming back over the Severn Bridge, I find that, strangely, I am now able to cope with the Christmas Dan absence. After all, I am lucky. Because Felix is in the Navy I have not had to share my children as much as I might have. Have hung onto them for most of our post-divorce Christmasses because their dad has no real place to put a tree. Mainly, I realise, one effect of Rose's traumas is that I'm experiencing a perspective shift of megalithic proportions. Getting a handle on the priorities in life. Coping even (dare think it?) with trying not to think about Adam Jones. Now that Ben is finally comatose, I turn the stereo down a bit and muse over a possible new bijou Christmas format, plus reflect that for first time in five years I will not have to drive over, get dad, ply dad with sherry all day while maintaining my own chauffeuresque sobriety, watch the first bit of the most looked forward to Xmas day TV special, command boys to tape the rest of the most looked forward to Xmas day special, drive dad home (so he can sleep in his own bed. Can *only* sleep in his own bed, apparently, despite umpteen naval years sleeping in hammocks, mud huts, oriental lap dancers' knickers etc.), sort dad out, drive back home, watch the closing credits of the most looked forward to Xmas special, moan at boys for failing to tape the most looked forward to Xmas day special, sling three glasses of port plus lump of stilton / stick of celery down throat, go to bed sick plus tipsy plus in highly belligerent mood.

This year, have father-plus-own-bed *in situ*. Will go nowhere, fetch no one, watch whatever I damn well please, drink myself to oblivion, at very least. Reflect that the cloud of twenty-four hour exposure to paternal foibles / eccentricities has a small silver lining after all. I feel suddenly in a decidedly Christmassy mood, and almost burst into a verse of Oh Little Town of Bethlehem for the toll-booth man, but desist on grounds of being considered a nit.

I do, however, take advantage of a change of tape manoeuvre to impart my revised festive arrangements to Ben.

'And how about next weekend,' I enthuse, 'you and me heading up to that Christmas tree farm near Brecon and getting ourselves a really mega tree? You could bring Francesca, if you like. And we could drive out somewhere nice for lunch. We could –'

'Do we *have* to?'

'I just thought it would be nice if you came with me for once. But if you don't want to – I mean, if you've got something else you'd rather be –'

Ben turns and looks at me, then slaps his Discman shut and shrugs.

'Yeah, yeah,' he says. 'OK. Whatever.'

Almost everything in my Christmas garden lovely, lovely, lovely.

Only when I return to the (heart-stoppingly fetid after our three-day absence) house, does googly ball (or whatever) hit my jolly mood and smash it into the boundary.

'Ah! Yon travellers! Ho!' says my father, hands astride hips, a cluster of jars steaming gently behind him. He has clearly been watching something in costume on TV. 'Hold fast, good fellows!' he then urges, with much flamboyant gesturing, before striding from the room.

He backs in, seconds later, carrying what looks perplexingly like some sort of children's party attire. It is only when he turns and I note the trio of plastic feet that sprout from the bottom that the unbridled horror of the situation engulfs me. What my father actually holds is a tree. A Christmas tree. A four-foot Christmas tree made out of tinsel. In silver.

'But –' I begin, rendered speechless by shock and by the ramifications of this distressing error of paternal judgement. Have twenty-years of my seven-foot, monster-girthed, living, breathing (*transpiring* in fact), pungent, glorious, heart-stopping, *real* Christmas trees not registered *anywhere* in my father's consciousness?

'Ten pounds, all in. What do you say to that?'

Consider 'aaarrrghhhh!'. Consider 'infidel!' Consider 'all in what? The worst possible taste?' But instead I just say;

'Um. Yes. Great. But –' again.

'No problem,' he adds, jiggling the top as he speaks. The tree, as if caught on the hop, jiggles back, causing flecks of tinsel to strew themselves beguilingly all over the kitchen floor. Look at me! says the tree. Look how I glisten and twinkle! How dare you cast scorn on my small silvery frame!

106

'Thought you'd be pleased,' continues my father, beaming. 'No needles, no mess, no fuss, no nothing. And what with Dan being off now, and you always so busy, it was the least I could do. My contribution, if you like.'

'Great,' I say weakly. I am not beguiled. 'Now, ho hum, must unpack. And email Dan, before I forget. And make sure Ben has a clean shirt for tomorrow, and –'

I leave the sentence gaping at its open end and flee to the sanctuary of the study, terrified lest I am followed by a job lot of flashing Santa's band musical light sets, or worse.

Note; I must brush up on proper psychology. (As opposed to psychology as practised by father: i.e. best thing to cheer up daughter would be to buy diminutive silver tinsel Christmas tree as probably shagged out by decades of humping huge real one home and spending hours and hours persuading it into upright position in bucket, and getting needle rash up arms, eyes gouged out, etc. and probably only too glad to have opportunity to spend pre-Christmas run-up making jams, chutneys and novelty stuffings instead.)

Oh no oh no oh no. Am owner of four-foot tinsel Christmas tree. In silver.

I sit in front of the computer and consider my options. The best option is to swallow my feelings of horror and make the four-foot silver tinsel Christmas tree the focal point in a retro Seventies-style kitsch living room, along with plastic poinsettias, colours-of-the-rainbow plastic baubles, metallic inverted fountain-spray two-foot dangling ceiling decorations, plastic flock-covered Rudolph with flashing red nose light, plastic bass-relief wall hangings of Santa, jolly snowman, elfin helpers, etc., plus plastic 'Joy to the World!' frieze-cum-Christmas-card-holder. Best option, as this will not hurt my father's feelings.

The other option would be to set fire to the Christmas tree (in freak jam boiling accident?), but this would be logistically difficult to achieve / extremely dangerous. But, if the ends justify the means etc … hmmm.

The other option would be to pretend I have already paid a

large sum of cash for a seven-foot, monster-girthed, etc., Christmas tree and that it is awaiting collection, and that I've not actually mentioned it as yet only as I wanted to try and extract a refund etc., and that I have failed to obtain a refund and that, regrettably, as I have paid such a large sum of money for it I have no choice but to bring it home, and that the silver Christmas tree can act as an additional festive icon in another location (say, toilet / hall), and – yes! very good! Has potential! Can see myself explaining it to father now. Except. Hmm. Suppose father says oh, well, we can always use seven-foot, monster-girthed, etc. tree as an additional festive icon in toilet – no, but hall / porch etc., or, *worse*, that we can donate the seven foot, monster- girthed, etc. tree to Cefn Melin community hall, deprived person or Eastern Bloc charity convoy? Uurgh! Can see father saying exactly that. And to argue would expose my real motive, and thus hurt his feelings.

Other option would be to go straight to father *now*, and say, 'Dad, that was really sweet of you, and I know ten pounds is a lot of money, but having a seven-foot, monster- girthed, etc. Christmas tree is one of those things that I really look forward to at Christmas, and lovely though *your* tree undoubtedly is, Christmas just won't seem the same if I don't have one. I know I'm a silly billy, but you do understand, don't you?'

And so on. So simple. But *so* difficult to do.

I decide to shelve the tedious moral maze dilemma for the moment and instead switch computer on to email Dan as arranged.

Compose thoughtful missive;

Dear Daniel,
It was <u>lovely</u> to see you, and absolutely horrible to meet Jack (as she calls herself). She seems opinionated, arrogant, obnoxious and snotty, and so full of herself that she's surely due to explode sometime soon (indeed, her eyes look as if they're on the way already). And I'm <u>so</u> cross that you're going to her house for Christmas. It's not fair! I want you to come home! I suppose the only good thing about 'her people' (yeuch!) having invited you for Christmas is that I won't be

108

forced to invite her to us. Wish I could fathom quite what it is you see in her, but, sadly, I'm groping for a reason. I can only assume she's good in bed, but, frankly, that's the last thing I want to think about.

Guess Ben had a brilliant time – he is mute and looks vaguely catatonic. Decided not to enquire, for my own benefit. What I don't know etc ...!! Miss you more than you can possibly imagine, but also happy beyond measure that you've grown into such a lovely, outgoing, confident, urbane, well-rounded young man (if with dubious taste in women so far, which I'm quite sure you will grow out of – and <u>soon</u>, God willing).

Tons and tons and tons of love and kisses and hugs,
Mummyxxxxxxxxxxxx
PS Perhaps you could let her know that I am perfectly fluent in restaurant punjabi etc., thank you very much. Indeed, I was eating peshwari naans while she was still sucking on rusks.

And delete. Send;

Dear Daniel,
It was lovely to see you. Missing you again already. Hope you weren't too embarrassed about the bag of underwear!

Thanks so much for having Ben to stay – he talked about his weekend all the way home (Just the edited highlights, I presume!). And sorry that we weren't able to hang around long enough to say goodbye to Jack. (She seems like a very nice girl, by the way.) Say hello to her for me, won't you?

It was good to see you looking so well and happy. I'm disappointed, of course, that you won't be home for Christmas itself, but look forward to seeing you on the fifteenth. Are you going to be here for New Year? (No pressure. Just wondered!)

Anyway, all home, safe and sound. Grandad has just presented me with a silver tinsel Christmas tree which he picked up at a boot sale this morning. Can't begin to think what to say to him. You know what I'm like about my trees, don't you? Any ideas?!!!!
Love Mumxx

Log on to the internet to get Dan's email off, and consider

again Rose's suggestion to email Adam about his mountaineering friend. I don't know if it's Rose, or Dad, or this whole Adam business, but suddenly, more than ever before, I realise just how much seeing Everest really means to me.

Why does a person fall in love with a mountain? What is it about that monolith of snow-gilded rock that exerts such a powerful effect? Is it beauty? Is it power? Is it sheer awesome scale? I pick up my much-thumbed *Trekking in Nepal* and scan its fact-packed, earnest pages. Monasteries, Buddhas, flat-faced smiling people, the strange, lunar landscape, those breathtaking peaks.

So perhaps I should email him. Get the ball rolling. Back seats, as Rose said, are not the place for dreams. But then again, why don't I simply forget it? After all, useful though it undoubtedly would be, it's not as if I really *need* any help. I can do this on my own. And what I *don't* need right now is to keep the Adam thing going. There are dreams and there are dreams, after all.

Needless to say, it's just while I'm having a very stern conversation with myself about all the reasons why it would be a *particularly* stupid course of action to email Adam (even for a Simpson) when *pop!* there's the message. That I have some new post. And yes, it's from him. I curse briefly at the small, hot (You see, Simpson? That's *exactly* why you shouldn't take that course of action) explosion in my stomach, then take a slow, deep breath and click tremulously on it.

thesimpsons@cymserve.co.uk

Hello Charlie,
I know you don't want me to email you any more, but I was watching a programme about earthquakes earlier and I remembered I was going to put you in touch with my friend Rhys. (Or had you forgotten, as I originally hoped you would?!) Obviously, I don't want you to mention it if I see you, and obviously, I'd be grateful if you'd keep it to yourself (!), but I decided what the hell and had a word with him about you, and

he said he'd be happy to help if he can. You can either call him at home, or if no luck (he's not in much!), you can get him at the General (he's a consultant gynaecologist there), in which case, dial the switchboard and ask them to bleep him.

Hope everything in your life is OK. (Though sounds like work's fairly stressful right now.) And really hope the trip takes shape.

Take care of yourself,
Adam.

Scribbling down the telephone numbers, I realise that we have both had the same thing on our minds at same time. That just as I was pondering the propriety of emailing Adam, Adam was doing the exact same thing about me. I realise also that I have an adrenalin surge in progress; that I am having a definite physiological response to his email. Also that I am feeling a familiar cocktail of diverse emotions. That, despite my best efforts, I am failing to consign my (ridiculous, inappropriate yet horribly potent) feelings for Adam to my virtual bin.

I hit the 'reply' icon and stare at the blinking cursor. Then type,

griffith@cymserve.co.uk

Dear Adam,
Thank you *so* much. That's really kind of you. I'm saving hard and of course I hadn't. Why on *earth* would you imagine I'd forget? I just wasn't sure if it was appropriate to ask, that was all. (*Obviously*!)

I will call Dr Hazelton (Mr Hazelton?) as soon as I get a minute tomorrow (though not on Willie JJ time, of course...).

Thanks again. I'm beginning to feel quite excited about it all.

With very best wishes,
Charlie.

As soon as I press 'send', of course, I regret it. Very much.

I click 'ok' to 'your email has been sent' message, and spend a distracted five minutes staring at the screen saver (this

111

week FS4BS4FS4BS4FS4BS4FS recurring) and experiencing specific regret over the italics in 'why on *earth* would you imagine I'd forget?'. They could, and should, be construed as a reference to the fact that my trip is a big thing on the horizon at present, but could also, and might, be construed as a reference to the fact that thinking about Adam Jones is a big thing on the horizon (indeed, foreground) at present. As both are patently true, I must expect rogue construing all round. Also regret '(*Obviously!*)', as confirmation that I understood the significance of griffith's own 'obviouslys; therefore my tacit agreement that our cyber-relationship is something to feel guilty about in the first place. As the only thing I have to feel guilty about is the size of my phone bill (and evening emailing is cheap rate anyway), then my guilt (our tacitly agreed guilt) *must* be about our relationship situation, even if it is only a cyber-relationship situation. Oh, *God*.

Regret mainly that I discovered a charming, witty, attractive, loveable virtual stranger before discovering his identity was Adam Griffith Jones.

Chapter 11

I can't help but wonder if a series of guilt-ridden 'obviouslys' have been transmitted, osmosis fashion, into Davina's psyche. She has behaved in an altogether un-Davina-like manner for most of morning. Though has to be said, un-Davina-like in all, not just Charlotte Simpson-related matters.

For a start she has brought the wretched Ianthe in with her, and they've spent much of the morning re-arranging the desks. They've moved mine, for example, to the back of the office, where chi energy will, so they tell me, give me ambition, direction, financial success, and (my own interpretation) a bloody great draught up my back. They have also – and couldn't bring myself to ask about this one – placed small bowls of sea salt all over the place. Weird upon weird, and distinctly unsettling. What next? Much relieved when Ianthe pushed off.

And then a *highly* curious episode with Hugh in the staffroom. This involved much muffled earnest-sounding conversation, plus scrapings and bangings of unidentifiable origin. If it were not for my firm opinion re Hugh's sexual orientation, I would have concluded that Davina and Hugh were having sex over the side of the armchair. But I am becoming paranoid. I am living in a constant state of fight-or-flight arousal and am consequently overly sensitive. But I am at least losing weight.

And work, on the whole, *is* looking infinitely more bearable, as I have had not one but *three* requests for details of Cherry Ditchling, following its appearance in the 'Homes of Character' slot in the local paper. Perhaps the Cherry Ditchling sale jinx is now inexplicably lifted, and I will be able to make a vast commission and be in good books all round. Which is especially important as I have decided Hugh

Chatsworth is making worrisome and somewhat unethical inroads into becoming the Willie JJ resident teacher's pet. Will arrange viewings, if possible, at back-to-back half hourly intervals in order to whip up a feeding-frenzy of enthusiasm and competitive spirit. Perhaps there is something to feng shui after all.

Anyway, I've done it. I have arranged to meet the mountaineering gynaecologist, Rhys Hazelton, after work, in the hyper-trendy 'Q' bar in the centre of the city. And at his suggestion. He is obviously a hip, happening guy. Personally, I would never have considered the 'Q' bar as being the type of venue middle-aged gynaecologists would frequent. (Would never consider it a place I'd frequent either, as it is almost exclusively the stamping ground of pre-pubescents with multiple piercings.)

But evidently I am wrong. The doorman greets him warmly. And he me.

'Well, hell-o, Mrs Simpson!'

'Charlie. Please.'

'In*deed*!' His note of celebration has heads turning already. Though they soon turn back upon realisation that I am neither famous nor youthful.

'So, what'll it be, Charlie? Better press on into the scrum, so to speak.'

Rhys Hazelton is a giant of a man. He has arms like legs of lamb and enormous brown hands with little blonde curls on the backs of the fingers. I cannot stop looking at them. I cannot help but remember that he's probably spent much of today using them to ferret around between women's legs and wave a speculum about.

He addresses his pint with one of them, once we're seated. The fingers curl around it like a laboratory clamp. But he *is* rather handsome. He has tanned skin and pale hair and the sort of long-limbed athleticism that probably passes for normal among cartoon superheroes. He is, in short, rugged. I can picture him wrestling a crocodile or lion.

'Well,' he says, ploughing his head of corn-coloured

commas with the other hand. 'Isn't this a turn up for the book?' My questioning face has him shaking his head. He leans closer. 'Adam neglected to tell me his intrepid friend was *fe*male, Charlie. It was only when you called that the penny dropped.'

'Oh,' I reply, and not wishing to invite any further speculation, add, 'Charlie's short for Charlotte, and … well … here I am.'

'And on a quest, I understand, to head up a mountain sometime soon. Done much climbing?'

'None,' I say. 'I have absolutely no mountaineering skills at all. I just have a big thing about rocks and mountains and plate tectonics and … well, I just want to, you know – *be* there. Actually see it for myself. Actually feel …' I can feel my face growing warm. As always, laid bare like this, seeing Everest sounds such a twitty, half-baked idea that I'm almost too embarrassed to talk about it. So I stop, and offer him a shrug instead.

But Rhys smiles and slides a little way along the bench seat towards me.

'He's right, then.'

'Right?'

'We *do* have a lot in common. The question of your sex notwithstanding, of course. Another drink? Or would you like to go on somewhere. Dinner?'

Oh.

11.45 p.m.

griffith@cymserve.com

Well, hello, Griffith with a capitla G griffith!

Just wanted to ring and thank you for putting me in touch with Rhys. We've had a super evening. I told him all about my plans for everest and he told me all aboutall the mountains etc. <u>and</u> other things he's been up. And that I should help shore up nepal's ecom=nomy by going in tea-houses a lot. All very edifyimng. All very nice. It's a shame he seems to thinki might like to go to bed with him at some stage andso on, but there you go. this is what happens, isn't it, when you get to our age. Rucsh rush rush as my fathercwould say. Trouble is, I have real problems in that department. smilesmisconstruings etc. in actualy fact, he's not **so** bad. Is rather good looking, if =n fact. if he lived locally (and Rose was still here, of course), we could discuss wht=ether he had sufficient qqq attributes to make him a contender for our shag lists (I know he'd be on Mjulia Potter's qqqq, for sure). But I dodn't have a shag list any more of course, for ***obvious*** reasons. **Do** I? been there, done that, and look where it got me.

In fact, speaking of obvious, what's with all the obviouslys? kept reading that email and wondering what it was all about – what the hiddne agenda was there. if there was one of course, which there mightn't have been By the way, did you notice how I can underline, bold and italicise all at once / it's really simple. you just click on all three of those bits at the top. \see? I'm not so information-technology-ology – challenged as you might think. or do think, I';m sure. or whatever.

Anyweay, just wanted to say hello goodbye and so on. and goodbye mainly.

Charliexxxxxx

PS I'm seriously stressedenough as it is, because my *father has bought me a four* foot.> horrible, horrible silver tinsel christmas tree made of tinsel.And it's horrible. And it cost him ten pounds. How can I bear it? I can't bear to put it in my lounge. But I feel really guilty, you know? mainly because ten pounds is a lot of money, but also becausewho am I to say that people who like four foot high silverTINsell christmas trees are any less tasteful than I am? And what is taste anyway?" Surely it's about having what you like and bollocks to everyone else. In which case, now I think of it, why ***shouldn't*** I want a great big lovely chrismas tree like I've always had. You know? Anye=way, i'm going to go to hell most probably unless I think of something else I can do with it and I should anyway because ten pounds would have bought him a heck of a lot of fruit and spices and other horrible smelly things and we must be grateful for that at leasmustn't we?

Going to bed now. Don't email back because it's much too stresssful.

**Obviously.** Goodnight. C.xx

Chapter 12

I wake up with a curious, inexplicable feeling of anxiety. Have eaten two extra strength brufen and drunk three mugs of rehydrating tea before I realise that the curious feeling is actually not simply alcohol-induced paranoia, but related to a dimly remembered drunken session at the computer last night. Boot up, log on and scroll madly through the filing cabinet. Find last email sent and bring it up on screen. Then gaze in gut-wrenching, toe-curling horror upon the rambling, inane, manic, puerile, typographically challenged absolute *garbage* that I have spewed out and sent off down a land-line to Adam. Oh no, and then some. Resolve that (as well as avoiding all human contact within Cefn Melin environs for rest of natural life) I must, in the fashion of a recovering alcoholic, not put myself in danger of an addictive relapse. As I take my shrivelled brain off to work, I decide I must take serious remedial action. Will buy a padlock for the study, and give Dad the key.

As if total humiliation were not enough, I cannot *believe* some people. No sooner had I returned to the (chiming, salty, be-mirrored, etc.) office after an exhausting, emotionally draining morning of accompanied viewings of Cherry Ditchling, than I had Mrs Rutland on the phone saying last straw, blah, blah, blah, etc., etc., as someone has brought dog poo in on their shoe and trod it over most of the house. Also that she was sick and tired of the whole business, very unimpressed with the level of interest generally, and that she was of the opinion that Willie JJ were not putting their backs into advertising, publicity, and expediting the sale generally. Finished by informing me that Mr Rutland was of the opinion that if we didn't pull our socks up forthwith he would be very tempted to tell Willie JJ to forget it and take his business to the more thrusting Metro instead.

Sod her.

As I was on my own in the office (Hugh – suspiciously – at the other branch dealing with – suspiciously again – typesetting and layout of a big Willie JJ ad campaign / editorial feature in *Homescene,)* I spent an enjoyable few minutes shouting 'Bollocks, bollocks, bollocks to you' at the telephone. Had an almost irresistible urge to call Mrs Rutland back and tell her that, as the carpets in her house were the colour of dog poo anyway, no one would notice, and that as the poo emanated from her own mangy dog and was never cleared away by its slut owner we could hardly be blamed for bits of it being squidged and brought into the house. And that if she was not so bloody insistent that we take everyone down to the far end of the garden in the middle of winter to appreciate the rustic (crappy) summerhouse built in eighteen forty-whatever by Mr Rutland's crappy great-whatever – that nobody gives a toss about anyway – then she would not have a dog-poo trauma in the first place.

Had an even greater urge to add that Mr Rutland was a dirty old git anyway, as whenever he had the chance of accompanying me on viewings he always made a big point of going 'you first!' up the stairs then hanging around at the bottom long enough to try to get an eyeful of backside etc., so the dirty dog-poo problem served them both bloody right.

But I resisted. Bad vibes (rotten chi?) seem to be whanging about the office in such abundance that I cannot move without risking getting lanced by one. In the back, most probably. Hmm. Am just debating a weapon of choice in a seventeenth-century-style misty duel at dawn scenario with Davina, when the phone rings again.

I pick up with a mixture of desperation and (as more often than not these days) fear, to hear a stressed social worker telling me that Minnie's friend Mr Williams died in the night unexpectedly, which, as well as being a shock, obviously, is also a potential disaster, Minnie-wise, as he will not now be able to have her cat after all.

But, oh! Relief! Relief! Relief!

I am, thankfully, spared the role of malevolent harpie in the four-foot silver tinsel Christmas tree debacle. I am liberated! I am able to embrace all those wonderful spirit-of-Christmas type feelings without a nasty stain on my character during the season of goodwill. Oh (With all due respect to the soul of Mr Williams, of course) joy!

Had had an entirely unhelpful email from Dan detailing the exact reasons why I should not flap and fuss about the Christmas tree situation; mainly that as an intelligent, focused, perfectly grown-up person of thirty-nine I should not feel stressed about telling my own father thank you very much but the Christmas tree arrangements are already in place. Chiefly because my father is, in Dan's view, being thoughtless in the extreme; he has spent the last twenty years coming for Christmas and failing to notice that to his darling only daughter, having a seven-foot, monster-girthed, etc. Christmas tree is of fairly profound importance.

Which is all well and good, but pretty hard on Dad. I think his motives are more along the lines of, no one in their right mind would spend the best part of a month planning / buying / shopping for decorations / spraying things for decorating / fussing generally over Christmas trees out of choice. He is, after all, a naval man.

But joy! Was taken aside by my father at 18.47 (window of opportunity between potatoes and curly kale).

'Trees,' he announced, causing the hairs on my nape to prickle. I braced myself against the worktop for another stressful encounter.

'Trees, Dad?' I prompted.

'Yes, trees.' He confirmed. 'I've been talking to young Ben and it seems he's rather disappointed –'

'Disappointed?'

'Indeed. About that little tree I picked up.'

I noted the choice of adjective. He has, I thought, at least got the concept of relative tree size in place. I said,

'Oh, really?'

'Indeed. Seems you'd planned to take him off out tomorrow. To buy a real tree. At a Christmas tree farm, he tells me. He says you do it every year. That it's a sort of family tradition.'

Yes, of course! The family tradition of me saying (plaintively, clutching pinny to bosom etc) 'Would anyone like to come with me to choose a tree this year?' And getting the traditional response of 'Mu-um! Do we *have* to?'

'Yes,' I said, beaming. 'Absolutely! Of course!'

'Well, bless him,' said my dad with a chuckle. 'Who'd have thought it at his age? But far be it from me to march in here and play fast and loose with your family traditions, dear. Anyway, the point is, you go right ahead and get his tree for him.'

I paused for some seconds, not believing my luck.

'Right then,' I ventured, finally. 'I'll do that, then. And I know!' I added, in a flurry of inspiration and gratitude. 'We could put your silver tree up in the porch.'

Rushed straight upstairs and went yes!yes!yes! with bobbing knee manoeuvre, as footballers do, then gave Ben a bumper kiss and hug and promised that a stunt bike was no longer entirely out of the realms of Christmas possibility.

Am now basking in an aura of warmth and love and gratitude for the frankly amazing show of astute yet sensitive grandparent management from my younger progeny. I am suffused with wonder at such an entirely unexpected display of sensitivity. (Indeed, display of having registered our conversation about the tree-procuring trip at all.) Am managing, obviously, to get some things right. And some wrong, of course, as I have not actually dealt with the situation at all. Still, having raised children to deal so effectively with maternal wimp difficulties must count for something.

Chapter 13

TWELVE OR SO SHOPPING days to go. Or whatever.

Heartwarming development.

Had an email from Dan tonight (*must* get another phone line installed).

Mum, hope you get this. Phone permanently engaged *again*. I know it's short notice but would it be OK if Jack came to us for Christmas instead? Her dad has had to change his plans at the last minute and he's going to be out of the country until the New Year (don't ask). Jack's pretty fed up, as you can imagine, but he's invited us both to join him at Klosters for skiing, in March, so can't say I'm too upset!!!!!!! But is that going to be OK with you? She can doss in my room.

I'll assume yes unless I hear from you.

Love Dan.

Very excited. Email straight back.

Hello darling!

Yes, <u>of course</u> Jack can come and spend Christmas with us! We'd love to have her! Will she be coming down with you, or is she making her own way here? Let me know when you can.

Wonderful news about both Christmas and skiing. You lucky thing you! And lucky old me! Looking forward to seeing you both,

Love Mumxx

Hah!

Wonderful, wonderful news in*deed*. Will have my baby son back in the bosom of his family and will be able to impress the snotty, goggle-eyed madam with fantastical, magical, sublime festive decor, Christmas-tree-to-die-for, and a best-roast-potatoes-in-the-world Christmas lunch. Even if it *is* eaten in a pokey, semi-detached hovel.

'I can almost hear him sitting there singing its praises,' I tell Rose, gleefully.

'You're pleased then, I take it? But I thought you couldn't stand the sight of the girl.'

'Ah, but that was in the Star of Bengal. The dynamic has shifted now. *I'm* in charge. Though, I have to say, I'm not quite sure what line to take about the sleeping arrangements. We don't have a spare room any more, of course, and it doesn't seem fair to turf Dad into Ben's room –'

'Hmm,' Rose says. 'I think I'd just leave them to it.'

'You would?'

'Well, you have to assume they sleep together, don't you?'

'Do I? I suppose so. They must do. It's not the sort of thing you'd ask.'

'Oh, I'm sure they are,' Rose decides, with the sublime nonchalance of one whose eldest is nine. 'So it's not like anyone's pretending otherwise, is it?'

'No, I guess not. But, still. I'm not sure I like the idea of them bonking away on the other side of my bedroom wall. Not sure I like the idea of them bonking, period.'

'Which reminds me. Any new developments with Adam?'

'Developments? Adam?' I trill disingenuously, while a small rodent gnaws at the pain in my gut. 'Can't imagine who you're talking about. Adam *who*?'

Thursday. In a spirit of joy (tinged only marginally by the bonk-question stress / Adam Jones thoughts-avoidance stress / respect for the newly departed etc.) I decide to put the tree up.

In fact; go into garage, remove argumentative protective netting from tree, spray tree with tree saver, have fifteen-minute coughing fit, find bucket, find bag of gravel, pour gravel into bucket, put tree in bucket, free hair from tree, take tree out of bucket, re-arrange gravel, put tree back in bucket, take tree out of bucket, raid perimeter of house for supplementary gravel, put tree back in bucket, free hair from tree, wonder why didn't put tree in bucket while netting still in place, drag bucket plus tree through kitchen, hall, lounge. Position tree in centre of lounge, move sofa, coffee table, magazine rack and standard lamp to other side of lounge, reposition tree in front of patio doors, wonder why didn't bring tree in via patio doors in first place, adjust tree in bucket, lash tree to radiator pipe for security.

Go back into garage, find decorative half barrel, bring decorative half-barrel inside, attempt to stand bucket in half barrel, remove half of gravel, attempt to stand bucket in half barrel, detach tree from radiator pipe, reposition tree in bucket, stand bucket in half barrel, put gravel back in bucket, re-lash tree to radiator pipe, step on assorted invertebrate life previously resident in half barrel, check tree for branch symmetry, hack off lower branch on right to achieve, hack off supplementary lower branch on left to balance, place hacked lower left branch on top of sparse lower right region to rebalance, add water to bucket, get kitchen roll from kitchen, mop carpet around barrel area.

Get decorations from loft, unwind lights, check lights, mend fuse in plug, replace five bulbs, re-check lights, wind lights around tree. Run out halfway down, unwind lights, rewind lights, run out of lights two-thirds way down, curse, go to local sweet shop, purchase supplementary light set, return, wind supplementary light set around bottom of tree, check lights, find lights don't work, replace bulb, go upstairs and look for adaptor, take adaptor from Ben's room, make note to replace later, switch on all lights, say ahhh!, switch off lights, get baubles out.

Put angel on top, adjust dress, hang baubles, dislike layout of baubles, curse, re-arrange baubles, hang last family heirloom delicate glass bird-of-paradise decoration, hang miscellaneous colour co-ordinated decorations, hang chocolate umbrellas, remember have tinsel, curse, get tinsel, weave tinsel carefully through lights, baubles, umbrellas etc., knock decorations off branches, curse, step on family heirloom delicate glass bird-of-paradise decoration, curse again, remember box of decorations made by Dan and Ben at nursery / infant / junior school, get box, hang falling to bits sugar paper plus glitter plus pasta and pulses decorations on inconspicuous parts of tree, feel guilty, re-hang in pride of place positions, groan, re-hang select few in compromise positions, return remainder to box, switch lights on, curse, check bulbs, curse again, check bulbs again, find culprit, replace bulb, eat chocolate umbrella.

Spray tree copiously with fake snow, have fifteen-minute coughing fit, realise not fake snow but tree saver again, curse, find snow spray, spray tree copiously with snow spray, get lametta, stand on chair and throw lametta artistically at tree, get down from chair, pick lametta up from floor, get on chair, throw lametta artistically at tree, get down from chair, pick up remaining lametta, chuck handfuls at lower branches, get hoover, hoover needles, lametta and invertebrate corpses from lounge, then hoover kitchen, hall and lower stairs, put hoover away, sit on sofa, fall asleep.

Wake to sound of insistent ding-donging of doorbell. Go to answer door to find Sheila Rawlins outside, wishing to deliver the Christmas edition of the parish newsletter, plus procure two pounds annual subscription.

I ask her in and pretend to have left my handbag in the lounge in order to lure her into the room to be impressed by my fantastical, magical etc. tree.

'Wow*ee*!' says Sheila. 'Your tree looks *stunning*!'

'Really?' I say. 'Oh you're *so* kind. It's nothing very exciting *really*' etc.

Give an extra pound for church fund.

Ahhh. Sleep the sleep of the just and self-righteous and dream (obviously unavoidable and possibly quite healing) dreams about hot sexual encounters with nameless GP. I even conjure up a grand scheme for a surreal, crystalline Lapland (uPVC) porch, based loosely on the four-foot high silver fake tinsel tree, plus cotton wool, polystyrene chips, branches and glitter. And the four million light set I saw in the market last week.

Lovely to come down in the morning, refreshed, uplifted and with the resiny scent of my majestic great fir putting paid to the last traces of father's most recent excursion into salsas and fermented fruit vinegars. Less lovely to endure a two-minute tirade from my younger son about the importance of not interfering with plugs, sockets and electrical equipment arrangements in his bedroom, particularly as the clock radio is the only sure method of waking for school in a house run by a dormouse mother.

But loveliness, on the whole, abounds. The post brings me a copy of *Intrepid Explorers! (Nepal and Tibet)* – *a personalised itinerary for Ms Charlotte Simpson,* which, following Rhys's advice, I requested, from a knowledgeable man with a business in Bolton, who, joy of joys! knows the difference between a *drokpa* and a *daal.* I take it off to work to enhance my good chi. And it's a morning of further good portents, as, hot on heels of the major downer of the Rutlands taking on Metro as well, in an unprecedented (in Cardiff) two-agency shoot-out at the OK Corral-type scenario, I have taken Mr and Mrs Habib for a second viewing of Cherry Ditchling and they seem, dare I say it, exceedingly keen.

'There's even a ha-ha,' he enthused to his wife. 'Jane Austen, I believe, thought very highly of those.'

But as ever, there is always scope for a disintegration of my luck, as Minnie is due to be moving to The Maltings today and I am scheduled to turn up and collect Kipling, just prior to (please, God) the completion. And I am not disappointed.

I arrive twenty minutes early in a persistent drizzle and am dismayed to find Austin Metro also in the street, picking wet leaves from the bonnet of his Jag. I lean in to grope around in search of an umbrella, and fully expect scorch marks to appear on the seat of my pond-weed skirt.

'Is there a problem?' I ask as I back out again.

He shifts his gaze from my bottom and then lopes across the road. 'Exactly what I was about to ask,' he says. '*I'm* here to see this completion completed. What about you? Bit above and beyond, this, isn't it, lovely?'

'If you must know, I'm having the cat,' I bark back. 'There is absolutely no problem with Minnie.'

Because I've also noted the social worker's car across the road, my words carry less than complete conviction. I'd been told that Minnie was to be collected at midday, by the sister from The Maltings, and that she would make sure Kipling was in his cat basket when I got there. Hmm. And less conviction still when a siren, closely followed by a shiny white bulk bearing down on us, heralds the arrival of what is clearly an ambulance. Somehow, I just know it's for Minnie. I bolt for the house, Austin Metro behind me. The front door is open so we both run inside.

'Ah, it's here,' says the social worker, glancing up as we enter. 'All right, Minnie. The ambulance is here, my love. You're all right now. Don't fret.'

I kneel on the floor beside her. Minnie is face-down on the hall floor, her head to one side and her eyes closed. There is a trail of dribble glistening at the side of her mouth. The social worker glances up and recognises me.

'Had a fall,' she confirms, with a sigh. 'As they do. Difficult to tell, of course, but I suspect her hip's gone. I've not tried to move her – ah, here we are.'

What little light there is disappears as two paramedics, plus stretcher (plus docusoap film crew?), fill the doorway. Relentlessly jovial, they move in and take over, and with disturbingly little protestation from Minnie, concoct some sort of splint, construct some sort of stretcher and soon have her outside and into the ambulance.

'I think I should go with her,' I tell the social worker, as we stand by and watch helplessly. She looks relieved.

'*Would* you? It would be nice to think someone could. I've got the Magistrates at one. I'll let the office know what's happened.' She checks her watch, then glances down the street. 'And that'll be the new people, I suppose. Oh dear.'

'What, already?' I turn to Austin, who has been standing nearby, gabbling into his mobile. I raise my eyebrows and point up the road. He shakes his head.

'Just the removal men,' he mouths. Then he nods and speaks. 'Just completed though. The Applebys'll be on their way to the office for the keys pretty soon. We clear here?'

The ambulance driver walks back up the path.

'You coming, love?'

'Yes, of course,' I say. 'But shouldn't I find her a nightie or something? *Is* there a nightie? The house has been cleared now, hasn't it?'

The social worker nods. 'But she has a couple of cases of personal bits to take with her, I believe. They'll be in the hall still. I suppose we could have a look through them, do you think?'

'Tell you what,' says the ambulance driver. 'We've given her a shedload of painkillers, so she's pretty well out of it at the moment. Why don't you get some bits together and follow us down? Come round to A and E and catch up with her there.'

The social worker nods again. 'That sounds best, doesn't it? If it's all right with you?'

'I suppose so, I say. 'What should I do with all her stuff though?'

She looks at her watch again. 'I suppose the best thing would be to have the person from The Maltings take it, wouldn't it? And she's due soon, is she not? Or should we telephone and stop her? Given the time. What do you think?'

I feel frazzled and fretty. I want to say 'I don't bloody know, you're the social worker,' but I don't, of course. Instead I say, 'Well, it is her new address now, so that would seem to make sense. Yes, righty-ho. Let's get on then, shall we?' I take the door keys the social worker then proffers and I head off back towards the house.

Austin follows.

'How about the keys then? D'you want to let me have them? Drop them off to Davina for you? I assume you'll be a while getting back to the office.'

I know it's the silliest thing, and I know it's not his fault, and I know he's only trying to get the details sorted and so on, and I know giving him the keys would be a sensible thing to do, but I feel quite unreasonably furious with him. As if, somehow, this mess is all of his making.

'I'm sorry,' I say sniffily 'but it's against company policy. I will find Minnie's nightie, give the cases to the sister at The Maltings, and then take the keys to the office myself. Once the solicitor confirms that the sale is completed, we will, of course, hand them over.' I step into the hall and pick up the cases. They are ridiculously light. As we arrive shall we go? The cat basket, however, is nowhere to be seen. 'I will,' I add, shutting both him and the rain out, 'return to the office as soon as I can.'

Cats and Simpsons don't mix. Never have. I am barmy.

'Your Minnie's a ninny,' I tell this one, conversationally, while trying to pretend that my purse is a juicy fat mouse. He's having none of it, of course. Ninny or not, she's been mother to him for as many years, I suspect, as I've been mother to Ben.

We spend a good twenty minutes engaged in no-claws-barred hostilities, but he is lured into the basket, in the end, by a small tin of cat food, which I remembered I saw in the bottom of one of Minnie's cases.

By the time we get home, my car smells like a fishmonger's toilet. But at least he's stopped spitting and lacerating the wicker.

'OK, Kipling,' I tell him. 'This is the deal for all four-legged Simpsons. No peeing, no crapping, no clawing the chair legs, no climbing on beds and no bringing in corpses. And make sure you keep your eyes off the sofa. Oh, and the worktops in the kitchen are right out of bounds. And one more thing –' I waggle my finger. 'Don't expect Whiskas at this house, OK?'

Kipling's ears flatten as I undo the buckles.

'Oh,' I add. 'And if you mangle the decorations, you're for it.'

He bolts from the basket and shoots straight up the tree.

My father appears while I am in the middle of trying to reassemble the carefully constructed tonal cascade that was my bauble arrangement this year. Luckily for him, he refrains from passing comment. He does, however, manage to rouse more than a little consternation (and a touch of angst), with a) a cravat, and b) the gleeful announcement that not only are he and Hester formally an item, but that he's invited her over for Christmas as well.

'So much for bijou,' I tell Rose, when I call her. 'I have Dan, I have Ben, I have Jack, I have Dad, I have Hester now too, I may yet have Francesca, and I have a psychotic cat with unbelievable breath.'

'You'll have fun!'

'All I'll have is a hundredweight of sprouts and a headache.'

'But I thought a big family Christmas was just what you wanted.'

'It was. So can I come to yours? I'd much rather bring the boys down and look after you.'

'You know you can, Charlie. My God, don't you know it. But I don't need looking after.'

'Yes you do. You need succour. You need someone to lean on.'

'I need no such thing, so stop this fussing, OK?' Something in her tone makes its point, and I take it.

'OK.'

'So, come on. Buck up. You'll enjoy yourselves. You're just feeling mopey. Get that sherry open early, is my advice.'

'I don't dare. I may just have to scarper. Can you really see Jack and that Hester together? Don't know why I don't just leave home myself and have done with it.'

'Tsh!' she says. 'Calm down. It's just this Adam business, isn't it?'

'No!' I say. *Yes.* 'I just feel like escaping.'

'You'll be OK,' she soothes. 'You'll all get along fine.'

I wish I could believe her. When I get into the study and boot up the computer, it is with the realisation that my air of festive jollity and *joie de vivre* is but a thin veneer over the fretwork of my stresses; that there isn't a bauble arrangement in the world that can lift this sort of low. And when I see he has emailed me, it is almost with a sense that none of this stuff is within my control. Cannot *believe* some people.

thesimpsons@cymserve.com

Dear Charlie,
Thought I would get in touch as Davina told me about Minnie. I'm sorry. Is she going to be OK?

Didn't respond to your last email because, well, you told me not to, of course, but also because I do take your point. But spoke to Rhys today and found myself stupidly dismayed by his (how shall I put this?) appreciation of your charms. In retrospect, not a particularly sensible position to have put myself in. None of which (I know you will tell me) is of the least concern to you. Yet here I am again. I seem unable to stop myself. A bit of a mess all round, eh? I'm sorry.
Adamxx

I am cross. I am more than a little cross. I am very, very cross.

I am cross at myself for having emailed him in the first place. I'm cross at him for having emailed me back. Mainly I'm cross that, despite me telling him in no uncertain tones not to, I'm secretly *so* thrilled and excited that he did.

But stuff that. When I was fourteen I received a Valentine card from a boy in my class that I was nuts about. It had been sent anonymously, of course, but I knew it was him because he had a left-handed italic fountain pen, which caused his thick strokes to be thin and his thin ones fat. He'd written 'Dear Charlotte, I think you're really lovely and I'd <u>really</u> like to go out with you.' I didn't say anything. He was already going out with my second best friend. Instead, I waited. I waited and waited. But still he went out with her. And I couldn't bring myself to give him a sign.

Still don't know why he sent it. What was the point? Sure as hell made me mad.

Rose, I tell you, this is bad. Think seismic activity (and you know how seismic activity is measured, i.e. *exponentially*) and you'll know what I mean when I tell you this email rates an eight. Forget San Francisco, forget Mount St Helens, forget, in fact, all the parameters you usually apply at a time like this, and that's how bad this is. This is real. This is not dreaming. This is not imagining. This is not reading things into things. Oh no. Nor fashioning a romantic epic from a few pedestrian encounters and writing myself the romantic lead. Nor fancying I noticed a particular nuance in his manner where there was simply a friendly smile. Nor telling myself I was being fanciful, period, while believing, inside, the reverse to be true. This is not about wishing, or hoping, or wanting. This is real. It's all real. It's all real. *It's all real.* It's – well, what it is, is – well, *mutual*, basically.

I couldn't actually email Rose, of course, as the last thing I wanted was to bother her with my problems right now. So, ho hum, off I went to bed, up my twinkly staircase, on my featherlight feet, with my gossamer, billowy negligee billowing, to lay my head on the soft pastel silk of my pillow and dream torrid dreams about making love in edelweiss-dotted grassy knolls. But this time the nameless GP grew some horns and had the words *forbidden fruit* stamped on his rump.

Chapter 14

I'VE DECIDED TO GO for a festive buffet-style Christmas Eve supper as I cannot face the stress involved in making the usual sit-down pig-out meal. In fact, I can't face the stress involved in making any sort of meal, given the amount of stress I've already expended in trying not to allocate ridiculous chunks of time to thinking; *yet here I am again. I seem unable to stop myself.* So have instead decided to splurge a big lump of my derisory Christmas bonus on buying everything in a black box that says 'Occasions' on it, in Sainsbury's.

Which proves to be something of a shrewd move early on, as there are no straining and plate warming agendas to adhere to and therefore no flash points of familial unease in the air. Until ...

Until some time after dinner, when we could all be happily watching an undemanding *Frost,* or *Morse,* or crappy TV Xmas special even, but instead Hester decides to regale us with her apocryphal tale about high jinks and much drama in the matter of the elderly person's seat on the bus going to Grangetown last week. Suddenly I'm whisked from our mundane but familiar dynamic and plonked down, hard, in the middle of a sit-com – a truly bad sit-com with terrible ratings, that is peopled (albeit in very twinkly surroundings) by a huddle of humourless numbskulls and geeks.

Hester; 'So I thought, well, it was only to be expected, wasn't it?'

Dad; 'How so, love?'

Hester; 'Well, he was a coloured chap, of course.'

Jack; 'Pardon?'

Hester; 'And it has to be said, some of them –'

Jack; 'I'm sorry, Mrs Stableford – did you say "and it has to be said"?'

Me; 'Who's for a hot chocolate?'

Hester; 'Don't get me wrong dear – I'm not saying that had anything to do with –'

Jack; 'And it has to be said that some of them *what?*'

Dan; 'Jack, drop it. It isn't important.'

Jack; 'I beg to differ, Dan. It's *extremely* important. This is exactly the kind of nasty latent racism that percolates through generations and infects everybody with its horrible canker.'

Me; 'Or a glass of something, perhaps?'

Hester; 'There's no need to point, dear. And I'm not saying it was anything to do with his colour. I have nothing against coloured people. I have friends who are coloured, and they are all *very* nice. It's just that, on this occasion –'

Jack (pointing); 'So why mention it? Why slip it into the conversation at all? Why give *him* (Ben) the impression that there is a correlation between the man's behaviour and his colour –'

Ben; 'Don't bring *me* into this!'

Me; 'Or a date? Piece of crystallised fruit, maybe?'

Dan; 'Come on Jack, let's leave it.'

Jack; 'Oh, so you think I'm wrong then, do you? That's not what you said at Deb. Soc. last week. It was all –'

Dan; 'Of *course* I don't think you're wrong. You're absolutely right. I *abhor* racism. You know that. It's just –'

Dad; 'Now come on, lad. Hester's no racist. I don't think we need to start bandying unkind words around.'

Dan; 'I *am* aware of that, Grandad. But Jack is simply making the point that sometimes these things are, well, innate. Not meant exactly. But nevertheless *there*. Latent. I don't –'

Jack; 'Exactly! Which makes her a racist! You can't go around making assumptions about people based on the colour of their skin, and then deny that you're a racist! God! This is exactly what I mean! Until we stand up and question that sort of behaviour in ourselves it will just go on and on and on!'

Dad; 'Bit of respect for your elders wouldn't go amiss here, young lady.'

Dan; 'There is no lack of respect here, Grandad. Jack is simply trying to –'

Jack; 'Yes there is! I hate all this respect your elders crap!'

Ben (tittering); 'Obviously!'

Me; '*Ben*!'

Jack; 'Since when do we have to respect people just because they are older than we are? I have respect for any number of people, believe me, but for their character, their intellect, their vision – not their ignorance!'

Dad; 'You're going to just sit there and let her speak to Hester like that, are you, lad?'

Dan; 'Grandad, it's not my place to –'

Jack; 'Quite. I am an educated, intelligent person and I do not need to be told-'

Hester (sniffing); 'Yes, well. Just goes to show what a waste of money all that so-called education is, doesn't it? Manners is as manners does, young lady, and I'm sorry to see how few you young people seem to have these days. When I was young we knew our place –'

Jack, (rising) 'Oh, yes, I'll bet. Riding roughshod over the colonies and exploiting the indigenous populations. That was about the size of it, wasn't it? Oh, and having nothing to do with niggers, of course.'

Me / Dan / Dad; 'Jack!'

Hester (reddening), 'I don't think I need to listen to any more of this, thank you very much. Leonard, I'm going to bed.'

Ben; 'Oh-er!'

Jack, (bursting into tears) 'Good! Good riddance! I'm fussy about the company I keep. Dan, I want to go home.'

Dan; 'Oh, for fuck's sake!'

Me, 'Dan!'

Dad (leaving); 'Well, I just hope you're both satisfied.'

Me (standing), 'Come on, Dad –'

Ben (grinning), 'Can I watch South Park on Sky now, Mum?'

Me, 'Ben, it's –'

Ping.

Me (again. Rubbing my eyes / blinking); 'Hmmm.

135

Evidently not.'

And cut.

When you suddenly find yourself standing in absolute impenetrable darkness the last thing you should do is start dashing around the room like a headless chicken, particularly when the room in question has played host to several people, a monster tree, a large quantity of glassware and the half-eaten debris from a buffet-style supper. At least two glasses and a meat dish fell victim.

I could hear Dan's voice from the hallway, closely followed by the jumpy yellow incandescence of a torch.

'Must be a power cut,' he said. 'Everything's off. Except, hold on –' the torchlight dimmed and disappeared momentarily. 'No. Can't be that. Next door's still got their lights on.'

'So what happened? Dan, find me the other torch, will you? It must be a fuse that's gone, something like that.'

He found me the torch and we went into the kitchen. The trip switches had all tripped, which told me nothing I didn't already know. I flicked up the big grey one and we peered for some seconds.

'To be honest,' I told him, 'I haven't a clue.'

He shook his head. 'Me neither. A short? I don't think we should touch it.'

Dad shuffled in. 'Get away from there, you two. Let *me* have a look.'

He took my torch and climbed up to inspect the meter box also. Some moments elapsed. There was much grunting and clucking. Then he clambered down.

'Well?' we both asked him. 'The verdict?'

'Don't know. A short? I don't think we should touch it.'

25th December. Ding dong merrily.

We have no electricity. We anticipate having no electricity for the rest of the day. So, to kill time, I will either kill the cat, or, if I fail to establish the whereabouts of the cat before the market re-opens after the Xmas break, I will kill the man who sold me a life-threatening set of outdoor festive four million winking fairy lights for my porch in the certain knowledge that they could not withstand the effect of even a pathetic single millilitre of liquid. Cat pee is surely not *that* dissimilar to rain. Or is it? Wish I had a more specific knowledge of acids.

I should not kill the cat, though, but the real culprits. Had Jack and Hester not spent the entire evening griping, grousing, niggling, fighting etc., I would doubtless have heard Kipling's miaow to go out. And would not have a pee puddle in the porch. Would still have power. Girlfriends. Who'd have them?

Speaking of which, have father's girlfriend in a sulk at the breakfast bar. Have son's girlfriend in a sulk in bed. Have younger son in a sulk in the lounge. Have elder son in a sulk in the study, and have father (who is a naval man and therefore a pragmatic sulk-free zone) in a pan-banging fury at the kitchen sink. I am about to preside over potentially the most harrowing Christmas day since the Great War. Wish I could defect *now*. Still small voice of calm too still, too small to register.

I decide to defect anyway, in an unprecedented yuletide on foot pre-lunch excursion to the Dog and Trouserleg, on (happy development) my elder son's arm. Village looking as it would do on any cold, drizzly midwinter late morning (i.e. cold, drizzly), except with the addition of an All Wales Leylandii Light Show in gardens and tantalising glimpses of the insides of adequately lit lounges, where festive board games and sherry-lubricated jolly veg preparation sessions are most probably already underway. But I also recall the year of the extended Simpson family Christmas brunch some years back and I'm reminded that my present covetous mood stems not from warm glowing memories of similar happy Yuletides, but from a highly selective memory re just how enjoyable it is spending the day with a bunch of discordant and hung over relatives. Particularly when said hung over relatives have spent a uncomfortable night on various unsatisfactory bed-type assemblages, and have queued for forty minutes to get into a bathroom that has been recently vacated by other hung over relatives who spent Christmas Eve eating a half ton of nuts. No wonder the sherry is generally gone before noon.

The pub is full, fuggy, warm and welcoming. The clientele are red-faced, chortling and predominantly male. I drink two very large glasses of wine before my seasonal *bonhomie* is restored.

'Isn't this nice?' I tell Dan, perching on a bar stool for safety and draining my third. 'So nice to have you all grown-up now and legal and able to escort your mother to the pub. Legally. And so on. And so forth.'

He glowers into his pint.

'I suppose,' he says. 'Would have been nicer if it wasn't with the knowledge that we've got to go back and face Jack and Grandad and Ben and that Hester woman and have to sit in the dark with no telly. It'll just happen all over again, I'm sure.'

I attempt a tut but it comes out as a 'tch!' *Bad* news.

'Dan, you really shouldn't call her "that Hester woman",' I berate. 'Anyway, all the more reason to hang out in here for a while. They could have come, couldn't they? So sod them. Besides, to tell the truth, I've about had it with Hester and Dad. They're beginning to cloy. And what about Jack?'

He turns. 'What about Jack?'

'What's the thing with her, *really*?'

'Thing?'

'Why is she so … well, so … so …'

'What?'

'Oh, you know. Uptight. Argumentative. As if …' Choose very *very* carefully here. 'As if she's, oh, I don't know … unhappy with life. She gave Hester a bit of a roasting, you must admit.'

He gulps another inch. 'Which she deserved.'

Give up *now*. He can't see it.

'You can't see it, but …'

'Mum, of *course* I can see it. But you have to know where she's coming from. She's had a shit life, basically. Oh, there may be plenty of money but her parents are both completely

138

hyper and self-obsessed and, well, sad. You know?' (*Do* I?)
'It's just the way she keeps it together. You should try *being*
her for once. She has such a lot of shit to put up with. And at
least she has some principles. You just don't – oh, look!
Doctor Jones is over there! I wanted to talk to him. We had
these amazing cadavers with –'

Rats. Why is that man so all bloody wise bloody nice
bloody friend-to-the-family bloody Dan's bloody hero bloody
perfect bloody *lovely*? He is wearing a black leather jacket.
With pockets. That his hands are in. Plus jeans again. Plus big
black boots. Boots! I hate him, I decide.

'Give him a break, Dan,' I lob into the body count. 'I'm
sure he doesn't want to talk shop today.' I force myself to
ignore his crestfallen look. Then spy Bill Stableford
approaching. 'Ah, Bill!' I beckon. 'How are you? Merry
Christmas and all that!'

'Hello, hello, hello!' says Bill. 'What brings the Simpsons
to the pub this fine morn?' He glances around. 'Not driven to
escape by my sainted mother, perchance?'

Dan chokes on his beer with such grace and aplomb that
the only evidence is a rush of crisp shards in the glass.

'As if!' I chortle merrily. (And having drowned my
conceptual grasp of irony in Chenin Blanc.) 'It's his and hers
G and Ts and a friendly tussle over the root veg. We thought it
best, Dan and I, to leave the love-birds to get on with it. That
and the lack of electricity.'

I explain, slightly manically. Bill chortles.

'It's a bit of a turn up, all this, though. Eh, what? Never
thought the old bird had the –' he makes a sound through his
nose like a rhinoceros farting. Which I presume means libido,
or virility, or horn, even. Who knows? 'Goodness me,' he goes
on. 'And what with your Ben and our Frankie, good grief,
Charlie, you and me'll soon be related!'

It's a sobering thought, so I pick up my wine.

And, of course, I forgot to keep a weather eye on the Doctor.
Always a bad move to second guess a GP. On this occasion,

particularly so, because when I decided I needed to lose some of the wine already on board, who should have decided to avail himself of the facilities at exactly that moment? Him.

I threw myself at the (heavy, unyielding) door to the Ladies and managed to dive out of sight just in time. The mirror reproached me. How, it said, could you go out in public with a face like the one you've just cobbled together? I turned my back on it and scowled at the warm air dryer. The toilets were busy but one flushed soon after, emitting Julia Potter, in black polo neck sweater and meringue-coloured jeans. Looking absolutely *perfect*. I'd not spotted Richard.

And wouldn't. She told me she was here agreeably husband-less.

'For the sake of my sanity,' she explained. 'You decided to get pissed as well?'

'It seemed sensible,' I replied. 'It was either that or chop my father and his girlfriend up and feed them to the cat.'

'Christ, me too! Richard, for quite unfathomable reasons, is making some sort of vegetarian loaf thing, and my mother is doing something despicable with giblets, as usual. So I bolted.' She ran her hand over the top of her hair and it sprung prettily forth in little snowy blonde peaks.

'You look great,' I said, feeling like a half ton of dog bones.

I spent a few moments loitering and pretending to be doing something constructive with a blunt eyebrow pencil (the only thing in my bag – the only hope for my face), then decided enough time had elapsed and emerged.

The secret, of course, was to time my exit so as not to coincide with his. Finally I inched the main door open. The corridor was empty. So far so good. I went back into the lounge.

Dan had got me another glass of wine, which he held out to me, smiling. But then I realised he wasn't smiling *at* me, but past me.

'Hi, Doctor Jones!' he said.

'Adam, *please*. Dan, it's good to see you. How's Med

140

School?'

Rats. *Rats*. Adam took the pint that Bill Stableford passed him. And didn't look at me *at all*. Which made it even worse.

'Mega,' said Dan. 'Harder work than I expected, but the anatomy's been great. I've been giving Mum all the gruesome details, haven't I?'

'Oh, absolutely. Yeuch!' I trilled, not looking at him either, and concentrating instead on downing my wine.

'Hard but enjoyable, I trust,' Adam ventured, tapping a beer mat on the bar top. 'Work hard but play hard –'

'Hem, hem!' I announced. 'Well, that's me! Let's be off!'

I slapped down my glass and they all turned to look at me.

'Mum, I've still got all this left to drink!' Dan exclaimed.

'Well, hurry up then,' I told him, looking pointedly at my watch. I couldn't, for some reason, make out what the hands said.

'In a hurry?' asked Bill. 'It's not even one yet. Thought you were anxious to –'

'No, no,' I answered, gesticulating wildly. 'I've got an old lady in hospital to visit.'

'You have?' Bill asked.

'Yes, I have. My friend, Minnie Drinkwater.'

Adam nodded. Dan frowned.

'First I've heard of it,' he said. 'Besides, you are pissed, Mum. There's no way you can drive anywhere.'

Ah.

I shook my head. 'I'm going by taxi.'

Bill laughed. 'Don't be daft. You'll no more get a taxi today than a ride on a donkey.'

Adam's hand brushed my arm. 'I can take you, if you like.'

His eyes, like the Thunderbirds mole, bored into me. 'No you can't.'

'Yes I can. We're not eating till four. I'm not expected back till three. So I can.'

'No you *can't*. I mean, I'd rather you didn't, actually. Look, er … it's terribly kind of you – Dan! Come *along*. We are going, and now.'

'But I don't want to go. You go off with Doct– Adam. I'll meet you back home. Where's the problem with that?'

I trained my eyes and hoped. It was obviously rusty and weak from disuse, but I gave him the zap anyway and, thank heavens, it worked.

His eyes dropped.

'OK, come on. Let's go then.' With a bemused shrug towards Adam, he steered me outside.

It suddenly seemed like a long walk home. A long disagreeable one.

'What *is* it with you, Mum? What was all that about?'

'Nothing.'

'But you never said anything about visiting anyone in hospital.'

'Yes I did.'

'When?'

'Oh, I can't remember, Dan. Does it matter?'

Evidently. He stopped on the pavement and propped the back of his hands on his hips, snorting little white clouds of angry breath into the drizzle.

'Yes, it does,' he said. '*Act*ually. Because if it was so important then why didn't you? And why were you so stroppy with Doct– *Adam*, when he offered to drive you there?'

I walked on, head down. Those *eyes*. 'I wasn't stroppy.'

He followed. 'Yes you were.'

'Was I? Was I really?'

'Yes. And he was only trying to be helpful. Honestly, Mum, just because you don't like Davina, doesn't mean you have to tar Adam with the same brush. You may not have noticed, but he's actually a very nice guy.'

My fit of pique is of such intensity that I find it leads me to the (entirely unrelated) conjecture that my elder son's sniffiness where the goggle-eyed witch is concerned is generated more by thoughts of a free winter sports holiday than by an excess of sociological distress. Which (I realise before we're even home) is just about the crappiest, most mealy-mouthed thought

142

I've had in a long time, and not in the least appropriate to my generally good and very principled son. More, a reflection on a juvenile mother. This is what happens, then, when you get bogged down in crap stuff. I feel like a maggot. Must wash my mouth out with soap.

Chapter 15

NEW YEAR'S EVE.

I remained bogged down and maggoty throughout the whole of Boxing Day, and decided to embark on a frenzied and full-time programme of mental self-flagellation. I hoovered obsessively, made any number of casseroles and cleared out six month's worth of odd socks from Ben's room. I instigated a family outing to the Sales, and even (cannot now believe that I *did* this) produced a carrot and walnut cake the size of a hatbox that I eagerly pressed upon Dan and Jack when they left. But even as the low cloud of self-reproach began lifting, New Year's Eve beckoned, to thrash me anew.

Into each life and so on.

Everybody has to have some downer in their life. Everybody has to have their own personal *bête noire*. A well-managed *bête noire* is like a dose of cod liver oil. Whatever social ordeal I find myself enduring, I can always remember I could be worse off. My most enduring *bête noire* is the habit of barn dancing, particularly as applied to the Cefn Melin community hall during a blizzard. And, boy, did we have a blizzard that night.

I have nothing against barn dances *per se*. This is not a blanket grievance. But neither do I have a fully toned pelvic floor. Plus, I don't care for cowboys, I don't much like hay, I loathe Country and Western music, and I can't doh-si-doh.

But despite that, we went. We went because Ben and Dad and Hester thought it would be fun to traipse through the snow and spend an evening in the village hall being bullied by a man with a fiddle. I, understandably, did not think it would be fun, and though that might lead me to suppose that everyone's needs would be best served by them going and me staying at home with a curry and a bottle of wine and the video of *Trainspotting* (for self-esteem restoration purposes), they, it seemed, did not subscribe to this view.

Their considered opinion was that it would be fun only if I came as well. Because (so the reasoning went) if I didn't come then they'd be forced to come home early and see the New Year in with me, because if they didn't come home early to see the New Year in with me they were convinced (to a man) that I would sulk or cry or feel quite unreasonably sorry for myself, and seeing as how I'd been so funny just lately, they all decided it was just too big a chance to take. And though my father had the good grace not to mention my hormones, I could tell he had not ruled early menopause out.

Thus it is with families. But I drew a firm line at Hester's spare gingham skirt.

And I had a fine time, as you very often do when your expectation is one of only stupefying boredom and wet pants. We did have to leave early, however, as Ben's asthma had grown steadily worse through the evening, not helped by the hay and the chilly night air. As the two of us walked the snowy half mile home, he was breathing in gasps and continually coughing, and had run out of discs for his inhaler as well.

'Doesn't matter,' I said. 'I'd had enough anyway. And there's bound to be something mindlessly entertaining on TV.'

Which no doubt there was, but by the time we arrived home, TV was the last thing on my mind. It was with some relief that I put my key into the lock.

The telephone was ringing as I opened the front door.

'Charlotte?'

My dad.

'Something up?' I replied.

'No, no, dear. Everything's fine. It's just that I've just brought Hester home, and the weather, quite frankly, well, it's looking rather nasty, and she suggested I stay the night. She has a Z-bed and a sleeping bag and we thought … well, what do *you* think? Will *you* be all right, dear?'

Bless him.

'Dad, I'll be fine. (I've been fine thus far, haven't I?) I'm going to call the GP out and get Ben fixed up with some steroids or something. I have Hester's number. If I need you, I'll call you. OK?'

'Are you sure? I mean if the lad's really poorly, then I think my place is there with you.'

'Dad, don't set out again now. You've just trudged a mile in the opposite direction. We'll be fine here. Really...'

'I don't know. Are you sure?'

'Dad, I'm *sure*.'

'In that case –'

'Night night.'

I realised that my father was no more in control of his primeval urges than Ben. And that the probable only difference between the wooing of Stablefords senior and junior was in the viability of the evolutionary outcome. So that was it. Here we were. All alone and being snowed on. Me and the cat and my poor sick child.

Since being on my own, I dreaded the boys being ill. It was the time when the fact that it was all down to me crystallised most sharply on my consciousness; became the most stark of all those stark parental realities. The doctor, the hospital, the emergency services; all were just a phone call or short drive away. But that overwhelming sense of being the one they relied on sometimes threatened to overwhelm me.

Tonight though, as I dialled the surgery and asked for a home visit, I realised I'd reached some sort of maturity watershed, because the fact that my father would not be back till the morning, made me feel, unaccountably, better, not worse.

But crikey! (And then some.)

What did I have forty minutes after this inspired realisation? Standing on my doorstep? Come to answer a call to attend my sick son? Not the taciturn Dr Spalding. Not the young Dr Pang. Not even a nameless and world-weary locum. Oh no. What the halogen had brought into being was Griffith. Was Adam. Was Dr Adam G Jones.

My maturity watershed collapsing around me, I stood there

146

and gawped at him, fifteen again.

I should have known, of course, shouldn't I? Because they didn't come to the Barn Dance. And when I rang the surgery, there should have been some part of me – some rational, functioning part, that said to itself, ah! Adam must be working! And wouldn't it be funny if he turned up here now? And yet the thought, despite the plethora of Adam thoughts already jostling and crowding it, never crossed my mind for the tiniest instant. Which in some ways was a blessing. Had it done so, I might have been tempted to abandon the surgery and take my chances with the no doubt over-stretched casualty department instead.

I couldn't, at first, take in that it was actually him on the doorstep, blinking, as I was, against the glare of my overstated uPVC white-out of a porch. The short walk from the car had crowned him with a cotton wool head-dress and he was wearing not the familiar jeans, but a suit.

'Oh!' I said. 'Adam!' I'd nearly said Griffith.

'Hmm,' he said. 'Yes. Do I get to come in?'

A tattoo started up in my chest then and there, and as I ushered him past my massed ranks of glittering white branches, my temple joined in with a beat of its own. What to do? How to play this? I tried a smile, which he didn't return. He looked very stern.

'Righty-ho,' he said, clearing his throat. 'Where's the invalid?'

I pointed upstairs and then followed him up. He had pearlescent glitter all over his jacket, and a tidemark of snow around the toes of his brogues. I mumbled the asthma attack's natural history, and hoped my tremulous larynx wouldn't give me away. We entered Ben's room.

'That's lovely,' said Adam, sounding not in the least like himself. Then, 'Hello, Ben. Thank you, Charlie.' All in one practised utterance. I was, I realised with relief, being dismissed.

Back in the kitchen while Adam attended to Ben, I flapped about in an agony of pinging nerve endings, surging hormones, and an alarming counter-current heat exchange in my face. I then realised (with a sudden, and thus worrisome, excitement) that a similar rush òf unwelcome proximity-related chemicals must also, *must* also, be ensuing for him. Except he had had thirty or so minutes to prepare himself, having been the GP to have accepted the call.

The kettle boiled just as he came back into the kitchen.

'Nothing to worry about,' he said, stuffing his hands in his jacket pockets and not looking at me. 'I put him on the nebuliser, and he's much better now. He'll be asleep soon I expect, so if you want to, I don't know, tuck him in or whatever –'

'I'll just go up then, ' I said. 'Would you, er – I mean, if you have time, of course, perhaps you'd like to –'

Complete paralysis of sentence-finishing neuronal pathway. Rats.

I flapped my hand about in the general direction of the kettle. He nodded.

'Er. Great. Yes. Yes, please. I could kill for a coffee.'

'Great,' I echoed. Stupidly. With the cringeworthy addition of an inane tinkling laugh. 'I'll just –'

He smiled a little then. Shrugged. Took one hand out of his pocket. Moved it across a chair back. Pulled an earlobe. Put a – Oh *God. Stop* it, Charlotte! 'Shall I get on and –' He gestured. I nodded. Laughed again.

Bloody *hell*.

'Yes. Absolutely. It's that cupboard. Fridge *here* and spoons *there* and – well. I won't be a moment.'

I bolted up the stairs to find that Ben was already asleep, his chest rising and falling with a reassuringly relaxed height and tempo. I perched on the edge of the bed and tried to still my own ridiculous pulse. Outside, the snow was falling in fluffy fifty-pence discs, tinged orange by the warm sodium glow in the street. Adam's car was parked not on the road, but beside mine on our drive, which lent a poignancy to the reason he was actually here.

The fact of our solitude resonating all around me, I counted out the twenty-two steps that took my feet back downstairs. Adam had gone into to the living room, and was standing in the middle of it, holding the coffees. He had dispensed them into a pair of horrible chipped mugs. The most horrible mugs in my entire mug dynasty. Typical. He turned as I entered.

'Just admiring your tree.'

'Oh. Thank you. It's a bit of a thing with me, the tree. All the sparkle. All the frippery. That's me. That's what I'm best at. All very insignificant and boring. Ha, ha. Though I don't admit to actually making my own stuffing.'

(Why not? What was wrong with making your own stuffing? Davina probably made two types of stuffing to ram up *her* festive bird's acquiescent bum.)

I heard myself embellish this rubbish with yet another self-conscious titter. I couldn't seem to think of anything else to add. *All* those emails. All that easy, comfortable talk about nothing. And now I had nothing whatsoever to say.

'I know,' he said, handing me my coffee and smiling properly at last. 'You told me all about it.'

So I had. At length. Ad nauseam. *Drunkenly*.

'And you shouldn't knock yourself,' he went on. 'You have a real talent for it. The room looks beautiful.'

I wanted to tell him that I wasn't knocking myself; that I thought tree decorating to be a fine and noble calling, and that my attempts at being self-effacing were simply the nervous ramblings of a woman completely fazed by the awesome possibilities inherent in her predicament. But I didn't. Instead I gestured to the sofa, which he obediently sat on.

'We don't make much of an effort at home, as you'd imagine. No kids to do it for, so we tend not to bother. And what with work and so on –' He shrugged and settled himself back against the cushions. His tie matched the upholstery perfectly. (The 'we', however, clashed dreadfully.)

I perched at the other end, clutching the chipped bit of my mug.

'Of course. You're both very busy, I'll bet. Three hundred lights,' I twittered, clinging on hopefully to the last vestiges of the topic, in case a more unsettling one should jump up and bite us. He made a face of approval. 'And those stars?' I pointed. 'They're new this year. I made them from preserved birch twigs. I'm particularly proud of them. Even if I have added a silver burnish to the kitchen table. Ha, ha.'

He smiled and nodded gravely, as if all this bilge was of desperate importance. As if my sad dalliance with glycerine-related floristry was of the least interest to a man who made life and death decisions on bank holiday evenings and carried a morphine vial around in his bag. Twit, twit, twit.

'Didn't know you had so many hidden talents,' he observed.

'Oh, none hidden, I assure you. This is it. The full range.'

He raised one eyebrow and then stood up again, filling the room. 'But no shell boxes on display, which is a little disappointing.'

He put his face in his coffee as he said this, so I couldn't quite catch his expression. And I hoped he'd keep it there a while, because a slow, warm, inexorable flush had found it's way out of the top of my (checked – yuk!) shirt and arranged itself tastefully over my cheeks. I waved my arms around as a diversion.

'Oh, I'm crap at those. But if you want one, I do know someone in Tenby.'

His next utterance, which began, 'Charlie –' was partly drowned out by my explosive guffaws, which were becoming more alarming by the moment.

So he said it again. 'Charlie –' On a rising note. Oh no.

'But he hasn't got a bucket,' I interrupted, avoiding his eye.

He sat again. About halfway up the sofa, this time. And turned back towards me, in a way that made it absolutely clear that this was no laughing matter. And certainly not an occasion for tittering or guffawing, and that he wanted me not to avoid his gaze but to make a connection with it, and that he wasn't going to be deflected by any amount of diversionary banter. I looked at him properly. Took in each perfect contour. And found myself quite unable, then, to look away.

150

'This is all a little difficult, isn't it?' he said.

'You're telling me!' I exclaimed, exhaling ten minutes' worth of backed-up gulps and swallows. 'You are *telling me*! I have to be the most embarrassed person I know right now. Which is why I'm not sure we should even be having this conversation. I'm finding it a little difficult to – oh, I don't know. It's –'

'The word 'strained' springs to mind.'

The eyes held fast, then he dropped his and sighed.

'Yes, doesn't it? ' I agreed. 'Which is so silly. Because actually there's no earthy reason why we should feel –'

'Yes there is.'

Just like that. *Yes there is.*

'Not really,' I said. 'It's not as if –'

'Charlie, you *know* there is.' He stopped. Then said. 'That's assuming I haven't entirely misread things from your end. In which case –' And then he ground to a halt again. Which was so exasperating. I couldn't be doing with all this huff-puff stop-start stuff. It was making me feel twitchy. But while I was chewing all this over, he chipped in with, 'Have I?'

To which I could have answered, 'Well of *course* you have! You didn't think – well, goodness me! Heavens! What on earth gave you the impression I was interested in *you*!' etc., but he knew very well that it was a load of compete tosh. I had my shag list to thank for that. I told him so. I said, 'I can hardly deny what's on a list in black and white on your hard drive, can I?'

Which sounded, I thought, impressively technical. For me, at least.

'All deleted,' he said. 'And quite beside the point.'

Ah.

'How d'you mean?' I asked, hoping to deflect the conversation down a more hypothetical avenue.

'What I mean is that I can hardly deny that if I had a shag list then Gwyneth Paltrow would probably be on it, and that up till a few months back, she'd have been higher up it than you. Which is why your shag list is beside the point, and what's been –' he made a circling motion with his hand – he seemed big on visual euphemisms. 'what's been *going on* since then is very much more to the point. And what I'm asking is ... well, *have* I misread where we've been going since then?'

'Wow,' I said. 'Can I have a half hour to deconstruct that, please?'

'You don't *need* to deconstruct it, Charlie. You know very well what I'm saying.'

I put my mug down on the carpet beside me, then regretted it. Without something to hold on to, my hands seemed to have developed a life of their own. I shoved them underneath my knees, where they busied themselves with picking at the stitching on the piping cord.

'You know I know,' I said finally. 'Of course you know I know. We both know the other one knows. And we know it's the same for both of us, don't we? All those 'obviouslys –'

He looked confused.

'You *know*,' I said. 'All that business about Rhys. *God*,' I groaned. 'And that drunken email.'

'So I'm not wrong.' The corners of his mouth twitched. 'I'm not *entirely* sure what you're on about, but I think I've understood that much correctly.'

I sighed. 'You have to understand I've had a couple of glasses of wine, a particularly fraught evening and, well, basically, this is all a bit difficult. You *know*?'

'I *know*,' he repeated gravely. Then laughed. A big laugh. A laugh that meant business. A laugh that in different circumstances could be endorsed by one of my own. A laugh that was full of warmth and affection. The same laugh I'd imagined he laughed when he read some of the rubbish I put in my emails. And then he stopped laughing. Abruptly. Which, in these particular circumstances, I supposed, was all he could properly do.

'And my fault,' he said.

I picked up my mug and shook my head.

'It's not a question of fault,' I said.

He stood up again, and walked across to the tree. Beyond it, the snowflakes outside continued to spin and dance. I wondered how he was going to manage the rest of his calls. Assuming more came, that was.

'Oh, but it is. And it's mine. Christ!' He peered out into the night. 'What was I thinking of? I'm a married man, for God's sake!. What possessed me?'

I couldn't answer that, so I didn't. 'It's not really important now, is it?' I tried instead.

'It was that shag list of yours,' he said, still on the track of his own internal dialogue. 'It just cracked me up. I didn't realise women *did* that kind of thing. *Do* women do that kind of thing? Or is it just you?'

He seemed to really want to know. He turned round and raised his eyebrows at me.

'Haven't a clue,' I said honestly. 'I've never really thought about it. Some women, I guess. But not in the way I think *you* think we do. It's just something we talk about over a few glasses of wine sometimes. We don't write it out and distribute it like a local newsletter or something. You only saw it because of Rose moving away and the whole email business. But it's just a bit of fun. I imagine, in time, we would have become bored with it. It's not the same when you're not together. Anyway, it's so unimportant. It means nothing really.'

'But it doesn't. It *hasn't*. It's meant all this! When I first read it and saw my name, yes, it amused me. Nothing more. And I thought it would be *amusing*, I suppose, to email you back. But then – well, you can imagine, can't you? It played on my mind. I – well, you know –' he gestured. At what? My hair? The shape of my eyebrows? Then shook his head. 'Heck – *fancied* you. But I don't think,' he went on, 'that it had ever really occurred to me that *you* might fancy *me*. You've never flirted with me. Never even danced with me at a party, as far as I can remember. Have you?' He raised a hand. 'You don't even have to answer. I know *unequivocally* that you haven't.

153

I've spent a ridiculous amount of time just trying to recall an encounter when the fact of you fancying me has ever even registered. And it hasn't. Which is why it was all so intriguing. I mean, yes, sure, lots of people flirt. Most people, in fact. It's what men and women do. All enjoyable, harmless stuff. But *you* haven't. Not with *me*, at any rate. I've known you for how long? Four years? Five?'

I nodded. Gulped. 'About that, I suppose.' Four years, seven months. Exactly. *Exactly*. Three weeks after starting at Willie Jones Jackson. Since a Stableford barbecue party, in fact.

'And you *never* flirted with me. Not once. So how come –'

'Because you don't. Not when you're on your own. Not unless you –' now it was my turn to circle my hand euphemistically. I regrouped. 'Not unless you hope to develop a relationship with someone. Not that I was in a hurry to get involved with anyone after Felix – I'd just ended a marriage, after all, but can you imagine how popular I'd be if I started chatting up all my friends' husbands? So you tend not to. Well, *I* tend not to. Not with men who are married. Not with men who are involved.'

He gazed for a moment into the twinkling depths of the tree, then freed the string from a bauble that had caught in some needles.

'I suppose so,' he said. 'I suppose that makes sense. In any event, it felt a little like I'd been told, oh, I don't know, that oh, Madonna or someone had told a mutual friend she fancied me –'

'Madonna!'

'Yes, well. OK, maybe not Madonna. Though – well, you know what I mean. That someone I thought barely registered my existence was all the time registering it a very great deal. You can't help but think about it.'

I found myself smiling now. 'I don't know about the "very great deal" bit. Registering it *amongst* others,' I pointed out. 'It wasn't as if I had a little shrine to you in my bathroom cabinet –'

He looked bashful. 'Fair enough, yes, yes. And I know I probably went up and down the charts a fair bit, but the point is I couldn't *help* but have it on my mind after that. Any time I saw you, I was seeing you differently. Quite apart from the fact that you were upset and everything, I couldn't help wondering what you were thinking about me. And you were still with Phil then, of course, which made it all the more –' He stopped and looked out of the patio doors again.

'All the more what?'

He came back and sat down on the sofa beside me, the empty mug swinging from the crook of his thumb.

'All the more erotic, basically.'

'Oh.'

Oh!

'All the more exciting. You wouldn't believe how many times I've –'

He stopped his sentence there. I wondered how he'd been going to finish it. With 'wondered what it would be like to have sex with you' maybe? Or 'imagined bundling you into a cupboard? Or onto an earthquake simulator even?' It didn't matter. I knew exactly what he meant.

So I nodded. 'It all became rather compulsive, didn't it?'

'Has be*come*,' he said, rolling the mug between his palms. It was distracting, and I wanted to reach out and take it from him, but was frightened to touch him in case my fingers got spot-welded to his. It really felt as if they might.

'*Is*,' he went on. 'The compulsion is still very much there.'

'Well,' I said, digesting this. 'I've actually been horrified. Since I worked out it was you, I've been horrified more or less constantly. Horrified about all the things I said to you when I thought I was talking to Rose. Horrified about all the things I said when I thought you were simply a stranger. But most of all, horrified since the moment when I found out who you were, that the day would almost certainly come when we'd be having a conversation exactly like this. Which is bad news all round.'

'We had to talk about it sometime.'

155

'No, we didn't. If we had any kind of sense, we wouldn't talk about it again, ever. And you're right. It is your fault. I can't be doing with going around feeling horrified all the time. And even though I won't be going around feeling horrified any more after this, I'm now going to have to go around feeling oh, I don't know, stressed, unsettled, *disappointed*, instead. Knowing how you feel about me and knowing how I feel about you and knowing it's all completely pointless and probably just down to a cocktail of lust and intrigue and guilty excitement anyway – and well, I just hope George Clooney shows up in the Dog and Trouserleg sometime soon and then we can forget all about it.'

'George Clooney? You fancy George Clooney?'

'Absolutely,' I said. 'You fancy Madonna.' Now I did, impulsively, reach out my hand for the mug. But he refused to let go of it, and then put his free hand on top of mine.

He leaned closer to me. 'Horrified?' he said. 'Is that *really* how all this makes you feel? Horrified?'

His hand stayed in place and I knew as readily as I knew that it wasn't going to stop snowing any time soon, that he was about to kiss me.

'Wouldn't it be funny if your bleep went off now?' I said. 'Wouldn't it be timely?'

He smiled. He didn't seem in the least bit tense all of a sudden. His hand was a still, warm presence on mine. 'That sort of thing only happens in films,' he said. 'So they can crank up the sexual tension a bit. In real life bleeps don't go off, telephones don't ring, door knockers don't knock and windows don't get blown in by unexpected explosions. In real life you just have to hang in there and accept the inevitable.'

I wished he wouldn't use words like "sexual tension". I said, 'Which means I get kissed, right?'

His smile became a grin. 'As kissee, you do have input. You can always say no.'

'Exactly. Which is why I feel horrified now.'

His face inched towards mine, and I felt my lips part.

'No,' I said.

'Fine,' he said.

And then I kissed him.

mnrgriffith@cymserve.co.uk

God, Rose! I did it! I kissed Adam Jones! I have to be the stupidest, most impulsive, most self-destructive woman on the entire planet. But I did it. I can't undo it. It is now, as they say, etched in my memory forever. Oh, God! *Why* did I do it? Help!

By the time you log on and read this I will doubtless have got myself together enough to put it (that one, beautiful, lovely, sexy beyond delirium type kiss, that is) into some sort of sensible perspective. I will probably be able to convince myself that it was nothing more than an expression of new year high spirits, and so on, though I have to tell you at the moment it feels like we just had sex on the living room carpet. That's how much that one kiss has done to me. I am a woman possessed. I am drowning in it all.

Bloody, bloody hell. Promise me it'll all be OK in the morning.

Ring or whatever and I'll tell you all.

Charliexx

First day of a new year. First day of the rest of my life. First day of my new incarnation as someone who has kissed someone else's husband and invoked passions in myself that I have not felt in years. First day of a sad, unfulfilling period in my life, for sure.

Having fallen asleep eventually, still dressed and above the covers, I awake cold and with a creased face and tramlines down the insides of my legs, where the seams of my jeans have spent two friction-filled hours. Friction, to boot, borne out of thrashing about mournfully. Not in any sense friction one could feel smug about.

Oh dear, oh dear, oh dear.

New Year's Day is fairy-tale beautiful. Silent, pink-tinged, and with a backdrop of misty-smudged hills. Snow is still falling in an intermittent, sluggish shower, and has entirely obliterated Adam's car tracks on the drive. I look down upon the sparkling, everything-just-as-it-was type scenario and feel like crying. Feel like crying mainly because despite my small-hours certainty that everything being just-as-it-was would be the most appropriate and manageable way to deal with this new situation, I find I am unable to consider the future without the addition of a hole where my heart should be and a sense that I will never, ever, be happy again.

Rats. I get up, strip off, and pull on my comforter dressing gown. Then consider moving to Kent. Then consider moving to Nepal. Then consider setting up an estate agency business in Kathmandu and / or devoting my life to the children of the Himalayas generally. Consider myself as a tragic heroine and am instantly reminded of our cyber-debate about the Brontë family, plus the fact that I am now in the same situation as Jane Eyre (except Davina is not mad or in an attic as far as I know) and that the best course of action would be to indeed hit Nepal and do improving works for a while. Except without the addition of a worthy male mentor, for which job Rhys Hazelton would, in all probability, champ at the bit, brandishing his thoughtfully warmed speculum. Recall griffith-word "*is*". Feel even more like crying.

But I am arrested from my damp and introspective chasm by the sound of paternal movements downstairs.

'Helloeeee!' calls Dad. His tone suggests the return from a happy, uncomplicated, sexually fulfilling encounter. With Hester. Who is with him. And has possibly come back for more. Bless them. Bless them, but yuk. Really, I do not wish to know. Would not wish to know under any circumstance. But particularly do not wish to know today.

Best to get out then.

'I'm going out,' I tell my father bluntly.

'Out?' they both chirrup.

'Yes, out,' I confirm, racking my brains for some plausible reason. The village store's closed, and they already know there's a community walk later. But what?

'Work!' I bellow at last, pulling on boots.

'*Work*?' Ditto chirrup.

'I've been hoping for snow,' I improvise. 'So I can get some decent shots of the Rutland's place. It's –'

'Work? On New Year's *Day*, Charlotte?' My father looks concerned. 'And what about lunch? Charlotte?' He follows me into the kitchen. 'Are you *sure* you're all right?'

I nod an affirmative, while I rummage feverishly in the kitchen drawer for gloves.

'So – what *about* lunch then?' he calls after me.

'Lovely. Look forward to it!' Then I make my escape.

'Season's greetings, Mr Rutland!' I hear myself chirrup twenty minutes later. 'And a happy and prosperous New Year to you both!'

Mr Rutland, who no doubt would consider himself a fine figure in his zip-up suede cardigan and leatherette slippers, emerges, grunting, from his Transylvanian porch. (Why does he always look as if he's just been masturbating? Don't accept angina explanation. Except as something exacerbated by former.)

'Charlotte,' he confirms. As if identifying a species. 'And to what do we owe this pleasant, if unscheduled, surprise?'

He thinks he's such a gent, and he's actually such a wanker.

'I know,' I say, waggling my new Willie JJ digital camera,' that it's a terrible liberty, on a bank holiday and so on, but it occurred to me this morning that a blanket of snow would be the very best thing to set off your lovely, lovely home, and that we could really capitalise on this lovely, lovely unexpected meteorological bounty. But it could all be gone by the weekend, couldn't it? So I thought, as I happened to be passing anyway –'

'You thought *what*?'

And stupid with it. But what *am* I doing here? 'That I might take a few photos,' I say sweetly.

'Photos?'

160

Of your house. You stupid git. The better to hide it.

'Of your beautiful home. Er …enhanced by the snow.'

Mrs Rutland appears. With the pooch under her arm. Which farts.

'Hmmm,' she says, tipping her face forward. 'Charlotte?'

'Come to take pictures, apparently,' says Mr Rutland.

'*Pictures*?'

'Some new ones,' I enthuse at her. 'Of the house. In the snow. The present ones are rather unseasonal, aren't they? What with the blossom and so on. I know it's not the best time, and if it's inconvenient, then –'

'In the *snow*?' she asks.

'Yes,' I say.

'*Why*?' she asks.

Jesus.

'Well,' I say, 'sometimes – *occasionally* – if the photograph of a house has very obviously been taken some time ago, people *sometimes* think that there might be something wrong – might be some reason why it's been on the market a long time, and so on, and that can *sometimes* – well, you know. I just thought Cherry Ditchling would look rather – *does* look rather –' (Plus the fact that Metro, whose tacky board has now been affixed outside lowering the tone of the streetlamp, has a more recent picture and a big advertising budget.) – well … *seasonal*. You know?'

'Hmm,' says Mrs Rutland, peering at my hiking boots. 'Outside, you say?'

'Back and front. Plus the garden.'

'Hmm,' says Mr Rutland. 'if you must, I suppose. But move the rubbish first.'

In the end, I persuade them. And, having relocated five bin liners containing a lot of swampy God-knows-what round the back, I spend ten frustrating minutes trying to convey, by means of a wide-angle lens and the power of digital, how a crumbling heap of unattractive spew-coloured masonry can be transformed by the addition of a dump of iced rain into something you can imagine yourself being happyish to live in.

161

Oh, I'm *not* in a happy mood, me.

By the afternoon I'm feeling marginally less frenzied. And cheered, at least, by Ben looking a great deal better. However, he sensibly submits to my dictate that the best place for shrivelled up bronchii is bed.

It's peculiar – if cinemascope dramatic – to be going on the Cefn Melin annual New Year's Day village walk up the mountain without Dan, without Ben, without a soul in the world. The landscape is glittering, perfect, captivating; an ideal partner to my intense and soulful mood. I feel like a heroine traversing a snow scene on the cover of a Thomas Hardy novel. Feel that, in spirit at least, I am wearing a voluminous hair skirt and lace-up boots; that tendrils of dark, curly hair are escaping from my bonnet and undulating, cloud-like, on a stiff winter breeze; that I have smouldering beauty, a resolute expression, a crippled great-aunt and a bundle of logs; that I'm on my way back to our hovel on the far edge of a sheep field, having learned of my dark lover's betrayal of trust; that I'm smitten by tumultuous and dangerous emotions; that I am tossed on a great tide of apocalyptic events. (I could, instead, have shared a prosaic discussion with my father about the preserve-related merits of whinberries, sloes and hedgerow fruit generally, but a stop was put to father coming on the walk by the kindly but firm Mr Prestwick, chair of the local walking society and person with whom the exercise-induced death-toll-buck stops.)

And I am *glad* to be a tragic heroine. I am glad for a chance to wallow in unhappiness and self-pity. I'm glad for the opportunity to drink in the drama of my surroundings and to compare them with the drama of the intractable problems of affairs of the heart. I concentrate, therefore, on maintaining a solitary front-end position, and immersing myself in sad thoughts.

My solitary front-end position turns out not to be particularly solitary, however, as the snow (coupled with laughably unrealistic personal fitness assessments in some cases) has encouraged a positive multitude of earnest ramblers.

Fortunately, the twin irritations of gradient and snow depth are such that, by the time we are fifteen minutes into our endeavour, the reality of hangovers and half tons of Quality Street have reduced all but a few to a slow creaking trudge. A few, however, is still more than one.

'Didn't expect to see you,' puffs Phil, as we head up the twinkling white slope. 'Thought you weren't keen on this sort of thing.'

Despite myself, I feel uncomfortable. And listen hard to see if I can detect a bitchy twang in his voice, but the observation seems genuine. Phil can't help it if he thinks I'm a couch potato. Why would he know any different? I spent most of the six months of our tepid encounter wheedling my way out of doing such things with him. I note the tilt of his Barbour and the bulge in his pocket. As Karen strides, red-faced (breathless, speechless, etc.), alongside him, I fancy a manual of outdoor sexual gymnastics, but logic tells me the bulge will be just as it always is – the Field Guide to the Flora and Fauna of Britain, carefully annotated and bristling with Post-its.

'Nice to meet you,' she says brightly, and I feel myself blushing. Not least for the curmudgeonly tone of my thoughts. I wonder what she knows of me. Though what's to know, really? 'You walk a lot?' she goes on, chattily. 'You look very fresh.'

'I'm gathering my thoughts for the year,' I tell them both. 'Doing what everybody does, I suppose. Getting fresh air into my lungs and resolutions into my psyche. Plus escaping my dad and his girlfriend for an hour. Hester Stableford, Phil? They've got a thing going on.'

Because I am embarrassed, I put the word "thing" into verbal quote marks, and as soon as I do so, I think; bugger! Because I don't mean this *at all*. And Phil – who is now nodding and going hmmm – will think I am pining and bitter and completely dried-up sexually. and someone who's life has been one long round of failed relationships. All of which is patently untrue. Right now I feel exactly as I *think* I remember I used to when I was young and full of simmering sexual appetites and had been shagged senseless by Felix when he came home on leave. Which is one mighty achievement for a simple kiss from a late thirty-something in a sensible suit. Which makes what happens next more than unfortunate.

'Hello there!' A vision in luminous Gore-tex. Addressing *me*. With a wave and a back-slap.

Davina! *Davina?* On a hike? In the snow?

Yes. Obviously. She extends her hearty greeting to take in Phil, Karen, and much of the surrounding population.

'Well, well! Quite a crowd today! Who would have thought it! And – aaaaahh! – why don't I do this more often?'

Oh *God*. Where is he? Is he here? Did he come too? Is he walking behind me? Has he seen me? Has he … oh, stop it!

'Nature,' announces Phil, once introductions have been effected 'is ambrosia for the soul.'

Karen nods happy agreement, then squeaks, 'Phil! Look over there!'

We look.

'It's a badger! Good grief! At this time of year! And in daylight! Do you see it?'

'Davina nods. 'I do!' Then looks back down the hill. 'Adam! Bill! Look! A badger!'

So, yes. YES. He *is* here. Bugger the badger. *He* is here. Uuurrrrgh. Cope, Simpson. Calm, Simpson. Eyes forward. Legs straight.

My pace slows (quite without my telling it to, which is disconcerting), while the soul food junkies speed up in pursuit of the badger. They take their noise with them and, apart from my heartbeat, all I can hear now is the soft flump and squeak of what I know are Adam's boots in the snow.

Bill strides on and past me. I feel like a sniper. I have Davina firmly in my cross-hairs as I sense Adam drawing level. He doesn't turn, doesn't smile. Just matches my stride.

'Hello,' he says, softly. 'Didn't think you'd be up here.'

'Why not?' I snap. 'I like hills. I like walking. You, of all people, should realise that. I come every year. I bring Dan. And Ben, usually. And I've never seen you on the New Year's day walk before.'

I turn as I say this. I'm so desperate to look at him.

He looks cold. The end of his nose is red. 'I didn't mean because you wouldn't want to. I meant because it was late, last night, and with Ben and so on. And I certainly *was* here last year.' He pushes his hands into his pockets. 'Though I did only get halfway. I had to come back. Jack Patterson You know him? The man from the video shop? That was asthma, too, funnily enough. I had to help him back down.'

Belatedly, this fact returns to my memory. It seems forever ago. Pre our … our … our … *this*.

I sniff. I feel cross. But I nod. 'So you did.'

'And the year before that.'

We toil on for some moments.

'Don't remember,' I say, finally. 'It was a long time ago.'

I hear him exhale. 'It's a funny thing, isn't it? All that time when we didn't … you know … *register* this.'

This. Aptly vague. Aptly oblique. I look ahead and say nothing, having thoroughly registered. Davina fluoresces a few yards up the hill from us. Her words float down in snatches, like quarrelling gulls.

'Don't you think?' he continues.

I stomp on and then glare at him. 'I wish I could laugh,' I say. 'Really I do.'

'Oh, Charlie –'

'Don't start.'

'Get my email?'

'What email?'

'This morning.'

'*What* email?'

'I just –'

'*Why* did you email me? We'd stopped that, remember?'

'Stopped what?' This is Phil again. Damn the man. Damn.

'Crossing the top field,' declares Adam, pointing. 'Drifts,' he adds, quickly. 'So we're going around it. How are you, Phil? Any new developments, rolling-stock-wise?'

I take the opportunity to quicken my stride now, and in

moments I've gained a good half-dozen yards. If I can keep my distance, I can cope with his nearness. If I can avoid his gaze I can maintain control of my own. If I don't have to talk to him I can turn my thoughts elsewhere. But as I clamber up minutes later to negotiate a stile, I can't resist turning back and scanning the group below for a glimpse of him. And when his eyes meet mine and I know he's been watching me, the thrill's so intense I know for sure I am lost.

What a mess. What a ridiculous, juvenile mess. I got home at four and practically ripped my snow boots from my feet. Then, panting and sweating, I wrestled myself from my coat. Couldn't breathe, couldn't focus, couldn't think straight, couldn't function. Could only chant bloody hell, bloody hell, bloody *hell*. Couldn't, mainly, get into the study fast enough, and careered across the hall in such a lather of excitement that I narrowly missed colliding with the recumbent Kipling, who, perhaps knowing his fate following Ben's obvious allergy, had developed a death wish, and decided to make door thresholds his location of choice. And never – *never, ever* – has the boot up, type password, dial, log-on process taken such an inordinate length of time.

But two emails! Not one. *Two* emails from Adam.

thesimpsons@cymserve.co.uk

Just in case you weren't absolutely clear where I'm at now, I just wanted to let you know who's on *my* list.

Charlie Simpson

That's it. That's all. The ball's in your court.

No names. No identifying detail. No fuss. Straight to the point. Ow*ee*. I mouth the words back at it. That's it. That's all. The ball's in your court. My court. *My* court. Scrabble with the mouse and bring the second email forth. Then spend several moments not daring to look at it – like a schoolgirl with her

166

very first note from a boy.

thesimpsons@cymserve.co.uk

Dear Charlie,
I feel bad about what I sent earlier. It somehow devalues what
this is really all about. I know what you said and I understand
why you said it, and I'm not about to kid myself that this is
anything other than entirely the wrong thing to do. But I can't
help myself. Have you managed to convince yourself that
these feelings are *really* going to go away? Well, they're not
going to go away for me, not even if you blank me from here
on in. Not now we've got to where we're at. You know that,
don't you?
Adam.

Of course I know that. Of course. I sit in the gloom and
consider the great crushing weight of morality. Consider the
unfairness of everything. Consider the unfairness, particularly,
of having feelings (and then some) thrust, hissing and spitting,
into the previously tepid water of my emotional life. Consider
mentally re-locating and spending the rest of my life in an
emotional desert and find the idea not without its merits.
Consider the tragic fact that I was thrust unwittingly into the
role of the other woman before I realised another woman was
even involved. Not fair.

Mad as hell.

Send;

griffith@cymserve.co.uk

Dear Adam,
What the hell am I supposed to do now? <u>I don't want to know</u>
that I'm on your list. I don't want to know about *any* of that.
OK? Don't you realise what you're putting me through here?
You are married. I am not. I don't have to get embroiled in <u>any</u>
of this stuff.

Yes, sure, it was nice. Yes, sure, I'm going to miss our little
chats (or whatever they were), but the bottom line is that I

can't even begin to contemplate having any sort of relationship with you. You are married, remember? Married to my boss. Let's just forget it, shall we?
Charliexxx.

Delete kisses. No kisses. But I so much want to do kisses. I sit with my cold face in my cold hands and await a response. Which comes – bing! – like lightening. Where is he sitting? Where is Davina? What does he tell her he's up to when he's doing all this?

thesimpsons@cymserve.co.uk

Charlie, can't we get this boss business out of the way? I know it's uncomfortable for you, but the fact that Davina is your boss is really nothing to do with our situation. I am married. You are not. Fine. <u>Fine</u>. Point taken, believe me. I really don't need telling, believe me. But I need to talk to you, to see you. <u>Can</u> I see you? Can we do something? Could we go for a drink? A walk? Sit somewhere? Whatever you want. I don't mind. You say. But please don't say 'it was nice' as if you've just been to see a show or something. Nice? Come *on*. You can't mean that.
Adamxxx

I scroll the email back and then read it again, slowly. Mouthing every syllable of every word and picturing him thinking it, tapping the words out. I can see his expression shift and change as he types it. Can see his long fingers as they cradle the mouse. Every syllable of every word. Can see his strong yet gentle face reflected in the monitor. Can see his heavy brow creased in anticipation. I print out the email and then slip it inside *Trekking in Nepal*.

What now? Now nothing. Do nothing, that's what. I sign off from Cymserve and, as the house is once again empty, I allow myself the bleak luxury of a last noisy cry.

Chapter 17

Whole two weeks post-kiss. I am coping. Just. And recovering, if not quite my equilibrium, at least a foothold on the pigeon-pooped seat-end of the seesaw.

But I'm concerned that I *am* suffering from SAD and must purchase daylight bulbs and so on. Would book a sunbed, but can't, because I would then stress about getting skin cancer, which would therefore negate the beneficial effect of UV rays on my psyche etc. Doubt that UV rays would have a sufficient beneficial effect anyway, as I am forced to admit the main cause of my sadness is not SAD but a broken heart. Am seriously blue, but in fact the same colour as my pond-weed suit plus similarly stagnant of temper. Were it not for the fact that I keep remembering that at least I have my health, and not fibroids query cervical cancer, and so on, I would be in a right strop all round.

'First week in Feb?' asks Davina, picking from her suit what I assume from her expression must be decomposing fruit fly corpses, or similar. 'You can't be off then. We'll be skiing.'

'Oh! But don't you usually go at Easter?'

She curls her lip as if I have the intellect of a slug. 'Only in North America, Charlie. Where we are not, unfortunately, going this year. My dear husband, in his infinite wisdom, has tendered the idea that a week of slush and queue-bargers in the Alps would be far more relaxing than ten days of good manners and decent snow in Aspen. Still, there you go. Can't have too much of a good thing, can we? Dear me, no. Wouldn't be seemly. So, no. In answer to your question. Not Easter this year. We're going the first week in Feb.'

Rats. Plus side-effect of intense, prickle-eyed moment of

yearning. Will have to get used to this, I suppose.

'Oh,' I say. 'Oh dear.'

'Oh dear is about right. I can't imagine anything more tedious. I can hardly be bothered, to tell you the truth.' She starts turning the crystals that Ianthe arranged on the windowsill last week. Perhaps something cosmic and useful will happen. 'Anyway,' she goes on. 'Why do you need *that* week off? Does it have to be that week?'

I nod. Or perhaps it won't. 'It's to help Rose out,' I say. 'I said I'd go down and help with the children for her. Her hysterectomy, remember?'

She raises her eyebrows. She obviously doesn't. In fact, she looks strangely alarmed.

'Rose? Rose Griffiths? Is she having a hysterectomy? Why on earth? Good God! She's only forty-odd, isn't she?'

'I told you. She's been having all sorts of symptoms. It may be cervical cancer, Davina. It's a major operation and she's going to need lots of help. Matt can manage the first couple of weeks, but then he's due to run some computer training seminar in Brussels or something, and rather than him cancel it, I offered to go down and help out for a week.'

She shakes her head, then moves back to my desk and picks up and flaps the latest copy of Cherry Ditchling details. The ones with the Christmas-card camouflage job. 'Well I simply can't spare you. Can't you bring them to Cardiff?'

I shake my head. 'Not in term time, I can't. But what about Hugh? Couldn't he manage for a week? I've managed alone before now. It's a quiet time.'

Which comment is obviously a mistake. Her withering look makes the weeping fig shiver.

'Hugh? On his own? Get *real*, Charlie. *Really*. Leave Hugh here on his own? Besides, if it's quiet –'

'Then there's all the more reason – yes. OK. Point taken. I shouldn't have asked.'

She nods. Says 'Exactly.' Then shrugs. 'Look, I'm sorry and all that. But it's going to be out of the question. I'm sure you'll be able to work something out.'

My own stupid fault, of course. I shouldn't have promised Rose before checking at work. Bloody hell. Big mess. Cock-up. Disaster. My best friend in the world is reliant upon my support in a time of a major crisis in her life, and I have failed her utterly. I scowl at *Homes Digest,* rant at computer, stomp round cold office, hate Davina, hate work.

'So what shall I do, then? Resign? Tell Davina to shove it? Believe me, just one tiny reason and I'll do it.'

I'm at the hospital, perched beside Minnie's bed. Her mouth makes a series of small, mouse-like nibblings and her tiny, white, paper-dry hands squeeze my own. She has a stray hair just tickling the edge of her eye. I smooth it back, but she doesn't wake.

'Hmm,' I say. 'Maybe you're right. Maybe the best thing would be to just ring Rose and tell her I'll come down and collect them and bring them up here to stay for the week. The children are still only young, after all. What's a missed week in school at their age? Just how much will they suffer? Besides, I could always give their old school a ring, couldn't I? They could visit. Maybe sit in on some lessons as well. Yes, that's what I'll do. No big problem.'

Minnie opens her eyes. I'm so pleased to see her.

'Did you bring me some tarts, then?'

'Of course I did. Dad made them specially for you.'

'And Edward.' She sinks back to sleep as she mouths it. 'Save a couple. Knowing him, he'll be here in a jiff.'

When I get back to the office, I telephone social services. After an interminable wait and connections to various concertos, I get through to a lady who at least knows Minnie's name. She's not the social worker I've met (that'll be Bernice, my lovely), but she knows Minnie's history and at least sounds as if she cares.

'I just thought,' I tell her, 'that it would be nice to find Edward –'

'Ah! The elusive Edward!' she answers. 'Believe me, we've tried, dear. But so far no luck. To tell the truth, we're

171

pretty much of the opinion that he simply can no longer be bothered with her. The last address we had for him is four or five years old now. And he hadn't responded to our letters for some months before that.'

'But you don't know that he actually received your letters, do you? For all we know, something may have happened to him.'

'I think you have a charming lack of cynicism, my dear. No use in this job, of course. No, dear. She gets plenty of postcards. From all sorts of obscure antipodean places. Sometimes you just have to accept the unacceptable. Could happen to any of us, truth be told.'

When I get off the phone, I resolve that even if the social services have given up trying to track him down there's certainly no reason why I shouldn't have a try instead. At the very least, it will help take my mind off Adam. I call the matron at The Maltings and ask if I can come down and pick up a few bits for Minnie. She can see, she says, no particular problem with that. It's not, she adds, quite in line with their policies, but admits that, as I brought the cases in the first place, then there's really no reason why I shouldn't rootle in them.

And speaking of rootling, I am suddenly reminded that I have agreed to go out with Rhys straight after work.

We've arranged to meet, not at the Q bar this time, but in a less aurally stressful Peruvian bar down by the station, the better to discuss the finer points of hiking, kit and relations with the locals. As I walk down St Mary Street, I feel welcome stirrings of excitement about my forthcoming trip. Even, surprisingly, a smidgen of positive feeling about spending a chunk of the evening with Rhys. Enough, at least, to lead me to check how I look in Howells window. And then again in the glass of a restaurant further down. It is here, however, that I find something more than my reflection; the unmistakeable outline of Hugh Chatsworth's back view.

I don't stop for long, but long enough to register that it's next to a rump of more generous proportions. Walking on, I consider the nipple ring situation. What *is* going on between Austin Metro and Hugh?

And then I spot Rhys on Wood Street, and our paths converge at the crossing.

'Hell-o!' he mouths, managing to convey with one glance that, for him at least, something's going on now with me.

'Did you kiss him?'

Rose, who with typical lack of fuss and flap has endorsed and applauded my revised childcare plans, now wants the gen on my latest encounter. Such as it is.

'Well, sort of,' I say.

'Sort of? What's sort of? Was it just the top lip, then?'

'I was thinking 'sort of' in more of a temporal sense.'

'A peck, then.'

'Not really. We were in his car. I didn't invite him in because I know he wants to sleep with me and that he'd be up the stairs like a whippet if I gave him the smallest indication I was up for it, so I told him I had an early start. And then he leaned over – like you do – and put his arm around my shoulder, and went to kiss me. So I let him.'

'And?'

'And nothing. Nothing happened. I mean, he's a perfectly nice, attractive man, and no doubt a very competent kisser, but I didn't find myself, well, responding, shall we say.'

Rose hoots with laughter.

'You are *such* a case, Charlie. And still utterly stuck on the doctor.'

'No, I'm not.'

'Yes you are.'

'No I'm *not*.'

'Yes you *are*.'

But at least one piece of good news. Paradoxically, from Davina.

'Ah, Charlie,' she says, just as I'm preparing to leave the

next day. 'Your week off. It's OK.'

'It is?'

She smoothes her honey-coloured ponytail and nods. 'Uh-huh. Because we're not going skiing.'

'You're not?'

She shakes her head. 'Adam can't make it. Some conference or other. And I can't say I'm disappointed. So there you are.'

'Well, that's brilliant. Oh, that's such a relief. Will you go later, as usual?'

'Hmm,' she says, collecting stray papers from her desktop. 'Hmm. We'll see.' Then she gets back to her phone.

I'm tempted to indulge in all sorts of wild and ridiculous speculations about *hmms*, but as soon as I begin to, I find myself in a state of extreme agitation caused not only by now familiar adrenalin surge but also by a scary vision of Davina screaming over the very same desk about Adam's passionate declaration of love for that Simpson woman and vowing to rip out her lower intestine from the top down. Must steel myself to avoid such flights of ridiculousness. Very bad habit, like picking the tops off scabs.

Chapter 18

I realise, as I tootle across the hospital car park with my cake tin, that I really look forward to visiting Minnie on the way home from work. It is the ultimate in symbiosis. I provide Minnie with a familiar face, company and a plentiful supply of patisserie items, and Minnie provides me with some kind of therapy – at very least, a kindly and non-judgemental (as largely non-comprehending) ear. Today I bring a treat – dad's state-of-the-art tarts.

'Oh, Minnie, Minnie, Minnie, what *is* a girl to do? I'm trying so hard not to think about him, but since all that business at New Year happened, I'm finding it really difficult, you know?'

'You've got that lovely titian hair, you have,' she says, battling with the tin lid. 'My Iris had hair just like that. Masses of it. Hopeless in the tropics. But there was no cutting of it. Not in those days. What are these, then? Are they from Tesco's? There's been things on TV about those people today.'

I look for the child in Minnie's leathery features. Imagine the beauty that once softened the frame. 'Was Iris beautiful? I'll bet she was,' I say. 'We'll have to find a picture some time.' I prise the lid off the tin and place the goodies on the bed for her.

Minnie, ignoring me, chooses a tart and starts her usual sniffing. 'Who's the lucky man, then? Anyone I know?'

'Well, yes, maybe. In fact, no, I don't think so, actually. He's, well, he's – oh, he's local, at any rate. But the point is I can't *have* him, Minnie.'

'And why, ye Gods, would you want him, dear? Nothing but trouble, men. Runner beans are the ticket. And courgettes. Grow like weeds. Hmmm. Best you don't plant courgettes, come to think of it. Mice, dear. God bless them. Does he have a good job?'

'Oh, I'm not in the least worried about that. I half wish he didn't.'

'But is he nice, dear? That's the nub of it. Is he? And why is this green – is it pea?'

'Gooseberry. And, God, yes. He *is* nice. He's – well, he's – well, he's everything, really. Tallish, dark, certainly, and handsome-ish, charming. No. Scrub handsome-ish. He's beautiful. And scrub charming. Charming's too pat. He *has* charm – you know? In that he doesn't *know* he has it. And he's considerate, and thoughtful and intelligent and, well –'

'Oh, *him*,' she says. 'That Jeremy Paxman off the wireless. You could do a lot worse.'

'No,' I say. 'Not *him*. Someone else. He's called Adam. He's not on the radio at all.'

'There you go, then,' she says, picking pips from the gooseberry jam. 'Adam and Eve. A bad lot, she was.'

'Oh, *you*, Minnie Drinkwater,' says a nurse, coming over. 'Crumbs in the bed again. What are you *like*?'

'Money and fair words, if you must know, young woman.'

'She's a poppet, your gran,' she adds, turning to me. 'A lovely old lady. No trouble to anyone.'

Which, as she hasn't got anyone to trouble, is really just as well, I suppose.

When I leave, as always, I feel one hundred per cent better. Our conversations, like gas molecules, touch only randomly, but despite this, I know we connect in some way. And there is nothing like having someone like Minnie in your life to put problems into their proper perspective. I step out into the hospital's main corridor; a long pastel spine connecting all the city's ills. I catch a glimpse of a sign that points the way to Dermatology. Does Adam realise, I wonder, just how far under my skin he's got?

'Hello,' says a voice. I turn around.

And it's him.

176

And he's walking my way. As he would be, knowing my luck.

I can do this, of course. There's no earthly reason why I can't just have a brief, ordinary, banal conversation with him. One of us, after all, will end it, sooner or later; this corridor doesn't go on for the rest of our lives, however much the analogy might appeal. The exit is still just a blur in the distance, but there's the Day Surgery Unit, the canteen, the theatres – and all the other wards, any of which could be where he is headed. And if not, and it all becomes too hard to deal with, then I'll just make a left, or a right, or whatever; there's X-ray just there, and Histology there, and further up, poignantly – Family Planning.

'Hello,' I say back. 'What are you doing here?' Helen Keller Ward. Admin. He clears his throat and then says,

'Asthma clinic. Wednesdays. Are you visiting someone?' I know he's turned to look at me, but I daren't look back.

'Minnie,' I say. 'Minnie Drinkwater.'

'Of course.' He moves a sheaf of what looks like patient notes from one arm to the other. His face is still angled towards mine as we walk. I can tell from the degrees of light and shade at the edge of my vision. 'How's she getting on now?' he continues.

Pharmacy. Pharmacology. WRVS Shop. 'Oh, OK, I think. She's been up, she's managing to get about a little on her frame, now.'

'Uh-huh. That's good. That's good. Look, er …'

'I took her some tarts. My father's. Gooseberry. Apricot and Whiskey. Something purple. Dad did say. I lose track.' *God.* Phlebotomy. Marie Curie Ward. Fracture Clinic. Morgue.

'Of course. Preserves. I remember. Er … um.' His face is back facing the way I prefer it. 'And Rose? How's Rose doing?' And now it's back again. Rats.

'Um, er.' (My turn.) 'Her hysterectomy is next week. Oh, but you didn't – or maybe you did – anyway, she –'

Somehow, I've been manoeuvred into having the sort of

177

conversation that can't help but involve the participants in looking at one another, and soon after that, I've stopped in the corridor and quite naturally made all the little gesticulations and facial expressions that generally accompany having a chat about someone's operation with someone else about whose precise knowledge (and right to knowledge) of the details of that operation are actually quite unclear. Should I have simply said 'women's troubles'? Should I instead have just opted for 'op'? But he's nodding. And is also a doctor, after all.

'Of course,' he replies. (Third 'of course'. Must be doctor speak, it's so automatic. Doctor, I'm depressed / stressed / obsessed and should really know better. Of course. Of course, my dear. Of course.) Then he adds, 'You're going down to stay with her, aren't you?'

I move off again. Pasteur Ward. Outpatient Toilets.

Go for Outpatient Toilets? But I should at least thank him. 'Oh, yes,' I say. 'Thank you. It's been a godsend for me, your conference. You're not skiing, I hear. Off to London instead.'

'Hmm,' he says, shifting the notes between arms again. Then silence, bar pulses. Lub dub, lub dub.

'Something interesting, is it?'

Now *he's* all eyes front. 'Palliative care in the community for the twenty-first century. It's … um … look, Charlie –'

And then he sort of swivels. And stops.

Mould Room. What's a mould room? Some sort of spore-ridden laboratory?

'Ah!' I say. 'This is me now.'

His eyes follow mine. And then narrow.

'In *there*?'

'Ha, ha, ha. Oh, look! Here we are. There's the exit!'

Followed by another. At some speed. My own.

'Did she like them, then?' asks my dad, when I return, irritable and churned up and with a rubber-band headache. He's made scones and a sponge cake and a big pot of tea. I'm beginning, I realise with no small measure of relief, to feel comfortable, pleased even, about having him around.

I plonk myself down and take the mug he holds out for me.

'Wolfed them down. Every last one,' I assure him.

'Excellent stuff. You've a message from Dan – says he sent you an email. And that Rhys chap telephoned. I've left his number in the hall. Oh, and I hope you don't mind but I've asked Hester for supper. She's made a pot-pie, which she thought she could road-test on us three.'

Addendum. Grrrr. I'll give him Hester for supper. In fact, no, will simply give supper a miss.

Take tea, wodge of cake, plus headache, to study. I'm in danger of Hester becoming a chronic irritant in my domestic balm. I am conscious also of a huge gulf beginning to gape in our respective expectation landscapes. I'm concerned that my father, as well as hoping for a wife substitute, is developing a sentimental yen for finding a mother substitute also. For *me*. I have not the slightest objection to any amount of grandmother substitute type behaviour toward Ben (birthday cards, small gifts of cash, tolerance and kindness in the face of maternal strops, etc.) But I manifestly do not require a new mother. Expect the domestic forecast to become changeable, turbulent, force ten, gales expected. In short, I expect the worst.

And I *did* expect the email. (Because, though cross, I had crossed my fingers.) Which reads;

thesimpsons@cymserve.com

Dear Charlie,

Yet another unsatisfactory encounter!

Truth is that yes, there is a conference and yes, I'm going (even speaking perhaps), but there is another truth, and that's that I hadn't originally intended attending the conference at all (if we went on every conference we had an opportunity to attend there would be a queue for the surgery that stretched way beyond Swansea). It was only when I found out about you and your trip to Canterbury that I decided I would perhaps go after all. The fact is that, given everything, I wasn't altogether enamoured with the idea of the skiing trip this year, and, well,

179

it seemed a perfect opportunity both to avoid it and to help you out at the same time. I have to go to the conference now, naturally, but I wondered if perhaps we could take the opportunity to meet up at some point? I don't know what your schedule is, but I'm going to be in London from the Wednesday to Saturday. You, presumably, will be travelling back to Cardiff at some point during that time. Could we get together, perhaps? Would you meet me in London? Would you, at the very least, give it some thought?

No pressure. No rush. I'll leave it with you.

Adamxxx

I mean. Bloody hell. What *is* a girl to do?

He simply isn't taking the slightest bit of notice of anything I've said to him. I consider ringing Rose, of course, as if she'd have all the answers. But it just wouldn't be fair. I have this picture of Rose in my head that I can't seem to shift. She's lying in bed – on her own because Matt's in the garden on midnight pest patrol or whatever – and she's imagining her own death. It's so clear in my mind's eye. She's lying there – possibly stroking her abdomen – and she's imagining what cancer would do to her body. Imagining her children attending her funeral, imagining – oh, it's too awful to contemplate – which is why, I guess people try not to spend too much of their lives worrying about other people's troubles – it's just too awful. Anyway, the main thing is that I can't ring Rose. My problems are way too trivial. Just love and hearts and stupid stuff like that.

But what the hell is it with him? What's with the jocular tone? What's with the 'given everything'? What's with the 'unsatisfactory encounter' nonsense? What's with the 'schedule' crap? And how could he attach exclamation marks to such a serious business? Ha bloody ha. But it was a nervous reaction I suppose. Classic male unease with intimacy. And what's with 'could we get together perhaps'? As if we were a pair of old school chums and do lunch type stuff. As if! Forget it.

Click, click. Log on. Find the post room and send;

griffith@cymserve.com

Dear Adam,
Don't be ridiculous. No way. OK? Yes, it's been a godsend
but, hey, there's a limit.
Charlie.

I hesitate about kisses, as ever. Then add some. What the hell;
observing moral propriety is all well and good and fine and so
on but there's no need to hammer it home so prissily all the
time. But hey, there's a thought. This is one of those times
when what you're supposed to do is to pretend to the person
you are in love with (yep, *am*) that really you can't stand the
sight of them, and tell them to go and clear off and get out of
your life, because you've got someone else, and so on. Like in
that film – when the deadbeat dad tells his son he doesn't want
him around. Do people do that? Do people really do that in
real life? Are people *really* that unselfish? Is love really that
unselfish? Am I, more to the point, really that unselfish? I
would like to think so, but on the whole I doubt it.

It's all a con anyway. All that crap about how if you love
someone all you want is for them to be happy and that it
doesn't actually matter if them being happy involves you or
not. All patent nonsense. All that 'you go, I'll be OK' stuff is
garbage. *Is* love ever like that? Guess with kids it probably is.
Love of kids is so utterly unconditional. You just can't help it.
You don't love your kids any less because they whizz off to
Australia, do you? Minnie sure doesn't. But partners stuff,
romantic love – that's so, so different. It's selfish. It has to be.
It's all about genes. I don't want Adam to be unhappy. Of
course I don't. But I don't want *me* to be unhappy either.

When I go to see Minnie at the end of the week, I ask what *she*
thinks re what I have now whimsically come to think of as my
Adam-love-tryst-thing. I am fully aware that this is of no more
use than slaughtering sundry livestock and examining their
entrails in order to divine the best course for the future of the

planet etc., but in my current frame of mind I find I am able to understand that just because much of what Minnie says has no basis in logical thought processes, doesn't mean there isn't (at some deeper, reflexology / iridology / acupuncture / tiger's bollocks / feng bloody shui-type level) a great deal of wisdom in the bizarre things she says.

I ask, 'What should I do, Minnie? I've been telling myself that I could go and see him – have lunch or whatever – with the intention of talking things through – discuss our feelings and so on, and make him understand that it would be so much better if he just stopped emailing me and that we made a strenuous effort to avoid one another – I've been thinking long and hard about changing my job anyway, which would help – but the thing is, I know myself. I know agreeing to meet him will signify no such thing. Agreeing to meet him will just crank the whole thing up even more. I cannot believe that I will be able to spend more than half an hour in his company without either him trying to kiss me, or me thinking about how long it will be before he tries to kiss me and looking for all those little signs and so on, and then – well, I just know it would all turn into the very thing I've been dreading it turning into. Sex, Minnie, will be on the agenda. If not then, not there, it will *be* on the agenda. Of that I am utterly sure.'

Minnie smiles and arrests the progress of her third macaroon.

'Sex?' she says. 'Sex? With a stranger? In *London*?'

'He's not a stranger, Minnie. I mean he was, as far as I knew initially, of course, but, no. Not a stranger, far from it. I've known him a long time. Liked him for a long time. Liked him as a person. As a friend. You know? And I don't mean it quite like that. I don't mean sex *then*, particularly. But just as a natural evolution if I let things go any further. D'you see?' She looks blank. ' OK. Yes, sex. Let's talk about that scenario.'

She puts the macaroon down. 'Let me tell you something, young lady. Last time I had sex that was just where *I* had it. Floating Discotheque, if I remember rightly.'

'With your husband?'

'Dear me, no. He was past all that years back. With an actuarial chap. At the Southern Area dinner cruise.'

'On the Thames?'

'On the floor of the cabin, by the galley.'

'Really? When was this?'

'1968.'

Chapter 19

TEN YEARS FOUR MONTHS. I have computed that I can reasonably be expected to enjoy no more than ten years four month's worth of sexually active life. I could, of course, meet another great love, get re-married, enjoy a rich and varied agenda of mutually satisfying sexual encounters commensurate with our age, flexibility, health status, etc., but, masochistically, right now I prefer to believe the former. The former sounds scarily plausible for a divorcee about town like me. Christ – Minnie was married but still redundant in the bonking department before decimalisation. A sobering thought. Plus (and mainly, if I'm being *scrupulously* honest here), it is a deeply compelling argument for a full-on shagathon with Adam in a Travelodge somewhere. Soon.

Things could be worse, I suppose. When I pack my case to go to Rose's, it is at least with the knowledge that I am getting ever closer to fulfilling my Everest ambition, because the last call I take before leaving work on the Friday, is one to let me know that the Habibs – hurrah, hurrah – have had a full asking price offer for their house from a corporate couple with nothing to sell. Which means they can make an offer for Cherry Ditchling. Though why they would want to is way beyond me.

When I arrive in Canterbury later that evening, it is to find my friend tired and sore and a little bit tipsy, and exuding a palpably false air of jollity.

'Gross!' she reports (with a laugh and a flourish). 'Gross is what it is, Charlie. I feel like a bloody combine harvester's been up there. Let me tell you, childbirth has *nothing* on this.'

We sit and drink some more while she outlines the gruesome details. Incontinence, bleeding, bizarre-sounding packing, plus nightmarish crises with catheter leads. Rose never seems to tire of the blood and guts re-runs. I don't mind. They're just her way, I think, of purging her brain of the fear that will lodge there till the pathology result is finally known. Which should be sometime this week.

'But it will all have been worth it,' I remind her. 'Whatever the pathology, at least the op's over. At least you can get on with your life now.'

She gulps back her wine – the second since I arrived, and judging by the bottle, her fifth, at least – and suddenly her expression becomes serious.

'But the funny thing,' she says, 'is that I have this huge, horrible, *nagging* sense of loss, you know? Of myself. Of myself as a *woman*. It's as if they've pulled a big shutter down on a whole chunk of my life. And I want to get back there. You know?' Her brows knit as she says this.

We are side by side on the sofa, so I put my arm around her.

'Of *course* you do,' I soothe. 'That's quite natural, isn't it?'

'Is it?' She sounds mournful. 'I'm not so sure. I certainly didn't *expect* to feel like this. It was all gung ho with me. It was all "whip it all out!", "toss those tampons out of the window with a merry whoop!" etc. I thought I'd feel free. Liberated. Up for it. You know? But I don't. I feel sad.'

'But Rose, you've just had a major –'

She swivels to face me and silences me with a finger.

'It's not *about* that, Charlie. It's not about cancer and stress and being ill and all that. It's about the finiteness of life. It's about stages and phases and looking back and regrets.' She pulls on a curl that's come loose from my scrunchie, pulls it straight and then winds it carefully around my ear. 'It's about being dragged on to the next bit when you don't feel ready. It's scary. It's bloody miserable.'

I take her hand. 'But it's not as if you want any more children, is it?' She shakes her head. 'So it's just a reaction. To everything. All perfectly understandable.' As if I'd know.

Rose sighs, then rests her head in the crook of my shoulder and snuggles up beside me.

'This isn't about having children,' she tells me.

'Then what?' I feel her shrug. There is something quietly

185

desolate in her manner, and there isn't, I realise, a thing I can do about it.

'Your life. My life. You and Adam, maybe. Fuck knows. I'm just sad and I need lots of hugs.'

So I hug her, and she is asleep mere moments later, snoring extravagantly, and warm and heavy against my chest. Matt, who has been 'leaving us to it' now enters, and beckons me silently.

'Come and join me outside,' he says. 'Come commune with a fag.'

There is little in the garden but grey-green rows of flaccid cabbage and root tops plus the wizened pre-blizzard breakfast debris from the bird table. I flick a nugget of bacon fat from the bench and sit down.

Matt lights a cigarette and sends blue smoke curling skywards.

'It's been a bugger, this snow,' he says. 'Put my cauliflowers back by weeks. And God only knows when the onions will sprout.' He flicks his ash off and stares mournfully skywards. Then sighs.

'You will keep an eye on things, won't you?'

I know what he means, but I stick with the garden. Matt has never been one for the baring of souls.

'Of course,' I reassure him. 'You just say what needs doing and I'll do it. Precisely, mind you. I haven't the first clue about vegetables. You can do me a timetable before you leave.'

'No sweat,' he says. 'I've already done it.' And we find ourselves laughing. Because we both know the only reason we're fussing about the garden is because it's infinitely better than discussing the real thing we're worrying about now.

I am glad to be sterilised, at least, as I am reminded daily that small children are knackering. Have taken to eating tea with the kids as I cannot be fagged to cook twice and would anyway rather flollop around in state of undress discussing weighty philosophical / esoteric matters over a similarly weighty quantity of wine. I've had a seriously bad hangover every morning this week. Possible iodine overload too, as I have rediscovered fishfinger sandwiches big time. Rose is now almost three weeks post-op and becoming bouncier and more cheerful daily, and revelling in lassitude and giving orders to everyone (me). But I don't care. I'm so glad to see her smiling. And for my part, I'm almost convinced that I could deal with whatever the rest of my love life lobs at me, if I could partake of regular female bonding sessions such as we have enjoyed this week. Such a shame that we can't, because despite feeling that, rather like vectors and quadratic equations, my knowledge of child-rearing must have dropped out of my neural net altogether, it's been a definite good move to drop out of my own life for a week and drop into one more grounded instead. Beginning to feel that I can lick the whole Adam problem; I'm more determined than ever to get to Nepal, carve out some new territory, take a firm line with my career, and hope the spin off from my aesthetic and holistic new lifestyle will reap an incidental bounty in the shape of a six-foot gentle hero, with whom I can explore (given constraints of age, flexibility and so on) an active physical union for a bit more than ten years. Though not Rhys Hazelton, probably.

In fact, I am so taken with the idea of finding my true self through developing a focused new life-plan that when I decide to telephone the office on Thursday afternoon to find out whether Habibs *have* made their offer for Cherry Ditchling, I find I am totally sanguine about a possible no-go. But not for long. (Obviously fooled myself about *that*.)

'Davina,' I tweet. 'How's everything going?'

'Tickety-boo,' she says. 'Is there something you want?'

'Oh, it's nothing important. I just couldn't bear waiting till Monday to find out.'

'Find out what?'

(Forgot that, in Davina-world, staff commission is less important than colour of tights.)

'Did they buy it?'

'Buy what?'

(Ditto.)

'Cherry Ditchling.'

'Cherry Ditchling?'

'The Habibs. Did they make a firm offer?'

'Oh, *them*. Yes, they did.'

Yes!

'For how much?'

'Four twenty-five.'

Excellent!

'And?'

'And nothing. The Rutlands –'

'Pardon? And *nothing*?'

'Like I just said. And nothing. The Rutlands said no.'

'No? They said *no*? But that's only five grand off the asking price. Why?'

'Because it wasn't enough.'

'Wasn't enough! Christ! But that's absolute rubbish. They knew they'd have to negotiate. Mr Rutland said as much to me only last week. Look, have you rung and discussed it with Mr Habib? The amount that we're talking here, I'm sure they'd be prepared to meet them halfway or something. They loved the house. They wouldn't want to lose it for the sake of a few thousand. Should I –'

'Charlie, I haven't rung them because there's no point. The reason Mr Rutland declined their offer is because he had a better one. An offer at the asking price, in fact. From a cash buyer.'

'*What?*'

'So, understandably, he took it.'

'Oh, God, that is *so* unfair! I don't believe it! How long have we been trying to sell that dump? Three years? I *can't* believe it. And – oh, God – don't tell me – it was Metro, wasn't it? Don't tell me it was Metro. Metro *have* sold it, haven't they?'

There is a silence so short that a flea would dwarf it. I hear it anyway.

'Not at all,' she purrs. '*We* sold it.'

'We *did*?'

'Hugh did.'

'*Hugh* did?'

'Uh-huh.'

Hugh did. Not me. *Hugh.* 'So,' I say finally, ice crystals misting the receiver, 'Willie JJ are happy. And Hugh's in the money. And the Habibs can't exchange as they've nowhere to go.' I laugh, and the mist superfreezes to minus two-seventy Kelvin. 'Well,' I add. 'I must say, I'm really glad I phoned.'

'You know how things work here, Charlie. You weren't here, he was. He has his own sales figures to think of.'

Then *I* think. 'Hang on,' I say. 'Surely we'd have been better off getting the Habibs to match the cash offer. That way, we'd still get the commission on Cherry Ditchling, but we'd get the commission on their sale as well. This way there's a chance that we won't get that sale now. It could be months before they find a new place to buy, and there's a strong possibility that their buyers might end up looking for somewhere else.'

'Charlie, you know the score. A bird in the hand, and so on. Besides, Hugh's out valuing a new property right now. An estate up on the hill. Could be perfect for the Habibs.'

'Then perhaps I'd better see if I can get back for tomorrow, before he has them, pens in hand, signing the contract.'

There is a small exhalation.

'Don't be churlish,' she simpers. 'Enjoy the rest of your break. See you next.'

Bitch.

Bastard.

Low-life scum.

Never trust a man with rings in his nipples. And more fool her. That boy is up to no good.

For ten seconds after I put the phone down I stare at it in appalled fascination, as if it, and not reality, was the orchestrator of my misery. My air of nonchalance, I manage to note, has dissolved along with the last traces of snow. Or perhaps not dissolved, but simply been buried alive under the malevolent bile that has risen phoenix-like from the ashes of my happy mood.

The point being, that it isn't really me that does what I do next.

It's a long number. Full of noughts and sevens and eights. And I'm still making sure I got it right when he answers.

'Hello,' he says.

I say it back.

'Hello. God! *Charlie*! Hello!'

And then I'm not sure quite what to say next. 'Adam, I –'

But he is. Or seems to be. 'How *are* you? How's Rose? Have you –'

'Um. Fine. She's fine. She's, er … fine, and, well, I … Well, I thought … well … I thought. Well, here I am, anyway. You wanted us to meet up. And, well –'

'So you changed your mind? I'm very glad, Charlie.'

'*Are* you? Are you sure we should do this? I mean, God, Adam, you know, *meet* like this?'

'Of course I'm sure, Charlie. Or I wouldn't have asked you.'

'I know that, but … well, you have … well, you have things to lose. I can't help but keep thinking …'

His voice is firm. 'Then don't. I suspect you could think yourself out of most things if you put your mind to it. So let's get on with it before you do exactly that, shall we? Where and when? You say.'

Me say. Oh God. 'I'm due to leave here tomorrow. I was going to set off early evening but Matt's due back at eleven, and Rose will … well, anyway, I could leave here in the morning and be in London by lunchtime. Would that be any good?'

'Fine. Absolutely. So where should we meet? Somewhere around here? I'm just off Portland Place. But what about your car? You don't want to have to bring that into town, do you?'

190

Someone (me, I guess) tells him I'll put it in the car park off Regent Street and we arrange that he'll meet me, just outside there, at one. Spit spot. All sorted.

'Charlie,' he says. 'Thank you.'

My heart goes kerplunk.

'Is that an underlined thank you?' I ask him.

'In bold.'

'Are you shocked?' I ask Rose, some minutes later, while still blowing the smoke from my mental revolver.

'Not in the least,' she assures me chattily. She pulls her legs up onto the sofa and smiles. In contrast to the beginning of the week, it is a happy, fulsome smile. The smile of a woman at peace with her career choice, at ease with her love life, and at one with her yin and her yang and so forth. And with a whole term's sick leave, to boot.

I blink. 'You're not? *I* am.' Indeed, I am as shocked as it's possible to be. Life seems one big round of unexpected behavioural tics just now.

'No, I'm not,' she re-iterates. 'Mainly because you already told me you have Adam's mobile phone number in your handbag. You don't make a point of carrying around the phone number of someone you don't ever intend ringing. You particularly don't carry it around if the agenda for the rest of your life is to make strenuous efforts not to communicate with the person in question ever again.'

'I said that?'

'More than once.'

'I did believe it.'

'No you didn't.' She puts her *Hello!* down and takes off her reading glasses. 'Charlie, Charlie, Charlie,' she says. 'Don't kid yourself about this. You've spent most of the week looking for an excuse to ring him. Now you've got one, so you've rung him. Seems pretty straightforward to me.'

'That's not true.'

'Yes it *is*. So stop beating yourself up about it.'

I sit down on the floor beside her, pull my legs up and cradle my knees in my arms. I'm conscious that even if Rose is having none of it, I seem to be creeping ever closer towards the tragic-heroine persona I've sketched out for myself.

'But what a crap reason for ringing him!' I wail. 'What a crap reason for *seeing* him. "Oh, hi, Adam! Just thought I'd call to say I've decided I will meet you after all, not because I think I should but because your wife is a bitch and I want to get even." Great.'

'But that's *not* the reason, is it? That's my whole point. You're desperate to see him. In fact you make desperation look like a *laissez-faire* option, quite honestly. You just needed something like this to happen so you wouldn't feel so bad about yourself.'

'So why *do* I feel bad, then?'

'Because you've convinced yourself otherwise. You've convinced yourself that you have to like Davina; that, as she's the wronged woman – though she isn't, not so far, remember – you have to feel some sort of benevolence towards her. Do the right thing by her. Make some sort of grand gesture of denial. Which is rubbish! You're not a saint. So you don't have to set yourself up as a martyr. And you never got on with her before, so why should you get on with her now? Plus she's made it pretty clear where her loyalties are, work-wise. You have every right to dislike her. *And* that Hugh. He sounds like a real piece of work.'

'I wish I could fathom what's going on there. Things are happening, but I just can't figure out what. Hey! You don't think Hugh and Davina –'

'No I don't think, quite frankly. *Far* too convenient. Just more wishful thinking on your part, Charlie girl.'

'No, you're right about that. But then again, there *is* Austin Metro –'

'Oh, come *on*, Charlie. Who *cares*? Who gives a stuff about any of them? You phoned Adam. You *did* it. *That's* what's important. That you're going to go and *meet* him.'

'Christ,' I say. 'My stomach's churning like you wouldn't believe.'

Rose grins broadly. 'Ha. Tell me about it,' she says.

Like most momentous, life-changing comments, this one, at first, goes straight over my head. Until much later, that is. It's a little before eleven and I am packed, plucked, waxed and polished. I feel like a little girl who's due to leave for holiday in the small hours. The excitement is palpable, but tinged with anxiety. Rose sips her wine and looks on benignly as I paint my nails purple.

'Chose the dress then,' she observes, noting the shade. 'Expecting an unseasonal heat wave?'

'It was either that or my hairy green trousers,' I tell her. Even talking about it sends my gut into freefall. And suddenly, another thought comes crashing down to join it. 'Tell me,' I ask, 'you know earlier, when I said about my stomach churning?'

She nods.

'Well, you said "tell me about it!". In a very pointed way. Not as in 'tell me what it feels like'. As in 'I *know* what it feels like.' It just came back to me. What did you mean exactly?'

Rose gazes into her wine for a full thirty seconds. Then narrows her eyes. *Ah*.

'Nothing,' she says.

'Liar.'

She smiles. 'I knew it.'

'Knew what?'

'That you'd notice.'

'So I'm right, then!'

Her expression changes. 'This must *never* –'

I tut. 'Oh, for God's sake! As if!'

'I know. I'm sorry. But you know what it's like. I've never told a soul. Anyway. Yes. You're right. Been there, done that. Etcetera.'

Been where? Done what? *Wow*.

'Wow!' I say, wide-eyed. 'You *what*?'

'Have been there and done that.' She drains her glass.

'When?'

'Oh, a long time ago now. Ellen must have been two when

193

it started.'

This is too much to take in. 'For how long? What happened? God, I would never have thought! I thought you and Matt – well, you know. Wow. This *never* occurred to me.'

I finish my wine too and reach for the bottle. Rose holds her glass out and says,

'Oh, it went on for over two and a half years. A lifetime at the time. Now I look back and it seems such a short chunk of my life. But it was very intense. I think I lived more life in that time than I ever did before or since.'

'But what happened? Who was he? How did it all start – did you end it or did he? Do you still –'

I take hold of my last sentence and retrieve its tail end. 'Do you really want to talk about this? Honestly, Rose? I mean, if you don't –'

She smiles. 'Funny. I never envisaged actually talking about it with anyone. Ever. Particularly you, the way you've been prattling on about morality all week.' She grins at me. 'Mrs Holier-than-thou. Mrs Righteousness-personified. But, yes. I do. Though there isn't actually that much to tell. I fell in love, had an affair, fell out of love – well, not out of love exactly, but out of the idea of that *sort* of love. Mainly out of love with myself, I suppose. The pull of everything else; Matt, the children, the awful, *awful* consequences of what I was contemplating – it did the trick, I can tell you.'

'But how did it happen in the first place? I thought you and Matt were like that.' I hold my thumb and forefinger together. She nods.

'We are. We are *now*. We weren't always. After Ellie was born we went through a really bad patch. Actually, I'm exaggerating. It wasn't so much a bad patch as just a dreary patch. Sex was hopeless – well, boring, infrequent. Matt was stressed about work, I hated being at home. I was climbing the walls. We didn't row much – we just couldn't be bothered with each other. Looking back, I guess if either one of us had been more motivated to do something about it, our marital doldrums wouldn't have lasted nearly as long. But the truth

194

was that it was simply easier not to communicate. We didn't have the energy. And then I met *him*, and what energy I did have was well and truly channelled elsewhere.'

I wonder how many calories are melting away for me. 'And I suppose you suddenly found plenty. But how did it start?'

'With a blazing row on a windy day outside Tesco. I'd put Ellie into her car seat and thought I'd shut the door, but she kicked it and it flew open and made a three-inch dent in his Volvo.' She laughs. 'He started banging on about people with kids having some consideration and being more careful, and I just blew my top and told him he could shove his Volvo up his arse. I was also very specific about where he could shove his crappy side-impact protection system, as I recall.'

'Very romantic.'

'Exactly. Which is why, I suppose, it caught us both off guard. One minute I was screaming at him and the next I was in floods of tears and railing against life, the universe and everything. And of course he was completely mortified. When I went round to his place to give him some money for the repairs, he wouldn't hear of it. And he asked me in for a coffee and said he'd been worried about me, and, well, wham! Bingo! I simply couldn't stop thinking about him. And then we seemed to find ourselves meeting almost every day. He worked nights then, of course, which made it all the more likely. If I went to the shops, he was there. Walked into the bank, he was there. Went to put petrol in the car, he was there. It took a couple of months – no more – before we took things that step further. I can't even remember now, how it happened exactly. But it did. We had sex. Just like that. In the Volvo. Fully clothed, as I recall. We were like animals. I tell you, Charlie, I never had sex like it. Haven't since, for that matter.'

I raise my eyebrows.

'Oh, don't fret,' she says, flapping a dismissive hand. 'Everything's just fine, *really*. You can't hope to maintain that level of excitement for a lifetime. Not even for a year. Not with *anyone*, can you? If I'd left Matt and the kids, it would have been no different. Worse, probably – guilt has a way of sapping your lifeblood.'

'You seem very sure.'

'I've had plenty of time to think about it.'

'So what happened?'

She reaches out her hand to put her wine glass on the coffee table and, as she does so, the stone in her engagement ring sparkles. She follows my eyes and smiles reassuringly.

'Oh, it was quite something, Charlie. We managed to spend the best part of three years living in cloud-cuckoo land; God knows how I kept things going at home. But you can, you know. Once you lose that connection as a couple, it's all too easy. You just exist on another level. It happens all the time. And I was completely obsessed. I didn't think about the future. It was like getting my next fix. Looking back, I can hardly believe myself, really. One minute dropping Ellen off at playgroup and chatting with the other mums about shopping and clothes, and next minute we'd be off in the car somewhere, and going at it like rutting stags. God, sometimes I'd go down to pick her up at twelve with my bra and knickers shoved in my handbag!'

'Cripes!' I cradle my wine in my hand and try to imagine jolly, down-to-earth, sensible Rose in the grip of an unbridled passion. And can't. 'Cripes!' I say again. 'But how did you *feel* about him? I mean with Adam, it isn't really about sex – no, that's stupid. It is partly. Of course it is. But it's not just about sex. It's much more about having that sense that we could be so – oh, listen to me. Now I'm beginning to sound like a Jane Austen heroine.'

'Which is exactly how I felt, so don't worry. I loved him, Charlie. I really loved him. But there was never a moment when I didn't love Matt, too. Except that at the time, it felt more like compassion than love. Just a deep-seated belief that there was always something there that we could rekindle. And that he couldn't really be the father of my children and me *not* love him. Which is silly, isn't it? But made me realise there must still be something in our marriage worth hanging on to.'

'So how did it end?'

'He left his wife.'

'*He* was married?'

'Oh, yes. Very much so. But no children, which made his situation way different from mine. And he wanted me to leave Matt. So everything changed.'

'He put you under pressure.'

'No. Not a bit of it. He was a quiet, gentle man. But him doing so made me realise things couldn't go on. If I wasn't about to leave Matt, then there was no way I could stomach the thought of this guy putting his life on permanent hold.'

'So you called it a day.'

'Sounds very prosaic, but, yes.'

'And he went back to his wife?'

'Nope. She wouldn't have him. Can't say I blame her. Can you?'

'I guess not. And Matt? Did he never find out? Never even have an inkling?'

Rose shakes her head. 'I think not. I hope not. Anyway, let's just say if he did, he never gave me that impression. Sometimes I wonder, but,' she shrugs. 'No. I don't think so. Like I said, I hope not.'

'So how did you get the marriage back on track? All the years I've known you, it never occurred to me that you were anything less than happy together. And we met when? Only a year or so after?'

She nods. 'I made the effort. I told him I thought we needed to take a long hard look at ourselves. I decided to go back to work full-time – Ellen was in school by this time, of course – and I generally took myself in hand. The rest, in time, followed quite naturally. Thank God.'

'And what about him? Do you ever see him these days?'

Rose now gives me a long hard look.

'Not these days.'

'But you have?'

'Not specifically. I used to see him around a fair bit.'

'So he was local? From Cardiff?'

She nods. 'Oh, yes.'

There is something in her tone that makes me realise she's uncertain whether to tell me who he is, which in turn makes me realise it's someone I know. For an instant, a horrible thought enters my mind. It must show on my face because she then snorts and says, 'Good God! It wasn't Adam, you numbskull!'

I release my held breath. 'But *who*?'

She considers for a few long moments more.

'Oh, well,' she says finally. 'What the hell? I suppose you've been tortured enough by mystery men lately. Yes. It *was* someone you know. And quite well, as it happens.' She looks me in the eye and, straight-faced, she says, 'Phil.'

Chapter 20

I WAS STUNNED. AND was speechless for sufficient seconds that Rose said 'Well, don't look so surprised – *you* went out with him, didn't you?' etc., which I then had to concede was actually true. But I was stunned nevertheless. Phil. An affair? Phil *and Rose* – an *affair*? I could not get my head round the enormity of it all. Could not get my head round the fact of Rose having had an affair period, let alone bringing Phil into the equation. And Karen! *Karen!* So much was now clear. So much previous 'don't want to talk about that, if you don't mind, Charlie' stuff was now explained. Phil's marriage was not a quiet fizzle-out like my own, but a bang-crash-wallop major-league bad business all round. And Karen was clearly not, I now realised, the person I had previously acknowledged her to be. Karen was a scarred, hurt person. Karen was a female cuckold. Karen was a person for whom the whole relationship arena was a bad scary place with lions etc.

Strenuously do not wish to be thrown to any lions.

On Friday morning I took the children to school and said my goodbyes to them, then hot-footed it back for more coffee and confessions. Rose, at last freed from her enforced isolation, was in bouncy, revelatory, talkative mood.

'But what about now?' I asked. 'What about the here and now? The last five years of seeing him around all the time? What about when *I* started seeing him?'

She poured the coffee and smiled.

'Really, Charlie, it hasn't been half as difficult as you'd imagine. Think back to old boyfriends of yours, for instance. Any old boyfriend. That one you told me you were passionate about before Felix, maybe. If you met him today do you think it would all still be there?' She shakes her head. 'Those feelings fade. Get superseded by new feelings. You just move into a different gear. It's like with you and Adam.'

199

Arrgghh! We are an *item*, I thought.

'There were years,' she went on, 'when you barely registered his existence. Oh, he may have been on our shag lists and so on, but you thought no more of having a relationship with him than you would with George Clooney. It was no more real than that. And with Phil, it was just like that in reverse. *Is* like that. We have an amazing capacity to consign feelings to boxes, don't we? I seem to, at any rate.'

'I suppose. But even so, there must be times when you think about him. There must have been times when I was with him and you, you know – had feelings about it.'

Rose shook her head.

'One thing I'm particularly good at,' she reminded me, 'is deciding to do something and sticking right to it. No. Thankfully, all that is way, way behind me. Mind you, I don't say I'm not glad you split with him. Quite apart from him being not remotely your type, I certainly wouldn't want to push my luck. No. I'm glad Karen's back with him. Order restored, as they say.'

She gathered toast crumbs into an orderly peak on the table, and we sat for some minutes digesting our thoughts. Mine drifted and spun then careered into something, like feathers caught and trapped against a newly tarred fence. Order restored, it said. Phil back with Karen. Order restored, it said. Rose still with Matt. What of Adam and Davina? How long before *they* ironed out all their wrinkles and furrows? Restored order. Got happy. And then what about me?

Rose must have sensed the way my thoughts were going, because she seemed suddenly anxious to divert them down a more positive route.

'You go for it, Charlie,' she urged. 'Guilt-trip all you like, but you can't escape fact. And the fact is that their marriage is dead in the water. I'd stake my life on it. He cares about you and, boy, do you care about him! You both have one life, remember, and you've already lived half of it. And what have either of you to lose that you haven't lost already?'

'Christ, Rose! Did you rehearse that chunk of philosophy?'

'Read it somewhere.' She waggled her finger. 'But listen, Charlie girl, it's no less pertinent for that.'

Before I left Rose's, I telephoned my father to check all was well at home. He told me he'd be going over to Hester's for dinner.

'What about Ben?' I asked.

'Coming with me, of course.'

'Bet that *really* made his week, Dad.'

'Oh, it most certainly did,' he corrected me. 'Francesca's coming too, and, between you and me, I think young Ben's got a bit of a thing going on there.'

Lovely, lovely, lovely. I don't think.

Everyone in their rightful place. Dad and Hester. Dan and Jack. Ben and Francesca. (Ben and someone, at any rate. Early days.) And me. Furtively meeting another woman's husband on a London street, to do goodness knows what. I scribbled Hester's number down, and promised to let everyone know what time (or *if*) I intended getting home.

'What's the occasion, then?' Dad asked, before I could hang up.

'Occasion?'

'I mean what's the shopping spree in aid of?'

'Nothing,' I told him. 'Just thought I deserved one.'

'And you do, my lovely,' he said warmly. 'You certainly do.'

When I finally swung in to the front of the five-star black marble car park portico, the sight of Adam leapt out at me, as if he was the subject of a magic eye painting and I'd spent the last two weeks squinting to see him. He was standing in a smoke-coloured suit, chatting to a man in some overalls who had a bucket and wiper thing and must valet the cars. They were laughing together as if the world's ills did not touch them. They were chortling. I fancied I could hear their guffaws through the glass.

Which did nothing to quell my increasing conviction that

201

what we were doing was horribly wrong.

I turned the car onto the ramp and then down, curling my way round the dark concrete spiral, my heart pumping wildly against my chest. By the time I had parked and walked back up to the entrance, the wash-man had gone and Adam was alone. 'Oh, God,' I said as he saw me. 'What am I *doing* here? This is all your fault, you know.' My legs were trembling from climbing the stairs and I could feel my face beginning to burn.

He shrugged and said 'Fair comment.' Then smiled a little and started moving towards me.

I put my hands to my face. 'This is such a bad, stupid, senseless thing for us to be doing. I can't believe I came. This is all going to end in tears, you know. It is.'

He was standing in front of me by now, examining my face. 'I'm inclining to the opinion that it already has,' he said. Then, 'Look, if you want to forget this, then just say the word.'

He shut his mouth and I opened mine, but couldn't find a suitable response to project into the gap. Other than what eventually came out, which was,

'God, you *know* I don't. I can't. Oh, God. If *only*.'

Which was not what I thought I'd intended to assert at all. So I shut it again quickly, before it could betray me some more.

'Me neither,' he agreed gravely. 'Shall we, er ...'

'Yes,' I said, following his lead to the exit. Like a dust mote caught up in a draught and swirled skywards. Or a polarised rock. 'Yes,' I said. 'Let's.'

He pulled open the heavy glass door and ushered me through it. Then nodded in the direction of a junction up the road. This was it, then. We were off on our little journey of discovery. We were going somewhere. Together. On our own. In secret. Strangely, I now felt a kind of relief. I'd stepped over the most significant moral threshold of my life to date, and now that I was on the inside and looking back out, the bit I'd left seemed cruelly judgemental and cold. Or was I now outside and looking back in? Whatever. A different place.

Somewhere new and compelling.

'So,' he said, as we began walking. 'What would you like to do?'

He said the words in the same, smooth, measured voice he'd used when attending to Ben over Christmas. Mouth dry, I put my car park ticket into the side pocket of my handbag and then shrugged my shoulders emphatically. What did one do? I had only the one infidelity scenario sorted. You met. You went to places to have sex. You had sex. You lay in bed smoking and eating stylish snack items. You didn't discuss the future. You didn't discuss the wronged partner. You didn't profess to higher feelings. You parted breathlessly, fumbling urgently with one another (as if your denial made you somehow less guilty). You said goodbye. You burned a memory of your naked selves onto one another's retinas. You recognised and acknowledged your mutual inability to break free from the slavery of your primeval drives. You arranged the next assignation. You counted the seconds until its time came around. You met. You did it all again.

Yet here we were in a Mayfair street, like a couple of office workers sharing the sandwich run, and self-consciously trying to have a workaday conversation with one another. No falling into each other's arms. No urgent kissing. No sexual imperative driving our actions. Another unsatisfactory encounter?

'I don't know,' I said, trying to still the inexorable surge of another hysterical outburst. 'I thought we were going to "do lunch" or something.'

He turned. 'Did I say that?'

'Did you not?'

'I don't think so. Not specifically. But, yes. It's lunchtime. We could have lunch if you like.'

Did I like? In actual fact, I didn't think so. My stomach convulsed at the prospect. Instead I said, 'What time do you have to be back in your conference?'

'Oh, whenever,' he offered, with an attempt at breeziness. 'Not today, even. There's a lecture I can happily miss and a

203

dinner wild horses wouldn't drag me to. My time's my own. So. Lunch, then?'

I had stalled on the first bit. Not *today* even? Oh, God. Sex after all. What else could he be implying? And what was I thinking! Sex *not* a feature here? I should cocoa, it wasn't. And clearly we couldn't do lunch. Not with all that legs under the table stuff and suggestive food consumption and smouldering looks and so on. But he was probably starving. Men generally were. Perhaps we could get a bun somewhere.

'Are you hungry?' I asked.

He paused on the pavement while he considered. He looked especially lovely against the pale Mayfair buildings; especially vulnerable yet especially strong. And much as I was aware that this was nothing more cerebral than simple sexual attraction, I couldn't help but feel sure the very loveliness of him was not about sex, but most definitely about love. Pathetic. And corny. But nevertheless real.

He patted his flat stomach and puffed out his chiselled cheeks. 'Big breakfast. Plus – well, you know. No. Not at the moment, to be honest. What did you say?'

'Pardon?'

He began walking again. 'To Rose. To your family. Where did you say you were going?'

We had reached the junction by now, and a car was approaching. Adam stopped on the pavement and turned to face me. A biscuit-coloured Rolls swept around the corner and away, but he made no move forwards. His hand moved lightly against my back, as a teacher's would in helping a small child cross the road.

'I told my father I was going to treat myself to a day's West End shopping.' He nodded. 'And Rose knows the truth, of course.'

'Of course.'

'Well, what there is of it, anyway.'

'Hmm. And what does she have to say on the subject?'

'Not much,' I said. 'She seems very relaxed about it. She has quite a strong conviction that I should do whatever is most

204

likely to make me happy.'

'Sounds reasonable.'

'Yes, doesn't it? Except that doing whatever makes you happy now isn't always in accord with what is going to make you happy in the long term.'

'Fair comment.'

'You said that once.'

'When you said this was all my fault.'

'I didn't mean to.'

'You did.'

'It wasn't anything personal. Just an observation.'

'About me.'

'About the situation you've put me in.'

'I didn't mean to.'

'Which doesn't help any.'

'I know that.'

Silence. A long one. A forty-week pause.

'Come on,' I said. 'Justify yourself. Give me something gritty and earnest about how we must, oh, I don't know, answer the call of our instincts and so forth. About being powerless to –'

'I don't subscribe to that view.'

'Oh.'

'So I'd be lying, wouldn't I?'

Which admission rather thrilled me, for some reason. Gave substance to the quality of the feelings *he* had.

'So,' I said. 'The fact is, you knew exactly what you were doing when you answered my email. You thought "I fancy her. Lets have a bit of a laugh here." That sort of thing.'

'Laugh?' he said. 'I don't know about laughs coming into it.' He paused. 'No, that's not true. Of course I thought it would be fun. But the attraction was part of it, from the very first instant.'

'Hrrmmph.' I said. 'Even though you were married.'

'Even though I was married.'

'Even knowing it might lead to –'

'Even *hoping* it might lead to – once I found out that you'd found out who *I* was.'

'Which doesn't paint you in a very good light.'

'No.'

'No. It doesn't, does it?'

'I'll have to learn to live with it. Can you?'

By the time I'd decided how to respond (bloody hell, what do you mean by *that?* etc.) we'd reached the end of the road. It had opened out onto a large square, in the centre of which was a tree-ringed garden. Flanked by cars, tethered like horses, to a necklace of meters.

'Hmm,' he said. 'Well. Hanover Square. What shall we do? We could sit in the square for a while, if you like. Or we could get ourselves a coffee somewhere. Or, well – what?'

He turned, his hand dropping back down to his side.

'I don't know,' I said, wanting suddenly to scoop him up and console him in his quiet disappointment with himself. 'I hadn't actually thought much beyond seeing you.'

He lifted his arms a little and smiled a self-conscious smile. 'Well, here I am. In the flesh. All fully visible.'

I nodded. 'I know,' I said. 'That's the problem. Now I've seen you, well, I don't seem to be able to – well.' I shrugged.

'What?'

'Here I am blushing again.'

'You don't need to.'

'Tell my face that.'

He stepped closer. 'You don't need to.'

Oh, God. 'Aha!' I said. 'A coffee bar! Coffee!'

When we got into the coffee house, which was bright and cheery and functional and looked like a room-setting from an *Ikea* catalogue, he said, 'My hotel's not far. We could stroll up there later, if you like.'

'We *what?*' I squeaked.

'Stroll up there. For a sandwich or something. And –'

God.

'Hold on,' I said. 'Perhaps you could run the "or something" by me again.'

He took possession of a café latté and stirred it thoughtfully.

'Charlie,' he said quietly (the waitress was wiping and humming nearby), 'you know very well that what I would most like to do now is to take you back there and spend the afternoon making love to you. I'm a man and that's the sort of thought that tends to occupy a fair-sized chunk of the average man's mind. Larger than average in this case, of course, as I have spent a considerably larger than average chunk of time lately imagining what it would be like to do exactly that. Particularly in tandem with the whole Stravinsky / seismic activity / mountaineering dimension you've sketched so alluringly for me. You know? But – and it's a serious but – I'm not about to make a big deal of it. If you want to go back there and do that, then I will be a very, very happy man this afternoon. If you don't, then I will accept it with good grace and remain hopeful. I'm good at that. But you can't blame me for trying, can you? Sugar?'

Bloody hell.

'That told me,' I said, waving the sugar bowl away and attempting the sort of no-nonsense look I hoped women more streetwise than myself would respond with. 'Are you generally this frank with your patients?'

'If appropriate.'

'With women?'

'Where possible.'

'Where possible?'

'Charlie –' He put his hand over both of mine. 'Don't think for a minute that I know what I'm about here. I don't. I'm floundering. *You* hold all the cards.'

'Pah!' I said. 'This isn't a James Bond film, you know.'

'I didn't say it was.'

'Then don't talk like you're in one.'

'What *is* it with you?'

'You know what I mean. Stop being so damned articulate.'

He sucked some coffee off his teaspoon.

'Articulate? Me?'

'As in "Male sexuality involves a chemical response to psycho-sexual stimuli. Discuss." And so on.'

'You *what*?'

'You know.'

'I don't understand a word of it.'

'Yes you do. Don't deny it.'

'Charlie, what *are* you on about?'

'This. You. Your, your –'

'What?'

'The way you keep cornering me. *Saying* things all the time. Making me feel so – so powerless.'

'*You*? *Powerless*?'

'There you go again. You disarm me all the time. I feel like a butterfly on the end of a pin. Like a beetle on its back. D'you know?' I freed my hands from under his and flapped them to illustrate. The sugar bowl skittered across the table towards him. He put out his hand as it slithered to a halt.

'See?' I said.

He sat back. 'Not at all. Not in the slightest.' He grinned, his smile alight with sudden joy. 'But it doesn't matter in the least.'

'You see? *That's* what I mean.'

His eyebrows moved upwards.

'Look,' I went on. 'When I got here today, and I saw you and so on, it was like – well, it was an intense physical thing, you know? I felt, oh, you know, hot, cold, shaky, self-conscious, like I wanted to throw my arms around you, like – there! You see? I'm blushing again already – like there were all these feelings whizzing around inside me that I couldn't get to grips with – *can't* get to grips with, and I didn't know what to say or do or –'

'So did I.'

'Oh, come *on*.'

'I *did*. I told you. I'm floundering here.' His smile faded. '*Every* bit as much as you.'

'So why do you seem so in control all the time?'

He grimaced. 'Practice.'

208

'No it's not. It's because you *are*.'

'I'm not, Charlie. *You* are.'

'Rubbish!'

'You are. I'm entirely at your mercy. I am here only because you agreed to it. I have been waiting, and hoping, and wondering whether to email you again, and –'

I put my finger against his mouth. Suddenly, somehow, I saw what was needed.

'How far's your hotel?' I said. 'Let's do the sex.'

Chapter 21

WE'VE ACHIEVED, I THINK, dynamic equilibrium.

Soames North Mayfair is a regency house hotel with knobs on. Exactly the place one would assume wealthy GPs would convene, as it has an almost palpable air of gravitas and sobriety, and is dripping with paintings of august-looking men.

All is not as it seems, however. On one of those red quilted boards in reception (which alerts the residents to the fact that it's 9 degrees C, overcast, chance of rain), the day's activities are carefully detailed in plastic gilt letters. 'Shelley Suite – Zipco Sanitary Installations (group two); The Keats Centre – Time of Your Life Photo Studios (Southern).' At the bottom, the Tennyson Suite does boast General Practitioners Consultative Forum (Palliative care and beyond – morals under the microscope), but in doing so, it has clearly cleaned out the hotel's stock of letters – the 's' in support is not an 's' but a 5, and microscope starts with a sideways-on E.

Were letters not at a premium I would be tempted to add; Upstairs – GPs Recreational Forum (Sexual athletics – moral code under stress).

A moment of pressure on my hand and we are heading off down one of the half-dozen or so dado-railed corridors that led from the heavily coved central area. Bar my brief concern about being seen by someone – which Adam dismissed instantly; I looked every inch a trendy Islington GP, apparently (must be the boots) – we have not really spoken since halfway up Great Portland Street. His confidence was based on fuzzy logic, however, as we have continued to hold hands like children throughout.

Adam took my hand as soon as we stepped out of the coffee house. Having confirmed that the sex thing looked like being the most practical way to spend a chilly afternoon (given that a. it was obviously what we both most wanted to do and b.

210

a comfortable West End hotel room was as convenient and well-appointed a venue as any), it seemed appropriate to make some sort of unequivocal statement of intent.

And it was unbelievably lovely to touch him at last. And so we remained thus coupled coming out of the square, crossing Oxford Street, threading through to Upper Regent Street, past the BBC and on up towards Regent's Park. Every so often we would exchange lingering glances. He would squeeze my hand, I would squeeze his in return. His fingers cradled my own; hard and warm and masculine; my own hand felt tiny and protected and safe.

But it was easier not to talk. It was *good* not to talk. I hadn't expected holding hands with Adam Jones, walking up a London street, on a cloudy day in February, to feel so intensely charged with emotion. I hadn't expected to find it so moving. I hadn't expected to find it so sexy. And, what was more, I had not the slightest idea about his thoughts, except through the transmission of the warmth of his skin. Did he feel as I did? This intense sense of excitable dislocation?

'Room twenty-four,' he says now, as we wait for the lift.

It glides down to meet us and opens its doors. We step into carpeted warmth and seclusion. Our own selves look back at us, bashful and mute.

'Well, Charlie,' he says next, smiling at my reflection and pushing a button. 'Here we are, then.'

I nod and squeeze his hand again and find absolutely nothing to say.

The lift deposits us on yet another corridor, down which he leads me, gilt key fob dangling in his hand. His room is at the end, adjacent to a tall window, through which a grey cloudbase rumbles over even greyer buildings.

I stand silent beside him while he deals with the lock. In a movie, of course, we would simply fall into the room, stumble frantically bedwards and get right on down to it. But this isn't a movie, so we get stuck in the doorway for just long enough for me to spy a pair of burgundy boxer shorts marooned over the side of the bath.

But it is a hotel room much like any other. Double bed, armchair, case stand, desk, wardrobe. There's a TV, a telephone, an elegant desk lamp, a trouser press and an en suite bathroom (door ajar). A laptop sits on the desk amid a muddle of papers and two bottles of mineral water. One is full. One half empty. As I take in the details, the hairs on my neck prickling, I am aware that Adam has now lost his former composure and is hovering beside me, unsure what to do next. I am pleased at this development. I don't want a seduction. I want him every bit as uncertain and tremulous as I've felt all day. I walk to the window. This one looks out over the park, where naked trees finger the low pewter fluff.

'Well,' he says, at last, switching the lamp on. 'I don't know about you, but I suddenly feel thirsty. How about I nip down to the bar and get us a drink. Soft drink? Wine or something?'

He looks flustered.

'Yes, why not,' I say. 'Coke sounds good. Can you get me a Coke?'

'Coke, then. Yes. Fine. OK. Right. Back in a jiffy.' He begins to reach for the key and then changes his mind.

'Ah,' he says, a wry smile escaping from underneath his grim expression. 'I don't need this, I suppose. I'll knock, shall I?'

I nod. 'Fine.'

The door sighs as it closes, then clicks shut behind him.

I can't afford to waste a window of opportunity like this so I sprint into the en suite and spend nine of the next ten minutes attending to all the little details a girl must attend to, borrowing at random from his M and S toiletry range. The last I spend sitting on the edge of the bath, wincing as I pluck out a few rogue bikini-line stragglers.

All too soon, there's a gentle tap tap at the door. He has brought up a tray with two glasses of Coke, two bottles of beer and two packets of honey-roasted cashew nuts. Stylish post-coital snack, perhaps?

'I got you Diet Coke,' he says. 'I presumed you'd want diet.' He bustles at the desk, sending papers and leaflets all over the place. I reach down to gather them up.

'Oh, don't worry,' he says. 'That's all junk. Promo stuff from drug companies, abstracts and whatnot. Nothing important.'

'Force of habit,' I say. 'Clearing up after men.' Then I straighten. He is now only six inches away from me.

'You smell nice,' he says suddenly.

Just familiar, I guess. But this is it, then, isn't it? I feel *sick*. 'I try to.'

'Coke OK?'

And faint too. 'Just fine.'

He rolls the bottle against his brow. 'God, I have to say, *I* feel *really* uncomfortable.'

And excited. Wow. 'So do I,' I agree.

'Do you?'

And then some. I gulp. 'Yes. I do.'

'Good,' he says, nodding also. 'That helps.'

'It does?'

'Greatly.' He then shrugs his jacket from his shoulders. I can see the fold marks across the front of his shirt. He yanks at his tie and undoes his top button. *God, I want to see his chest.*

'I'm glad,' I say. 'Not that you're feeling uncomfortable, of course. But that you've admitted to *me* that you're feeling uncomfortable. Makes me feel much better.'

He says 'Good' again, but looks no less tense. He tips his head back and pours some beer down his throat. His neck muscles move as he swallows. *He is too, too beautiful.* 'Though I wouldn't,' he adds, 'like to think you were feeling difficult about this. If you are, well, like I said before, we don't have to do this.'

'Oh,' I say. 'Don't *you* want to, then?'

'*God*, yes. But if you don't –'

I sit down on the bed, the '*God*, yes' spreading inside me like a large slug of rhino horn soup.

'Adam, I do. Believe me, I do. I think I might implode if I

don't get my hands on you pretty soon.'

He doesn't seem to know how to respond to this. I have no jacket to remove – I've already taken off my coat – and I don't want to plunge in and whip my dress off, but something tells me he needs tangible evidence. Something to break the inertia. I reach up and pull the scrunchie from my pony-tail.

'There,' I say. 'Take me.' He looks alarmed. I shake my head a little, so that my curls flop forward and frame my face. I know this looks good because I've had twenty years mirror practice. 'All right,' I coo. 'Kiss me, then. That'll be a start.'

He sits down – finally – on the end of the bed beside me. His weight shifts my own so I lean slightly towards him and his arm moves tentatively around my shoulder. He doesn't seem to want to kiss me properly, however, just brush my face with his lips and touch my cheek with his fingers. It's so gentle and tender that I begin to wonder if I am not being teased – the urge to crush my lips against his is almost irresistible.

I must be squirming or grunting because he then pulls back and inspects me.

'You OK?' he asks anxiously.

'Christ, yes,' I pant. 'OK and then some!'

Which seems sufficient reassurance because he then pulls me to him and kisses me properly; the whole bit, for some minutes, with much lust and abandon. Plus limbs, swirly hand movements, and plenty of frantic head rolling and breathlessness. This is it, I think, as he twiddles enthusiastically with my buttons. We're going to make love this afternoon. Adam is going to make love to me. *Is*. I help him by shrugging my arms from their sleeves, and then undoing his shirt. He hauls it from inside his trousers and lets it hang loose and unbuttoned, while his hand slides, inch by agonising inch, towards my bra. His fingers arc over the lace and he sighs. And I sigh, and he sighs some more, then we both sigh.

Point taken, the same hand sweeps round to the clasp.

Our eyes meet and hold. 'May I?' he asks.

And then, proprieties observed and respected, Adam changes gear. Suddenly, he has misplaced his shyness; indeed, he is now like a creature possessed. And I – well, forget all that old crap about waves crashing against beaches and fireworks exploding and twinkling eternity and the unbearable lightness of being and time stopping and drowning in stuff and spiralling and floating and velvet caresses and doves and stars and asteroids *and* earthquakes – Forget *all* that dreary euphemistic metaphorical metaphysical blah blah blah bilge – I am desperately, desperately, *desperately* horny and *nothing* I've wanted has ever come close to the wanting that grips me for Adam right now. My bra hits the ceiling, my head hits the bedspread and Adam's grey trousers hit the floor with a flump. His pants – the same boxers, but this time in navy – are ripped from his torso, by my own frenzied fingers, in less time than it takes to whip a contact lens out. And then there he is. The whole man. My hero. Glorious. Wild-eyed. Quivering. Huge.

'Christ!' he says, 'Charlie! OhGodOhGod! *Charlie*!' then crushes me to him and consumes me with kisses and finds his way in and then moans through my hair. I can't tell what he's saying now, and couldn't give tuppence; all my energies are focused on the exquisite sensation that I've never *ever* felt loved as intensely as this.

Of course, being flippant about the more romantic aspects of having a shag are strictly the preserve of the pre-coital phase. Once I'm curled up beside him (and the aftershocks have quietened), I feel as dizzy and dazzled and breathless and swoony as any self respecting eighteenth-century heroine would. Adam's chest hair, I note, as we meld and caress, is exactly the hue of the hair on my head. And his lips, still hell bent on more seismic activity, are so seamlessly fused to my own trembling skin now, that it's only the pulsing deep down in my stomach that alerts me to how much – oh, Adam! Oh, Adam! Oh, *Adam! OH, ADAM!* –

Then his mobile phone rings.

'Oh, bloody hell,' he groans. 'Ignore it.'

But we can't because immediately it stops ringing, it rings again.

I feel his sigh escape in a warm stream against my throat.

'Don't worry,' he reassures me. 'It'll go on divert if they ring for long enough.' He returns his attention to kissing my breast.

Silence falls again – bar our again ragged breathing – but within minutes the tootling noise starts up again.

'Why don't you just answer it?' I ask him. 'Then it's dealt with, isn't it?'

What a silly, silly thing to say.

He pushes himself up onto his knees and reaches across to the chair for his jacket.

'I can't believe it,' he groans. 'The last call I had on this was you, yesterday. Why now? I'm at a bloody conference, aren't I? Who the hell can it be?'

He slips the phone from his jacket pocket and peers at the display. It must, I realise, be one of those phones that indicate the number that's called, because his expression suddenly changes and he climbs off the bed. Then he wordlessly presses the button to answer and takes his naked self to the en suite to talk.

Davina, then. Has to be. Bloody hell. Why her? Why now?

I sit up on the bed, feeling suddenly vulnerable, and meet my reflection in the reproduction mirror. I am pink and my hair is a seething great wasps' nest. I look like a badly permed extra from *Cats*. I lie back down again and roll over, dragging the paisley bedspread protectively around me. Adulterers, I suppose, do get used to this stuff. Either that or they organise their deceit so efficiently that when they're together their phones are switched off. What babies we two are. What sad, fumbling people.

Adam's voice rumbles out through the tiling and plasterboard. I can't make out the words but the tone is clear enough. He doesn't sound cross. Or irritable, either. Just quietly pissed off. Which is just how I feel. I turn over again.

Stand up. Get my Diet Coke. Drink some. Then begin the slow process of retrieving my clothes.

He emerges.

'Davina.'

I nod at him. 'Guessed so.'

He sees what I'm doing and starts doing likewise. 'Wanted to know if we're free Friday fortnight. Jesus! There's some big charity dinner dance we've been invited to, apparently. And she has to know *now*, of course, because there's going to be some big-noise planning types there or something. Who need impressing. *Jesus*. As if I'm some bloody mascot she trails round behind her. And like dinner-dances are *so* important in the scheme of things, aren't they?' He waves his hand to take in me, the bed, himself. All *this*. 'As if they're so *fucking* important, you know?'

He downs the rest of his beer in one long swallow, then picks up the second bottle and slams off the top against the side of the desk. The metal disc rattles and spins for a moment. Then is still. Adam stares at it, hand on his forehead, a faint sheen of moisture still wet on his brow.

I don't know what to say to him. I have never heard him swear. I have never seem him angry. I cannot recall a time when he's said anything bad about his wife. I feel suddenly as if I'm in the room with an absolute stranger. And that I most want to do, all of a sudden, is go home and cry. But he must see the chasm of reality that has now gaped between us, because he comes and sits down beside me again and holds me very tight.

'I'm so sorry,' he says into my hair. 'I'm so, so, *so* sorry. What a mess.'

'Yes.' It comes out as a whisper. Not my voice at all. A small, desolate thing.

He moves to look at me. Touches my face. 'And you were right, of course. About it all ending in tears. Except –'

'What?'

'Except, Christ. Is that it?' His eyes bore into mine then he's up and off again, prowling around me, pulling on his boxers, donning the shirt which means next time I touch him, it won't smell of him, feel of him – won't *be* him any more. 'I don't know where we go now,' he says. 'I don't know what we do.'

I don't either. Except I should do, but can hardly bear to give the thought credence.

'I think I go home,' I say, wrenching my clothes on. 'And you go back to your conference, and then we make that effort I've been banging on about. You know, the one that involves not seeing one another. Not communicating with each other any more.'

He shakes his head. 'Don't say that, Charlie. I don't think I can.'

'But you have to. You are married. And I,' I am up now, 'can't live with this.' I point to the phone, which, its treachery done, now lies abandoned on the desktop, in the spotlight of the Tiffany lamp. 'I can't live with any of it. And neither can you.'

We are facing each other across six inches of tasteful pastel carpet. He runs gentle fingers across my forehead and loops my hair behind my ears. Such a physical, *intimate* thing to be doing.

'I can't *not*, Charlie. Not now.' He moves forward to kiss me.

Instinctively, I find myself pulling away. 'God, Adam. I told you! I can't do this! It's as if she's in the room with us now, for God's sake. *Isn't* it? Doesn't it feel like that to you?'

I step back, leaving him framed by the window, his beautiful broad shoulders sloped in defeat.

'No! It isn't! You're here, I'm here. No one else is! Forget it, can't you? *Can't* you?'

'No, I can't. Not when you'll be going back to her tomorrow! Not when you'll be going home and slipping into bed beside her! You don't have to deal with *any* of that stuff! Oh, you can concoct all your little fantasies about *me*. Imagine what *I* might be doing. Reinvent me as some sort of irresistible siren. Keep me chaste in your head. Whatever! There are no grim realities to deal with. No wonder you were so bloody keen to see Phil packed off! Well, from *this* end of the deal, it's not quite so rosy, believe me.'

He moves a step closer to me.

'I don't sleep with her, Charlie.'

'Oh, diddums! I wondered when we were going to get around to that old chestnut. And do we get the next one? That pigs bloody fly.'

'I don't. We haven't. Not for over a year now. We even have separate bedrooms, for God's sake.'

He looks as if he'd like me to pop round and confirm it. 'Oh, please –'

'Look, I'm not trying to justify anything, Charlie. Just stating a fact.'

'Ah! And don't tell me. She doesn't understand you?'

He pulls on a sock and then shakes his head. 'I'm not sure understanding me is high on her list of priorities. I'm just *there*. But that isn't the point. What's important is that I no longer understand her.'

'And what *exactly* am I supposed to do about that?' I snort. 'As if I much care anyway. And don't talk to me about her not understanding. You should try working for her some time.'

As soon as I say it, I bitterly regret it. The one thing I really don't want to do is bitch about Davina. I feel quite low enough. But before I can get my retraction worded and spoken, he says. 'That wasn't worthy of you, even if it is true.'

Which makes me mad.

'I bloody well know that, thank you. I'm not myself. Can't think why. Perhaps it's because I haven't been making too many successful life choices lately. Bit like you, I guess. But while we're on the subject, just for the record, she certainly isn't worthy of you.'

He sits down again and pushes his hands though his hair. 'What a mess.'

'You already said that.'

'No, I mean my *life*. What a fuck-up.'

'I don't need to hear this. I don't need the run-down on

why we got to here, thank you. Or, more specifically, why *you* got to here. Don't try tugging at my heartstrings about it. If your marriage is a cock-up then you should go home and sort it.'

I nearly said 'end it', but thank goodness I didn't.

'Believe me, I've been trying,' he said. 'Year in, year out. Trouble is, we've never been able to work out what the problem is. It's just got steadily worse.'

I recall Rose's words about her and Matt's problems.

'Then you should try harder,' I hear someone say. Can't be me. 'You should deal with it. You should talk. Not spend your time sending flirtatious emails to strangers.'

His eyes flick up but he doesn't rise to it. He shakes his head. 'Oh we've done plenty of talking. Still do, as it happens. I say "what's the matter" and she says "I don't know." It gets a touch repetitive, you know? She's seeing someone now though. Has been for some months.'

I gape. '*Seeing* someone?'

'A therapist. To work through her problems.'

'And?'

'And nothing. Not much, anyway. The only progress we seem to have made is acknowledging that Davina has some sort of deep-rooted psychological problem that we need to make progress with. But that, apparently, *is* progress.'

His words chill me so much that I can feel the winter afternoon drawing its frosty tendrils around me. This doesn't sound dead in the water to me. The word 'progress' hangs between us like a starched white hankie on a washing line.

'But she still loves you?'

'She says so. Just doesn't want to have sex with me. And wants children – badly. Just doesn't want to do what you need to do to get them.'

God, I think, you just never know. This new Davina is surreal.

'And you're sure there's no one else?'

He shakes his head. 'This isn't like that, Charlie. She says not. I believe her. She's in a mess. She's ill. She's –'

220

'And you still love her.' My voice has dropped a whole octave.

His eyes meet mine and hold them.

'I care about her. I do care about her, Charlie. God, wouldn't it all be so easy if I didn't? And, Christ, I *married* her. But since meeting you –'

'You mean emailing me.'

'Yes, of course. Everything's changed.'

I turn away, so he can't see the tears sloshing about in my eyes, but he turns too and pulls my face around. Suddenly I no longer care if he sees it.

'And not just for you!' I shout. 'I don't need all this grief! I'm not going to be the sex in your bloody stale marital sandwich!'

'Look, I know what you want from me. I know how you feel. God, if only I could –'

'Turn the clock back?' I start collecting up the small evidences of my passing. My boots, my handbag. My swizzled-up scrunchie. I feel dirty.

'Please don't do this.'

'Do what? Leave this situation with some modicum of dignity?' The tears are tracking down my face now. I sit on the bed and zip up my boots, then start rummaging for my Handy Andies. He kneels in front of me.

'Charlie, we can't just draw a line under this. It's not going to go away. Not now.'

I snap my body back upright. 'How many more times are you going to spin me that line? We're both adults! We can draw a line under any bloody situation we like! It just takes a little strength of character. It just takes knowing what you want, for goodness sake!'

He stands up as well.

'I know what *I* want,' I tell him. 'I want out of this. You go and tend your sick wife and leave me to go climb my mountain.' I yank my handbag over my shoulder and head towards the door.

'But I need you –'

No, not that. I swivel. 'So leave *her*!'

His eyes drop. Six unhappy seconds thump by.

They rise again briefly. 'Charlie, I can't.'

Adam's words, now released from their home in my nightmares, seem to flutter and dance in the light from the lamp.

'Exactly,' I say, quietly, pulling the door open. 'I'm done here, I think.'

I go down via the stairs.

It is barely five but already the February night is reclaiming the city. Car headlamps stream back and forth in the murk, and the offices are beginning to spew out their gaggles of typists and clerks. It's far enough to the car park that I don't want to walk. I can't seem to stop the huge gulping sobs that have accompanied my flight down the hotel stairs, and I can't face the curious looks of commuters. When I see the welcome orange glow of a taxi *for hire* light, I don't care that it's headed the wrong way.

'Cost you, darling,' the cabbie says, incurious, yet smiling. 'Traffic like this, you'd be quicker to walk.'

I climb in regardless and we head off through the car-scape, my fistful of tissue a tight ball in my lap.

He is right, of course. It takes close to twenty minutes to double back through the side streets, but I've at least dried my eyes and regained some sort of control. I pay my parking fee – a king's ransom for four such deeply miserable hours – and take the lift down to where my car waits. All I want to do now is get home, get my life back. It'll take a good hour, I suppose, to get out of London, but with luck and dry weather, I should be home before nine.

Another unsatisfactory encounter.

I recall little of the journey home. Ten minutes out of London and I remember that I left my mascara and tweezers and coconut ChapStick on the shelf in the en suite in Adam's room. And I start crying again. And then I cannot stop crying.

I simply *cannot* stop crying. I cry hot salty tears till my throat feels like gravel, curse Adam, curse me, curse Davina, curse marriage, curse the moon and the stars and the inky night sky. I feel alone in a way that I could never have imagined; a remnant of myself; a small ragged scrap.

But, somehow, I get there.

I finally slew into the drive, still sniffing, and yank the hot car to a shuddering stop. As well as all the cares in the world, I have returned, I remember, with a smelly Sainsbury's plastic basket, which Rose has thoughtfully filled with some of Matt's organic bounty; three cabbages, some parsnips, and about a million fat sprouts. My lot now, my prize. My foreseeable future. Making sprout soup, or hotpot, or sweet parsnip batons. Not love. Not with Adam. Not with *Adam*.

After dumping the basket on the doorstep, I am just returning to the car for my suitcase when I become aware of my front door opening and someone coming out of the house.

'Ah,' says a male voice. '*There* you are. Thank goodness!'

But it is not Dad, and not Ben and (as if it would be) not Adam.

The voice is joined by a body.

'Good God!' I say. '*Phil?*'

'Charlie,' he says, waving.

'Phil!' I say, boggling.

'Yes, it *is* me' he confirms. Then says, 'Charlie, it's your dad.'

Chapter 22

FOR A MOMENT MY ears must have seized up or something. 'What are *you* doing here?' I asked, quite unable to fathom. Was it a development in the Rose / Phil affair?

Phil took the case from me and trundled in through the front door. He had already deposited the veg in the hall. I followed him, mute and uncomprehending.

'Your father, Charlie,' he said gently.

'Dad?'

'Yes.'

'*Dad?* What about him?'

'He's in hospital. Look, you mustn't worry –' He took my arm at this point and squeezed it reassuringly '– he's not in grave danger, or anything. They think he went into a diabetic hypo – or was it hyp*er*? Anyway, whatever it was, he hit his head. Come on. I'll drive you to the hospital. Karen's down there with Ben.'

By the time I had digested this sufficiently to obliterate traces of the sudden, violent and terrifying image of my father lying dead in the hospital morgue, Phil had already steered me to his car and fed me into the passenger seat.

'But Dad doesn't have diabetes,' I said.

He shrugged as he switched the ignition on.

'Apparently, he does. So they said, anyway. But we'll know more, I'm sure, soon.' He glanced across at me. 'Don't *worry*. He's OK.'

I tried to work out why all this meant I was sitting in Phil's car.

'But when did this happen? And why are *you* here? And Karen, and –'

'Ben called me. He's such a sensible lad. He said you were away and that his grandad had collapsed and hurt his head and that he wasn't sure what to do. He was very calm, very grown-up about it.'

'But when was this?'

'About three. Maybe earlier.' He manoeuvred the car around a mini roundabout. God, what had *I* been doing at about three? Oh, Lord.

'So I came straight over,' he said. 'Lucky we were in, as it happened. We were supposed to be going on a coppicing weekend, but they'd cancelled it because of some local flooding. Anyway, Ben told me you'd spent the week at Rose's – how is she, by the way?' Not a pause, not a flicker. 'And she told me about you visiting the embassy and so on, and that she doubted you'd be home much before ten –'

Embassy? So on? Jesus. *What?*

'Um. Yes. She's fine. Um. Traffic wasn't too bad. But was Ben OK? Oh, *poor* Ben. What a dreadful thing to happen with me not here. Oh, poor Ben. If only –'

His hand brushed my arm. 'Don't fret about it. You were doing your bit down at Rose's. You had no way of knowing something like this would happen, did you?'

'Yes, but – oh, *poor* Ben. Poor *Dad*.'

'But everything's *fine*, Charlie. So don't beat yourself up about it.'

Rose said that. Rose did. Her expression, or his?

'I know, but –'

'But nothing. What are friends for?'

If only he knew.

We drove on in the darkness for a few minutes. Funny to be sitting here in Phil's familiar car (the same Volvo?) with Phil's familiar profile beside me, Phil's familiar pale hands on the steering wheel. In some ways it all seemed a lifetime ago. Yet, for a moment, I could half see myself back with him. The gentle pace of an undemanding relationship, the lack of expectation; the absence of stress. Yet now I knew what I knew he seemed completely unfathomable. As if there was a whole chunk of him I'd never quite managed to find. If only he *did* know, I pondered. He'd been there, hadn't he? He'd surely know how to cope. We stopped at the lights by the hospital entrance. He turned.

'Charlie, are you OK? You look –'

'Like shit. I know. Tell me about it.'

He looked closer. Nodded.

'Your eyes –'

I tutted dismissively. 'You know London. Pollution Central.'

Which explanation he made a good attempt at looking like he believed. Not good enough, but his best shot, I supposed.

'OK,' he said.' Here we are, then. Your Dad's been taken to Helen Keller ward. I'm not sure what the plan for the head injury is. Still, we'll sort all that out now. Now you're home safely.'

We thread our way up and onto the ward. I see Karen first. She's in smiling conversation with the sister. Belatedly, I remember that she's a nurse. A good person to have around in a crisis. A good person, full stop. Which makes me feel wretched. Because I too am now a defiler of marriages. I have colluded and deceived. I have lied. Phil beckons.

'Here we are then,' he says again brightly. As if we've assembled for an interval drink in the theatre. Do I detect now the merest hint of discomfort in his voice? On my behalf, I suspect, given the logistics of our relationships. He knows nothing of the maelstrom that my life has been since him. I thank them both, profusely, persuade them that Ben and I really will be fine getting a cab home, and hurry off to see my father. I turn to wave as I reach the bed, but they are just turning the corner. Hand in hand. OK. Happy even, I suspect.

Ben stands as I arrive and straight away shoves his hands in to the pockets of his jeans. This means he wants a cuddle but cannot bring himself to instigate it. His expression tells me not to touch him. Not yet. But compassion almost overwhelms me. He is trying so hard not to cry. How many hours of being brave, being together? My poor baby. I bustle and fuss and don't offer too much gushing sympathy. I know he'll hold out if we're matter-of-fact about things. My father, understanding, does likewise and clucks at me. The short term-plan for his head injury, it seems, is to make him look like a comedy toothache poster. He resembles the little fat pig from Bugs Bunny.

'Charlotte, *there* you are,' he chides. His voice is warm and reassuring. 'Trust you to be off gallivanting when I'm busy falling over.' He laughs. 'And trust me to do it, eh? Eh, Ben? Trust your silly old grandad!' He grins. 'What a palaver! All this nonsense for the want of a little sugar. Then he stops. And peers at me. 'Charlotte? What on earth's happened to your face, dear? You look absolutely dreadful – like you've collided with a tree!'

At which point I have no choice but to abandon my composure. Because, quite without meaning to, I flop down on the bed with him and try as I might not to, I howl and howl and howl.

But he's going to be fine. The X-rays confirm it. And Ben and I, relieved, make our way home not long after. What we both need is sleep; him for growth, me for oblivion, but if telephones could get up and tap people insistently on shoulders, the Simpson telephone would be doing just that as we tumble, exhausted and drained, into the house. It's Rose.

'God, there you are! What's been going on? Is your father OK?'

I say, 'Yes, yes, yes,' and collapse in a heap by the telephone table. Ben steps over me and heads into the kitchen, clutching the burger and chips we picked up for him on the way home.

'So what happened?'

'He had a diabetic hypo, apparently. And then fractured his skull just to finish the job.'

'Poor old sod.'

She's been drinking, obviously. It's now eleven thirty. Fourteen hours since she waved me off, full of vicarious excitement. Fourteen hours. How many of them has she spent rewinding her life? Then I remember that Phil phoned her to find out what time to expect me. How untimely. What a shock

227

to have to talk to Phil just as she's dredged out his memory and dusted it off.

'Look,' I say. 'Can I call you back in a minute? I must get poor Ben sorted.'

But Ben's voice rattles out from the other side of the kitchen door. He is anxious to reassert his masculine autonomy after his little cry in the car.

'Mum, I'm *fine,*' he mumbles through his mouthful. 'Talk to Rose. I'm going to bed now. I really don't need any sorting.'

So I do, blowing kisses as he thunders up the stairs.

'You OK?' I ask Rose.

'Me? What you asking *me* for, stupid? I'm fine. Fine and dandy. Clear, Charlie. OK. It's you lot I'm worried about.'

'OK? As in –'

'As in no cancer. You see? Nothing to worry about.'

'Oh, Rose! Thank *God!* You must be so relieved!'

' –ish, Charlie. Relieved-*ish*. It's as if it was all a dream now. Funny.'

There is a silence. A cough.

I wish I could wave a wand and bring her here instantly. I know what she most needs is someone to be with. But not Matt. Not right now.

'Oh, Rose –'

'Come on.' She says sternly. 'Buck up, Charlie girl. I want to know all about *you*.'

'I'm OK,' I say. 'And Ben's fine. And Dad's got his head bandaged.

'Poor old love. And diabetic. What's with the diabetic? You never said he was diabetic. Christ, the man lives on jam!'

'Quite. I didn't *know* he was diabetic. I can't believe he never got around to telling me about it. But he's not very accepting of illness at the best of times, so I guess not discussing it is his way of dealing with it. Anyway, it's not as bad as it sounds. It's controlled by tablets. No insulin injections or anything. Just tablets and a careful observance of diet. Which he obviously failed to observe today.'

'Careful observance. I like that. Sounds faintly fetishistic.' She laughs. A bit wildly. I wish *I* was drunk. I make a mental note: must get drunk very soon.

'And what about you?' I say. 'Are you alright *really?*'

She knows what I mean. 'For God's sake!' she snaps. 'Don't start on that again. If I thought for one instant I'd have this sort of nonsense from you, Charlie, I'd never have told you the first thing about it.' There's another silence, into which she's struggling not to put sobs, then she rallies.

'It's all frothing on the surface a bit, actually. But don't worry; it'll subside again soon.'

'Oh, Rose –'

'Oh, nothing. It's just sentimentality. It doesn't mean anything. Just, well, you know –'

'Phil ringing you like that must have been a bit –'

'Tosh, Charlie Simpson, and you just stop all this right now! I phoned up to find out what it is *you've* been doing all afternoon. At least, the edited highlights. I don't need the squishy bits. Come on. Let's have the debrief.'

I have as little stomach for talking about it as she has for talking about Phil. But I have to say *some*thing. But what?

'Which reminds me,' I stall her. 'What was all that embassy stuff? I didn't have a clue what Phil was on about.'

'God, yes! I just didn't know what to say! It was the first thing that came into my head!'

'An *embassy*?'

'The Nepalese one. A bit of inspired invention on my part, actually, now I come to think of it. You know, to go and sort out your visa or something.'

'Do I need one?'

'God, I don't know! But it sounded plausible. You might do.'

'I suppose. Shame I told Dad I was on a shopping spree.'

'Oh, he won't have said anything. Would he now, *really*?'

'I suppose not.' I wasn't sure if she meant my Dad or Phil. Either way, I supposed it didn't really matter. There would be no further need for deceptions such as these.

'So?' she says. 'Well? Go on then, tell all.'

Saturday. Bluuurrrrghhh.

When I finished telling Rose the sorry story of my encounter with Adam, I felt so tearful and distressed again that I didn't even dare go in and kiss Ben goodnight, for fear of drowning him. Reason enough, I thought ruefully, not to do this stuff again. Ever. But he should be, I hoped fervently, already asleep.

Instead, I stripped off and buried myself under my duvet, where a party of nocturnal bed-living insects had some sort of illegal rave disco on my face.

At least that's the only reasonable explanation I could come up with for the state of the face that greeted me when I woke up the next morning. To say I looked the pits would be to cast a stain on the entire South Wales coal-mining heritage.

'Wow, Mum, you look dreadful! Ha!' said Ben, clearly recovered from his traumas. He chomped cheerfully on a toasted chocolate spread sandwich, shaking his head from side to side, like a masticating camel.

'Why "ha!"?' I said. 'Thanks.'

'How d'you get like that anyway?'

'Stress.'

'Stress? What stress have you got?'

For once I was glad of his lack of adult insight. He'd have more than enough of this sort of stress yet to come.

'By the way,' he said. 'Dan called yesterday. He's coming to stay next weekend if it's OK with you.'

Which made me feel a bit better, and needed, and focused, and that order, of a sort, could now be restored.

No cakes baked today, of course, but I manage to unearth four serviceable raisin flapjacks, so take those instead, wrapped in a square of tinfoil. I visit Dad first, but I have been usurped, armchair-wise, by the proprietorial Hester, who is making something unidentifiable from some brown wool and a crochet hook. And rather than hover at the foot end and feel

230

irritable, I decide I will detour to see Minnie instead.

'My lovely girl!' she greets me. I'm tempted to feel sniffy about the lack of similar gushy felicitations from my own flesh and blood father, but I am trying to nurture sufficient maturity to take it in my stride, like thread veins. Minnie looks well and fit and can now, she says, shuffle to the day room and back. She's still barking, of course, but no less dear for that.

'Minnie, look at you!' I say. 'Haven't you come on!'

'I've no truck with bedpans,' she observes, with some acuity. 'And you'll not find me lacking where a bit of grit is concerned.' She points to my package. 'Victoria sponge?'

'Flapjacks.'

'Don't eat them.'

'You do.'

'Not since the business with the war memorial. I always said they'd be hard pushed to capture Albert. And I was right, wasn't I? No telling, you see.'

'Absolutely.'

'And not one of them found, you know. The British Museum will have something to say about it. It's the Elgin Marbles all over again, you mark my words. So what have you been up to? Did you water my euphorbia?'

'I've been staying at my friend's house. She's been poorly, like you, so I went down to help her out with her children. You know Rose. I've mentioned her before, Minnie. The one who moved down to Canterbury.'

'And that young lad of yours?'

'Ben?'

'No!' she tuts. 'Your young chappie. Are you married yet? There's nothing to be gained by a long courtship these days.'

She's been fighting with the foil, so I take it and open it for her. 'D'you know what,' I say. 'I've come to the conclusion just lately that there's nothing to be gained in courtship at all. Just grief. I'm done with it.'

She hands me a flapjack.

'Do as you would be done by and you'll get your reward in heaven. Now, can you pick out the raisins, dear? Darned things always play merry hell with my plate.'

As I walk back down the ward again, the sister's voice reaches me.

'Who's that then, Minnie? A friend from The Maltings?'

I hear Minnie chuckle.

'That's my Iris,' she answers.

I find myself smiling. I mean, who does that hurt?

As Hester has also brought a box of Thornton's diabetic selection and a copy of *The People's Friend* with her, I do not feel it wise to stay long with my father. More than five minutes' worth of hearing about how a shirtwaister flatters the more mature figure, and I know I'll be weeping and wailing again. Cannot believe I've been crying so much. Decide, instead, that I will drive down to The Maltings for the spot of detective work I'd promised myself.

Minnie's room is at the end of a short carpeted corridor, with a window that looks over an expanse of flat lawn. There's a forsythia in bloom, which will please her no end, and, in the distance, a radio mast, which will obviously not. Her two cases stand in the corner, unopened, beside a chest of drawers topped off with a small bunch of early daffodils. Despite knowing they probably have a policy on the subject, I feel a stab of irritation; given the circumstances, it seems a pity the staff didn't bother to unpack.

I pull the cases onto the bed and clunk them both open. A musty smell mushrooms up; more evocative than unpleasant. There is little here in the way of clothing, but what there is I transfer on to the small clutch of hangers, or fold and find homes for in the large chest of drawers. I'd taken Minnie's washing bag and nightwear down to the hospital, and all that's left in one case now is an old onyx soap dish, inside which is a ring and a tiny dry sliver of soap. I close the lid and push the case under the bed. In the other however, is a large shoe box full of papers; most of which date back over the last fifty-odd years. I have no wish to pry, so I flick through these quickly; it's only references to Edward that I'm interesting in finding.

There are photographs too, some of them so old they look nibbled, and pretty soon I find myself looking into the dark eyes of a little girl whom I know must be Iris; her hair tumbles to her hips and she is barefoot. The picture is black and white, but I can see she's quite tanned, and the foliage around her is tropical and lush. I put it to one side to take back to the hospital, and continue my search for the mysterious son.

Which bears fruit before long. Inside an envelope I finally come upon the postcards; the ones the social worker had told me Edward periodically sends. She is right – they're from a wide variety of locations. Sydney Opera House, Ayers Rock, what looks like Easter Island, and all are written in a small, round, backward-sloping hand. They're signed Ted, although Minnie always calls him Edward. But then my father would no more call me Charlie than fly. I flick through a few of them, scanning the sentences. I'm aware again that the words are really none of my business, but there is little here, bar the usual touristy stuff.

There are a good thirty-odd postcards in the envelope, and my short inspection reveals four scribbled addresses; two in Australia, one in New Zealand, and one from somewhere unpronounceable in Singapore. Any of which could be a start. And all of which I can write to. I have no dates, of course; Minnie has ripped off all the stamps, and in doing so, the top right-hand chunk of each card.

I gather up the postcards and the photo of Iris, clear the cases away and head for home.

Chapter 23

SUNDAY.

'How went the Florence Nightingale bit, then?'

Make a mental note never again to answer a ringing phone. I will in future leave it to ring itself to exhaustion, before availing myself of the convenient 1471 facility and making a policy decision whether to pursue the conversation or otherwise. Because really don't feel like talking to Rhys right now.

'Hello,' I say, wondering how he knows about it. Or even, in fact, which 'it' he refers to. He expands.

'Your lad told me last week you were off down in Kent. Good time? Not too frazzling?'

'Fine,' I say. 'Tiring. But, yes, lovely to see her.' I can't seem to find any conversation to use. He clears his throat.

'Well,' he says, 'reason I called was to ask if you'd had any thoughts yet.'

'Any thoughts?'

'About the dinner. My invite? Week before last?'

'I'm sorry?'

A pause. Then, 'Thought so. Didn't get the message. Which would explain why you didn't answer my email as well.'

Email? Groan. I *don't* want emails. 'No,' I say. 'No. I didn't get either. Well, certainly not an invitation. I haven't looked to see if I had any emails last week.' (Will eat a spider sandwich before doing *that*.)

'Not to worry,' he says. 'Just that there's a bit of a charity bash in town weekend after next and I er … wondered if you'd like to er … dust a frock down or something and, er … come along to it with me. I recall you telling me how you could do with a bit of … well, anyway, what do you think? Are we on for it? I don't want to press, of course, but I'm off to a conference in Denver on Thursday, and I should really RSVP before I go.'

Dinner. Hmmm. Charity dinner. Hmmm. *That* dinner.

Gulp.

'So what do I do, Rose? What do I *do*?'

'Go to it.'

'Bah! How can I? I'm just going to burst into tears all over the place and get myself in a complete state. Besides, it's not fair on Rhys.'

'Then don't go.'

'But I feel I should, now he's asked me. Especially as he's been so kind. And if he's going off on a conference now, it's going to be a bit late for him to ask someone else, isn't it?'

'I shouldn't flatter yourself that your going is the biggest deal in his life to date, Charlie. He's a grown-up. I'm sure he could go on his own.'

'Which is all the more reason to go, come to think about it. If it's not such a big deal, then I don't need to feel so guilty about it, do I?'

'Then do go. Show Adam what you're made of. Show him you mean what you say. Show him it's over.'

'Over? It hardly even started! Anyway, this is not supposed to be *about* Adam, is it? This is supposed to be about me moving on, isn't it? So I *should* go with Rhys, shouldn't I?'

'I don't *know*! Look, Charlie, do you actually *like* Rhys Hazelton?'

'Yes. Yes, I do. We have a lot in common. And he's a nice, friendly, intelligent, uncomplicated, *single* bloke.'

But not Adam.

Monday. Nine ten.

First day of the rest of my life, in yet *another* new (and, this time, more sensible) incarnation. As a person for whom the sanctity of marriage is far more important than the selfish pursuit of personal gratification without regard to the consequences. I can kid myself if I like. I am in full PMT

235

flow. And I have also decided. Await Davina.

But cannot *believe* some people. Particularly cannot believe Hugh bloody Chatsworth, as he has left a card (a nasty soft focus photo of a croissant and coffee pot), plus a box of Bendicks Bittermints from Sainsbury's on full view at the front of his desk, the card carefully angled so that the name Rutland leaps out of the mire of his cess-pit desk-top, like a malevolent enemy periscope. I pick it up and read it.

My dear Hugh,

Just a quick note to thank you so much for expediting the sale of our darling Ditchers. Can't tell you what a weight it is off our minds to know that it's going to be home to such <u>lovely</u> people. Hope they will know as much joy as Mr Rutland and I have. Keep in touch. And thanks again – you've been a treasure. Best wishes, Meredith.

Meredith? I am tortured momentarily by an image of the Rutlands screwing on the grass in their ha-ha, then reflect that a woman who is named after a biscuit and who also calls her house "Darling Ditchers" probably doesn't screw; just has daddy's special cuddles or some such bilge. And I get it. I *get* it. They are complete racist bastards. Their reluctance re Habibs' offer all falls into place. Hope it turns out that a previously unrecorded plethora of public highways is scheduled for the locale forthwith. Hope a new international airport is in consultation stage as I read. I take two Bendicks Bittermints to consume with my morning coffee. Hope the flavour doesn't infect my psyche too much.

Ten twenty.

Reorganise the window display to ensure that properties on my own file are in prominent positions and properties on Hugh's are in dim corners at base. I realise that this is an utterly pointless exercise, but feel markedly better for doing so. Decide to fill a quiet moment by telephoning Social Services to discuss the Minnie / Edward situation. Feel not the slightest smidgen of guilt about use of the company phone, as I am, by rough reckoning, no small amount down on my deserved commission status, plus a zillion points up on the martyrdom scale.

Get through to Bernice via a few bars of *Finlandia*, an exhortation to hang on, and only four people. The rest must be herding the current week's jobseekers into pens.

'Hello, my lovely,' she says. 'Funny you should call today. I was just filing the paperwork for Mrs Drinkwater's house sale. Have you seen her?'

'On Saturday. And she's doing really well. She's almost mobile again.'

'Fair play, she's a one!'

She pauses for a benevolent titter. As people generally do where old mad ladies are concerned. Sometimes not even mad ones.

'I was calling about Edward,' I say. 'I had a chat with your colleague the other week, and I thought I'd have a go at trying to track him down for her. I've managed to find some postcards with addresses on them, but I thought I should ring you before sending a letter, because I believe there are a couple you've already tried. That's if it's not too much trouble, of course.'

'Not at all, lovely. Hold on and I'll dig out the file.'

I spend the five minutes while waiting for Bernice to return adding a cartoon tadpole to the logo on my Willie JJ scrap pad.

'Here we are,' she says at last.

I read out the addresses I have. Only two match with hers. So there are two still worth trying.

'That Singapore one,' she says, 'sounds quite hopeful, actually. I remember Minnie showing me a card from Singapore quite recently. No address on that one, though, as I recall.'

Mine certainly has one. 'Right,' I say. 'I'm on the case. I'll let you know if I hear anything.'

I feel like Philip Marlowe. Feel I am going to open a fat can of selfish bastard absentee son worms. Eat third and fourth Bendicks Bittermints and practise a dour and sleuthy expression. Find doing dour easier than it used to be, somehow. Practice smiling instead.

Await Davina.

Eleven fifteen.

Draft a short letter to the absentee Edward, and print out four copies. Address as per postcards. Still feel dour, so frank same.

Await Davina.

Twelve twenty. Right.

'Good morning' she says. 'Good week? Good weekend? How's Rose? Bearing up? Everything as it should be?'

In spite of the fact that I know she's not remotely interested in the answers, I tell her in some detail (where appropriate) how things went. Or perhaps because of. My mind is no more on this than hers.

'Right,' she says, jauntily, pinging her PC to life. 'Busy, busy, busy! Partners meeting at one thirty, Ianthe and her swatches at three, plus the dear old BM at four. So I'll need you on the case here, Charlie. Oh, and Hugh's at Brian's branch for the rest of the day now, so you'll have to hold the fort and get the ad copy done. Any viewings?' I nod. 'Then call Brian's PA, will you? You'll need to put the phone on divert.'

She's so jolly I half expect her to add tra-la, tra-lee and dance a little reel or something.

Davina,' I say. 'I need a word, if I may.'

Her head swivels.

'A word?'

I nod again.

'If I may.'

'About what?'

'About this.'

She is suddenly listening.

'My resignation,' I tell her. 'I'm handing it in.'

'You're what?'

'I'm leaving.'

I give her the letter. Which she takes, with a nod, and then, in a spooky re-run of Rose the week earlier, she screws up her face and promptly bursts into tears.

So much crying!

The telephone rang almost immediately after, so I turned around, walked back to my desk and took the call. It was Hugh, for Davina, but I told him she was busy and that she'd call him back just as soon as she could. Then I turned back, expecting the moment to have passed, but to my dismay, consternation and utter astonishment, not only had Davina not recovered her composure, but she was sinking ever more noisily into huge gulping sobs.

This? Over me? Over me leaving Willie JJ? Bloody hell. What a turn up. Unless … *Oh dear*.

Of course, I did the only thing humans can reasonably do in such situations. I walked back to her, said 'come here', bent down and put my arms around her. She sobbed against my shoulder for a good five minutes, then sighed heavily, released me and transferred her head to her hands.

'Ohh,' she said. 'Ohhhhhh. Oh, God. Oh, Charlie!'

I found my Handy Andies and gave her the whole pack.

I didn't know what to say, so I said, 'Davina, I don't know what to say. I never thought in a million years that you'd –'

'Ohhh,' she said again, dabbing at the tramlines in her foundation. 'It's just, ohh. Oh, *Charlie*.'

And started crying again.

I pulled a chair up. 'What's the matter?'

'Nothing. No, fuck it! *Every*thing!'

'I mean, you know, if this is a bad time, then –'

'Charlie, please. You *can't* leave.'

'But it's not as if –'

'It *is*. Please, not right now. I just don't think I could cope. *Seriously* –'. She gripped my hands in her own. She was very strong and it hurt. '*Seriously. Please*.'

She gave me my hands back.

'Well –'

'Thank God. Thank *God*.'

The face went back into the hands now and I could hear her sobbing again behind them. I picked up the notion of Charlie Simpson, utterly indispensable estate agent. Then tried it on for size and found it simply didn't fit. I twiddled the pen pot. I patted her arm. All my instincts were beginning to scream at me. Ask her what's the matter! *Ask* her, Simpson! Ask her what the matter is! That's what you *do*!

A sense of grave foreboding found its way into the office. Then singled me out and did what such senses do best. Thus, like the young girl in the nightie with the tiny stub of candle, I pulled the creaking door open and stepped out to find the ghost.

'What is it?' I said. 'What's *really* the matter, Davina?'

She sobbed some more into her hands.

'Efefeng,' she mumbled. 'sifly efefeng urg.'

I waited. Did some more patting and there-there-ing. Then said, 'Do you want to talk about it?' in that way that you do.

She spread her hands out and laid them palms down on the desktop. Then looked up and sighed heavily, which I took to mean yes.

'*Is* it work?' I said hopefully.

She dashed that. 'I wish it were that simple! No. It's not *work*. I mean, yes, in a way it is, I suppose. What's going on here is pretty much all I need right now, I can tell you. It certainly isn't helping matters. But no. If I'm honest. Not really, no. Except in so far as I've been so fucking obsessed with it. Jesus! Don't do it, Charlie. Don't think for a moment that all this,' she threw her arms wide, by which I assumed she meant the whole Willie Jones Jackson empire, 'will make you happy. *Oh*, no. Don't think that. OK?'

As if! I'd just handed my notice in, hadn't I? I waited while she took another tissue.

'Something else, then,' I said.

Deep breath. She nodded. 'It's me, Charlie. Me and Adam. *Adam*. No. Bollocks. It's *me!*'

While she gulped back the next bout of tears, I spent ten seconds trying to think how I'd respond to this situation were this situation entirely unfamiliar to me. But the time was wasted because in reality, you can't do that stuff.

'You?' I said, trying to keep the warble out of my voice.

'Me. God, it's hopeless, all of it. Hopeless!'

'What is?'

'My life.'

What a mess. You said that. No. I mean my life. What a fuck-up. I don't need to hear this.

Here we were again.

'Your life? In what way?'

Davina leaned forward and cradled her forehead in her fingers. As if she was studying a chess problem in the paper. Which she could have been. It must have felt like one. Intractable, frustrating, utterly perplexing. Then she looked at me.

'How old were you when you had Daniel, Charlie?'

Oh, God. The baby thing. I took a deep breath. 'Twenty-one…'

'God, *young*. And Ben?'

'A bit older. Almost twenty-seven.'

'And then?'

'And then nothing.'

'Then your marriage broke up.'

'Not quite then. A bit after.'

'Why?'

I didn't know where this came from or where it was going; only that I rather wished it wasn't going there with me lashed to the bumper. 'We just fell out of love,' I said.

Her face crumpled again. And this time I fancied mine might start having a go at it too.

I took her arm. '*What*, Davina? Tell me. What is it?'

'I'm thirty-seven,' she sobbed. 'And it's too late! And it's just all so, so … Oh, God. What's the use?'

'In what?'

'In talking about it. It's as if it's the biggest thing in a

241

woman's life, isn't it? It's such a big thing to have to let go of. It's so hard to have to come to terms with the fact that you've missed the boat. Got it wrong. Fucked up. That *I've* fucked up, and that it's all too late now!'

'But it isn't! It needn't be! Women even have children in their fifties, these days! You know that!'

I was trembling with the agony of forcing those words out, but she didn't notice. She was shaking her head again. And though she didn't realise it, we both knew why.

'Not me,' she said softly. 'Not me.' Then her voice began to rise again. 'And Adam! What about him? He's nearly forty, for God's sake! He's got –'

But she didn't tell me just what it was that he had. Though I did have a bit of an inkling, of course. Instead she said, 'What about you? How did it happen? How could you just fall out of love like that? *How*?'

Oh, Christ.

I exhaled. 'We just did, Davina. It happens. Felix was in the Navy – *is* in the Navy. I suppose we just didn't spend enough time together. It was a gradual thing. You know, you start off wishing the time away when you're apart and counting the days till you're together again and then one day you wake up and you suddenly realise that you're doing the opposite. I was wishing him away again, so I could get on with my life.' I shrugged. 'And he was doing the same. It wasn't acrimonious or anything. Just horrible for the kids and, well, sad.'

She stared at her tissue. Then sniffed.

'And that was that?'

'Pretty much. Looking back. Which I generally try not to. I don't find it helps.'

She nodded.

'It was never like that for us, you know? Never passionate. Never urgent. I see that now. But it didn't mean I didn't love him. I just – I just wasn't very good at all that. You know? It wasn't *me*. And we weren't young like you were. So we didn't *expect* it to be like that. You know? We'd got beyond all that.

242

Or so *I* thought. I thought it would all work out fine. I thought we'd get married, have babies, settle down, do all that stuff. But we never quite seemed – *I* never quite seemed to – oh, you know. There was always work, and developing the business and everything. And I didn't realise –' she pushed the tissue into her face as she spoke, 'I didn't *realise*, Charlie. And now look at all these years we've wasted – *I've* wasted. Shit, *he's* wasted! On me! And now look at us! I can't blame him for hating me, can I? God, it's all such a mess!'

Hating her? Suddenly something that had up to now not occurred to me, occurred to me like a right hook in the face. Had Adam said something to her? *Done* something? Oh, God! What?

But there weren't any clues. And I wasn't about to start asking.

'It isn't too late to sort it out, Davina,' I told her. 'Not if you really want it to work. Not if –'

She was shaking her head again.

'Yes it is,' she said slowly.

Then she stood up, abruptly, checked the time, blew her nose. So that was it. For the moment. I felt wrung out. She looked it.

'Coffee?' she asked me.

We exchanged a wan smile.

'Yup. Too late,' she muttered, heading for the staff room. Then she turned in the doorway, her hand on the jamb.

'Funny, isn't it?' she said. 'When we were first together, and Adam was still a junior doctor; you know, exams, ridiculous hours and so on, I used to say how much I'd like a daughter – I always wanted a little girl – and he'd say, "Oh, no. Not yet. There's only room for one tyrannical woman in this family." That sort of thing. And now look at us.' She thrummed her nails against the woodwork. 'Ironic, isn't it?'

Something in me wanted to put a hand up and confess. But then she laughed. Said 'Huh! Three *is* a crowd. No doubt about that.'

So she knew. She knew very well. The fact, if not who the

actual female was. I don't know why, but I answered, 'Like Princess Diana said.'

She cocked her head to one side, as if considering, and then nodded.

'Yeah,' she said, the door closing behind her. 'I suppose.'

Should I telephone Camilla? Compare notes? See if she has any handy tips for keeping a profile that's low enough below the parapet that you don't get picked off by a sniper? I know there is nothing in my father's little books to cover this overwhelming sense of guilt and anguish. Know as I have read all father's books from cover to cover and have reached the conclusion that people who read such books are generally people in need of only a gentle prod to excel at almost every aspect of their saintly personal interactions, and for whom an overwhelming sense of guilt and anguish is not part of life. Or so much a part of life that they think fuck the books and call the Samaritans instead.

Have become a very drunk person. Have become a very drunk person on a Monday night. Have become a very drunk person on a Monday night that is to be shortly followed by a Tuesday with six viewings (including one in a house where I am sure they eat composted crustacean remains for breakfast) before 11 a.m. Have become a very drunk person on a Monday night followed by a Tuesday with six smelly viewings and without a cheering, devil-may-care, have-handed-in notice-and-don't-give-stuff-any-more cushioning. Because I haven't handed in my notice after all and give a great deal more stuff than an ordinary, perfectly nice person can be reasonably expected to cope with.

And so much want to see myself as an ordinary, perfectly nice person, but cannot. Have been an irresponsible absentee mother, leaving poor younger son no doubt traumatised permanently, and have been a self-serving, cavalier, absentee daughter, leaving my father to flail helplessly at death's very jaw. And now have confirmation that I have utterly wrecked a marriage; the marriage, moreover, of a person for whom life is

244

already, clearly, one big crock of shit. That I am totally alone, bar the cat, seems appropriate (Ben at a sleepover), though it can only be a matter of time before the cat also shuns me, and desists from returning to poo in the porch.

Very much want to send a rambling, self-pitying email to Rose, but dare not enter the study as will be sucked in by log-on tractor beam like Starship Enterprise. Could call Rose, of course, but cannot in all conscience bring myself to as is very late on Monday night and normal people do not wish to be telephoned late on Monday night by drunk women with intractable personal problems. Except the Samaritans. And cannot in all conscience call the Samaritans as will clog the line with my own piffling (in scheme of things so fucking important, I don't think) problems and will perhaps as a consequence cause a suicide off the Second Severn Crossing by a person with real problems who couldn't get through. Like Davina. Oh *God.*

Strange to be feeling so awful about Davina. Strange and humbling. I have worked for Willie Jones Jackson for almost five years and in all that time I have never really got to know her at all. Have never looked beyond her brusqueness and temper; never wondered why she relates to the world as she does. And even though I know it's as much her fault as mine, I can't help thinking the onus was on me. As if everything bad in my small sphere of influence is suddenly my responsibility to put right, to make better. Ergo, Tuesday;

'Yes, Rhys. I'd love to. Thank you so much for inviting me.'

'Well, that's splendid!'

He sounded so pleased I suddenly wished I'd flipped heads and said no. But he, was, I reflected, a fully grown man with more opportunity than most for a shag (not patients, obviously, but given proximity to female environment generally ...). And a fully grown man with control of his feelings. I wasn't leading him on. Just attending a dinner dance. That was all. No strings. Zippo.

'By the way,' he added. 'Just read an absolutely

unputdownable book about an Everest summit attempt. It's called *The Death Zone*. You will *love* it. So I've given it to Adam to pass on to you for me. He said he'd drop it round to you. See you Saturday week.'

Cross, cross, cross. Was tempted to ring back and cancel the dinner dance date altogether, as the Adam / Rhys / *Death Zone* juxtaposition plunged my mood into such an abyss of jangly monsters, buzzy stingy things, ghoulies, etc., that I doubted I would conjure sufficient composure to even open the front door. But I didn't, as it was utterly not Rhys's fault. I resolved, instead, that when the book delivery happened, I would be mature, be calm, answer the door, say hello, accept the book, say thank you, shut the door. Done.

Oh, but what hard work life could be.

Davina arrived in the office at midday.

'Hello!' she chirped, as if absolutely nothing had happened (though I was now deeply suspicious of her new, jaunty tone).

'Hello!' I chirped back, with equivalent trill. She picked up the phone and called Austin Metro. I knew it was him because she said 'Austin, *por favor*!' to the telephonist, but regrettably, I was unable to establish the details, as was called myself then, by Mr Habib. But it was, I could tell, an acrimonious exchange.

She slammed the phone down and went straight out again. Thirty seconds later, she was back for her briefcase. Which she grabbed wordlessly, then stalked back to the door. She yanked it open, then turned.

'Tell me,' she said, eyes flashing, hair like a golden windsock, 'tell me *absolutely* honestly. Do you *like* your uniform, Charlie?'

Uuurgh. 'Well, I –'

'Stop! No procrastination! Just a simple yes or no.'

'No.'

'Not at all?'

'No. Not really. It's –'

'Uh-huh,' she said. 'Right. See you.'

And was gone.

Spookily reminiscent of my time down in Canterbury, Rose rang just as I was shovelling the last of my *brussels con lardons* into the swing-bin.

'Where the bloody hell have you been?' she demanded.

'Out.'

'Out where?'

'Um, let me see. The RSPCA, the hospital, the dry cleaner's and the twenty-four-hour Tesco store.'

'Why?'

'Um, let me see. Cat, Dad, Minnie, dress, trainers. Not necessarily in that order. Oh, yes, and Burger King. For dinner.'

'Busy.'

'I should say! Actually, no. Just pathetic.'

'In what way?'

'In going out.'

'Why?'

'I've been out because of Adam'

'Why because of Adam?'

'Because of the book.'

'What book?'

'The book that Rhys is lending to me and that he's given Adam to drop round to me. I can't face him, Rose.'

'Pah! Of course you can, you ninny. You just get Ben to answer the door and tell him you're out.'

'I can't do that! I can't have Ben colluding with low-life deceit!'

'Hardly low-life deceit.'

'It's the thin end of the wedge, believe me.'

'Oh, rubbish! D'you get my email?'

'Not you as well.'

'What?'

'No, I didn't get your email. I don't do emails any more. I don't do computing. I am returning to my natural state of technological indifference. In preparation for harmonising more fully with the Nepalese way of life.'

'Don't be daft.'

'It's not daft, Rose. It's self-preservation. And what's with everyone these days? Why do people keep sending me emails all the time? God, I wish I'd never given out my email address. Davina will be emailing me next, asking for marriage guidance. Or my father, God love him, requisitioning socks.'

'When's he home?'

'Thursday. Anyway, what was *your* email about?'

'I think we'll draw a veil over my email, Charlie. Doesn't matter. Forget it. What are you going to wear for the do?'

Rats. Veil over what?

Eleven thirty-seven.

Best friends are a bloody pain in the arse at times.

Take a firm line. I am *not* going to log on and read Rose's email. Tomorrow perhaps. One day at a time.

Wednesday

Hmmm. Another worrisome Metro development. After work (two sales – Everest fund now truly amazing £1574.39; my broken heart is financially heart-warming, at least) drive to the hospital via the dry cleaner's. And spot a familiar Jag parked outside swish 'Zone' bar nearby. I peer in and spot Austin Metro at the counter, sporting mobile, cigar, and stupid Mexican beer. Think nothing of it (other than that Austin Metro is way too old and crabby to be swigging speciality lagers with scorpions in) until I see Hugh bloody Chatsworth is in there as well. *With* Austin. Laughing. Hmmm.

'I think they're in cahoots,' I tell Dad at the hospital. 'I think something's going on. Something I don't like the look of.'

'Not liking the look of things never won any wars,' he says obliquely.

'And there's the uniform business. It's all rather

disquieting.'

He taps his nose. 'Intelligence. You need facts, Charlotte, facts. Now then,' he adds, brandishing a Sainsbury's carrier. 'That Dr Jones friend of yours dropped this bag off.'

Dr Jones chap. Asthma clinic. Hospital. Wednesday. Sensible. Of course. Of course. Of course. All that fretting! What a silly billy!

I open the bag in the privacy of my car, in the hospital car park. As well as a colossal lump of extreme disappointment in my throat, I find the book, as promised, plus toiletry items; mascara, coconut ChapStick and tweezers. Plus a small bag with a CD in it. From HMV Oxford Street. Tchaikovsky. Symphony No. 1; Winter Daydreams.

No note. No message. No nothing.

No need.

Thursday.

In a seriously dangerous frame of mind. And I am not unobserved.

'Hugh?'

He starts. Looks shifty. Puts the phone down. Scowls.

'Hugh, tell me something. Just what's going on around here?'

He picks up a silage-hued Willie JJ ballpoint. 'Going on?'

'You heard me. What exactly is going on around here?'

He clicks it. Click, click. Click, click. 'What d'you mean – going on?'

'I mean what's going on between you and Austin Metro?'

He stops clicking. And blushes. A lovely carmine on khaki. 'Nothing,' he says.

'Don't lie.' I walk around to the front of my desk and sit against the edge of it, arms folded. 'I've seen you and Austin Metro out together. Twice. What's it all about?'

He rallies a little. 'None of your business, *frankly*. What I do in my private life is –'

'I don't give a stuff what you get up to in your private life, Hugh. I don't care if you and Austin like to spend your evenings beating each other with damp loofahs, *frankly*, but this isn't about your private life, is it? This is work. *You,'* I point, 'are up to something with Austin Metro and *I* would like to know what it is.'

He is now puce under the glow, but is also an estate agent. Estate agents are not noted for their meekness of temperament and lie down and die fear. He rustles up what I'm sure he presumes is an authoritative and threatening masculine attitude. But he is nineteen and has nipple rings and Mr Men plasters. Doesn't matter how much he poses. He cannot but fail.

'Like I said,' he says gruffly, 'it's none of your business. If I were you I'd just keep my head down and my mouth shut.'

'Ah! the wheels of commerce on a go-slow, are they?' quips Davina, who has appeared, bearing cakes, and looking jaunty again.

We exchange a silent three-way conference appraisal. Hugh looks shifty, Davina looks curious / suspicious, and I sincerely hope Simpson looks suitably cool and unfazed.

Hmm, I think. Definite worrisome development. But what to do about it? Davina has enough on her plate without shifty goings-on between Austin Metro and Hugh. Will buy the *Western Mail* and scour the job ads on the way home from work.

Evening. About time.

'The black dress, the green dress or the gold suit? What d'you think?'

My father, complete with bald patch, steri-strips and a whole new outlook on sucrose, is home from hospital and re-establishing territorial rights. There's a sponge in the tin and a smell in the kitchen. Order and odour are, for the moment, restored.

'The green dress,' says Ben.

'The black,' says my father.

'Oh, the suit,' Hester says, pausing mid-loop in her crochet. 'I've always said a well-cut suit takes you anywhere. Besides, at your age, dear, you shouldn't expose your upper arms.'

Which makes it the green, of course, as the black has sleeves. Even though I actually *was* going to opt for the suit, as I did not want to lead Rhys down any avenues of carnal expectation. I know it's immature beyond belief to be attempting to score points off a well-meaning, if irritating, pensioner, but I feel if I don't have some outlet for feelings of a baser nature (and I'm definitely entitled to a few right now) I will quite possibly have to resort to saying fuck off you old bag. And given my rumbling suspicion that the Hester / Dad union is showing signs of encroaching even further on the household, I concede that screaming and profanity are not the best course of action, if family harmony is to be maintained at all times.

I am particularly keen to maintain family harmony. I'm now more than halfway through *Trekking in Nepal* and finding it spiritually beneficial to ponder, as the book requests, questions of culture and morality. The Nepalese obviously benefit from their Himalayan lifestyle. Unlike me, they seem to have a handle on life.

I am just considering the concept of mountaineering as metaphor, and how much concern one should feel regarding its vestiges of imperialism and so on, when the telephone rings. It is Dan.

'Didn't you get my email?' he asks.

'What email?' I am, I realise, becoming repetitive.

'The email I sent you on Tuesday, about this weekend.'

'What about it?'

'Well, just to let you know I'll be coming on my own, really.'

'No Jack?'

'No Jack.'

'Oh.'

'Yeah, well. You know how it is.'

'You've split up?'

'Yes. So it'll just be me. Thought I'd better –'

'Did *she* –'

'Mum, I don't want to talk about it.'

'Oh. Right. OK. Of course. Oh, but your skiing holiday!'

'I know. Never mind. There'll be others.'

'But, oh, it's such a shame! Couldn't we – couldn't you – I mean, can't you rustle up a friend or something, and –'

'Mum, no one has any cash, me included.'

'But I could give you some. Oh, you were so looking forward to it, Dan –'

'Mum, it's fine. Really.'

'But are *you* all right – *really*?'

'Mum, stop fussing.'

'I'm sorry. I know. It's just that … No. You're quite right. You're better off without her, in any case. There are plenty –'

'Mum, don't. OK?'

'Don't what?'

'Please don't start on about fish.'

Bitch witch goggle-eyed stroppy gruesome argumentative harpy from the brimstone and hell-hole of Hades. How dare she! How *dare* she!

Wish I could go to London and bash the bitch to pulp.

Am just pondering the relative advantages of a cultural landscape that prohibits the free expression of maternal angst vis-a-vis filial distress perpetrated by goggle-eyed bitches and so on, when the telephone rings, *again*. It is Matt. Matt! Of all people! Matt doesn't *do* telephones.

'Charlie, did you get my email?' he says.

Chapter 24

THAT'S IT. EMAILS. GOING to have to bite the bullet.

Can put off logging on just to read Rhys and Daniel's. And as Rose mentioned veils, I am more than happy to oblige. But I cannot, in all conscience, given the grave tone of his whisper, ignore an email from the pathologically taciturn Matt.

Though I wish I could. Matt's email reads,

Charlie,
I'm so sorry to bother you with this, but I've been a bit concerned about Rose just lately and I wondered if she'd said anything specific to you. I know I shouldn't have even looked, but I came across an email she sent you recently and which rather worried me. I think she's very depressed, but you know Rose, she won't have it. Any thoughts?

I scroll down and click on the offending email, wondering what dire sentiments so needed a veil.

Rose's email runs to two screenfuls and I can clearly see how, to the untutored eye, it may look like the work of a woman in a state. To an experienced Simpson, however, it's a familiar missive; a garbled treatise on the psychology of life, love and shagging, with a smattering of sundry (and often unrelated) quotations, which she's plucked from a book and typed in at random. All bog-standard stuff for the post-modern woman with an absentee husband and free rein at the wine.

Charlie, Charlie, Charlie, (she begins)
   Whither love? Whither?

All the seven deadly sins are self-destroying, morbid appetites, but in their early stages at least, lust and gluttony, avarice and sloth know some gratification, while anger and pride have power, even though that power eventually destroys itself. Envy is impotent, numbed with fear, never ceasing in its appetite, and it knows no gratification, but endless self torment. It has the ugliness of a trapped rat, which gnaws on its own foot in an effort to escape. Which isn't strictly relevant, but has a certain penetrative gravity about it, wouldn't you say? So! Think on!

Oh, and remember; Morality is what the majority there and then happen to like and immorality is what they dislike. Oh, and morality's not practical. Morality's a gesture. A complicated gesture learned from books. So stuff it, I say! <u>We've been here, have we not?!!</u>

And so on and so forth. Then;

I've been thinking a lot. A very great deal. And I think sometimes, in life, you have to do the thing that your core being demands; be it grand gesture, or a simple acceptance of the vagaries of fate. Who are we to know what fate holds for us, Charlie? Who are we, but mere pawns on the chessboard of life?

And her an English teacher. But there's more;

We all have our moment. We all have a time that is ours. And who is to say that we can't seize that moment? Why should the petty dictates of our peers and our consciences rob us of the desire to achieve spiritual relief? You are a precious jewel in God's creational necklace. Think on!

The 'think on' is a new slant. I recall vaguely that Rose may well have the dales somewhere back in her ancestry. And someone in the performing arts, given the tone.

Hmm. I'm not in the habit of feminist carping, but I've said it before, and I'll say it again, a man without the benefit of a classical education is a man with insufficient tools to understand the female psyche.

But thank God she didn't mention the name Phil.

After some minutes of reflection and consideration, I reply;

Matt, you big noodle! You have <u>nothing</u> to worry about. Least of all the state of your wife's mental health. The email was simply her kind contribution to the solving of the problems in my own shambolic life. Oh, and the result of a not inconsiderable post-operative thirst. Fear not. Everything's *fine*.

Dan's email is short, sharp and to point as always.

Hi Mum, just to let you know that Jack won't be coming down with me for the weekend. Oh, and make a note of my new email address, will you? It's the college one, but I check my pigeon hole most days.

Oh, my poor, poor baby. Wicked bitch, goggle-eyed low-life cow.

I find myself taking stock of Rose's grand gesture directive, and send an email back, saying;

My darling, darling Dan, can't *wait* to see you. And, guess what? I've had a most brilliant idea! Will tell you all about it when you get home.
Oodles and oodles of lovexxxxx

Dump both 'oodles' and substitute singleton 'lots'. Then add signature 'Mum', in case a censorship system is employed and Dan is considered someone who hangs out with morons.

But nothing from Adam. Nothing. Have spent the whole week visualising a screen-length list of envelope icons, and cannot quite believe none are actually there. So much cannot believe it that I spend several minutes zipping hither and thither; personal filing cabinet, post room, download manager (romantic attachment?), recycle bin, favourite places, post room again. But nothing. *Nothing*. My griffith – my *Adam* – has accepted instructions and decided never, ever, to email me again. Though I can hardly believe it, I can too easily believe it. I find the last email. Read and digest and re-read it. Only four weeks have passed but it seems like a lifetime. And nothing. *Nothing at all.*

Rats.

Dan arrives on Saturday morning in a flurry of laundry and nonchalant posturing, and I do what all good mothers should do in times of emotional torment, I say nothing, do nothing, avoid giving him anxious inspections, and instead, cook him fried eggs, sausages, bacon, tomatoes, fried bread, baked beans, mushrooms and fried potatoes (which I thoughtfully boiled earlier). All of which he eats in the kitchen, in silence, while I run the new improved Simpson idea past him.

'So,' I say. 'What do you think? You, me and Ben, eh? On the piste together? I'm sure I can find somewhere happening and groovy. Somewhere with plenty of happening and groovy *après ski* too. Which I won't come to, if you don't want me to, of course, and I'll probably have a broken leg anyway, and in any case, I have a whole stack of novels to catch up with – just bought one called *Julia Gets a Life* in fact; sounds perfect for me, don't you think? Ha ha. And Ben and I will be off at the rookies ski-school of course, so we won't cramp your style or anything, but we will be able to enjoy a proper family holiday, and –'

He chews on, nodding, while I witter on hopefully. 'Of course, if you'd rather go on your own, or see if you can find some mates who might like to go with you, then of course you could just have the money – *have* it – and take yourself off and have a really good time. Absolutely. I won't mind. You say. I haven't said anything to Ben yet. It's just that I thought it would be – well, it's been a long time since we did something together, just the three of us and so on.'

He stops chewing, shakes his head, picks up his mug, drinks some coffee.

Then nods. 'Yeah,' he says thoughtfully. 'Yeah, thanks. Great. OK.'

Great OK is certainly good enough for me.

256

Black Monday.

Another pyroclastic moment in geological / Simpson time. A small skiing trip (six days, low alps, hovel apartment, no food, 4 a.m. flight, eight hour transfer, etc.) will cost appreciably more than I have in the entire world. Not including lift passes, or ski hire or boot hire, which I can get, it seems, only if I'm prepared to shag the bank manger, or at least make a big pretence of being desirous to do. As I emerge triumphant from his office, I reflect that where shag lists are concerned generally, it's far better to be on one than to have one oneself.

Feeling mysteriously euphoric after having blown my entire Everest fund, I decided I was robust enough to run the gauntlet of the Wednesday Asthma clinic and pop in to visit Minnie in my lunch break. With Dan being home I hadn't seen her since before the weekend, and with the prospect of her move to The Maltings now looming, I worried that she might become anxious and stressed. My dad made a batch of new low-sugar drop scones, forty-eight of them, no less, which I'd brought in a tin. But Minnie wasn't there. So I tracked down a nurse.

'Has she gone, then?'

We'd never met. She asked, 'Are you a relative?'

'No,' I said. 'She doesn't really have any family. I'm her friend.'

'Oh,' she said. 'Right.'

'So has she already been moved to The Maltings?'

She shook her head. Her expression changed, and I knew immediately what she was about to say.

'I'm sorry. Mrs Drinkwater passed away on Sunday. Peacefully, in her sleep. Heart failure, I believe.'

I stood, clutching my cake tin, imagining Minnie's little bits and bobs waiting for her at the rest home. The place she'd so dreaded going to. Where she now wouldn't have to.

'Does The Maltings know?'

'I assume so. We rang Social Services.'

'Of course,' I said. 'Well, thank you. I know you took good care of her. Um. Shall I leave you the scones I brought?'

There seemed nothing else useful I could do, other than go to The Maltings and gather her things together. So with half an hour to kill still, that was what I did.

Nothing had changed when I entered Minnie's bedroom, except that the window had been opened and the flowers removed. I repacked her few scraps of pale crackly clothing, and gathered up the soap dish and ring as well. Then I sat on the bed with the battered old shoebox and began sifting through the contents. If Edward rang now I'd have nothing but bad news to tell him. Anger swelled inside me. As if he cared much anyway. Perhaps if he'd been around, none of this would have happened. He was doubtless still cavorting through the tropics, oblivious.

It was this thought that possibly alerted my eyes to the envelope – to the word Singapore on the postal frank. The document inside was pristine, as if new, but even before I could make out the translation (in small print beneath all the lines of Chinese), one thing jumped out that replaced my anger with sadness. This was Edward's death certificate, and it was eleven years old.

'Oh, I am glad you phoned, lovely,' said Bernice. 'Speak of the devil. We were about to try and contact your estate agency firm.'

'Why?'

For your name and address – we don't have them on file here.'

'Do you need them?'

'Well simply to tie up the file, dear. All the legal bits and bobs. And you've got her things, so the nursing home tell me. And we do have a will, as it turns out. Old, but valid nevertheless. Not that her son will be seeing any of it, of course. I don't think it was a great deal, but the main beneficiary is a hospital in India, apparently. Ahmenabad, or something? Plus the Cat's Protection League, of course. But if we do make contact, we thought you'd –'

'That's why I'm ringing. You won't,' I say.

'Won't?'

'Because Edward's no longer with us. I have his death certificate right here.'

'Goodness! *Really?* Good Lord.'

'And it's dated eleven years back. He died in Singapore. Pneumonia, it says.'

'Oh, dear, dear me. And *all* that time, Minnie waiting and hoping and not knowing. Makes you weep, doesn't it? Oh, dear, what a shame.'

'That's just it. I think she *did* know. This didn't come in the post. It was in her box of papers. Which completely threw me, of course, given all the postcards and so on, but then I found her stamp pot, with all the ripped off corners. When you match them up you realise they're all really old.'

'Well, how bizarre!'

'Not really,' I answered. 'And that's a point. When was the will made?'

'Oh, about five or six years ago, I believe.'

'So she *did* know. So that proves it. I think she preferred to make believe he was still alive. And I suppose if you kid yourself about something enough, you eventually believe it yourself. But who knows? So much unfathomable stuff went on inside her head, didn't it? Poor thing, though. She had no one, did she?'

'She had you, dear, at least.'

'Hmmm. Not much consolation for two lost children though, is it? When is the funeral?'

'Not arranged as yet, lovely. We have to sort out the finances and so on –'

'But you'll make it a good one, won't you?' I didn't like to think of Minnie going to her rest in a coffin made of plywood with a retinue of one. 'And you will let me know? I'd like to be there.'

'Of course, lovely,' Bernice assured me. 'Just a question of unravelling all the ravels, then we'll be on to it. Leave it with me.'

Back at work I find myself wondering just how much ravelling I want going on in *my* life. Seems to me that ravels are not good things to have. Nor are secrets.

'That's wonderful news!'

Davina is looking jaunty again. It has become though, I've noticed, a subtly different calibre of jauntiness; a jauntiness symptomatic of actually *feeling* jaunty, as opposed to just staving off a lurking hysteria. She refers to my news that Mr Habib has just called, and made an offer for Ty Willow, to which the owners have said yes. It's a half-million sale, and our highest one yet. Though a calculator inside my head gives thanks for the cashflow, I'm still underwhelmed. I wish I could share whatever the thing is that drives her. Truth is, our moods now are too closely correlated. The happier she seems the more sad I get.

'Wonderful,' I agree. For the Habibs' sake, really. And almost add 'and not a Hugh bloody Chatsworth for miles.'

She bounces out of her chair and comes over to my desk.

'Listen,' she says. 'About Cherry Ditchling, Charlie. You know I really am sorry about all that. I mean not about the commission – though I do appreciate how hard you worked and so on – but that, well, I know I could have spoken to Hugh, come to some sort of arrangement with him. It wasn't on, really, was it? I know business is business and all that but, well. I do feel a bit bad about it. Even though I did have my reasons. As you know.'

I start to speak; to tell her to forget it, but her hand comes up. 'Speaking of which,' she says. 'I didn't get a chance to thank you for the other day. Not like me to dump that sort of thing on people, ha ha. You know me, bottle it all up! Onwards and upwards! Anyway, it helped a *lot*.'

'I didn't do anything.'

'You were there. You listened. It made me feel better.'

'I'm glad.'

'I feel I've really got things together now. Got a life-plan sorted – isn't that what they say? And thanks for staying on. I know this job isn't the be all and end all in your life, Charlie, but it's not *so* bad, is it?' She smiles and flaps the details of Ty Willow in the air. 'Buy some really swanky outfits with the commission on this, eh?'

Even as I sit before her in my pond-weed suit with my stagnant pool bow, she doesn't seem to realise the irony in this.

'Absolutely!' I trill though, because it seems po-faced not to. She checks her watch.

'Cripes!' she says. 'Which reminds me, I was due at Velda's for a fitting ten minutes ago.'

'A fitting?'

'For a ball gown. For the CancerCope dinner. It's going to be a pretty swish do, by all accounts. Mustn't let the side down.'

As if. 'Oh,' I say, 'CancerCope? I'm going to that one.'

'*Really?*' I find I don't hold her astonishment against her.

'Yes, with Rhys Hazelton. Have you come across Rhys?'

'So she thinks you've been having treatment for some sort of gynaecological problem, no doubt,' laughs Rose. It's reassuring to hear Rose laughing and jolly. I haven't quite decided whether to say anything to her about Matt's worries. Haven't really even completely decided if he's wrong to have them. My instinct, for the moment, is to leave things as they are.

'Which I do have, ironically.'

'What?'

I recall the fruitless cyber-scramble through my personal email filing cabinet. 'It's called utterly hopeless fixation syndrome – I'm sure there must be a pill I could take.'

'You don't need a pill. You've got the top man. I'd make use of him, if I were you. Distraction therapy – I'll bet he's a really well-informed shag.'

'Oh, *please,* Rose. Don't! I can no more think of shagging

Rhys Hazelton than taking up crochet. Not at the moment, anyway. And possibly never. Nice as he is, I regret to inform you that he's not yet lit any of the Simpson boilers. Anyway, it's not funny.'

'What's not funny?'

'The realisation that I made a point of telling Davina I was going to this bloody dinner dance with Rhys, simply because I knew she'd pass the information straight on to Adam. Hardly progress, is it?'

'Don't be so hard on yourself, Charlie. These things take time.'

'But I should have left, shouldn't I? I should have stuck to my guns and given myself a bit of space. It was one thing having Davina make me come to my senses last week – it's quite another having to see her so happy. It's like bing! Everything in the Jones house is suddenly rosy. And it's not that I begrudge it –'

'Yeah, you do.'

'OK, a *part* of me does, but I have this big other bit that keeps patting me on the back and telling me to buck up because I did the right thing. Which everyone knows should make you feel better. But it still feels like shit. She thanked me today, you know. For being so kind and understanding. And apologised about the Cherry Ditchling business. What a laugh! If only she knew how that particular scenario turned out ... Well. Bad news, anyway, this new incarnation. I can't handle her like this. I should go and get a job in a sweet shop or something.'

'You'll be fine.'

'I know I will, but when?'

'Platitude time, my dear. A lot sooner than you think.'

On Thursday Davina is so jaunty that I half expect her to pop up on a GMTV dawn charity special. Too jaunty by half, and clearly oblivious to worrisome developments at work, another of which occurs when I return from picking up lunch. Hugh has propped the door open to allow the fumes from his saveloy and chips to escape, and he has his back to me, so he doesn't hear me come in. He's on the phone, talking in a synthesised voice. Recalling my father's intelligence directive, I hover for a while by the franking machine.

'Yup,' he says. 'Yup, yup. Whatever you say, Austin.'

Then, after a pause. 'Well, this is exactly my *point*. You know what she's like. She can be a bit, well –'

A longer pause. 'No, absolutely! No, I was simply pointing it out. No, you're right. You *can't* take that away from her. I don't mean *that*. Of course I don't. And I do respect her experience, believe me. Absolutely I do. But you can't deny she's been a bit, well, funny, lately – you don't know; she might have –'

And then a very short one. 'Fine. You're the boss. Whatever you say. Ha ha ha. Nice one!'

And a blip. 'Oh. OK, bye.'

And down goes the phone. Hmmmm.

I rustle the bag with my tuna baguette in.

'Tell you what,' I say. 'I'm fairly quiet for an hour or so. If you want to pop round and lick his arse for good measure, you go right ahead, Hugh. I'll hold the fort.'

Hugh's face fills with red like a dip-dyed pashmina.

'Pah!' he says.

'Well?' I ask.

'Bollocks to you!'

Not much scope for a frank exchange of views there, then. But hmmm. Do I tell Davina? Or do I not tell Davina? Or do I phone Austin Metro?

In the end I take an executive decision that I will telephone Davina in the evening on her mobile and just mention that I keep seeing Hugh and Austin together. Very light, very matter-of-fact, very; "Oh, just thought I'd mention it as I've been a little concerned lately though you probably know all about it anyway, don't you, ha, ha, ha," etc. and so on and so forth. I cannot, in all conscience, continue to do nothing. I'm deeply worried that Austin Metro is up to big-time no good.

Dial.
Then wait.
And wait some more.
'*Yes!*'
Adam. Shit. *Adam*. Adam brusque. Adam breathless.
Hang up.
And feel sick.

Chapter 25

'THIS,' SAYS AUSTIN METRO, gravely, 'is a very important day.'

I am tempted to point out that yes, this is indeed a very important day, as I have, in theory, taken the afternoon off to visit the hairdressers to have my hair coaxed into believing itself glamorous and chic. Not to stand in an expectant huddle while the fat man bangs on. I have, in fact, only ninety-six minutes until my appointment time. Will be most aggrieved if I fail to arrive. I decide that, though I'm obviously keen to be present at the worrisome-development denouement, I will happily leave, never to return, if needs be.

We are assembled at the other office of Willie Jones Jackson (Independent Estate Agents), where Brian Jackson and his team have put on a bit of a spread. The staff from both branches, all summoned, are present, and Brenda Willie has popped on her David Shilling and come. We've even been graced by our style guru, Ianthe, which doesn't bode well image-makeover wise. Speaking of which, as we swarm over the buffet, I realise that passing pedestrians may mistake the gathering for the unexpected arrival of a new aquatics emporium, as the stagnant pond effect is exponentially increased when *en masse*.

Davina is very much present today, as she is wearing a suit that appears to be an eighteenth-century map of the northern hemisphere, over a frock horror tangerine turtleneck sweater. I've noticed a definite trend for less austere power dressing; in hindsight, a clue to today's *coup de grâce*. Indeed I speculate about a post-Christmas colour analysis. With Ianthe, perhaps? Wonder if colour analysis is possibly a side arm of her profitable corporate image enhancement line. I have been watching Davina closely since her arrival at nine forty-seven this morning; for jauntiness, suspiciousness and most anxiously, evidence of recent sexual abandon. Though have not the slightest idea what signs might signal such antics, so it's hard to say whether a loud suit is post-orgasmic or not.

Austin shrugs off his jacket and gestures expansively. 'And an auspicious one too,' he continues, somewhat unimaginatively. 'Because today marks the start of a new era in realty. The conjoining of Metro and Willie Jones Jackson to form a fresh, thrusting force in the property world. Independent estate agency has never looked so good!'

We try to arrange our expressions into suitably reverent configurations while Austin battles manfully with a bottle of champagne.

We then, for some reason, toast our long-deceased senior partner.

'Peter Willie!' we enthuse, even though most of us never met him.

Brenda Willie acknowledges the ripple of applause as if she is accepting a BAFTA, though in truth what she's getting is a great deal more useful. Brian Jackson knocks back his drink in one gulp. I can't help but wonder how much coercion's involved.

And that's that. We are to have a new name, a new image, and (oh, God) a new uniform. And, doubtless, a shiny new mission statement too.

As I turn to leave, Austin sidles up, smiling broadly.

'So!' he booms. 'Charlie! Here we are then! First thoughts? Management appeal? New horizons in Rural?'

'To be honest,' I say archly, 'depends on the suit.'

'That's a bit of a do,' quips Hester when I finally get home. 'I'd always maintained a high chignon was rather ageing, but I have to say, somehow, you do manage to carry it, even without the benefit of a long neck.'

I am tempted to lengthen it a fraction by nutting her, but desist on account of the risk of flying pins.

'So it's a takeover, then, basically,' says my father.

'Exactly. He's buying all Brenda Willie's shares, plus two-thirds of Brian Jackson's. And as Brenda had forty percent, and Brian thirty, that gives Austin sixty per cent in all. And control of the company, of course.'

'Hmm. And what will *they* do?'

'I think Brenda's going to give the money to her daughter. Brenda only hung on to the shares in case her daughter wanted to go into the business, but as she's currently living in a traveller's commune near Andover, I guess she's decided there's really no point. As for Brian, I don't know. He and Austin have always been at loggerheads – he was one of Metro's top managers before joining Peter and Davina. But he's still keeping some shares so I guess he'll still be involved.'

'And what about Mrs Jones?'

My gut jink-a-jinks a bit. Exactly. Mrs Jones. What *about* Mrs Jones?

'You could have floored me with a wet lettuce,' I tell them. 'She's selling half her shares to Hugh Chatsworth, of all people! And where is he getting the money to buy them? He's barely twenty, you know. Anyway, no longer my problem, whatever I decide. He's going to run Brian's branch now.'

'And what's she going to do, then?'

'Stop work, apparently.'

'Ahhh! Start a family, I expect,' coos Hester.

OK, I know. I *know* she doesn't know. But it doesn't stop me wanting to wring her bloody neck.

I telephone Rose while my bath water's running.

Hello! says her voice. *We're not around at the moment. Matt's probably outside pretending he knows the difference between cutworms and root rot, and I'm no doubt asleep.*

I decide there can't be much awry in a marriage where such a lively interplay of humour exists on the ansafone front. Can't say why; it's such a little thing really. But seems to me the little things make the best barometers.

I'm just onto the buff and polish stage when there's a light knock on the bedroom door.

'Charlotte?'

My father. 'Come in, Dad!' I tell him.

He stops in the doorway, tea and fruitcake in hand.

'Well!' he says. 'You look quite, quite magnificent. And do you know, when you walked in earlier with your new hairdo, it quite took my breath away. It was almost as if I'd gone back thirty years. Your mum often used to wear her hair up like that for an evening out. D'you remember?'

Vividly; her warm fragrant powdery kisses, my father in uniform, smelling faintly of Scotch. And Mrs Binks from next door, who'd more often than not baby-sit, and make dresses for my Sindy from her material scrap bag. I nod and smile and slurp at the tea.

'Have some cake, dear,' he urges.

'I'm not really hungry, Dad.'

He sits on the bed. 'Tch! Take a tip from an expert. Never go out on an empty stomach.'

'It's a dinner.'

'And before you get so much as a sniff at a melon ball, there'll be cocktails, aperitifs, buckets of wine. Best you eat something.'

I'm about to tell him not to fuss, when I realise he's right. I have shunned the buffet, spent the afternoon stressing, and cannot wait to get the first glass of wine down my throat. Left to myself, I will be legless by nine. So of course he's right. And why shouldn't he be? He's lived a bit, hasn't he? Why does that fact so often elude me?

'This Rhys chap's certainly a lucky fellow.'

Hmm. Not where I'm concerned. Not so lucky, really.

'It's not serious, Dad.'

He laughs.

'Wasn't about to marry you off again, dear. But I'm glad to see you back with someone. Girl like you shouldn't be on her own.'

I'm beginning to feel fairly ambivalent about that. But is there another agenda lurking within this conversation? A Hester announcement perhaps? I hand him a necklace to fasten for me. Not the one I'd originally intended, but this one was my mother's and, though the style isn't quite mine, and the length not quite right for the dress, I suddenly have an urge to put it on. For luck, maybe? A talisman to make everything turn out right?

'Dad,' I say. 'You and Hester – you're pretty serious, aren't you?'

His big rough hands manage the tiny clasp easily.

'Tch, Charlotte! Goodness me! One day at a time. There's only a few things I take seriously at my time of life, dear, and they're good health, peace and quiet, and the state of Welsh Rugby. The 'serious' you refer to isn't nearly as pressing; it's not so engrossing when you get to my age. There,' he then says. 'You look lovely. A picture.' He proffers the cake again and this time I take it. 'Why d'you ask?,' he says. 'Trying to get rid of me, are you?'

'On the contrary,' I say, and despite his wide grin, I don't think he realises quite how much I mean it. I don't think I did until now. '*Really*,' I add, 'I'm getting worried that she's going to whisk you away.'

He picks up my cup and saucer and chuckles.

'The only whisking around here will be done by your Kenwood Chef. We're fine as we are, Charlotte. Right, ready for the off?'

With that knowledge on board, I realise I feel infinitely more gracious and well-disposed towards Hester. Unbelievable, with so much grown-up stuff under my belt now, that I have still so many odd bits of growing up yet to do.

Sitting, some twenty minutes later, in the leathery gloom of Rhys's Mercedes (250 GYN – his weekly tally of internals?), I decide I shouldn't be so tough on myself. It's not that I have anything against my father getting it together with someone – and I know Hester is essentially a well-meaning old lady. It's just that, having got him, and with us finally having adjusted to one another, I find I'm reluctant to lose him again. And not only for myself; he's important to Ben; much as his own father loves him, he's away more than at home, and often not when it counts. And though I don't have any axe to grind with Felix about it, I'm glad Ben has a positive male role model around permanently, and without so much testosterone zipping around.

'Your father seems a very nice chap,' observes Rhys. 'Navy, you say?'

'Second Lieutenant. He was on the Ark Royal,' I tell him proudly.

Not just an old man who makes jam and times vegetables.

'Nice to have him around?'

I nod. 'He's the best.'

The CancerCope ball is one of the highlights of the local glitterati circuit. The event all the socialites want to be seen at. We are not they though. We are, Rhys explains, invited guests; he has been involved in research with the charity for some years, and has fronted some major fundraising campaigns. As such, he is here as a guest of the charity. Most of the rest of the two hundred-odd people are paying over £60 for the privilege of being here.

So this is high-falutin company indeed. I recall Davina's words, via Adam, about all the big noises. There's big noise aplenty. I feel relieved about my last-minute fake-fur addition. An extravagance from Felix during the phase when we thought that extravagant gestures might solve things, it only got used for mess dos once an aeon. I've worn it no more than twice since being on my own.

Once inside and divested of it, however, I suddenly feel insubstantial again. And uncomfortable around all this loud *joie de vivre*. And not just psychologically. Fat cats abound. Men with big paunches that bowl around like bumper cars, and big-bosomed ladies so dripping with sequins and suntans it feels like an outsize shop sale preview night.

God, what am I *doing* here?

Well, hello *there*!' says a voice; boomy, masculine. Bill Stableford's.

'Hi Bill,' I say. Then 'Bill, this is Rhys.'

'Hello there,' Rhys replies, shaking hands, peering. 'Already acquainted, aren't we?'

Bill nods. 'Indeed we are. Via Carolyn.'

Rhys nods too. 'Absolutely. Keeping well, is she?'

Bill nods again. 'Splendid. Great job.'

Rhys nods again too. 'Good, good,' he says.

Oh dear. I think I have arrived at hysterectomy central. I realise that I may be forced to spend the evening with a succession of people whose main opening conversational gambit will be related to the ill-health of North Cardiff's collective reproductive tract.

Rhys, who is beginning to exhibit a proprietorial touchy-feeliness, bends his head and groans in my ear.

'Hmm,' he says. 'Sorry. Occupational hazard. Thing with this type of shindig is the tedious business of having bland conversations with men you don't really know, with their wives' genitalia hanging between you like a pair of metaphysical curtains. Course, it's not so bad with the women themselves.' He winks at me and slides a hand over my shoulder. 'I find women are generally far less euphemistic about these things.'

He smells nice. He *is* nice. I so wish he could have the effect he desires. Instead, I find the word 'genitalia' makes me feel edgy and stressed, rather like the word 'stiffy' did when I was ten. It's just a tiny chemical signal that's needed, but without it, I find real, pukka sexual overtures become anxiety-inducing in the extreme.

'Rhys, old chap!'

'Lord, here's another one,' he mutters. 'Don't worry, we'll be safe once we get to our table. Michael! How *are* you?'

'Would you excuse me?' I ask them. 'I've just seen someone over there I need to speak to.'

Hugh is at the bar, where he blends in rather more readily than he probably thinks he does with the only just post-pubescent bar staff. The Willie / Metro contingent are some distance beyond him. Austin in white tux, but no Joneses as yet.

'Thanks, low-life,' I say mildly. His eyes narrow.

'Thanks for what?'

'For that good word you put in for me with Austin.' He looks blank. 'That was all about *me*, wasn't it? All that stuff I heard you say?'

He sips the froth off his lager. And adds a white moustache to his fluff one.

'Well,' he says finally. 'It was all true, wasn't it?'

'I don't know – you tell me. You're the one who knows what I'm like. Knows how funny I am and so on.'

'Look,' he then says. 'What *is* it with you? You've had it in for me since the day I fucking started. Mrs Bloody know-it-all. Mrs Mother Superior.'

I'm genuinely surprised. Me? Superior?

'What on earth are you on about?'

'You know very well. The Pringle business.'

'The *what* business?'

'You ratted on me.'

'I certainly didn't.'

'Don't lie.'

'I didn't! Hugh, I may not have approved of your 'tactics' as you called them, but I never saw it as my responsibility to tell anyone else about it. Yes, I have principles, but I'm not a snitch.'

He looks suspiciously at me.

'Hmm,' he grunts. 'Anyway. You've done all right. You've got your branch, haven't you?'

He sounds exactly like the petulant juvenile he is. He should go far with Metro.

I can't be bothered to talk to Hugh Chatsworth any more. Possibly never will. So I return to where Rhys is now holding court to a huddle of matronly women. All post-hysterectomy, presumably, as the snatches of conversation that reach my peripheral point in the throng, seem mainly to be about pipework and plumbing. Rhys isn't right about a female

272

distaste for euphemism – as I acknowledge his smile, I hear one woman explain what a relief it is not to have all that downstairs plumbing clanking around, because the hot-water system is now firing up nicely.

I leave them to their titters and look around hopefully. The Willie Jones Jackson table consists of Austin, Brian Jackson, his wife and Hugh, plus a Metro manager I recognise, and the stylish Ianthe. I belatedly recognise an un-Davina-like Davina and then cast my eyes over the remaining chairs. There are twelve to a table and the remaining five on theirs are all taken, presumably by the very same big noises in planning that were instrumental in the cessation of my inopportune tryst. But – I scan wildly – there is no sign of Adam. He's not there. No Adam. *No Adam*. Why not?

But then Rhys steers me off to our table, where we are separated by six feet of starched linen plus several diners, and then we say grace.

Thank you, Lord, for this excellent repast and so on and so forth. And thank you for Rhys because he's such a nice guy, oh, but by the way, can you find him someone else for me? And I'm so sorry for all the times I use your name in vain, and it isn't *really* in vain, you understand, but oh, *God*, why isn't Adam here? What have you done with him? Why didn't you send him? Was it all too much? Could he simply not bear to be around me? Well? *Well?*

God sends back message; he's a doctor, you silly cow. He's probably on call or something. *God,* you're self-important, Simpson! Don't flatter yourself! And in any case, didn't he make it absolutely clear where he stood? *Didn't* he? Didn't he tell you he loved his wife and was intent on making progress with her? And hasn't he? *Hasn't he*? Is she not the very *incarnation* of progress? Is she not progress *personified*? Is she not the embodiment of what a dogged persistence and much love can achieve? Does she not look like a woman who has bloomed and ripened and thrust forth her pistils? Has she not, in fact, intimated as much? This very day, in fact? This

273

very day?'

Go into sulk.

I open my eyes to find there is already something edible in front of me. A small pinkish disc, like an ice hockey puck, but with a dribble of sauce and a thimbleful of red caviar. A fishy hors d'oeuvre, which I really don't fancy. But eat anyway, as I know small children have emptied their money boxes to pay for it. Hmmm. I am becoming dangerously chopsy. I almost want to refuse to eat. Don't people realise where their hard-earned donations are going? Don't people care? I think of Minnie's little pot of stamps for the blind, and all those gold and red milk bottle tops that my mother would rinse off religiously each morning and put on the kitchen windowsill to dry. They would glint in the sun like oversized sequins – treasure, to help all the sick children feel better. Not to pay for the likes of me to sit here. Which is ludicrous, I know, as this ball will make thousands, but I can't seem to help it. I push it away.

The plate is removed and as the diners who flank me are both engaged in conversation with more personable people, and because it is in the nature of such functions that there is generally a twenty-minute wait between courses, I excuse myself and head off to the loo.

Where my blooming and ripening ex-boss has gone too.

'Well,' says Davina, as we exit our cubicles and our reflections make contact. 'Now that *is* nice, Charlie. That greeny-blue really is *you*.'

Right about the colour analysis, then.

'Thank you. So's yours,' I reply, finding that much as I want to dislike it, I actually mean it. Davina's looks, normally leached from her by the wet roof-slate colours she generally favours, are enhanced by the soft pastel hues in her dress. And the straight honey hair that she usually ties back is tonight a big glitter-flecked cascade of curls. In short, she looks beautiful. I want to go home.

'You like this?' she asks. I nod again. At it. 'Ah!,' she says.

'It's the Ianthe effect. It's after Monet, you know. And she helped me choose it. I would never have dreamed I'd wear something like this! Just goes to show, eh?' She smiles at herself in the mirror. 'She has *such* taste, doesn't she? A natural artist.'

Jesus. Scrub colour analysis. This is serious stuff. Progress, I guess. Davina slips her lip gloss back into her handbag, and turns her smile on me.

'You look great,' I repeat. And then, despite my absolute, *absolute* rule never to bring him into any conversation with Davina ever again in my life, and despite the fact that as soon as I bring him into *mind*, let alone larynx, in public, I know, that I will turn the colour of a freshly cropped radish, and despite the fact that even as I think about formulating a sentence with his name in, I emit saline in sufficient quantity to make my eyeballs look like a pair of marbles in a puddle – despite *all that*, I smile and say;

'Shame Adam's not here to show you off to everyone.'

She's been beaming and smiling pretty much throughout. So much so that when her face suddenly changes back into something approaching its usual configuration (shifty, suspicious, trifle with me at your peril eyebrows etc.) I am jerked back to reality with a twang. She adds some penetrating eye contact and stares at me with it. While inside I'm going sixteen shades of puce.

'Yes,' she says finally. 'It *is* a shame, isn't it?' She pokes at her hairdo. I poke at mine. 'But just,' she adds, 'the way that things sometimes work out.'

'Hmmm,' I reply. And then her beam reasserts itself.

'So,' she says. 'Shocked?'

She knows, then. She *knows*. But she means work now. She must do.

'Um. Yes. A little. Though I did know there was something going on. Funny,' I eject a laugh to illustrate, but it comes out as a squawk. '*I* thought that *you* didn't know about it. I kept seeing Hugh and Austin Metro together, and I thought they were plotting something behind your back.'

275

She roars with laughter at this. She has become so, *so* strange.

'Oh, bless!' she says, shaking her head. 'No, you know what these things are like. We had to keep covert. But, my God, it *has* been stressful. And it was a pretty tough decision for me, I can tell you. If you'd asked me six months ago how I would have responded to Austin's proposal, well! Phew! You know me! And what with everything else,' she embellishes the words "everything else" with a grimace. 'I would rather have died. Well. *You* know, Charlie, don't you? Work was all I had left.'

I feel I have entirely lost the plot of this conversation. I get the look again briefly, then she's once again smiling as we head to the exit.

'So what changed?' I ask. 'I could never have imagined you leaving.'

She puts a hand on my shoulder and beams again – *really* beams – at me.

'*I* changed,' she says, holding the door open for me. '*Me.*'

There is little time to gather my thoughts into anything resembling an understanding of the situation, because when we come out of the toilet we bump into a large man with a moustache whom Davina introduces as Mr Routledge – the gentleman who bought Cherry Ditchling.

'Ah,' I say, slightly light-headed with confusion. 'You fell in love with the beautiful gardens, no doubt.'

I have no idea why I have said this, but am soon to be pleased beyond measure that I have, because he replies,

'Gardens? What gardens? Har, har, har, har. Show me five acres of prime flat land, and I'll show you covered hard standing for twenty-five cars.'

'Mr Routledge,' Davina explains, 'has the biggest collection of Classic Jaguars in Wales, apparently. He was particularly keen on Cherry Ditchling because of its lack of gradient.'

'Oh,' I say, nodding. 'You'll not be keeping the ha-ha,

then?'

'Bugger the ha-ha, my lovely,' he says sternly. 'Gone the way of the summerhouse. Bulldozed. Ptchung!'

Elevenish. Elizabeth Shaw Mint Crisps *et* comedian.

What am I *doing* here?

On the way back to my table, I passed the Harris-Harpers, who looked as if they'd only just arrived. David Harris-Harper (big noise in conveyancing, presumably), was at the bar, ordering drinks. His dinner suit jacket was made from a bronze-coloured brocade, and six months ago, I would have thought what a catch he looked. Top three material, always, David. Tonight all I saw was a man.

Kim Harris-Harper (big noise, period) came across and waved an arm towards Davina's departing form.

'That's some dress,' she observed. 'Hmmm. How the other half lives, eh?'

I nodded. 'Yes, it's beautiful, isn't it? (Blah, blah, blah. Gush, gush, gush. Go with it. Just learn to cope. Grow up). Ianthe designed it, apparently. Ianthe's the woman who did the Willie JJ makeover.'

Kim nodded and went; 'Ah! The legendary Ianthe! Hmmm. Still, Davina looks happy, I suppose.'

I nodded back. 'Yes, doesn't she? Very.' Then tagged on, for effect, 'which is nice.'

Kim sipped her drink.

'Hmm. I suppose so. Bit of a shock though.'

Here we were again. 'Shock?'

'This whole giving up work, earth mother, Romania *thing* she's embarked on. Bit of a turn-up, isn't it?'

'*What?*'

'The baby bit. You wouldn't have thought it, would you? I mean, she's always been so –well, so utterly not *into* that sort of thing. And even if you accept the bio logical countdown argument – and the physical constrictions, *obviously* – you still can't help but be a touch fazed. I mean, orphanages?

277

Foreigners? Squalor? *Davina*? Can *you* see it?'

I was still trucking through eastern Europe. I'd turned left at baby and got lost straight after constrictions.

'It's a turn-up.' And then some. Though not totally incredible.

'Well, precisely! I know it's all very fashionable these days, but *really!* You'd think she'd exhibit a little more *sangfroid* – I mean she's pushing forty, for God's sake! And can you really see Davina hunkered down on the Axminster playing Tootles the Taxi with some two-year-old sprog? Even given a perfectly adapted sprog, it's hard to imagine. And these children have *problems*, don't they? In fact, barely function, most of them, from what I've heard. And that's quite without all the other malarky, isn't it?' She shook her head. 'I just can't see it. There are limits and there are limits. I mean no one's saying she doesn't have a right to be happy. Of course they're not. And I'm as broad-minded as the next person. But, well, some things really are beyond the pale. It'll be mendhi and a black wig next, *a la* Madonna.'

'Is that a wig? I thought it was her own hair.'

'Does anyone's hair *really* grow that fast? I don't think so. And don't tell me those biceps aren't steroid enhanced. Anyway, I just think you can take these things a little too far. Don't you?'

'Doesn't she what?' said David Harris-Harper, from behind me. Which was handy, as I'd not the slightest idea what to say next. Kim flapped her hand dismissively.

'Oh, nothing. We were just talking about Davina.'

He rolled his eyes. 'Oh, leave the poor woman alone, Kim,' he said. 'Don't be so judgemental all the time. I don't know. You girls – gossip, gossip, gossip. At least she's doing something useful for society.'

'*Useful?*' countered Kim irritably. 'Useful for who? Useful for which society? Don't we have enough dysfunctional families already? Don't we –'

'No,' he said, winking at me. 'Useful as in giving up work. Useful as in one less estate agent around.'

Apart from his time-expired joke about estate agents, (for which I immediately and unreservedly forgave him as soon as he had the grace to realise its impropriety in my company) David Harris-Harper was really a perfectly nice guy. Why did perfectly nice guys so often end up with baggages?

And how on earth did his baggage *know* all this stuff?

There was a limit to how much time I could spend wandering around during a formal dinner without someone coming up and asking me for an extra bread roll or something, and I didn't want Rhys to think I was stuck in a toilet, so I went back to the table and sat down again. Another plate had arrived in my absence, this one playing host to a piece of brown meat, a stick and green gravy. The man on my left proffered a vegetable dish.

And we had, I believe, an ordinary conversation. He asked me what I thought about GM foods and I said I had mixed feelings about them, though not, of course, mixed in a centrifuge ha ha, and with double helixes unravelling like crazy all over the place and recombining to form triangular carrots and blue sweetcorn and so on, ha ha, and he said hmm, in the manner of someone who knew a great deal about the subject and really couldn't be fagged to have a conversation with a maniacal dimwit about it and then I thought, shall I just make my excuses and go home? The person on the other side of me said, if you ask me this whole assembly nonsense is just another bloody excuse for another bloody quango and bloody cars and expense account orgies and did I see all that imbroglio about the Lord Mayor's stash of booze just recently, and wasn't it disgraceful? And did I have a stance on the assembly myself? And I said, actually, I thought it was all fundamentally ideologically sound and so on, but that in reality there had to be a question mark over its efficacy given the small extent of its actual remit and so on, and he looked at me in the sort of way that made it perfectly obvious that he couldn't be arsed having a conversation with someone who just memorised chunks out of the broadsheets at random, and I thought should I go and speak to Kim Harris-Harper again, because she seemed to know everything about everything, and how did she know everything about everything? Surely not just because they shared the same acupuncturist, and then I thought, because she made it her *business* to know everything about everything, whereas I'd spent the last six months making it my business to pretend to know *nothing* about anything; particularly where Davina was concerned. It was no wonder I had as much nous as a pea pod, and what was the point anyway? Because hearing any more about it was liable to make me sick anyway, and then they took the plates away and I thought I *should* in fact go and speak to Davina, to at least let her know that I really didn't think I could face working for Willie Metro or whatever they were going to call themselves, any more because even if she *was* going to go off in a truck to get a baby and so on, she was still my boss at the moment. Then someone put more red wine in my glass which I drank and then the man on my left said, so what is it you do then? and I told him I was *formerly* an estate agent and even more formerly a housewife, and even more formerly than that a lab technician in a high school which is why I knew about centrifuges and so on and that I was now doing a PhD on indigenous Himalayan peoples and did he know that Everest was originally named Chomolungma by the Tibetans, which meant goddess mother of the earth, and that it was long before western people found out it was the highest peak on the planet, and wasn't that interesting? And then the pudding came and it was something meringuey with hot sauce and lots of little fru-fru berries scattered all over it and it looked very pretty and I ate most of it because I thought blood sugar! blood sugar! possible genetic pre-disposition! etc., and then I drank some of the dessert wine I was given and it was really disgusting and I wondered if I should tell Rhys why I wanted to go home, or should I just pretend I was ill? Given that if I drank any more of the wine I probably would be anyway, but if I did the latter I would still have to deal with telling Rhys I didn't want to see him again at some other point anyway, and then I had some disgusting coffee and a mint crisp and then I thought that ill or not I *should* maybe be honest with him, as it would be all too easy to find myself in another unsatisfactory Phil-type situation, simply because of my inability to deal with things in a firm and decisive way, plus also if I told him I was ill he would insist on coming back with me, which was the last thing I wanted, and then they wheeled out some minor TV comedian who was very funny, I'm sure, but I couldn't hear a word he was saying because I couldn't get my head around the idea that Adam was actually going to go along with this ridiculous baby plan, because everyone knew you didn't repair marriages by putting babies into them, particularly profoundly damaged children with Victorian skin diseases and no visas and so on, and then they brought more coffee, and Rhys leaned across the table and said 'All right?' and 'Can I get you a liqueur to go with that, Charlie?' and I said no thank you, and then the man on my left, who turned out to be the director of the charity, and was probably a political appointment and wouldn't know a centrifuge from a deep fat fryer anyway, said let me press you on that and I said no again and then the comedian started getting into his stride and everyone started guffawing enthusiastically and I thought *should* I go and speak to Davina? And then the guy on my right who didn't like the assembly said how about you and me taking a turn around the dance floor in a while and his breath smelt of dog hairs and I thought, crikey – *what am I doing here?*

After I had the thought, it suddenly seemed very easy to answer. I was wasting everybody's time. And Rhys's in particular. All I really wanted to do was go home and cry. It was after eleven; not embarrassingly early. So that, I decided, was what I would do.

Chapter 26

'I'M SO SORRY, RHYS. But I have to leave. I don't feel too well.'

'Then I'll come with you.'

'No, really.'

'Nonsense! Of course I will!'

'*Really,* please- I'd much rather you didn't. You go back and enjoy the rest of the evening. I've been lousy company anyway.'

'Nonsense. Besides, I've hardly spoken to you yet.'

'Wisely.'

'Charlie, why is it I get the feeling there's something else going on here?'

'There isn't. No. OK, yes. Yes. You're right. This is stupid. There is.'

'Which is?'

'I shouldn't have accepted your invitation.'

'Why not?'

'Because I feel I've given you the impression that I'd – well, that I'd like to take things further than I – well, than I actually would.'

'Hmm. OK. Fair enough. But that doesn't mean *I* was inferring anything from your acceptance. I did say as much, didn't I?'

'I know. But I still feel I've implied it. But I realise I don't. And it's not because I … well, I mean I *do* feel …. well, actually, I *don't* because I feel …. well, it's not that. It's just that I've been –'

'There's someone else.'

'Not strictly speaking. There's –'

'Adam Jones. It is Adam, isn't it?'

'Well –'

'I'm not stupid, Charlie. And I've known Adam for fifteen years.'

'But how –'

'The whole bit. The book. His ... well, let's say I just knew. Like I said, I've known him a long time.'

'It's all academic, Rhys. It's not happening. It's just that I don't feel able, at the moment, to – well – you know.'

'I know. Wrong place, wrong time. And shall I tell you something? When Adam phoned me and asked if he could put someone in touch with me, before I got the wrong end of the stick about your name, do you know what my very first thought was?'

'What was it?'

'Girlfriend.'

'Has he had one before then?'

'Not to my knowledge, never. He's really not like that.'

I know.

We stood awkwardly, like two candidates attending the same interview, while the lady in the cloakroom went and sought out my coat. The deed done, I felt a mixture of relief and great sadness. I'd untangled myself from the web of his affections but, like a fly with one wing left and half its legs missing, once free, it seemed pointless. I'd only fall down and get squished on the floor.

A burst of noise from the ballroom reached us, as the giant beech doors let a small group escape. A group of three, two of them lilac and turquoise; Davina, Ianthe and my old mucker, Hugh.

'Hello, you two!' Davina said, a little too chattily. 'You off then?'

I nodded. 'I'm not feeling well. But Rhys is staying. Davina – you know Rhys, don't you?' She acknowledged him briefly. 'And Rhys, this is Hugh Chatsworth.' They shook hands and grimaced. I left the Ianthe introduction to them. Which Davina duly did.

Rhys nodded. 'Hello, Davina,' he said levelly. 'No Adam? On call, is he?'

I stared at the counter.

'Erm, yes,' she said. 'What a life, eh?' Looking at me and not him. She seemed funny, but that was becoming the norm now. Rhys just looked as if he wished he could be somewhere else. As he would, knowing what I'd just confirmed. The cloakroom attendant was still rootling for my coat. I wondered if she'd got lost and turned up in Narnia.

I had to say something, because nobody else did. 'Off home as well?' I asked.

'God, no!' said Davina. 'The night is still young! We're off clubbing.'

'Clubbing?' She made it sound more like a seal-cull. Plus, I never imagined she *did* things like that. She nodded gaily.

'Ianthe and I are. Poor Hugh's all worn out.'

'Too much excitement,' Ianthe announced, grinning.

Hugh scowled at her. 'God, Mum! Button it, will you?'

Button it, will you? Button it, *Mum?*

The lady brought my coat and flopped it across the counter. It lay there, black and corpulent, between us while various Hugh stuff all dropped into place in my head.

'Well,' said Rhys. 'Let's get you into a taxi. Goodnight, all.'

He draped my coat over my shoulders.

'Night, night,' said Davina. 'Charlie – see you next?'

The air outside was crisp and salty, with a chilly breeze cajoling the surface of the bay into flecks. We walked the few steps down to the cab rank in silence. Then Rhys sighed.

'I'll stay and wait with you,' he said.

'Please, I'd rather you didn't.' I tried a laugh. 'After all, what on earth would we talk about? We've done the big scene now.'

I immediately regretted the unintended flippancy. 'Well,' he said. 'It's been a pleasure – what there's been of it. And you know you can call on me any time if there's anything you need to know for your trip. Anything – I'd be happy to help.'

I shook my head.

'That won't be a for a long time yet now. I've blown all my

savings. I'm taking my boys skiing instead. Next week, in fact. I must be mad.'

It must have been my night for fatuous chit-chat, and I immediately regretted the 'mad' tag as well. I didn't feel mad at all. I felt like I was getting a grip on things, finally. But he ignored it anyway.

'Lovely. You ski?'

I shook my head. 'Hardly. I've only been twice. And that was years ago.'

'It's enough. Well. I hope our paths cross again – though not professionally, ideally. But if they do –'

'Absolutely.'

His lips brushed my cheek, then he strode back into the lobby. Somehow I didn't think there was much chance that they would.

I watch Rhys go back inside, and am just digesting the wide-ranging implications of Davina-as-mum / Ianthe-as-*Hugh's*-mum concepts, when the mums in question emerge, coated, from the hotel, and begin to stroll along the railing looking out over the bay. They look like twin prows, with their Pre-Raphaelite curls streaming behind them, and their pale Monet dresses peeking out of their coats, the hems rippling in colourful cuttlefish waves. I wonder how the image makeover will hold up in Davina's eastern European truck adventure. But I do not wonder for long. I'm too tired.

A taxi slides up.

The driver says, 'Simpson? Cefn Melin?'

I climb into the back while he footles in his footwell and fishes out a pale dog-eared Cardiff A-Z. He then stabs at a meter button that presumably clocks a pound for it being after midnight, a pound for it being windy, a pound for there being an R in the month and a further pound, I suspect, for just being in the cab. I gaze out into white-sprinkled black night and care little.

'Where to in Cefn Melin?' he asks.

But I'm miles away. Davina and Ianthe move back across

the forecourt to the cab rank. I can hear the click clack of their heels on the stone. The cabbie turns around.

'Where to, my lovely?'

'Ah,' I say. 'Right. Yes. Of course.'

The moon and stars flicker as Davina dips down to wave to me.

I wave back. Then speak my address and head home.

As with pretty much everything I do, what I then did seemed like a pretty good idea at the time. Twenty minutes or so after leaving the hotel, I was back in my own chutney jar of a kitchen, resolving a) never to have anything to do with affairs of the heart ever again and b) not to knock crochet as a fulfilling pastime. In fact, to ask Hester to show me how to do it. And while I was at it, to ask Sheila Rawlins if I could go to her floristry class with her as well. And then I saw the note.

7.47. Charlotte, (it said)
Message from Dr Jones.
Will call back in the morning.

What? *What?*

Because I had had more than a little wine by this time, I read the note six times to see what else I could glean from it. But only one fact readily presented itself. And that was that the note lacked a telephone number. I turned it over, but it being, as it was, on an Indian takeaway menu, the words on the other side were of little practical use. Unless I'd been hungry. Which I absolutely was not.

I fumed at my father. What a ridiculous message! What, pray, was the point of even writing it down? I returned to the hall and snatched up the phone book, knowing even as I did so that I was wasting my time.

Alrighty, I thought. (I was, by now, half delirious.) I could call directory enquiries and get the number from them.

But I couldn't, of course. They would be ex-directory. Even so, I spent some minutes proving the point.

There seemed no point in waking my father to ask him. If the note said no more then no more had been said. I sat down at the foot of the stairs and tried to make some rational sense of the situation. Why did Adam telephone? Why did Adam telephone at 7.47 on the night when he knew I'd be at the CancerCope ball with Rhys? What did he want to say to me? What was it all about? And why did he phone me? Why didn't he email? Or did he?

12.37. No.

At twelve thirty-eight I decided that perhaps the best thing I could do would be to go to bed and try to sleep and then get up in the morning and put a total ban on any member of the Simpson household using the phone all day. Yes. That would be best. The sensible thing to do. Except that a mounting excitement inside me had got to the top and was waving a flag. I would no more fall asleep than make Welsh cakes tonight. So I plucked up the phone again

'Yes, now, if that's possible.'
    'All right, my lovely. It'll be on its way soon.'

12.49.
    'Oh, it's you!'
    'Hello there!' the cabbie said. 'You timed that well. Off out again?'
    I opened the car door and got in the front with him.
    'Absolutely,' I said. 'Never a dull moment around here!'

1 a.m.
    Feel monumentally stupid.
    Am standing outside Adam and Davina's house and am experiencing a degree of consternation about the course of action I have just taken that I deeply regret I did not feel half an hour ago. Moreover, I am standing outside Adam and Davina's house in the small hours of a cold Saturday morning,

in pitch black, in a fur coat and stupid kitten heel shoes. Am not It girl, but Twit girl. And not even a girl anymore.

Adam and Davina's is a big posh house, as expected given their big posh jobs, their big posh lifestyle, big posh mortgage capability, etc. A big posh house at the end of a drive at the end of a creepy lane flanked by trees and dark and possibly large mammals and rapists and jabberwockies. A big posh house at least two miles from my own home (may as well be six, given footwear), and without a sign of human habitation *at all*. I march up front path in a purposeful way as advised to in the Tufty Club, and bing-bong the doorbell before the urge to scuttle away under a stone gets the upper hand.

Silence.

Bing-bong again, plus add a rattle of the door knocker for emphasis.

Silence.

Bing-bong, rattle knocker, slap flat of hand against door, twice.

Silence.

An owl hoots in the distance. Things kind of *rustle*.

I realise that I am perhaps the most stupid, impetuous, imbecilic nonce in North Cardiff, and will possibly pay the ultimate price and be found assaulted and dead in the lane in the morning, while people eat breakfast and shake their heads and say why oh why oh why do they do it? Why do women put themselves in such ridiculously vulnerable situations? What a tragic, tragic waste of a life and her with two boys and a diabetic father to consider etc. I decide that I will burst into tears and scream mightily if I spend one moment more speculating about my own violent death. Instead I retrace my steps halfway up the path, then split off down a tributary of stepping stones that leads to the side gate of the house.

Which opens with a bloodcurdling Edgar Allan Poe creak. The side passage is, if anything, even darker and more scary, as it runs between the house wall and the garage, and smells of goblins and trolls. I edge forwards and blink into the inscrutable distance. A few hundred micrograms of good quality alcohol take fright and evaporate with each mincing step. It's bad enough being scared in a dark alley in the small hours. Far worse being scared in a dark alley in the small hours *sober*. But I'm most definitely sober – bar rustling things rustling, the entire landscape is now unmoving.

But sober has its compensations. Once halfway down the house wall (big house and then some) I realise that the area of brightness in the far distance on the patio, is not a desperation-generated mirage after all, but actually a photon-based puddle of light. I trip towards it and find myself in a black hole back garden, adjacent to a window from which a blue light emits.

The light, it turns out, comes from a computer monitor. I'm outside what looks like a second division sitting room. There are wall-to-wall books, a big desk, a plaid armchair. And the room has a decidedly masculine feel. And an empty one. As it would, as there's nobody in it. And even as I rap on the patio door, I know that I've just done a ridiculous thing, and will now have to walk all the way home, in the dark, on my own.

Chapter 27

TO SING OR NOT to sing?

When I was a little girl, accepted wisdom was always that you sung if you were scared. Singing, the idea went, would keep your mind occupied, strengthen your resolve, bolster your courage, and advertise your lack of fear.

And advertise your existence to any passing serial killers at a loose end. I break off my wavering *Ghostbusters* tribute (the one with the proper words, not the crappy Metro ad version), and squelch on in silence. Such a little thing, changing into more sensible footwear, but, nevertheless, too large for a Simpson to manage.

The trouble with people who live in lanes off lanes is that they generally have several reliable cars, thus don't feel the need to make any concessions to pedestrians. Even the post around here comes in a van. And, goodness, a lane is a long scary prospect when you're traversing it in black and impenetrable darkness at the speed of a hamster on crutches.

I'm just deciding to treat slugs with a lot more respect and a good deal less salt, when a white beam arcs over the top of the far hedgerow and outlines the hawthorn in a soft pearly light.

My first thought, obviously, is 'Ah! It's Adam!' but as I have already passed at least four more big houses, plus a couple of farms, plus a side-lane to God knows where, plus, ominously, a lay-by, my second and third thoughts are far less promising ones. As the headlamps get nearer, I take a policy decision. I can either flatten myself, face first, against a small gap in the hedgerow, or stand boldly in the lane and flap my arms about. Given the time of night the first course of action is less risky, but I am an optimist (drunk still?), so opt for the flap.

I am just positioning myself when a car sweeps around the corner. Then brakes hard (much mud), and slews left, against the hedge. I cannot see which car as I am blinded by headlamps, but I can certainly hear the sharp scrape of bramble on wing. I cross my fingers.

A man jumps out. Who, though? (Still blinded.) He says, 'Jesus!' then, 'Good God!' then, 'What on earth?' then, 'Hello? Who's there?''

'Erm …' I begin. Then he gets a bit closer.

'*Charlie*? Charlie, is that you? God, I thought you were a bear!'

I am so utterly, totally, overwhelmingly grateful to see him that I answer, with feeling,

'Don't be so stupid! Everyone knows that there aren't any bears left in Britain. Besides, do I *look* like a bear?'

He is standing close to me now, hands on hips, in front of the bumper. His hair has a small golden halo around it, where midges pay homage in the shimmering light. His expression (one of mild shock) tells me nothing.

'Yes, you do, quite frankly. And would it be presumptuous to enquire why you are walking along the outer reaches of Cefn Melin at – he checks his watch – twenty past one in the morning?'

He has a trace of a smile at the edge of his mouth. But then he hasn't inspected his nearside as yet.

'I'm here,' I reply, feeling my confidence ebb, 'in response to your phone call earlier this evening. You neglected to leave a number. And it might have been urgent so I hurried straight round.'

He peers at me closely. As if there is, after all, something a little bizarre about having this conversation, at this time, in this place. Oh, I wish such a thought had occurred to me earlier.

'*Really?*' he asks.

'Really.'

He shakes his head. 'Then where's your car?'

'At home. I couldn't drive here. I'd had too much to drink at the ball.'

He nods. 'Of course. Yes.'

'Though I have to say, right now, I've never felt so sober.'
I pull my coat a little tighter around me.

'God, yes!' He moves towards me. 'What am I thinking!
You must be frozen. Come on, let's get you in the car and
home.' He ushers me around to the passenger door and helps
me inside. 'Wow, Charlie, you are something else, you know
that?'

He slides back into the driver's side, pulls the door shut
and, grinning at me now, re-starts the car. The warm air is
suddenly filled with the scent of him, and low music pours out
and swirls in the space. Stravinsky. Stravinsky! We begin to
purr back up the lane.

My mind is seething with all sorts of desperate questions.
Most of which I'm too scared to even think about asking.

'So,' my mouth manages. 'What was the phone call
about?'

As I say it, I realise it's never occurred to me that it may
have been something entirely unrelated to the dizzying
prospect of what I so want it to be about. A new asthma
breakthrough. Some geological news. Sponsorship (uurgh) for
his and Davina's Romania campaign? Stupid twit, Simpson.
Even so, his small hesitation feels like an aeon.

'I was hoping to catch you. I wanted to talk to you –'

'About what?'

'About everything, really. About Davina and me. And,
well…'

We're in the driveway already. My lips feel as if a
puppeteer is holding a string.

Oh, God. I got it wrong. He's going to start on some
earnest apology.

'I think I know all I want to about Davina and you.'

The engine dies and he pulls the key from the ignition.

'Do you?'

Bad move, Simpson.

'You said "And well". And well *what*?'

'And well, *us*, of course,' he says, turning.

'Which us?'

'*Us* us. Which other *us* is there?'

I'm hot in my coat now. Hot and light-headed.

'The Davina us. The you and Davina bit. The dress, the crying, the giving up work, the euphoria, God, the *dress*, the hair, the excitement, the clubbing, the baby nonsense – Adam, the *baby* nonsense. What *is* all that *baby* nonsense?'

Adam pauses for a moment with one hand on the steering wheel, then smiles again and opens his door. Then he gets out, comes round, opens my door, helps me out. Then, finally, *finally*, he answers my question. Is he on some different time plane to mine?

'The baby nonsense – if nonsense it is, and I'm inclined to go with you on that one – is nothing to do with me, Charlie. God, you don't actually know, do you? You don't know any of it.'

'Know what?'

'About Davina.'

'All I know is that I've been through all kinds of horrors in the past few weeks. *Horrors,* I can tell you. We made love, Adam. God! Was I just supposed to forget about it? I've been in *agony*. So, no, I don't know. You tell me. Or, rather, don't. I don't think I can stomach any more tonight.'

Tears spring in my eyes. This is like pulling a plaster off, slowly. We should either get back in the car or go in. It's late, it's dark, and it's very cold out here. But we don't. Instead, we continue to stand face to face by the passenger door. Me in my fur coat. Him in his Barbour. Like we're posing for *Hello!* Or advertising the car. Looking, at any rate, like two plastic dummies. His reticence with me is breaking my heart.

Except it's already broken. *C'est la vie. Que sera.*

He reaches around me and clunks the car door shut. I can *breathe* him beside me. I fill my cold lungs.

'Davina's gone to live with Ianthe,' he says. 'You know Ianthe? The –'

'Of course I know Ianthe,' I snap, blinking hard. 'I can't see a pond or a frog without her springing instantly to mind.'

Then my brain slips back into gear.

Wham.

'You mean *gone*? You mean permanently? You mean you've split up? With *Davina*?'

He spreads his hands. Nods. While I wipe my eyes and struggle to assimilate this wonder.

'Of course I have,' he continues. 'I just told you, she's gone to live with Ianthe. *Live* with her, Charlie. As in ... Look, what about Rhys? I thought you and he ...'

I shake my head. 'You thought wrong.'

'So did he, then,' he tells me.

'He didn't, you know. He'd guessed all about us.'

He holds up a finger. Touches it lightly to my face. And smiles.

'Ah! Would that be *you* us, or *us* us?'

'What do you think, you wuss?'

'In that case ...' He moves closer. Slips his keys in his pocket. Slides his cold lovely hands between the edges of my coat, 'At the very least I think I should have a share of that pelt.'

'It's not real,' I tell him.

'So what?' Now he's laughing. 'Your clam digger from Tenby isn't real either.'

His lips find my own.

'But *this* is,' he says.

THE END

Epilogue

EVEN THOUGH IT WAS *more than eighty kilometres away, Everest felt close enough to be touched. The fine details of the North Face, more perfectly triangular than I had imagined, were easily visible to the naked eye even at this long distance. Now I could understand why to the Tibetans Everest was 'Chomolungma', the goddess mother of the earth, long before western surveyors determined its status scientifically as the highest summit in the world.*

Seen from the Tibetan Plateau, Everest's greatness does not need theodolites for confirmation; it is, indisputably, head and shoulders above everything else on earth, with a grandeur, a presence, that far outweighs that of the other Himalayan giants.

From the north, Everest does not hide behind any veil, it reveals itself in all its glory with no preamble or guile. It just sits there alone, proud and magnificent, a pyramid of rock, sculpted by the most powerful forces on earth over millions of years. No other peak encroaches on it: none would dare. It effortlessly fills what seems to be half the horizon. Seen from where we stood, there was no room for any doubt at all: this was the ultimate mountain.

Sounds from outside interrupt my reading. The clattering chit-chat of boots on loose stones. I look out. The huge sky is marine-dark and cloudless, and colours the spaces between the majestic shoulders of blue-white and charcoal. Then there's shadow.

'Ah! Awake at last! What are you reading?'

'*The Death Zone*. I can't put it down. It's brilliant.'

'Sounds harrowing.'

'It will be. But no less good for that.'

'Two minutes, OK? I'll go bag us some drinks.'

'Two minutes. No problem.' I unzip my bag.

The open flap admits a swirl of cold air that glitters with crystals of bright dancing ice. I slip my book under my pillow, slide my pen between the pages of my diary, and restore Minnie's coin to its home in my purse. Then I pull on my own boots and wriggle out into the sunshine, where my own Sherpa Tenby awaits me, for tea.

Author's Note

The epilogue extract, taken from *The Death Zone*, by Matt Dickinson, describes the North Face of Everest, as seen from Tibet, and not Nepal. Everest straddles China and Nepal, and climbers of the North Face begin their ascent from the Rongbuk glacier, at the edge of the Tibetan Plateau.

Most successful Everest attempts, however, have been on its South West Face, the one that the mountain shows to Nepal. Trekkers who wish to see the foot of Everest for themselves would journey by bus from Kathmandu up to Jiri, and then trek there, via Namche Bazaar and Pheriche. Everest Base Camp sits at the foot of the Khumbu Icefall, at a little over seventeen and a half thousand feet.

Acclimatisation is essential.

LBL

About the author...

Lynne Barrett-Lee is the author of five novels and has taken part in the Quick Reads initiative with her book, *Secrets*.
Lynne lives in Cardiff with her husband and three children.

For more information please visit
www.lynnebarrett-lee.com